The Author

ANNA BROWNELL JAMESON was born Anna Brownell Murphy in Dublin, Ireland, in 1794. Her family moved to England in 1798, settling first in Newcastle-upon-Tyne, and moving in 1806 to London, which became the family's permanent home. Her father, Denis Brownell Murphy, was a miniaturist and portrait painter.

Anna Murphy worked as a governess from the age of sixteen until her marriage in 1825 to Robert Jameson. When he left England in 1829 for an appointment as chief justice of Dominica, his wife, already aware of their incompatible relationship, stayed in England, where she was gaining increasing fame as a writer of biography and travel literature.

In mid-December 1836, Anna Jameson joined her husband, somewhat reluctantly, in Toronto, where in 1833 he had become attorney general of Upper Canada (Ontario) and was hoping to become Vice-Chancellor of the Court of Chancery, the highest legal post in the province. In September 1837, having reached a separation agreement with her husband, Anna Jameson left Upper Canada for England. Written in the form of a journal to an absent friend, *Winter Studies and Summer Rambles in Canada* (1838) records both her winter in Toronto and her summer trip through Ontario.

Upon her return to England, Jameson devoted most of her time to art history, and her impressive art catalogues and art history books commanded her scholarly attention for the final decades of her life.

Anna Brownell Jameson died in London, England, in 1860.

ANNA BROWNELL JAMESON

Winter Studies and
Summer Rambles in Canada

"Leid, und Kunst, und Scherz."
RAHEL

With an Afterword by Clara Thomas

M&S

This edition is an unabridged reprint of the first edition of
Winter Studies and Summer Rambles in Canada, published in
London, England, by Saunders and Otley in 1838.

New Canadian Library edition copyright © 1990 by
McClelland & Stewart Inc.
Afterword copyright © 1990 by Clara Thomas

Canadian Cataloguing in Publication Data

Jameson, Mrs. (Anna), 1794–1860
Winter studies and summer rambles in Canada

(New Canadian Library)
Bibliography: p.
ISBN 0-7710-9962-2

1. Ontario – Description and travel – 1764–1850.*
2. Indians of North America – Ontario I. Title.
II. Series.

FC3067.2.J3 1990   917.13′042   C89-093655-2
F1057.J3 1990

Typesetting by Trigraph Inc.
Printed and bound in Canada

McClelland & Stewart Inc.
The Canadian Publishers
481 University Avenue
Toronto, Ontario
M5G 2E9

Contents

Preface

In venturing to place before the public these "fragments" of a journal addressed to a friend, I cannot but feel considerable misgiving as to the reception such a work is likely to meet with, particularly at this time, when the country to which it partly refers is the subject of so much difference of opinion, and so much animosity of feeling. This little book, the mere result of much thoughtful idleness and many an idle thought, has grown up insensibly out of an accidental promise. It never was intended to go before the world in its present crude and desultory form; and I am too sensible of its many deficiencies, not to feel that some explanation is due to that public, which has hitherto regarded my attempts in literature with so much forbearance and kindness.

While in Canada, I was thrown into scenes and regions hitherto undescribed by any traveller, (for the northern shores of Lake Huron are almost new ground,) and into relations with the Indian tribes, such as few European women of refined and civilised habits have ever risked, and none have recorded. My intention was to have given the result of what I had seen, and the reflections and comparisons excited by so much novel experience, in quite a different form – and one less obtrusive: but owing to the intervention of various circumstances, and occupation of graver import, I found myself reduced to the alternative of either publishing the book as it now stands, or of suppressing it altogether. Neither the time nor the attention necessary to remodel the whole were within my own power. In preparing these notes for the press, much has been omitted of a personal nature, but far too much of such irrelevant matter still remains; – far too much which may expose me to misapprehension, if not even to severe criticism; but now, as heretofore, I throw myself upon "the merciful construction of good women," wishing it to be understood that this little book, such as it is, is more particularly addressed to my own sex. I would fain have extracted, altogether, the impertinent leaven of egotism which necessarily mixed itself up with the journal form of writing: but, in making the attempt, the whole work lost its original character – lost its air of reality, lost even its essential truth, and whatever it might possess of the grace of ease and pictorial animation: it became flat, heavy, didactic. It was found that to extract the tone of personal feeling, on which the whole series of action and observation depended, was like drawing the thread out of a string of beads – the chain of linked ideas and experiences fell to pieces, and became a mere unconnected, incongruous heap. I have been obliged to leave the flimsy thread of sentiment to sustain the facts and observations loosely strung together; feeling strongly to what it may expose me, but having deliberately chosen the alternative, prepared, of course, to endure what I may appear to have defied; though, in truth, defiance and assurance are both far from me.

These notes were written in Upper Canada, but it will be seen that they have little reference to the politics or statistics of that unhappy and mismanaged, but most magnificent country. Subsequently I made a short tour through Lower Canada, just before the breaking out of the late revolt. Sir John Colborne, whose mind appeared to me cast in the antique mould of chivalrous honour, and whom I never heard mentioned in either province but with respect and veneration, was then occupied in preparing against the exigency which he afterwards met so effectively. I saw of course something of the state of feeling on both sides, but not enough to venture a word on the subject. Upper Canada appeared to me loyal in spirit, but resentful and repining under the sense of injury, and suffering from the total absence of all sympathy on the part of the English government with the condition, the wants, the feelings, the capabilities of the people and country. I do not mean to say that this want of sympathy *now* exists to the same extent as formerly; it has been abruptly and painfully awakened, but it has too long existed. In climate, in soil, in natural productions of every kind, the upper province appeared to me superior to the lower province, and well calculated to become the inexhaustible timber-yard and granary of the mother country. The want of a sea-port, the want of security of property, the general mismanagement of the government lands – these seemed to me the most prominent causes of the physical depression of this splendid country, while the poverty and deficient education of the people, and a plentiful lack of public spirit in those who were not of the people, seemed sufficiently to account for the moral depression everywhere visible. Add a system of mistakes and mal-administration, not chargeable to any one individual, or any one measure, but to the whole tendency of our Colonial government; the perpetual change of officials, and change of measures; the fluctuation of principles destroying all public confidence, and a degree of ignorance relative to the country itself, not credible except to those who may have visited it; – add these three things together, the want of knowledge, the want of judgment, the want of sympathy, on the part of the government, how can we be surprised at the strangely anomalous condition of the governed? – that of a land absolutely teeming with the richest capabilities, yet poor in population, in wealth, and in energy! But I feel I am getting beyond my depth. Let us hope that the reign of our young Queen will not begin, like that of Maria Theresa, with the loss of one of her fairest provinces; and that hereafter she may look upon the map of her dominions without the indignant blushes and tears with which Maria Theresa, to the last moment of her life, contemplated the map of her dismembered empire, and regretted her lost Silesia.

I have abstained generally from politics and personalities; from the former, because such discussions are foreign to my turn of mind and above my capacity, and from the latter on principle; and I wish it to be distinctly understood, that whenever I *have* introduced any personal details, it has been with the express sanction of those most interested, – I allude particularly to the account of Colonel Talbot and the family at the Sault Ste. Marie. For the rest, I have only to add, that on no subject do I wish to dictate an opinion, or assume to speak as one having authority: my utmost ambition extends no farther than to *suggest* matter for inquiry and reflection. If this little book contain mistakes, they will be chastised and corrected, and I shall be glad of it. If it contain but one truth, and that no bigger than a grain of mustard-seed, it will not have been cast into the world in vain, nor will any severity of criticism make me, in such a case, repent of having published it, even in its present undigested and, I am afraid, unsatisfactory form.

Winter Studies

And over that same door was likewise writ,
Be bold, Be bold, and everywhere *Be bold;*
That much she mus'd, yet could not construe it
By any riddling skill or common wit:
At last she spied at that room's upper end
Another iron door, on which was writ,
Be not too bold.

FAERIE QUEEN, book iii.

Winter Studies in Canada.

Sind denn die Bäume auch so trostlos, so verzweiflungs voll in ihrem Winter, wie das Herz in seiner Verlassenheit?

Bettine v. Arnim.

Dec. 20th.

TORONTO, – such is now the sonorous name of this our sublime capital, – was, thirty years ago, a wilderness, the haunt of the bear and deer, with a little, ugly, inefficient fort, which, however, could not be more ugly or inefficient than the present one. Ten years ago Toronto was a village, with one brick house and four or five hundred inhabitants; five years ago it became a city, containing about five thousand inhabitants, and then bore the name of Little York; now it is Toronto, with an increasing trade, and a population of ten thousand people. So far I write as *per* book.

What Toronto may be in summer, I cannot tell; they say it is a pretty place. At present its appearance to me, a stranger, is most strangely mean and melancholy. A little ill-built town on low land, at the bottom of a frozen bay, with one very ugly church, without tower or steeple; some government offices, built of staring red brick, in the most tasteless, vulgar style imaginable; three feet of snow all around; and the grey, sullen, wintry lake, and the dark gloom of the pine forest bounding the prospect; such seems Toronto to me now. I did not expect much; but for this I was not prepared. Perhaps no preparation could have *prepared* me, or softened my present feelings. I will not be unjust if I can help it, nor querulous. If I look into my own heart, I find that it is regret for what I have left and lost – the absent, not the present – which throws over all around me a chill, colder than that of the wintry day – a gloom, deeper than that of the wintry night.

This is all very dismal, very weak, perhaps; but I know no better way of coming at the truth, than by observing and recording faithfully the impressions made by objects and characters on my own mind – or, rather, the impress they *receive* from my own mind – shadowed by the clouds which pass over its horizon, taking each tincture of its varying mood – until they emerge into light, to be corrected, or at least modified, by observation and comparison. Neither do I know any better way than this of conveying to the mind of another, the truth, and nothing but the truth, if not the whole truth. So I shall write on. Hitherto I have not been accused of looking on the things of this world through a glass darkly, but rather of a contrary tendency. What have I done with my spectacles *couleur de rose?* – the cheerful faith which sustained me through far worse than anything I can anticipate here; – the desire to know, the impatience to learn, the quick social sympathies, the readiness to please and to be pleased, – derived, perhaps, from my Irish blood, and to which I have owed so much of comfort when I have most needed it, so much of enjoyment when least I could have hoped for it – what! and are all forgotten, all gone? Yet am I not quite an icicle, nor an oyster – I almost wish I were! No, worst of all, is this regretful remembrance of friends who loved me, this heart-sick longing after home, and country, and all familiar things and dear domestic faces! I am like an uprooted tree, dying at the core, yet with a strange unreasonable power at times of mocking at my own most miserable weakness. Going to bed in tears last night, after saying my prayers for those far away across that terrible Atlantic, an odd remembrance flashed across me of that Madame de Boufflers, who declared "*avec tant de sérieux et de sentiment*," that she would consent to go as ambassadress to England, only on the condition of taking with her "*vingt-cinq ou vingt-six de ses amis intimes*," and sixty or eighty persons who were *absolument necessaires à son bonheur*. The image of graceful impertinence thus conjured up, made me smile – but am I so unlike her in this fit of unreason? Everywhere there is occupation for the rational and healthy intellect, everywhere good to be done, duties to be performed, – everywhere the mind is, or should be, its own world, its own country, its own home at least. How many fine things I could say or quote, in prose or in rhyme, on this subject! But in vain I conjure up Philosophy, "she will not come when I do call for her;" but in her stead come thronging sad and sorrowful recollections, and shivering sensations, all telling me that I am a stranger among strangers, miserable inwardly and outwardly, – and that the thermometer is twelve degrees below zero!

There is much, too, in first impressions, and as yet I have not recovered from the pain and annoyance of my outset here. My friends at New York expended much eloquence – eloquence wasted in vain! – in endeavouring to dissuade me from a winter journey to Canada. I listened, and was grateful for their solicitude, but must own I did not credit the picture they drew of the difficulties and *désagrémens* I was destined to meet by the way. I had chosen, they said, (Heaven knows I did not *choose* it,) the very worst season for a journey through the state of New York; the usual facilities for travelling were now suspended; a few weeks sooner the rivers and canals had been open; a few weeks later the roads, smoothed up with snow, had been in sleighing order; – now, the navigation was frozen, and the roads so broken up as to be nearly impassable. Then there was only a night boat on the Hudson, "to proceed," as the printed paper set forth, "to

Albany, *or as far as the ice permitted*." All this, and more, were represented to me – and with so much apparent reason and real feeling, and in words and tones so difficult to resist! But though I could appreciate the kindness of those persuasive words, they brought no definite idea to my mind; I could form no notion of difficulties which by fair words, presence of mind, and money in my pocket, could not be obviated. I had travelled half over the continent of Europe, often alone, and had never yet been in circumstances where these availed not. In my ignorance I could conceive none; but I would not lightly counsel a similar journey to any one – certainly not to a woman.

As we ascended the Hudson in the night, I lost, of course, the view of that superb scenery which I was assured even winter could not divest of all its beauty – rather clothed it in a different kind of beauty. At the very first blush of morning, I escaped from the heated cabin, crowded with listless women and clamorous children, and found my way to the deck. I was surprised by a spectacle as beautiful as it was new to me. The Catskill mountains which we had left behind us in the night, were still visible, but just melting from the view, robed in a misty purple light, while our magnificent steamer – the prow armed with a sharp iron sheath for the purpose – was *crashing* its way through solid ice four inches thick, which seemed to close behind us into an adhesive mass, so that the wake of the vessel was not distinguished a few yards from the stern: yet in the path thus opened, and only seemingly closed, followed at some little distance a beautiful schooner and two smaller steam-vessels. I walked up and down, from the prow to the stern, refreshed by the keen frosty air, and the excitement caused by various picturesque effects, on the ice-bound river and the frozen shores, till we reached Hudson. Beyond this town it was not safe for the boat to advance, and we were still thirty miles below Albany. After leaving Hudson, (with the exception of the rail-road between Albany and Utica,) it was all heavy, weary work; the most painfully fatiguing journey I ever remember. Such were the roads, that we were once six hours going eleven miles. What was usually a day's journey from one town, or one good inn, to another, occupied sometimes a day and a night, or even two days.

One dark night, I remember, as the sleet and rain were falling fast and our Extra was slowly dragged by wretched brutes of horses through what seemed to me "sloughs of despond," some package ill stowed on the roof, which in the American stages presents no resting-place either for man or box, fell off. The driver alighted to fish it out of the mud. As there was some delay, a gentleman seated opposite to me put his head out of the window to inquire the cause; to whom the driver's voice replied, in an angry tone, "I say, you mister, don't you sit jabbering there, but lend a hand to heave these things aboard!" To my surprise, the gentleman did not appear struck by the insolence of this summons, but immediately jumped out and lent his assistance. This is merely the manner of the people; the driver intended no insolence, nor was it taken as such, and my fellow-travellers could not help laughing at my surprise.

After six days and three nights of this travelling, unrelieved by companionship, or interest of any kind, I began to sink with fatigue. The first thing that roused me was our arrival at the ferry of the Niagara river, at Queenston, about seven miles below the Falls. It was a dark night, and while our little boat was tossed in the eddying waters, and guided by a light to the opposite shore, we could distinctly hear the deep roar of the cataract, filling, and, as it seemed to me, shaking the atmosphere around us. That mighty cataract, the dream and vision of my childhood and youth, so near – yet unseen, – making itself thus heard and felt, – like Job's vision, consciously present, yet unrevealed and undiscerned! You may believe that I woke up very decidedly from my lethargy of weariness to listen to that mysterious voice, which made my blood pause and thrill. At Queenston we slept, and proceeded next morning to the town of Niagara on the shore of Lake Ontario. Now, as we had heard, the navigation on the lake had ceased, and we looked for nothing better than a further journey of one hundred miles round the head of the lake, and by the most execrable roads, instead of an easy passage of thirty miles across from shore to shore. But Fortune, seized with one of those freaks which, when we meet them in books, we pronounce improbable and unnatural, (and she has played me many such, some good, some bad,) had ordered matters otherwise. A steam-vessel, making a last trip, had called accidentally at the port, and was just going off; the paddles were actually in motion as I and my baggage together were hurried – almost *flung* – on board. No sooner there, than I threw myself down in the cabin utterly overwhelmed with fatigue, and sank at once into a profound and dreamless sleep.

How long I slept I knew not: they roused me suddenly to tell me we were at Toronto, and, not very well able to stand, I hurried on deck. The wharf was utterly deserted, the arrival of the steam-boat being accidental and unexpected; and as I stepped out of the boat I sank ankle-deep into mud and ice. The day was intensely cold and damp; the sky lowered sulkily, laden with snow, which was just beginning to fall. Half-blinded by the sleet driven into my face and the tears which filled my eyes, I walked about a mile through a quarter of the town mean in appearance, not thickly inhabited, and to me, as yet, an unknown wilderness; and through dreary, miry ways, never much thronged, and now, by reason of the impending snowstorm, nearly solitary. I heard no voices, no quick footsteps of men or children; I met no familiar face, no look of welcome. I was sad at heart as a woman could be, – and these were the impressions, the feelings, with which I entered the house which was to be called my *home!*

There is some need – is there not? – that I allow time for these sullen, unkindly influences to melt from my mind and heart before I judge of what I behold around me. The house – only a temporary residence while another is building – is ill provided with defences against the cold, and altogether comfortless; it has the advantage of commanding one of the principal roads entering the town and a glimpse of the bay, – but at present all objects wear one hue. Land is not distinguishable from water. I see nothing but snow heaped up against my windows, not only without but within; I hear no sound but the tinkling of sleigh-bells and the occasional lowing of a poor half-starved cow, that, standing up to the knees in a snow-drift, presents herself at the door of a wretched little shanty opposite, and supplicates for her small modicum of hay.

Dec. 27.

With regard to the society, I can as yet say nothing, having seen nothing of it. All the official gentlemen have called, and all the ladies have properly and politely left their cards: so yesterday, in a sleigh, well wrapped up in furs and buffalo robes, I set out duly to return these visits. I learned something of the geography of the town – nothing of the people. Those whom I did see, looked somewhat formal and alarmed, but they may be very excellent people for all that. I returned trembling and shuddering, chilled outwardly and inwardly, for none of my fur defences prevailed against the frost and the current of icy air, through which we glided, or rather flew, along the smooth road.

The appearance of the town was much more cheerful than on my first landing, but still melancholy enough. There was little movement or animation; few people in the streets; some good shops and some brick houses, but the greater number of wood. The very different appearance of the town and bay in the summer season, the blueness of the water, the brightness of the verdure, the throng of vessels, the busy crowds along the piers, were often described to me, but without conveying to my mind any very definite or cheering picture. The very novelty of the scene before me, by strongly impressing my imagination, seemed to shut out all power of anticipation.

The choice of this site for the capital of the Upper Province was decided by the fine harbour, the only one between Burlington Bay and Cobourg, a distance of about a hundred and fifty miles. General Simcoe, the first governor after the division of the two provinces, and a man of great activity and energy of character, entertained the idea of founding a metropolis. At that time the head quarters of the government were at Niagara, then called Newark, on the opposite shore; but this was too near the frontiers to be a safe position. Nor is Toronto much safer: from its low situation, and the want of any commanding height in the neighbourhood, it is nearly defenceless. In case of a war with America, a few boats sent from the opposite coast of New York could easily lay the fort and town in ashes; and, in fact, during the last war, in 1813, such was the fate of both. But the same reasons which rendered the place indefensible to us, rendered it untenable for the enemy, and it was immediately evacuated. Another objection was, and *is*, the unhealthiness of its situation, – in a low swamp not yet wholly drained, and with large portions of uncleared land immediately round it: still the beauty and safety of the spacious harbour, and its central position about half-way between Lake Huron and the frontier line of Lower Canada, have fixed its rank as capital of the province and the seat of the legislature.

When the engineer, Bouchette, was sent by General Simcoe to survey the site, (in 1793,) it was a mere swamp, a tangled wilderness; the birch, the hemlock and the tamarac-trees were growing down to the water's edge, and even into the lake. I have been told that Toronto, the Indian appellation of the whole district, signifies *trees growing out of water*. Colonel Bouchette says, that at this time the only vestige of humanity for a hundred miles on every side was one solitary wigwam on the shore, the dwelling of a few Missassagua Indians. Three years afterwards, when the Duc de Rochefoucauld was here, the infant metropolis consisted of a fort and twelve miserable log huts, the inhabitants of which, as the duke tells us, bore no good reputation. The town was, however, already marked out in streets running parallel with the shore of the bay for about two miles, and crossed by others at right angles. It is a pity that while they were about it, they did not follow the example of the Americans, in such cases, and make the principal streets of ample width; some hundred feet, or even furlongs, more or less, would have made little difference where the wild unowned forest extended, for all they knew, from the lake to the north pole, – *now*, it would not be so easy to amend the error. King-street, the principal street, looks narrow, and will look narrower when the houses are higher, better, and more regularly built. I perceive that in laying out the *fashionable* or west-end of the city, they have avoided the same mistake. A wide space between the building lots and Lake Ontario has been reserved very properly as a road or esplanade, but I doubt whether even this be wide enough. One of the most curious and inexplicable phenomena connected with these immense inland seas is the gradual rise of the waters; and even within these few years, as I am informed, great part of the high bank has been washed away, and a carriage-road at the foot of it along the shore has been wholly covered. If this process goes on, and at the same rate, there must be a solid embankment, or quay, raised as a barrier against the encroaching waters, or the esplanade itself will in time disappear.

Thus much of knowledge I gained in the course of my cold drive – bitter cold it was every way, and I returned without being much comforted or edified by my visits.

New Year's Day – colder than ever. This morning the thermometer stood at eighteen degrees below zero, and Dr. R—— told me that some chemical compounds in his laboratory had frozen in the night, and burst the phials in which they were contained.

They have here at Toronto the custom which prevails in France, Germany, the United States, (more or less everywhere, I believe, but in England,) of paying visits of congratulation on the first day of the year. This custom, which does not apparently harmonise with the manners of the people, has been borrowed from the French inhabitants of Lower Canada.

I received this morning about thirty gentlemen – to gentlemen luckily for me the obligation is confined – two-thirds of whom I had never seen nor heard of before, nor was there any one to introduce them. Some of them, on being ushered into the room, bowed, sat down, and after the lapse of two minutes, rose and bowed themselves out of the room again without uttering a syllable: all were too much in a hurry and apparently far too cold to converse. Those who did speak, complained, sensibly enough, of the unmeaning duty imposed on them, and the danger incurred by running in and out from over-heated rooms into the fierce biting air, and prophesied to themselves and others sore throats, and agues, and fevers, and every ill that flesh is heir to. I could but believe and condole. These strange faces appeared and disappeared in succession so rapidly, that I was almost giddy, but there were one or two among the number, whom even in five minutes' conversation I distinguished at once as superior to the rest, and original minded, thinking men.

In London society I met with many men whose real material of mind it was difficult to discover – either they had been smoothed and polished down by society, or education had overlaid their understanding with stuccoed ornaments, and figures historical and poetical – very pretty to look at – but the coarse brick-work or the rotten lath and plaster lay underneath: there being in this new country far less of conventional manner, it was so much the easier to tell at once the brick from the granite and the marble.

Jan. 12.

We have had another considerable fall of snow, and the weather is milder. They say here that the weather never remains the same for more than three days together; and all agree that the atmospherical changes are violent and sudden at all seasons. Yet the medical men assure me that the climate of Canada, take it altogether, is one of the healthiest in the world, though the immediate vicinity of Toronto be for the present, from local circumstances, an exception. The winter in the upper province is infinitely less severe and trying than the same season in Lower Canada.

Jan. 14.

It should seem that this wintry season, which appears to me so dismal, is for the Canadians the season of festivity, and if I were not sick and a stranger, – if I had friends near me, I should really enjoy it. Now is the time for visiting, for sleighing excursions, for all intercourse of business and friendship, for balls in town, and dances in farm-houses, and courtships and marriages, and prayer-meetings and assignations of all sorts. In summer, the heat and the mosquitos render travelling disagreeable at best; in spring the roads are absolutely impassable; in autumn there is too much agricultural occupation: but in winter the forests are pervious; the roads present a smooth surface of dazzling snow; the settlers in the woods drive into the towns, supply themselves with stores and clothing, and fresh meat, the latter a luxury which they can seldom obtain in the summer. I stood at my window to-day watching the sleighs as they glided past. They are of all shapes and sizes. A few of the carriage-sleighs are well appointed and handsome. The market-sleighs are often two or three boards nailed together in form of a wooden box upon runners; some straw and a buffalo skin or blanket serve for the seat; barrels of flour and baskets of eggs fill up the empty space. Others are like cars, and others, called *cutters*, are mounted on high runners, like sleigh phaetons; these are sported by the young men and officers of the garrison, and require no inconsiderable skill in driving: however, as I am assured, they are overturned in the snow not above once in a quarter of an hour, and no harm and much mirth ensues: but the wood sleighs are my delight; a large platform of boards is raised upon runners, with a few upright poles held together at top by a rope, the logs of oak, pine, and maple, are then heaped up to the height of six or seven feet. On the summit lie a couple of deer frozen stiff, their huge antlers projecting in a most picturesque fashion, and on these again, a man is seated with a blanket round him, his furred cap drawn down upon his ears, and his scarlet woollen comforter forming a fine bit of colour. He guides with a pole his two patient oxen, the clouds of vapour curling from their nostrils into the keen frosty air – the whole machine, in short, as wildly picturesque as the grape wagons in Italy, though, to be sure, the associations are somewhat different.

Jan. 16.

This morning, before I was quite dressed, a singular visit was announced. I had expressed to my friend Mr. Hepburne a wish to see some of the aborigines of the country; he had the kindness to remember my request, and Colonel Givins, the principal Indian agent, had accordingly brought some Indians to visit us. Those to whom the appearance of these people is familiar and by no means interesting, were surprised by a curiosity which you will at least allow was very natural and *feminine*.

The party consisted of three – a chief named the White Deer, and two of his friends. The chief wore a blanket coat, and leggings, and a blanket hood with a peak from which depended a long black eagle plume; stout mocazins or shoes of undressed deer-skin completed his attire: he had about fifty strings of blue wampum round his neck. The other two were similarly dressed, with the exception of the wampum and the feathers. Before I went down I had thrown a chain of wampum round my neck, which seemed to please them. Chairs being presented, they sat down at once, (though, as Colonel Givins said, they would certainly have preferred the floor,) and answered with a grave and quiet dignity the compliments and questions addressed to them. Their deportment was taciturn, and self-possessed, and their countenances melancholy; that of the chief was by far the most intelligent. They informed me that they were Chippewas from the neighbourhood of Lake Huron; that the hunting season had been unsuccessful; that their tribe was suffering the extremity of hunger and cold; and that they had come to beg from their Great Father the Governor rations of food, and a supply of blankets for their women and children. They had walked over the snow, in their snow-shoes, from the Lake, one hundred and eighty miles, and for the last forty-eight hours none of them had tasted food. A breakfast of cold meat, bread, and beer, was immediately ordered for them; and though they had certainly never beheld in their lives the arrangement of an European table, and were besides half famished, they sat down with unembarrassed tranquillity, and helped themselves to what they wished, with the utmost propriety – only, after one or two trials, using their own knives and fingers in preference to the table knife and fork. After they had eaten and drunk sufficiently, they were conducted to the government-house to receive from the governor presents of blankets, rifles, and provisions, and each, on parting, held out his hand to me, and the chief, with a grave earnestness, prayed for the blessing of the Great Spirit on me and my house. On the whole, the impression they left, though amusing and exciting from its mere novelty, was melancholy. The sort of desperate resignation in their swarthy countenances, their squalid, dingy habiliments, and their forlorn story, filled me with pity and, I may add, disappointment; and all my previous impressions of the independent children of the forest are for the present disturbed.

These are the first specimens I have seen of that fated race, with which I hope to become better acquainted before I leave the country. Notwithstanding all I have heard and read, I have yet but a vague idea of the Indian character; and the very different aspect under which it has been represented by various travellers, as well as writers of fiction, adds to the difficulty of forming a correct estimate of the people, and more particularly of the true position of their women. Colonel Givins, who has passed thirty years of his life among the north-west tribes, till he has become in habits and language almost identified with them, is hardly an impartial judge. He was their interpreter on this occasion, and he says that there is as much difference between the customs and language of different nations, the Chippewas and Mohawks, for instance, as there is between any two nations of Europe.

January 16.

Some philosopher has said or written, that our good and bad qualities, our virtues and our vices, depend more on the influence of climate, than the pride of civilised humanity would be willing to allow; and this is a truth or truism, which for my own part I cannot gainsay – yet which I do not much like to believe. Whatever may be the climate in which the human being is born or reared, can he not always by moral strength raise himself above its degrading, or benumbing, or exciting influence? and yet more, rather than less, easily, when, at a mature age and with habits formed, he is subjected accidentally to such influences? Is there most wisdom, in such a case, in passively assimilating ourselves, our habits, and our feelings, to external circumstances, or resisting and combating them, rather to defend the integrity of our own individual being, than with the hope of changing or controlling the physical or social influences around us?

How I might have settled this question with myself, long ago, when in possession of the health and energy and trusting spirit of my young years, I know – but now it is too late. I could almost wish myself a dormouse, or a she-bear, to sleep away the rest of this cold, cold winter, and wake only with the first green leaves, the first warm breath of the summer wind. I shiver through the day and through the night; and, like poor Harry Gill, "my teeth they chatter, chatter still;" and then at intervals I am burned up with a dry hot fever: this is what my maid, a good little Oxfordshire girl, calls the *hager*, (the ague,) more properly the lake fever, or cold fever. From the particular situation of Toronto, the disorder is very prevalent here in the spring: being a stranger, and not yet *acclimatée*, it has attacked me thus unseasonably. Bark is the general and unfailing remedy.

The cold is at this time so intense, that the ink freezes while I write, and my fingers stiffen round the pen; a glass of water by my bed-side, within a few feet of the hearth, (heaped with logs of oak and maple kept burning all night long,) is a solid mass of ice in the morning. God help the poor emigrants who are yet unprepared against the rigour of the season! – yet this is nothing to the climate of the lower province, where, as we hear, the thermometer has been thirty degrees below zero. I lose all heart to write home, or to register a reflection or a feeling; – thought stagnates in my head as the ink in my pen – and this will never do! – I *must* rouse myself to occupation; and if I cannot find it without, I must create it from within. There are yet four months of winter and leisure to be disposed of. How? – I know not; but they *must* be employed, not wholly lost.

The House of Assembly is now sitting, and the question at present agitated is the appropriation of the clergy reserves – a question momentous to the future welfare of the colony, and interesting to every thinking mind. There are great differences of opinion, and a good deal of bitterness of spirit, prevailing on this subject, so often brought under discussion, and as yet unsettled. When Upper Canada was separated from the Lower Province (in 1791) one-seventh part of the lands was set apart for the maintenance of the clergy, under the name of Clergy Reserves: and the Church of England, as being the church by law established, claimed the entire appropriation of these lands. The Roman Catholics, under the old conditions by which the maintenance of their church was provided for on the conquest of the colony, also put in their claim, as did the Presbyterians on account of their influence, and the Methodists on account of their number. The inhabitants, meantime, through the legislature, petitioned the government that the whole of the clergy reserves should be appropriated to the purposes of education, for which the funds already provided are wholly inadequate, and are ill managed besides – but of this hereafter. If the question had been left to be settled by the House of Assembly then sitting, the Radicals of 1832, there is no doubt that such would have been the destination of these reserves, which now consist of about two millions of acres out of fourteen millions, settled or in course of cultivation, and indefinitely increasing as more and more land is redeemed from the unmeasured, interminable forest. The government at home sent over to the legislature here a cession of the crown lands, and a recommendation to settle the whole question; but we have now a House of Assembly differently constituted from that of 1832, and the preponderance is altogether the other way. I am now aware that there exist three parties on this subject: –

First, those who would appropriate the whole of these reserves solely to the maintenance of the Church of England. This is a small but zealous party – not so much insisting on their own claim, as on the absolute inconsistency and unrighteousness of allowing any other claim. The Church of England, as the archdeacon observed last night, being the only true church, as well as the church by law established, to maintain any other religion or form of religion, at the expense of the state, is a manifest rebellion against both the *gospel* and the *law*.

A second party represent that the Church of England consists of but a small number of the colonists; that as no profession of belief (quakerism excepted) can exclude a man from the provincial legislature, so each religion tolerated by the state should be by the state maintained. They exclaim against disuniting religion and education, and insist that the reserves should be divided in shares proportionate to the number of members of each church, – among the Episcopalians, Presbyterians, Roman Catholics, Wesleyan Methodists, and Baptists. This party is numerous, but not unanimous. In hostility to the exclusive pretensions of the episcopal church they are agreed, but they seem to agree in nothing else; and some numerous and respectable sects are altogether excluded.

A third party, and by far the most numerous, require that the maintenance of the clergy should be left, as in the United States, to the voluntary aid of their congregation, and the entire produce of the lands reserved for the education of the people.

I have not been long enough in the country to consider the question practically, as applying to the peculiar wants and circumstances of the people; but theoretically I do not agree with any of these parties, and at present am content to listen to all I hear around me. With regard to the petition forwarded to the home government, it has been an ample source of ridicule that a house of parliament, of which many members could not read, and many more could not spell, should be thus zealous on the subject of education. In truth, I have seen some specimens of the writing and spelling of honourable members, men of influence and property too, at which it was impossible not to laugh; but I felt no disposition to join in the ridicule freely bestowed on the writers: it seemed anything but ridiculous, that men who had not themselves received the advantage of a good education, should be anxious to insure it to their children. Mr. H. told me the other day, that in the distant townships not one person in twenty or thirty could read or write, or had the means of attaining such knowledge. On repeating this to Mr. B., a native Canadian, and perfectly acquainted with the country, adding some expression of incredulity, he exclaimed laughing, "Not one in twenty or thirty! – Madam, not one in seventy!"

The question, as a mere party question, did not interest me; but the strange, crude, ignorant, vague opinions I heard in conversation, and read in the debates and the provincial papers, excited my astonishment. It struck me that if I could get the English preface to Victor Cousin's report (of which I had a copy) printed in a cheap form, and circulated with the newspapers, adding some of the statistical calculations, and some passages from Duppa's report on the education of the children of the poorer classes, it might do some good – it might assist the people to some general principles on which to form opinions; – whereas they all appeared to me astray; nothing that had been promulgated in Europe on this momentous subject had yet reached them; and the brevity and clearness of this little preface, which exhibits the importance of a system of national education, and some general truths without admixture of any political or sectarian bias, would, I thought – I hoped – obtain for it a favourable reception. But no; cold water was thrown upon me from every side – my interference in any way was so visibly distasteful, that I gave my project up with many a sigh, and I am afraid I shall always regret this. True, I am yet a stranger – helpless as to means, and *feeling* my way in a social system of which I know little or nothing; – perhaps I might have done more mischief than good – who knows? and Truth is sure to prevail at last; but Truth seems to find so much difficulty in crossing the Atlantic, that one would think she was "like the poor cat i' the adage," afraid of wetting her feet.

Another fit of illness and fever of four days' duration happily over; but it has left me more good-for-nothing than ever – more dejected and weak.

Mr. Campbell, the clerk of the assize, has politely offered to drive me over to Niagara in his sleigh. Good-natured Mr. Campbell! I never saw the man in my life; but, in the excess of my gratitude, am ready to believe him everything that is delightful; my heart was dying within me, gasping and panting for change of some kind – any kind! I suppose from the same sort of instinct which sends the wounded animal into the forest to seek for the herb which shall heal him. For here is Dr. R., who assures me that change of air is the only thing which can counteract the effect of these successive fits of aguish fever: so it is fixed that on Tuesday next, at eight o'clock in the morning, I shall be ready to step into Mr. Campbell's sleigh. Five days – five times twenty-four hours of frost and snow without, and monotonous solitude within – and my faculties, and my fingers, and my ink, all frozen up!

> "So slow the unprofitable moments roll,
>   That lock up all the functions of my soul,
>   That keep me from myself."

Slow? – yes; but why unprofitable? that were surely my own fault!

January 21.

There is some diminution of the intense cold yesterday and to-day. The thermometer is above zero.

I begin to be ashamed of recording idle days and useless days, and to have a conception of what those unfortunate wretches must suffer, who are habitually without an interest and without an occupation. What a life is this!

> "Life which the very stars reprove,
>   As on their silent tasks they move."

To me it is something new, for I have never yet been *ennuyée to death* – except in fiction. It is like the old-fashioned torture patronised by that amiable person, Queen Elizabeth, when a certain weight was placed on the bosom of the criminal, and increased gradually every day till the life and the heart were crushed together. Well! patience and resignation are still at hand: – but Patience, "the young and rose-lipped cherubim," seems to have borrowed the features of grim Necessity, and, instead of singing an angel's song, clanks her fetters in my ear; and Resignation comes in a form which reminds me of Ottilie's definition – "Resignation, my dear, is only a despair, which does not beat people." Yet there remains DUTY, which is, far more than Love –

> . . "The star to every wandering bark,
> That looks on tempests, and is never shaken."

It is the upholding law through which the weakest become strong, without which all strength is unstable as water. No character, however harmoniously framed and gloriously gifted, can be complete without this abiding principle; it is the cement which binds the whole moral edifice together, without which all power, goodness, intellect, truth, happiness, love itself, can have no permanence; but all the fabric of existence crumbles away from under us, and leaves us at last sitting in the midst of a ruin – astonished at our own desolation.

January 21–22.

While ranging my German books this morning, I fell upon the Correggio of Oehlenschläger, and Die Schuld of Müllner; and I read both through carefully. The former pleased me *more*, the latter struck me *less*, than when I read them both for the first time a year ago.

One despairs of nothing since the success of "Ion;" but would it be possible, think you, that the tragedy of "Correggio" could be exhibited in England with anything like the success it met with in Germany? Here – in England I mean – it might indeed "*fit* audience find, though *few*," but would it meet with the same sympathy? – would it even be endured with common patience by a mixed audience – such as hailed its appearance in Germany?

Here is a tragedy, of which the pervading interest is not low ambition and the pride of kings; nor love, nor terror, nor murder, nor the rivalship of princes, nor the fall of dynasties, nor any of the usual forms of tragic incident – but ART, high art – its power as developed within the individual soul – its influence on the minds of others. This idea is embodied in the character of Correggio: yet he is no abstraction, but perfectly individualised. All those traits of his life and peculiar habits and disposition, handed down by tradition, are most carefully preserved, and the result is a most admirable portrait of the artist and the man. His gentleness, his tenderness, his sensitive modesty, his sweet, loving, retiring disposition, are all touched with exquisite delicacy. The out-break of noble self-confidence, when he exclaimed, after gazing on Raffaelle's St. Cecilia, "*Anch' io sono Pittore!*" is beautifully introduced. The sight of the same picture sent La Francia home to his bed to die, so at least it is said: but Correggio was not a man to die of another's excellence, though too often doubting his own. The anecdote of the man who was saved from the rapacity and vengeance of a robber, by an appeal to one of his pictures, and the story of his paying his apothecary with one of his finest works,* are also real incidents of the painter's life, introduced with the most picturesque effect.

Those who have travelled through the forests of Catholic Germany and Italy, must often have seen a Madonna, or a Magdalen, in a rude frame, shrined against the knotted trunk of an old oak overshadowing the path; the green

* The Christ on the Mount of Olives, now, if I remember rightly, in possession of the Duke of Wellington.

grass waving round, a votive wreath of wild flowers hung upon the rude shrine, and in front a little space worn bare by the knees of travellers who have turned aside from their journey to rest in the cool shade, and put up an *Ave Maria*, or an *Ora pro nobis*. I well remember once coming on such a Madonna in a wild woodland path near Vollbrücken, in Upper Austria. Two little, half-naked children, and a gaunt, black-bearded wood-cutter, were kneeling before it; and from afar the songs of some peasants gathering in the harvest were borne on the air. The Magdalen of Correggio, the same which is now in the Dresden gallery, and multiplied in prints and copies through the known world, is represented without any violent stretch of probability as occupying such a situation: nor are we left in doubt as to the identity of the picture; it is described in three or four exquisite lines. It is beautiful, – is it not? – where Correggio comments on his work, as he is presenting it to the old hermit: –

> "Ein sündhaft Mädchen, das mit Reu' und Angst
> Wie ein gescheuchtes Reh zum Dickicht floh,
> Um der nachstellung ferner zu entgehen.
> Doch ist es schön von einem Weibe, meyn ich,
> Einmal gefallen wieder sich zu heben;
> Es gibt sehr wen'ge Männer, die das können."*

And the reply of Silvestro places the lovely form before us, *painted* in words.

> Welch schön Gemählde!
> Der dunkle Schattenwald, die blonden Haare,
> Die weisse Haut, das himmel blau Gewand

---

* An erring maiden, that in fear and penitence
  Flies, like timid hind, to the deep woods,
  Seeking t'escape the snares around her laid –
  And it is good to see a hapless woman
  That has once fallen redeem herself; – in truth,
  There be few men methinks could do as much.

Die Jugendfülle und der Todtenkopf,
Das Weiberhafte und das grosse Buch,
Ihr habt mit vieler Kunst die Gegensätze
In schöner Harmonie hier auf-gelöst."*

The manner in which Correggio betrays his regret on parting with his picture, is also natural and most exquisite.

"Die Dichter haben's gut; sie können immer
Die Kinder alle in der Nähe haben.
Der Mahler ist ein armer Vater, der
Sie in die weite Welt aussenden muss;
Da müssen sie nachher sich selbst versorgen."†

Grouped around Correggio in every possible degree of harmony and contrast, we have a variety of figures all sufficiently marked, each in itself complete, and all aiding in carrying out the main effect, the apotheosis of the artist hero.

Nor has Oehlenschläger made his tragedy the vehicle for mere declamation, nor for inculcating any particular system of art or set of principles. In Michael Angelo and in Giulio Romano we have exhibited two artist-minds as different from each other and from Antonio Correggio as can be imagined. The haughty, stern, arrogant, but magnanimous and magnificent Michael Angelo, can with

---

*   .   .   .   What a fair picture!
This dark o'er-hanging shade, the long fair hair,
The delicate white skin, the dark blue robe,
The full luxuriant life, the grim death's head,
The tender womanhood, and the great book –
These various contrasts have you cunningly
Brought into sweetest harmony.

† Well for the poet! he can ever have
The children of his soul beside him here;
The painter is a needy father; he
Sends his poor children out in the wide world
To seek their fortune.

difficulty be brought to appreciate, or even look upon, a style so different from his own, and thunders out his rules of art like Olympian Jove. The gay, confident, generous, courteous Giulio Romano is less exclusive, if less severely grand, in his taste. The luxuriant grace of Correggio, the blending of the purely natural with the purely ideal, in his conceptions of beauty, are again distinct from both these great masters. Again the influence of art over minds variously constituted is exhibited in the tender wife of Correggio, the favourite model for his Madonnas; the old hermit Silvestro; the high-born, beautiful enthusiast, Celestina, who places the laurel-wreath on the brow of the sleeping painter; and the peasant girl, Lauretta, who gives him drink when fainting with thirst; and the penitent robber; and the careless young noble, with whom art is subservient to his vanity and his passions; and the vulgar villain of the piece, Battista, who alone is absolutely insensible to its influence; – all these form as beautiful a group, and as perfect in keeping, as we can meet in dramatic literature. Then there are such charming touches of feeling, such splendid passages of description and aphorisms on art, which seize on the fancy and cling to the memory! while the allusions to certain well-known pictures, bringing them before the mind's eye in a few expressive and characteristic words, are delicious to the amateur.

The received account of the cause of Correggio's death rests on a tradition,* which later researches render very problematical; but it remains uncontradicted that he lived and died poor – that his health was feeble and delicate – his life retired and blameless; – and the catastrophe has

---

* That of Vasari, who states that he died in extreme poverty; that, having received at Parma a payment of sixty crowns, which was churlishly made to him in copper, he walked to the city of Correggio with this load on his back from anxiety to relieve his family, and died in consequence of the effort. Lanzi and other of his biographers distrust this story, and have pointed out its improbability. Whatever the cause of his death, the expressions of Annibal Carracci are conclusive as to the neglect and poverty in which he lived.

been so long current and credited, that the poet has done well to adhere to the common tradition. In the very moment that Correggio sinks into death, a messenger arrives from the Duke of Mantua, with splendid offers of patronage. He comes too late. Art and the world are the heirs of the great man's genius; his poor family follow him heart-broken to the grave.

The Schuld of Adolf Müllner does not produce such an overpowering effect on the imagination the second time of reading, because we are not hurried forward by the interest of the story; but in one respect it has affected me more deeply than at first. Hugo says,

> "Mich dunket, nie
> Sollten Nord und Süd sich küssen!"*

And all through this fine play the spirit of the North and the spirit of the South are brought into beautiful yet fearful contrast. The passions which form the groundwork of the piece are prepared amid the palaces and orange-groves of the glowing South; the catastrophe evolved amid the deserts and pine-forests of the North; and in the fair, still-souled, but heroic Scandinavian maid, Jerta, and the dark, impassioned Elvira, we have the personified *sentiment* of the North and the South.

Has it ever occurred to you that Coleridge must have had this tragedy in his mind when he wrote his "Remorse?"

What a slight touch upon an extreme link will send us back sometimes through a long, long chain of memories and associations! A word, a name, has sent me from Toronto to Vienna; what a flight! what a contrast! – it makes even Fancy herself breathless! Did I ever mention to you Madame Arneth? When the "Schuld" was produced at Vienna, she played the Scandinavian Jerta, and I have heard the effect of her representation compared, in

---

* Methinks,
  That North and South should never kiss each other.

its characteristic purity and calmness, and mild intellectual beauty, to the "moonlight on a snow-wreath," – a comparison which gave me a vivid impression of its *truth*. Madame Arneth was herself not unlike the fair and serious Jerta.

The question has been often agitated, often controverted, but I am inclined to maintain the opinion elsewhere expressed, that there is nothing in the profession of an actress which is incompatible with the respect due to us as women – the cultivation of every feminine virtue – the practice of every private duty. I have conversed with those who think otherwise, and yet continue to frequent the theatre as an amusement, and even as a source of mental delight and improvement; and this I conceive to be a dereliction of principle – wrong in itself, and the cause of wrong. A love for dramatic representation, for imitative action, is in the elements of our human nature; we see it in children, in savages, in all ages, in all nations; – we cannot help it – it is even so. That the position of an actress should sometimes be a false one, – a dangerous one even for a female, is not the fault of the profession, but the effect of the public opinion of the profession. When fashion, or conventional law, or public opinion, denounce as inexpedient what they cannot prove to be wrong – stigmatise what they allow – encourage and take delight in what they affect to contemn – what wonder that from such barbarous, such senseless inconsistency, should spring a whole heap of abuses and mistakes? As to the idea that acting, as a profession, is incompatible with female virtue and modesty, it is not merely an insult to the estimable women who have adorned and still adorn the stage, but to all womankind; it makes me blush with indignation. Unreflecting people – the world is full of such – point to the numerous instances which might be cited to the contrary. I have been perplexed by them sometimes in argument, but never on consideration and examination; and with regard to some other evils, not less, as it appears to me, in a moral point of view, I do not see their necessary connexion with the stage as a profession. Vanity, jealousy, selfishness, the spirit of intrigue, the morbid effects of over-excitement, are not confined to actresses; if women placed in this position do require caution and dignity to ward off temptation, and self-control to resist it, and some knowledge of their own structure and the liabilities incurred by their profession, in order to manage better their own health, moral and physical, then they only require what all women should possess – what every woman needs, no matter what her position.

But to return to Madame Arneth.

At Vienna, some years ago, there lived three celebrated actresses, all beautiful, and young, and gifted. Sophie Müller was first mentioned to me by Schlegel; he spoke of her with rapturous admiration as the most successful representative of some of Shakespeare's characters that had yet been seen in Germany, and she seems to have left an ineffaceable impression on those who saw her play Chrimhilde in the "Niebelung." She was surrounded by admirers, adorers, yet I never heard that one among them could boast of being distinguished even by a preference; austere to herself, devoted to her art, which she studied assiduously, her ambition centered in it; in the mean time she was performing all the duties of a daughter to an aged father, and of a mother to a family of younger brothers and sisters; and her house was a model of good order and propriety. She died in 1830.

Not long before died Anna Krüger, equally blameless in her conduct and reputation as a woman, but in all other respects negligent of herself and of her own interests. She was remarkably free from all selfishness or jealousy, charitable and good, and universally beloved. Her representation of spirited or heroic characters, in comedy and in tragedy, has been described to me as wonderfully fine. Schiller's Joan of Arc was her *chef d'oeuvre*.

The third was Antoinette Adamberger, now Madame Arneth, whom I am happy and proud to number among my friends. Her former name cannot be unknown to you, for it has a dear yet melancholy celebrity throughout all Germany, and is inseparably associated with the literature of her country, as the betrothed bride of Theodore Körner, the poet-hero of the war of deliverance. It was not till we had been for some time intimate that I ever heard her allude to Körner. One evening as we were sitting alone, she gave me, with much feeling and graphic power, and even more simplicity, some particulars of her first interview with him, and the circumstances which led to their engagement. I should tell you that she was at the time a favourite actress of the Court Theatre, and excelled particularly in all characters that required more of delicacy, and grace, and dignity, than of power and passion; those of Thekla in the "Wallenstein," and Jerta in the "Schuld," being considered as her masterpieces. Of her judgment as an *artiste* I could form some idea, from the analysis into which I once tempted her of the Beatrice in Schiller's "Braut von Messina," a character in which she is said to have excelled, and which, in its tender delicacy and almost evanescent grace, might be compared to Perdita. To analyse all the passive beauty and power of Schiller's conception, must have required a just and exquisite taste, and to render them with such felicity and effect, a person corresponding in girlish delicacy. Yet, perhaps, in her youthful years, when she played Beatrice divinely, Madame Arneth could not have analysed the character as ingeniously as she did when a ripened judgment and more cultivated taste enabled her to reflect on her own conception. This, however, is digressing; for the moral qualities, not the intellectual powers, of the actress, are what I am contending for. Theodore Körner came to Vienna in 1813, bringing with him his "Grüne Domino," a piece composed expressly for Anna Krüger and Antoinette Adamberger. These two young women, differing altogether in character, were united by the most tender friendship, and a sincere admiration for each other's particular talent. I have been told that it was delightful to see them play together in the same piece, the perfect understanding which existed between them producing an effect of harmony and reality which was felt, rather than perceived, by the audience. At the period of Körner's arrival, Antoinette was ill in consequence of the extreme severity of the winter of that year, and the rehearsal of the "Grüne Domino" was put off from day to day, from week to week, till Körner became absolutely impatient. At this time he had not been introduced to Antoinette, and it was suspected that the beauty of Anna Krüger had captivated him. At length, the convalescence of the principal actress was announced, the day for long-deferred rehearsal arrived, and the performers had assembled in the green-room. Now, it happened that in the time of the late empress,* the representation of Schiller's "Marie Stuart" had been forbidden, because her imperial majesty had been greatly scandalised by the indecorous quarrel scene between Queen Elizabeth and Queen Mary, and particularly by the catastrophe of the latter, regarding the whole play as extremely dangerous and derogatory to all crowned heads, more especially female ones. On her death it was hoped that this prohibition would be repealed, and the performers presented a petition to that effect. The emperor, however, steadily refused, on the plea that he had *promised* the empress never to permit the representation of the tragedy.† The refusal had just been received, and the whole *corps dramatique* were in a state of commotion, and divided on the merits of the case. Körner, in particular, was in a perfect fever of indignation, and exclaimed, in no measured terms, against the edict which deprived the public of one of Schiller's masterpieces, in tenderness to the caprices of an old woman now in her grave, *et cetera*. The greater number of those present sympathised

* Maria-Theresa-Caroline of Naples, who died in 1807.

† I do not know whether the emperor was ever induced to break this promise. It was *after* his death that I saw Marie Stuart performed at Vienna, where Madame Schroeder and Madlle. Fournier appeared as Queen Elizabeth and Mary Stuart.

with him. The dispute was at its height when Antoinette entered the room, still weak from recent illness, and wrapped up in cloaks and furs. Her comrades crowded around her with congratulations and expressions of affection, and insisted that the matter in dispute should be referred to "Toni;" Körner, meanwhile, standing by in proud silence; he had not yet been introduced. When the affair was stated, and the opinions of the majority vehemently pressed on her, she replied in her gentle manner, "I do not pretend to judge about the injury done to the public, or the expediency or inexpediency of the matter; it is a simple question between right and wrong – between truth and falsehood. For myself, I can only say, that if I had made a promise to a person I loved, or to any one, I would keep it as long as I had life myself, and the death of that person would render such a promise not less, but more binding, more sacred, if possible."

This simple appeal to principle and truth silenced all. Körner said no more, but his attention was fixed, and from that moment, as he told her afterwards, he loved her; his feelings were interested before he had even looked into her eyes; and it is no wonder that those eyes, when revealed, completed her conquest.

Within a few weeks they were betrothed lovers, and within a few months afterwards the patriotic war (die Freiheits-Kriege) broke out, and Körner joined Lutzow's volunteers. His fate is well known. Young and handsome, a poet and a hero, loving, and in the full assurance of being loved, with all life's fairest visions and purest affections fresh about his head and heart, he perished – the miniature of "Toni" being found within his bosom next to the little pocket-book in which he had written the Song of the Sword – the first shattered by the bullet which had found his heart, the latter stained with his blood; I have seen it, – held it in my hand! Now, will you believe, that within three or four months afterwards, when Antoinette was under the obligation to resume her professional duties, the first character she was ordered to play was that of Thekla? In vain she entreated to be spared this outrage to every feeling of a heart yet bleeding from her loss; the greater her reluctance, the greater the effect which would be produced on the curiosity and sympathy of the public; – this, I suppose, was the cold calculation of the directory! She was *not* excused; and after going through the scene in which the Swedish captain relates to Thekla the death of her lover,* the poor Antoinette was carried from the stage by her aunt almost lifeless, and revived only to give way to such agonies of grief and indignation as threatened her reason.

Madame Arneth is remarkably calm and simple in her manner, and more than twenty years had elapsed since she had been thus insulted and tortured; but when she alluded to this part of her history, she became gradually convulsed with emotion, trembled in every limb, and pressed her hands upon her eyes, from which the tears *would* gush in spite of an effort to restrain them. And to this, you will say, an actress could be exposed? Yes; and I remember another instance, when under circumstances as cruel and as revolting, a young and admired actress was hurried before the public in an agony of reluctance; but still I do say, that such exhibitions are not necessarily or solely confined to the profession of the stage; woman, as a legal property, is subjected to them in her conventional position; a woman may be brought into a church against her will, libelled and pilloried in an audacious newspaper; an English matron may be dragged from private life into a court of justice, exposed, guiltless and helpless, to the public obloquy or the public sympathy, in shame and in despair. If such a scene *can* by possibility take place, one stage is not worse than another.

Antoinette had suffered what a woman of a quiet but proud temper never forgets or forgives. She had made up

---

* It will be remembered that the death of Theodore Körner was similar to that of Max Piccodomini.

her mind to quit the stage, and there was only one way of doing so with honour. Four years after the death of Körner she married Mr. Arneth, one of the directors of the Imperial Museum, a learned and amiable man, considerably older than herself,* and with whom she has lived happily. Before I left Vienna she presented me with a book which Körner had given her, containing his autograph and the dramas he had written for her – "Die Toni," "der Grüne Domino," and others. I exclaimed thoughtlessly, "O how can you part with it?" and she replied, with a sweet seriousness, "When I married a worthy man who loved me and trusted me, I thought there should be no wavering of the heart between past recollections and present duties: I put this and all other objects connected with *that* first period of my life entirely away, and I have never looked at it since. Take it! and believe me, even *now*, it is better in your hands than in mine." And mine it shall never leave.

Madame Arneth once described to me the admirable acting of Schroeder in Medea, when playing with her own children: she treated them, however, with savage roughness, and when remonstrated with, she replied, "the children were her own, and she had a right to do what she liked with them." "That was certainly her affair," added Madame Arneth, "but I would not for the whole world have exhibited myself before my own children in such a character."

Is not this a woman worthy of all love, all respect, all

---

* Madame Arneth is now *Vorleserin* (Reader) to the Empress Dowager, and entrusted with the direction of a school, founded by the Empress for the children of soldiers. In Austria only two soldiers in each company are allowed to marry, and the female children of such marriages are, in a manner, predestined to want and infamy. In the school under Madame Arneth's direction, I found (in 1835) forty-five children, well managed and healthy. The benevolence which suggested such an institution is, without doubt, praiseworthy; but what shall we say of the system which makes such an institution necessary?

reverence? and is not this the sentiment of duty which is, or should be, "the star to every wandering bark?" And thus I have read and scribbled away two long days. The eve of my intended excursion is come at last; I am looking forward to to-morrow with almost childish pleasure and impatience. The weather is most ominous; but I shall see Niagara in all its wintry magnificence – a sight granted to few. O! in this moment I do not envy you the blue Mediterranean, nor the summer skies and orange-groves of your southern island!

Niagara in Winter.

Merrily dash we o'er valley and hill,
  All but the sleigh-bell is sleeping and still;
O bless the dear sleigh-bell! there's nought can compare
To its loud merry tones as they break on the ear.

Our horses are staunch, and they dash o'er the snow;
Our bells ring out gaily the faster we go;
The night breezes sing with an answering swell
To the melody rude of the merry sleigh-bell.

Canadian Song.

January 23.

AT HALF-PAST eight Mr. Campbell was at the door in a very pretty commodious sleigh, in form like a barouche, with the head up. I was absolutely buried in furs; a blanket, netted for me by the kindest hands, of the finest lamb's-wool, rich in colour, and as light and elastic as it was deliciously warm, was folded round my limbs; buffalo and bear skins were heaped over all, and every breath of the external air excluded by every possible device. Mr. Campbell drove his own grey horses; and thus fortified and accoutred, off we flew, literally "urged by storms along the slippery way," for the weather was terrific.

I think that but for this journey I never could have imagined the sublime desolation of a northern winter, and it has impressed me strongly. In the first place, the whole atmosphere appeared as if converted into snow, which fell in thick, tiny, starry flakes, till the buffalo robes and furs about us appeared like swansdown, and the harness on the horses of the same delicate material. The whole earth was a white waste: the road, on which the sleigh-track was only just perceptible, ran for miles in a straight line; on each side rose the dark, melancholy pine-forest, slumbering drearily in the hazy air. Between us and the edge of the forest were frequent spaces of cleared or half-cleared land, spotted over with the black charred stumps and blasted trunks of once magnificent trees, projecting from the snow-drift. These, which are perpetually recurring objects in a Canadian landscape, have a most melancholy appearance. Sometimes wide openings occurred to the left, bringing us in sight of Lake Ontario, and even in some places down upon the edge of it: in this part of the lake the enormous body of the water and its incessant movement prevents it from freezing, and the dark waves rolled in, heavily plunging on the icy shore with a sullen booming sound. A few roods from the land, the cold grey waters, and the cold, grey, snow-encumbered atmosphere, were mingled with each other, and each seemed either. The only living thing I saw in a space of about twenty miles, was a magnificent bald-headed eagle, which, after sailing a few turns in advance of us, alighted on the topmost bough of a blasted pine, and slowly folding his great wide wings, looked down upon us as we glided beneath him.

The first village we passed through was Springfield, on the river Credit, a river of some importance in summer, but now, converted into ice, heaped up with snow, and undistinguishable. Twenty miles further, we stopped at Oakville to refresh ourselves and the horses.

Oakville stands close upon the lake, at the mouth of a little river called Sixteen-mile Creek; it owes its existence to a gentleman of the name of Chisholm, and, from its situation and other local circumstances, bids fair to become a place of importance. In the summer it is a frequented harbour, and carries on a considerable trade in *lumber*, for so they characteristically call timber in this country. From its dock-yards I am told that a fine steamboat and a dozen schooners have been already launched.

In summer, the country round is rich and beautiful, with a number of farms all in a high state of cultivation; but Canada in winter and in summer must be like two different regions. At present the mouth of the creek is frozen up; all trade, all ship-building suspended. Oakville presents the appearance of a straggling hamlet, containing a few frame and log-houses; one brick house, (the grocery store, or general shop, which in a new Canadian village is always the best house in the place;) a little Methodist church, painted green and white, but as yet no resident preacher; and an inn dignified by the name of the "Oakville House Hotel." Where there is a store, a tavern, and a church, habitations soon rise around them. Oakville contains at present more than three hundred inhabitants, who are now subscribing among themselves for a schoolmaster and a resident clergyman.

I stood conversing in the porch, and looking about me, till I found it necessary to seek shelter in the house, before my nose was absolutely taken off by the ice-blast. The little parlour was solitary, and heated like an oven. Against the wall were stuck a few vile prints, taken out of old American magazines; there was the Duchess de Berri in her wedding-dress, and as a pendant, the Modes de Paris – "Robe de tulle garnie de fleurs – coiffure nouvelle, inventée par Mons. Plaisir." The incongruity was but too laughable! I looked round me for some amusement or occupation, and at last spied a book open, and turned down upon its face. I pounced upon it as a prize; and what do you think it was? "Dévinez, madame! je vous le donne en trois, je vous le donne en quatre!" it was – Don Juan! And so, while looking from the window on a scene which realised all you can imagine of the desolation of savage life, mixed up with just so much of the commonplace vulgarity of civilised life as sufficed to spoil it, I amused myself reading of the Lady Adeline Amundeville and her precious coterie, and there anent.

> Society is smoothed to that excess,
> That manners hardly differ more than dress.
> Our ridicules are kept in the background,
> Ridiculous enough, but also dull;
> Professions, too, are no more to be found
> Professional, and there is nought to cull
> Of Folly's fruit; for tho' your fools abound,
> They're barren, and not worth the pains to pull.
> Society is now one polished horde,
> Form'd of two mighty tribes – the *bores* and *bored*.

A delineation, by the way, which might almost reconcile one to a more savage locality than that around me.

While I was reading, the mail-coach between Hamilton and Toronto drove up to the door; and because you shall understand what sort of a thing a Canadian mail is, and thereupon sympathise in my irrepressible wonder and amusement, I must sketch it for you. It was a heavy wooden edifice, about the size and form of an old-fashioned lord mayor's coach, placed on runners, and raised about a foot from the ground; the whole was painted of a bright red, and long icicles hung from the roof. This monstrous machine disgorged from its portal eight mencreatures, all enveloped in bear-skins and shaggy dreadnoughts, and pea-jackets, and fur-caps down upon their noses, looking like a procession of bears on their hindlegs, tumbling out of a showman's caravan. They proved, however, when undisguised, to be gentlemen, most of them going up to Toronto to attend their duties in the House of Assembly. One of these, a personage of remarkable height and size, and a peculiar cast of features, was introduced to me as Mr. Kerr, the possessor of large estates in the neighbourhood, partly acquired, and partly inherited from his father-in-law Brandt, the famous chief of the Six Nations. Kerr himself has Indian blood in his veins. His son, young Kerr, a fine boy about ten years old, is the present acknowledged chief of the Six Nations, in his mother's right, the hereditary chieftainship being always transmitted *through* the female, though passing *over* her. Mrs. Kerr, the eldest daughter of Brandt, is a squaw of unmixed Indian blood, and has been described to me as a very superior creature. She has the good sense to wear habitually her Indian costume, slightly modified, in which she looks and moves a princess, graceful and unrestrained, while in a fashionable European dress the effect is exactly the reverse.

Much mischief has been done in this neighbourhood by beasts of prey, and the deer, driven by hunger and the wolves from their forest haunts, have been killed, near the settlements, in unusual numbers. One of the Indians whom I saw at Toronto, on returning by this road, shot with his new rifle eight deer in one day, and sold them at Hamilton for three dollars each – no bad day's hunting. The venison in Canada is good and abundant, but very lean, very unlike English venison; the price is generally four or six cents (twopence or threepence) a pound.

After taking some refreshment, we set forth again. The next village we passed was called, oddly enough, Wellington Square; it has been recently laid out, and contains about twenty wooden houses; – then came Port Nelson, Mr. Kerr's place. Instead of going round the head of the lake by Hamilton, we crossed that very remarkable tongue or slip of land which divides Burlington Bay from Lake Ontario; these were, in fact, two separate lakes till a channel was cut through the narrow isthmus. Burlington Bay, containing about forty square miles, is now one sheet of ice, and on the slip of land, which is near seven miles in length, and about two hundred yards in width, we found the snow lying so deep and in such irregular drifts, that we proceeded with difficulty. At length we reached Stony Creek, a village celebrated in these parts as the scene of the bloodiest battle fought between the English and Americans during the last war. We had intended to sleep here, but the inn was so uncomfortable and unpromising, that after a short rest we determined on proceeding ten miles further to Beamsville.

It was now dark, and the snow falling thick, it soon became impossible to distinguish the sleigh-track. Mr. Campbell loosened the reins and left the horses to their own instinct, assuring me it was the safest way of proceeding. After this I remember no more distinctly, except that I ceased to hear the ever-jingling sleigh-bells. I awoke, as if from the influence of nightmare, to find the sleigh overturned, myself lying in the bottom of it half-smothered, and my companions nowhere to be seen; – they were floundering in the snow behind.

Luckily, when we had stretched ourselves and shaken off the snow, we were found unhurt in life and limb. We had fallen down a bank into the bed of a rivulet, or a millrace, I believe, which, being filled up with snow, was quite as soft, only a little colder, than a down-bed. Frightened I was, bewildered rather, but "effective" in a moment. It was impossible for the gentlemen to leave the horses, which were plunging furiously up to the shoulders in the snow, and had already broken the sleigh; so I set off to seek assistance, having received proper directions. Fortunately we were not far from Beamsville. My beacon-light was to be the chimney of a forge, from which the bright sparks were streaming up into the dark wintry air, visible from a great distance. After scrambling through many a snowdrift, up hill and down hill, I at last reached the forge, where a man was hammering amain at a ploughshare; such was the din, that I called for some time unheard; at last, as I advanced into the red light of the fire, the man's eyes fell upon me, and I shall never forget his look as he stood poising his hammer, with the most comical expression of bewildered amazement. I could not get an answer from him; he opened his mouth and repeated *aw!* staring at me, but without speaking or moving. I turned away in despair, yet half laughing, and after some more scrambling up and down, I found myself in the village, and was directed to the inn. Assistance was immediately sent off to my friends, and in a few minutes the supper-table was spread, a pile of logs higher than myself blazing away in the chimney; venison-steaks, and fried fish, coffee, hot cakes, cheese, and whiskey punch, (the traveller's fare in Canada,) were soon smoking on the table; our landlady presided, and the evening passed merrily away.

The old landlady of this inn amused me exceedingly; she had passed all her life among her equals in station and education, and had no idea of any distinction between guests and customers; and while caressing and attending on me, like an old mother or an old nurse, gave me her history, and that of all her kith and kin. Forty years before, her husband had emigrated, and built a hovel, and made a little clearing on the edge of the lake. At that time there was no other habitation within many miles of them, and they passed several years in almost absolute solitude. They have now three farms, some hundred acres of land, and have brought up nine sons and daughters, most of whom are married, and settled on lands of their own. She gave me a horrid picture of the prevalence of drunkenness, the vice and the curse of this country.

I can give you no idea of the intense cold of this night; I was obliged to wrap my fur cloak round me before I could go to sleep. I rose ill and could eat no breakfast, in spite of all the coaxing of the good landlady; she got out her best tea, kept for her own drinking, (which tasted for all the world like musty hay,) and buttered toast, *i.e.* fried bread steeped in melted butter, and fruit preserved in molasses – to all which I shall get used in time – I must try, at least, or "thank Heaven, *fasting*." We proceeded eighteen miles farther, to St. Catherine's, the situation of which appeared to me very pretty even in winter, and must be beautiful in summer. I am told it is a place of importance, owing to the vicinity of the Welland Canal, which connects Lake Ontario with Lake Erie: it contains more than seven hundred inhabitants. The school here is reckoned the best in the district. We passed this morning several streams, which in summer flow into the lake, now all frozen up and undistinguishable, except by the wooden bridges which cross them, and the mills, now still and useless, erected along their banks. These streams have the names of Thirty Mile Creek, Forty Mile Creek, Twenty Mile Creek, and so on; but wherefore I could not discover.

From St. Catherine's we proceeded twelve miles farther, to Niagara. There I found some old English or rather Irish friends ready to welcome me with joyous affection; and surely there is not a more blessed sight than the face of an old friend in a new land!

January 26.

The town of Niagara presents the same torpid appearance which seems to prevail everywhere at this season; it is situated at the mouth of the river Niagara, and is a place of much business and resort when the navigation is open. The lake does not freeze here, owing to the depth of its majestic waters; neither does the river, from the velocity of its current; yet both are blocked up by the huge fragments of ice which are brought down from Lake Erie, and which, uniting and accumulating at the mouth of the river, form a field of ice extending far into the lake. How beautiful it looked to-day, broken into vast longitudinal flakes of alternate white and azure, and sparkling in the sunshine!

There are dock-yards here lately erected, dry docks, iron works of some extent, and a steam-engine for hauling up vessels for repair; the chief proprietor is a good-natured and public-spirited gentleman, Captain Melville. He tells me that upwards of twenty thousand pounds have been expended on these works, and they employ constantly about fifty workmen; yet, in spite of this, and in spite of its local advantages, as a frontier town and the oldest settlement in Upper Canada, Niagara does not make progress. The population and the number of houses have remained nearly stationary for the last five years. I find the people complaining much of the want of a good school.

The land all round Niagara is particularly fine and fertile, and it has been longer cleared and cultivated than in other parts of the province. The country, they say, is most beautiful in summer, taxes are trifling, scarcely felt, and there are no poor-rates; yet ignorance, recklessness, despondency, and inebriety, seem to prevail. A—— , who has been settled here five years, and B—— , himself a Canadian, rate the morality of the Canadian population frightfully low; lying and drunkenness they spoke of as nearly universal; men who come here with sober habits quickly fall into the vice of the country; and those who have the least propensity to drinking find the means of gratification comparatively cheap, and little check from public opinion.

> Men learn to drink, who never drank before;
> And those who always drank, now drink the more.

Though I parody, I do not jest; for in truth, if all, or even half, of what I heard to-day be true, this is a horrible state of things. I asked for a bookseller's shop; there is not one in the town, but plenty of taverns. There is a duty of thirty per cent. on books imported from the United States, and the expense on books imported from England adds at least one-third to their price; but there is no duty on whisky. "If government," said B—— , "were to lay a duty on whisky, we should only have the province overrun with illicit stills, and another source of crime and depravity added to the main one."

Sir Francis Head recommended to me, playfully, to get up a grievance, that I might have an excuse for paying him a visit. I think I will represent to his Excellency the dearness of books and the cheapness of whisky. I could not invent a worse grievance either in earnest or in jest.

The opposite shore, about a quarter of a mile off, is the State of New York. The Americans have a fort on their side, and we also have a fort on ours. What the amount of *their* garrison may be I know not, but our force consists of three privates and a corporal, with adequate arms and ammunition, i.e. rusty firelocks and damaged guns. The fortress itself I mistook for a dilapidated brewery. This is charming – it *looks* like peace and security, at all events.

January 29.

Well! I have seen these Cataracts of Niagara, which have thundered in my mind's ear ever since I can remember – which have been my "childhood's thought, my youth's desire," since first my imagination was awakened to wonder and to wish. I have beheld them, and shall I whisper it to you? – but, O tell it not among the Philistines! – I wish I had not! I wish they were still a thing unbeheld – a thing to be imagined, hoped, and anticipated – something to live for: – the reality has displaced from my mind an illusion far more magnificent than itself – I have no words for my utter disappointment: yet I have not the presumption to suppose that all I have heard and read of Niagara is false or exaggerated – that every expression of astonishment, enthusiasm, rapture, is affectation or hyperbole. No! it must be my own fault. Terni, and some of the Swiss cataracts leaping from their mountains, have affected me a thousand times more than all the immensity of Niagara. O I could beat myself! and now there is no help! – the first moment, the first impression is over – is lost; though I should live a thousand years, long as Niagara itself shall roll, I can never see it again for the first time. Something is gone that cannot be restored. What has come over my soul and senses? – I am no longer Anna – I am metamorphosed – I am translated – I am an ass's head, a clod, a wooden spoon, a fat weed growing on Lethe's bank, a stock, a stone, a petrifaction, – for have I not seen Niagara, the wonder of wonders; and felt – no words can tell *what* disappointment!

But, to take things in order: we set off for the falls yesterday morning, with the intention of spending the day there, sleeping, and returning the next day to Niagara. The distance is fourteen miles, by a road winding along the banks of the Niagara river, and over the Queenston heights; – and beautiful must this land be in summer, since even now it is beautiful. The flower garden, the trim shrubbery, the lawn, the meadow with its hedgerows, when frozen up and wrapt in snow, always give me the idea of something not only desolate but dead: Nature is the ghost of herself, and trails a spectral pall; I always feel a kind of pity – a touch of melancholy – when at this season I have wandered among withered shrubs and buried flower-beds; but here, in the wilderness, where Nature is wholly independent of art, she does not die, nor yet mourn; she lies down to rest on the bosom of Winter, and the aged one folds her in his robe of ermine and jewels, and rocks her with his hurricanes, and hushes her to sleep. How still it was! how calm, how vast the glittering white waste and the dark purple forests! The sun shone out, and the sky was without a cloud; yet we saw few people, and for many miles the hissing of our sleigh, as we flew along upon our dazzling path, and the tinkling of the sleigh-bells, were the only sounds we heard. When we were within four or five miles of the falls, I stopped the sleigh from time to time to listen for the roar of the cataracts, but the state of the atmosphere was not favourable for the transmission of sound, and the silence was unbroken.

Such was the deep, monotonous tranquillity which prevailed on every side – so exquisitely pure and vestal-like the robe in which all Nature lay slumbering around us, I could scarce believe that this whole frontier district is not only remarkable for the prevalence of vice – but of dark and desperate crime.

Mr. A., who is a magistrate, pointed out to me a lonely house by the way-side, where, on a dark stormy night in the preceding winter, he had surprised and arrested a gang of forgers and coiners; it was a fearful description. For some time my impatience had been thus beguiled – impatience and suspense much like those of a child at a theatre before the curtain rises. My imagination had been so impressed by the vast height of the Falls, that I was constantly looking in an upward direction, when as we came to the brow of a hill, my companion suddenly checked the horses, and exclaimed, "The Falls!"

I was not, for an instant, aware of their presence; we were yet at a distance, looking *down* upon them; and I saw at one glance a flat extensive plain; the sun having withdrawn its beams for the moment, there was neither light, nor shade, nor colour. In the midst were seen the two great cataracts, but merely as a feature in the wide landscape. The sound was by no means overpowering, and the clouds of spray, which Fanny Butler called so beautifully the "everlasting incense of the waters," now condensed ere they rose by the excessive cold, fell round the base of the cataracts in fleecy folds, just concealing that furious embrace of the waters above and the waters below. All the associations which in imagination I had gathered round the scene, its appalling terrors, its soul-subduing beauty, power and height, and velocity and immensity, were all diminished in effect, or wholly lost.

I was quite silent – my very soul sank within me. On seeing my disappointment (written, I suppose, most legibly in my countenance) my companion began to comfort me, by telling me of all those who had been disappointed on the first view of Niagara, and had confessed it. I *did* confess; but I was not to be comforted. We held on our way to the Clifton hotel, at the foot of the hill; most desolate it looked with its summer verandahs and open balconies cumbered up with snow, and hung round with icicles – its forlorn, empty rooms, broken windows, and dusty dinner tables. The poor people who kept the house in winter had gathered themselves for warmth and comfort into a little kitchen, and when we made our appearance, stared at us with a blank amazement, which showed what a rare thing was the sight of a visitor at this season.

While the horses were cared for, I went up into the

highest balcony to command a better view of the cataracts; a little Yankee boy, with a shrewd, sharp face, and twinkling black eyes, acting as my gentleman usher. As I stood gazing on the scene which seemed to enlarge upon my vision, the little fellow stuck his hands into his pockets, and looking up in my face, said,

"You be from the old country, I reckon?"

"Yes."

"Out over there, beyond the sea?"

"Yes."

"And did you come all that way across the sea for these here falls?"

"Yes."

"My!!" Then after a long pause, and eyeing me with a most comical expression of impudence and fun, he added, "Now, do *you* know what them 'ere birds are, out yonder?" pointing to a number of gulls which were hovering and sporting amid the spray, rising and sinking and wheeling around, appearing to delight in playing on the verge of this "hell of waters" and almost dipping their wings into the foam. My eyes were, in truth, fixed on these fair, fearless creatures, and they had suggested already twenty fanciful similitudes, when I was roused by his question.

"Those birds?" said I. "Why, *what* are they?"

"Why, them's EAGLES!"

"Eagles?" it was impossible to help laughing.

"Yes," said the urchin sturdily; "and I guess you have none of them in the old country?"

"Not many eagles, my boy; but plenty of *gulls!*" and I gave him a pretty considerable pinch by the ear.

"Ay!" said he, laughing; "well now you be dreadful smart – smarter than many folks that come here!"

We now prepared to walk to the Crescent fall, and I bound some crampons to my feet, like those they use among the Alps, without which I could not for a moment have kept my footing on the frozen surface of the snow. As we approached the Table Rock, the whole scene assumed a wild and wonderful magnificence; down came the dark-

green waters, hurrying with them over the edge of the
precipice enormous blocks of ice brought down from
Lake Erie. On each side of the Falls, from the ledges and
overhanging cliffs, were suspended huge icicles, some
twenty, some thirty feet in length, thicker than the body of
a man, and in colour of a paly green, like the glaciers of
the Alps; and all the crags below, which projected from the
boiling eddying waters, were encrusted, and in a manner
built round with ice, which had formed into immense
crystals, like basaltic columns, such as I have seen in the
pictures of Staffa and the Giant's Causeway; and every
tree, and leaf, and branch, fringing the rocks and ravines,
was wrought in ice. On them, and on the wooden buildings erected near the Table Rock, the spray from the
cataract had accumulated and formed into the most beautiful crystals and tracery work; they looked like houses of
glass, welted and moulded into regular and ornamental
shapes, and hung round with a rich fringe of icy points.
Wherever we stood we were on unsafe ground, for the
snow, when heaped up as now to the height of three or
four feet, frequently slipped in masses from the bare rock,
and on its surface the spray, for ever falling, was converted
into a sheet of ice, smooth, compact, and glassy, on which
I could not have stood a moment without my *crampons*.
It was very fearful, and yet I could not tear myself away,
but remained on the Table Rock, even on the very edge of
it, till a kind of dreamy fascination came over me; the
continuous thunder, and might and movement of the
lapsing waters, held all my vital spirits bound up as by a
spell. Then, as at last I turned away, descending sun broke
out, and an Iris appeared below the American Fall, one
extremity resting on a snow mound; and motionless there
it hung in the midst of restless terrors, its beautiful but
rather pale hues contrasting with the death-like colourless
objects around; it reminded me of the faint ethereal smile
of a dying martyr.

We wandered about for nearly four hours, and then
returned to the hotel: there my good-natured escort from

Toronto, Mr. Campbell, was waiting to conduct us to his house, which is finely situated on an eminence not far from the great cataract. We did not know, till we arrived there, that the young and lovely wife of our host had been confined only the day before. This event had been concealed from us, lest we should have some scruples about accepting hospitality under such circumstances; and, in truth, I *did* feel at first a little uncomfortable, and rather *de trop*; but the genuine kindness of our reception soon overcame all scruples: we were made welcome, and soon felt ourselves so; and, for my own part, I have always sympathies ready for such occasions, and shared very honestly in the grateful joy of these kind people. After dinner I went up into the room of the invalid – a little nest of warmth and comfort; and though the roar of the neighbouring cataract shook the house as with a universal tremor, it did not quite overpower the soft voice of the weak but happy mother, nor even the feeble wail of the new-born baby, as I took it in my arms with a whispered blessing, and it fell asleep in my lap. Poor little thing! – it was an awful sort of lullaby, that ceaseless thunder of the mighty waters ever at hand, yet no one but myself seemed to heed, or even to hear it; such is the force of custom, and the power of adaptation even in our most delicate organs.

To sleep at the hotel was impossible, and to intrude ourselves on the Campbells equally so. It was near midnight when we mounted our sleigh to return to the town of Niagara, and, as I remember, I did not utter a word during the whole fourteen miles. The air was still, though keen, the snow lay around, the whole earth seemed to slumber in a ghastly, calm repose; but the heavens were wide awake. There the Aurora Borealis was holding her revels, and dancing and flashing, and varying through all shapes and all hues – pale amber, rose tint, blood red – and the stars shone out with a fitful, restless brilliance; and every now and then a meteor would shoot athwart the skies, or fall to earth, and all around me was wild, and strange, and exciting – more like a fever dream than a reality.

To-day I am suffering, as might be expected, with pain and stiffness, unable to walk across the room; but the pain will pass: and on the whole I am glad I have made this excursion. The Falls did not make on my mind the impression I had anticipated, perhaps for that reason, even because I had *anticipated* it. Under different circumstances it might have been otherwise; but "it was sung to me in my cradle," as the Germans say,* that I should live to be disappointed – even in the Falls of Niagara.

Toronto, February 7.

Mr. B. gave me a seat in his sleigh, and after a rapid and very pleasant journey, during which I gained a good deal of information, we reached Toronto yesterday morning.

The road was the same as before, with one deviation however – it was found expedient to cross Burlington Bay on the ice, about seven miles over, the lake beneath being twenty, and five-and-twenty fathoms in depth. It was ten o'clock at night, and the only light was that reflected from the snow. The beaten track, from which it is not safe to deviate, was very narrow, and a man, in the worst, if not the last stage of intoxication, noisy and brutally reckless, was driving before us in a sleigh. All this, with the novelty of the situation, the tremendous cracking of the ice at every instant, gave me a sense of apprehension just sufficient to be exciting, rather than very unpleasant, though I will confess to a feeling of relief when we were once more on the solid earth.

B. is said to be a hard, active, clever, practical man. I liked him, and thought him intelligent and good-natured: we had much talk. Leaving his servant to drive, he would

---

* "So war mir's in der Wiege gesungen," is a common phrase in the north of Germany to express something to which we are seemingly predestined.

jump down, stand poised upon one of the runners, and, thus gliding smoothly along, we conversed.

It is a remarkable fact, with which you are probably acquainted, that when one growth of timber is cleared from the land, another of quite a different species springs up spontaneously in its place. Thus, the oak or the beech succeeds to the pine, and the pine to the oak or maple. This is not accounted for, at least I have found no one yet who can give me a reason for it. We passed by a forest lately consumed by fire, and I asked why, in clearing the woods, they did not leave groups of the finest trees, or even single trees, here and there, to embellish the country? But it seems that this is impossible – for the trees thus left standing, when deprived of the shelter and society to which they have been accustomed, uniformly perish – which, for mine own poor part, I thought very natural.

A Canadian settler *hates* a tree, regards it as his natural enemy, as something to be destroyed, eradicated, annihilated by all and any means. The idea of useful or ornamental is seldom associated here even with the most magnificent timber trees, such as among the Druids had been consecrated, and among the Greeks would have sheltered oracles and votive temples. The beautiful faith which assigned to every tree of the forest its guardian nymph, to every leafy grove its tutelary divinity, would find no votaries here. Alas! for the Dryads and Hamadryads of Canada!

There are two principal methods of killing trees in this country, besides the quick, unfailing destruction of the axe; the first by setting fire to them, which sometimes leaves the root uninjured to rot gradually and unseen, or be grubbed up at leisure, or, more generally, there remains a visible fragment of a charred and blackened stump, deformed and painful to look upon: the other method is slower, but even more effectual; a deep gash is cut through the bark into the stem, quite round the bole of the tree. This prevents the circulation of the vital juices, and by degrees the tree droops and dies. This is technically called *ringing* timber. Is not this like the two ways in which a woman's heart may be killed in this world of ours – by passion and by sorrow? But better far the swift fiery death than this "ringing," as they call it!

February 17.

"There is no *society* in Toronto," is what I hear repeated all around me – even by those who compose the only society we have. "But," you will say, "what could be expected in a remote town, which forty years ago was an uninhabited swamp, and twenty years ago only began to exist?" I really do not know what I expected, but I will tell you what I did *not* expect. I did not expect to find here in this new capital of a new country, with the boundless forest within half a mile of us on almost every side – concentrated as it were the worst evils of our old and most artificial social system at home, with none of its *agrémens*, and none of its advantages. Toronto is like a fourth or fifth rate provincial town, with the pretensions of a capital city. We have here a petty colonial oligarchy, a self-constituted aristocracy, based upon nothing real, nor even upon anything imaginary; and we have all the mutual jealousy and fear, and petty gossip, and mutual meddling and mean rivalship, which are common in a small society of which the members are well known to each other, a society composed, like all societies, of many heterogeneous particles; but as these circulate within very confined limits, there is no getting out of the way of what one most dislikes: we must necessarily hear, see, and passively endure much that annoys and disgusts any one accustomed to the independence of a large and liberal society, or the ease of continental life. It is curious enough to see how quickly a new fashion, or a new folly, is imported from the old country, and with what difficulty and delay a new idea finds its way into the heads of the people, or a new book into their hands. Yet, in the midst of all this, I cannot but see that good spirits and corrective principles are at work; that progress is making: though the march of intellect be not here in double quick time, as in Europe, it does not absolutely stand stock-still.

There reigns here a hateful factious spirit in political matters, but for the present no public or patriotic feeling, no recognition of general or generous principles of policy: as yet I have met with none of these. Canada is a colony, not a *country;* it is not yet identified with the dearest affections and associations, remembrances, and hopes of its inhabitants: it is to them an adopted, not a real mother. Their love, their pride, are not for poor Canada, but for high and happy England; but a few more generations must change all this.

We have here Tories, Whigs, and Radicals, so called; but these words do not signify exactly what we mean by the same designations at home.

You must recollect that the first settlers in Upper Canada were those who were obliged to fly from the United States during the revolutionary war, in consequence of their attachment to the British government, and the soldiers and non-commissioned officers who had fought during the war. These were recompensed for their losses, sufferings, and services, by grants of land in Upper Canada. Thus the very first elements out of which our social system was framed, were repugnance and contempt for the new institutions of the United States, and a dislike to the people of that country, – a very natural result of foregone causes; and thus it has happened that the slightest tinge of democratic, or even liberal principles in politics, was for a long time a sufficient impeachment of the loyalty, a stain upon the personal character, of those who held them. The Tories have therefore been hitherto the influential party; in their hands we find the government patronage, the principal offices, the sales and grants of land, for a long series of years.

Another party, professing the same boundless loyalty to the mother country, and the same dislike for the principles and institutions of their Yankee neighbours, may be called the Whigs of Upper Canada; these look with jealousy and scorn on the power and prejudices of the Tory families, and insist on the necessity of many reforms in the colonial government. Many of these are young men of talent, and professional men, who find themselves shut out from what they regard as their fair proportion of social consideration and influence, such as, in a small society like this, their superior education and character ought to command for them.

Another set are the Radicals, whom I generally hear mentioned as "those scoundrels," or "those rascals," or with some epithet expressive of the utmost contempt and disgust. They are those who wish to see this country erected into a republic, like the United States. A few among them are men of talent and education, but at present they are neither influential nor formidable.

There is among all parties a general tone of complaint and discontent – a mutual distrust – a languor and supineness – the causes of which I cannot as yet understand. Even those who are enthusiastically British in heart and feeling, who sincerely believe that it is the true interest of the colony to remain under the control of the mother country, are as discontented as the rest: they bitterly denounce the ignorance of the colonial officials at home, with regard to the true interests of the country: they ascribe the want of capital for improvement on a large scale to no mistrust in the resources of the country, but to a want of confidence in the measures of the government, and the security of property.

In order to understand something of the feelings which prevail here, you must bear in mind the distinction between the two provinces of Upper and Lower Canada. The project of uniting them once more into one legislature, with a central metropolis, is most violently opposed by those whose personal interests and convenience would suffer materially by a change in the seat of government. I have heard some persons go so far as to declare, that if the union of the two provinces were to be established by law, it were sufficient to absolve a man from his allegiance. On the other hand, the measure has powerful advocates in both provinces.* It seems, on looking over the map of this vast and magnificent country, and reading its whole history, that the political division into five provinces,† each with its independent governor and legislature, its separate correspondence with the Colonial-office, its local laws, and local taxation, must certainly add to the amount of colonial patronage, and perhaps render more secure the subjection of the whole to the British crown; but may it not also have perpetuated local distinctions and jealousies – kept alive divided interests, narrowed the resources, and prevented the improvement of the country on a large and general scale?

But I had better stop here, ere I get beyond my depth. I am not one of those who opine sagely, that women have nothing to do with politics. On the contrary; but I do seriously think that no one, be it man or woman, ought to talk, much less write, on what they do not understand. Not but that I have my own ideas on these matters, though we were never able to make out, either to my own satisfaction or to yours, whether I am Whig or Tory or Radical. In politics I acknowledge but two parties – those who hope and those who fear. In morals, but two parties – those who lie and those who speak truth: and all the world I divide into those who love, and those who hate. This comprehensive arrangement saves me a vast deal of trouble, and answers all my own purposes to admiration.

---

* A very clever paper on this subject was published in the Quebec Mercury, Sept. 14th, 1837.

† Viz. Upper Canada, Lower Canada, Nova Scotia, New Brunswick, and Prince Edward's Island.

February 18.

Toronto is, as a residence, worse and better than other small communities – *worse* in so much as it is remote from all the best advantages of a high state of civilisation, while it is infected by all its evils, all its follies; and *better*, because, besides being a small place, it is a *young* place; and in spite of this affectation of looking back, instead of looking up, it must advance – it may become the thinking head and beating heart of a nation, great, and wise, and happy; – who knows? And there are moments when, considered under this point of view, it assumes an interest even to me; but at present it is in a false position, like that of a youth aping maturity; or rather like that of the little boy in Hogarth's picture, dressed in a long-flapped laced waistcoat, ruffles, and cocked-hat, crying for bread and butter. With the interminable forest within half a mile of us, – the haunt of the red man, the wolf, the bear – with an absolute want of the means of the most ordinary mental and moral development, we have here conventionalism in its most oppressive and ridiculous forms. If I should say, that at present the people here want cultivation, want polish, and the means of acquiring either, *that* is natural – is intelligible – and it were unreasonable to expect it could be otherwise; but if I say they want honesty, *you* would understand me, *they* would not; they would imagine that I accused them of false weights and cheating at cards. So far they are certainly "indifferent honest" after a fashion, but never did I hear so little truth, nor find so little mutual benevolence. And why is it so? – because in this place, as in other small provincial towns, they live under the principle of fear – they are all afraid of each other, afraid to be themselves; and where there is much fear, there is little love, and less truth.

I was reading this morning* of Maria d'Escobar, a

---

* In the Life of Sir James Mackintosh.

Spanish lady, who first brought a few grains of wheat into
the city of Lima. For three years she distributed the produce, giving twenty grains to one man, thirty grains to
another, and so on – *hence all the corn in Peru*.

Is there no one who will bring a few grains of truth to
Toronto?

February 21.

The monotony of this, my most monotonous existence,
was fearfully broken last night. I had gone early to my
room, and had just rung for my maid, when I was aware
of a strange light flashing through the atmosphere – a fire
was raging in the lower parts of the city. I looked out; there
was the full moon, brighter than ever she shows her fair
face in our dear cloudy England – bright and calm as you
now behold her in the Mediterranean, looking down upon
the snowy landscape, and the icy bay glittered like a sheet
of silver; and on the other side of the heavens all was
terror and tumult – clouds of smoke mingled with spires
of flame rose into the sky. Far off the garrison was beating
to arms – the bells tolling; yet all around there was not a
living being to be seen, and the snow-waste was still as
death.

Fires are not uncommon in Toronto, where the houses
are mostly wood; they have generally an alarum once or
twice a week, and six or eight houses burned in the course
of the winter; but it was evident this was of more fearful
extent than usual. Finding, on inquiry, that all the household had gone off to the scene of action, my own maid
excepted, I prepared to follow, for it was impossible to
remain here idly gazing on the flames, and listening to the
distant shouts in ignorance and suspense. The fire was in
the principal street, (King-street,) and five houses were
burning together. I made my way through the snow-
heaped, deserted streets, and into a kind of court or garden at the back of the blazing houses. There was a vast

and motley pile of household stuff in the midst, and a poor woman keeping guard over it, nearly up to her knees in the snow. I stood on the top of a bedstead, leaning on her shoulder, and thus we remained till the whole row of buildings had fallen in. The Irishmen (God bless my countrymen! for in all good – all mischief – all frolic – all danger – they are sure to be the first) risked their lives most bravely; their dark figures moving to and fro amid the blazing rafters, their fine attitudes, and the recklessness with which they flung themselves into the most horrible situations, became at last too fearfully exciting. I was myself so near, and the flames were so tremendous, that one side of my face was scorched and blistered.

All this time, the poor woman on whose shoulder I was leaning, stood silent and motionless, gazing with apparent tranquillity on her burning house. I remember saying to her with a shudder – "But this is dreadful! to stand by and look on while one's home and property are destroyed!" And she replied quietly, "Yes, ma'am; but I dare say some good will come of it. All is for the best, if one knew it; and now Jemmy's safe, I don't care for the rest." Now Jemmy was not her son, as I found, but a poor little orphan, of whom she took charge.

There had been at first a scarcity of water, but a hole being hewed through the ice on the lake, the supply was soon quick and plentiful. All would have been well over, if the sudden fall of a stack of chimneys had not caused some horrible injuries. One poor boy was killed, and some others maimed – poor Mr. B. among the number. After this I returned home rather heart-sick, and nigh to the house a sleigh glanced by at full gallop, on which I could just perceive, in the moonlight, the extended form of a man with his hands clenched over his head – as in agony, or lifeless.

Talking this morning of the incidents of last night, several people have attempted to comfort themselves and me too with assurance, that whatever might be the private loss

or suffering, a fire was always a *public* benefit in Toronto –
a good brick house was sure to arise in the place of a
wooden one. It may be so – brick houses are better certainly than wooden ones – safer too; but as a general argument, I never can bear to think that any public benefit can
be based on individual suffering: I hate the doctrine, and
am not convinced by the logic. In these days of political
economy, it is too much a fashion to consider human
beings only in masses. Wondrous, and vast, and all-impor-
tant as is this wide frame of human society, with all its
component elements variously blended – all its magnificent destinies – is it more important in the sight of God,
more fearful, more sublime to contemplate, than that
mysterious world of powers, and affections, and aspirations, which we call the human soul?

In what regards government and politics, do we not find
the interest of the many sacrificed to the few; while, in all
that regards society, the morals and the happiness of individuals are sacrificed to the many? and both are wrong. I
never can bring myself to admire a social system, in which
the honour, rights, or happiness of any individual, though
the meanest, is made to yield to a supposed future or
general good. It is a wicked calculation, and it will be
found as inexpedient as it is wicked.

We women have especial reason to exclaim against this
principle. We are told openly by moralists and politicians,
that it is for the general good of society, nay, an absolute
necessity, that one-fifth part of our sex should be condemned as the legitimate prey of the other, predoomed to
die in reprobation, in the streets, in hospitals, that the
virtue of the rest may be preserved, and the *pride* and the
passions of men both gratified. But I have a bitter pleasure
in thinking that this most base, most cruel conventional
law is avenged upon those who made and uphold it; that
here the sacrifice of a certain number of one sex to the
permitted license of the other is no general good, but a
general curse – a very ulcer in the bosom of society.

The subject is a hateful one – more hateful is it to hear it sometimes alluded to with sneering levity, and sometimes waved aside with a fastidious or arrogant prudery. Unless we women take some courage to look upon the evil, and find some help, some remedy within ourselves, I know not where it is to come from.

F. told me yesterday a story which I must try to note down for you, if I can find fit words in which to relate it. It is another proof that the realities of life transcend all fiction. I have known – have seen with these mine own eyes, more of tragedy and romance than I would dare to reveal – and who has not?

F. told me, that when he was serving in the army in the Lower Province, a young officer, one of his own friends, (mentioning his name,) seduced from her parents a very pretty girl, about fifteen or sixteen. F. knew something of her family, which was respectable, and tried to save her, but in vain. After some months, the officer S. became tired of his victim, and made her over to a brother officer. F. again interfered, and the poor girl did for a time return to her parents, who gladly and gratefully received her; but she was spoiled for her home, and her home was spoiled for her; the sources of innocent pleasure were poisoned, and why should we wonder and exclaim, if a woman who has once known the flatteries and caresses of love, find it hard – most hard – to resign herself to days and nights, solitary, toilsome, joyless, unendeared? After a while, the colonel of the regiment found means to allure her again from her home; he became strongly attached to her, she was faithful and devoted to him, and he took her with him to England.

Years had passed away, when S., who had left the army, also returned to England. While he was roaming about London, amusing himself as young men are wont to do after a long absence from the central mart of pleasure and dissipation, he betook himself one evening, after a tavern dinner, to some house of infamous resort, and one of the wretched women of the establishment was sent to him as a companion. As she entered the room, S. started from the sofa to encounter in the impudent, degraded, haggard, tawdry thing before him, the poor child who had been his victim in Canada; but long years of vice and misery had not yet utterly hardened her. They stood face to face for a few seconds, and looked in silence upon each other, (and who can tell what in those few seconds may have passed through the minds of each?) and then the miserable girl fell senseless on the floor.

He raised her up, and, in the remorse and agony of the moment, offered her all he had in the world; – poor, poor compensation! He urged her return to Canada: – he would pay all her expenses – place her beyond the reach of want – but it was all in vain.

After the first burst of feeling was over, the wretched girl shook him from her with sullen scorn and despair, and not only refused to return to the home she had disgraced, but even to accept from him anything whatever – and thus she left him. He it was – *himself* – who described the scene to F.

"Poor fellow!" said F., in conclusion, "he did not recover it for a long time – he felt it very much!"

Poor fellow! – and yet he was to be pitied; he did not make the system under which he was educated.

"What became of Captain S.?" I asked.

"O, he married well; he is now a very respectable and excellent man – father of a family."

"He has children, then?"

"Yes; several."

"Daughters?"

"Yes."

"No doubt," thought I, "he will take care of *them*."

And yet one word more before I throw down my pen. I have wandered far from the fire in King-street – but no matter.

How often we hear repeated that most false and vulgar commonplace, that the rakes and the libertines of the other sex are sure to find favour with women – even the most virtuous women! This has been repeated over and over again by wits and playwrights till foolish women take the thing for granted, and foolish men aim at such a reputation as a means of pleasing us. O the folly in them, – the insult to us! No man ever pleased a woman because he was a libertine. What virtuous woman has the least idea of what a libertine really is? What fair, innocent girl, who hears a very agreeable and perfectly well-bred man stigmatised as such, images the thing to herself? Does she know what it means? Can *she* follow such a man into his daily life, his bought pleasures, his shameful haunts? Luckily – or shall I not say unluckily? – she has no knowledge, no conception even, of all this. If the truth were laid open to her, how she would shrink away from all contact with such a being, in the utter disgust which a pure-hearted and pure-minded being would naturally feel! Her idea of a libertine is about as near the truth as poor Minna's idea of a pirate. And so that which is the result of the ignorance, the innocence, the purity of women, is oddly enough converted into a reproach against us.

No; there is no salvation for women but in ourselves: in self-knowledge, self-reliance, self-respect, and in mutual help and pity; no good is done by a smiling abuse of the "wicked courses" of men, while we trample into irrecoverable perdition the weak and erring of our own sex.*

---

* I cannot forbear quoting here a passage from Harriet Martineau, printed since this little journal was written: –

"In the present case, the course to be pursued is to exalt the aims and to strengthen the self-discipline of the whole of society by each one being as good as he can make himself, and relying on his own efforts after self-perfection, rather than on any fortunate arrangements of outward social circumstances. Women, especially, should be allowed the free use of whatever strength their Maker has seen fit to give them; it is essential to the virtue of society that they should be allowed the freest moral action, unfettered by ignorance and unintimidated by authority: *for it is an unquestioned and unquestionable fact, that if women were not weak, men would not be wicked; that if women were bravely pure, there must be an end to the dastardly tyranny of licentiousness.*" – *Society in America*

February 24.

"Ce qui est *moins* que moi, m'éteint et m'assomme: ce qui est *à côté* de moi m'ennuie et me fatigue: il n'y a que ce qui est *au-dessus* de moi qui me soutienne et m'arrache à moi-même."* This is true – *how* true, I *feel*, and far more prettily said than I could say it; and thus it is that during these last few days of illness and solitary confinement, I took refuge in another and a higher world, and bring you my ideas thereupon.

I have been reading over again the Iphigenia, the Tasso, and the Egmont of Goëthe.

Iphigenia is all repose; Tasso all emotion; Egmont all action and passion. Iphigenia rests upon the grace and grandeur of form – it is *statuesque* throughout. Tasso is the strife between the poetic and prosaic nature. Egmont is the working of the real; all here is palpable, practical – even love itself.

I laid down the Tasso with a depth of emotion which I have never felt but after reading Hamlet, to which alone I could compare it; but this is a tragedy profound and complete in effect, without the intervention of any evil principle, without a dagger, without a death, without a tyrant, without a traitor! The *truth* of Leonora d'Este's character struck me forcibly; it is true to itself, as a character, – true to all we know of her history. The shadow which a hidden love has thrown over the otherwise transparent and crystalline simplicity of her mind is very charming – more charming from the contrast with her friend Leonora Sanvitale, who reconciles herself to the project of removing Tasso with exquisite feminine subtlety and sentimental cunning.

Why do you not finish your translation of the Egmont? who will ever do it as you *can?* What deep wisdom, what knowledge of human nature in every scene! And what can be finer than the two female portraits – the imperial,

* Mademoiselle de l'Espinasse.

imperious Margaret of Austria, and the plebeian girl, Clärchen? The character of Clärchen grows upon me as I study it. Is she not really a Flemish Juliet, in her fond impatience, her wilfulness, and the energy of resolve arising out of the strength of passion? And her tenderness for her poor discarded lover, Brackenberg, whom she cannot love and cannot hate, is all so womanly natural!

Iphigenia is an heroic tragedy – Tasso, a poetical tragedy – Egmont, an historical tragedy. Clavigo is what the Germans call a bürgerliche, or domestic tragedy (tragédie bourgeoise.) I did not read this play as I read the Tasso, borne aloft into the ideal, floating on the wings of enthusiasm between the earth and stars; but I laid it down with a terrible and profound *pain* – yes, pain! for it was worse and deeper than mere emotion. Yet it is difficult to speak of Clavigo as a work of art. The matter-of-fact simplicity of the plot, the every-day nature of the characters, the prosaic sentiments, the deep homely pathos of the situations, are almost too real, – they are brought home to our own bosoms, our own experience, – they are just what, in feeling most, we can least dare to express. The scene between Carlos and Clavigo, in which Carlos dissuades his friend from marrying the woman to whom he was engaged, is absolutely wonderful. If Clavigo yielded to any mere persuasion or common-place arguments, he would be a despicable wretch, – we should feel no interest about him, and it would also belie the intellect with which he is endowed. It is to that *intellect* Carlos addresses himself. His arguments, under one point of view – that of common sense – are unanswerable. His reasoning, springing from conviction, is reason itself. What can be more practically wise than his calculations – more undeniably true than his assertions? His rhetoric, dictated as it is by real friendship, and full of fire and animation, is even more overwhelming from its sincerity than its eloquence; and his sarcastic observations on poor Marie Beaumarchais, on her want of personal attractions, her ill health, her foreign manners; on the effect she will produce on society as his wife, and the clog she must prove to his freedom and ambitious career, are all so well aimed, so well meant, so well founded, that far from hating Carlos and despising Clavigo, we are impressed with a terror, a sympathy, a sort of fearful fascination. Every one who reads this play must acknowledge, and with an inward shuddering, that it is possible he might have yielded to this conventional common sense, this worldly logic, even for want of arguments to disprove it. The only things left out in the admirable reasonings and calculations of Carlos are nature and conscience, to which, in their combination, the world have agreed to give the name of *Romance*. But never yet were the feelings and instincts of our nature violated with impunity; never yet was the voice of conscience silenced without retribution. In the tragedy, the catastrophe is immediate and terrible; in real life it might come in some other shape, or it might come later, but it *would* come – of *that* there is no doubt.

February 25.

The accusation which has been frequently made against Goethe, that notwithstanding his passionate admiration for women, he has throughout his works wilfully and systematically depreciated womanhood, is not just, in my opinion. No doubt he is not so universal as Shakspeare, nor so ideal as Schiller; but though he might have taken a more elevated and a more enlarged view of the sex, his portraits of individual women are true as truth itself. His idea of women generally was like that entertained by Lord Byron, rather oriental and *sultanish;* he is a little of the bashaw persuasion. "Goethe," said a friend of mine who knew him intimately, "had no notion of heroic women" (Heldenfrauen;) "in poetry, he thought them unnatural, in history, false. For such delineations as Schiller's Joan of

Arc, and Stauffacher's wife (in Wilhelm Tell) he had neither faith nor sympathy."

His only heroic and ideal creation is the Iphigenia, and she is as perfect and as pure as a piece of Greek sculpture. I think it a proof that if he did not understand or like the active heroism of Amazonian ladies, he had a very sublime idea of the passive heroism of female nature. The basis of the character is *truth*. The drama is the very triumph of unsullied, unflinching truth. It has been said, that Goethe intended this character as a portrait of the Grand Duchess Louise, of Weimar. The *intention* of the poet remains doubtful; but it should seem that from the first moment the resemblance was generally admitted; and what a glorious compliment to the Duchess was this acknowledgment! It was through this true-heartedness, this immutable integrity in word and deed, and through no shining qualities of mind, or blandishments of manner, that she prevailed over the angry passions, and commanded the respect of Napoleon, a man who openly condemned women, but whose instructions to his ambassadors and ministers always ended with "Soignez les femmes," a comment of deep import on our false position and fearful power.

February 27.

I have had a visit this morning from a man I must introduce to you more particularly. My friend Col. F. would have pleased me anywhere, but here he is really invaluable.

Do you remember that lyric of Wordsworth, "The Reverie of Poor Susan," in which he describes the emotions of a poor servant-girl from the country, whose steps are arrested in Cheapside by the song of a caged bird?

'Tis a note of enchantment – what ails her? she sees
A mountain ascending, a vision of trees;
And a single small cottage, a nest like a dove's,
The one only dwelling on earth that she loves!
She looks, and her heart is in heaven!

And how near are human hearts allied in all natural instincts and sympathies, and what an unfailing, universal fount of poetry are these even in their homeliest forms! F. told me to-day, that once, as he was turning down a by-street in this little town, he heard somewhere near him the song of the lark. (Now, you must observe, there are no larks in Canada but those which are brought from the old country.) F. shall speak in his own words: – "So, ma'am, when I heard the voice of the bird in the air, I looked, by the natural instinct, up to the heavens, though I knew it could not be there, and then on this side, and then on that, and sure enough at last I saw the little creature perched on its sod of turf in a little cage, and there it kept trilling and warbling away, and there I stood stock-still – listening with my heart. Well, I don't know what it was at all that came over me, but everything seemed to change before my eyes, and it was in poor Ireland I was again, and my home all about me, and I was again a wild slip of a boy, lying on my back on the hill-side above my mother's cabin, and watching, as I used to do, the lark singing and soaring over my head, and I straining my eye to follow her, till she melted into the blue sky, – and there, ma'am – would you believe it? – I stood like an old fool listening to the bird's song, lost, as in a dream, and there I think I could have stood till this day." And the eyes of the rough soldier filled with tears, even while he laughed at himself, as perfectly unconscious that he was talking poetry, as Mons. Jourdain could be that he was talking prose.

Colonel F. is a soldier of fortune – which phrase means, in *his* case at least, that he owes nothing whatever to fortune, but everything to his own good heart, his own good sense, and his own good sword. He was the son, and glories in it, of an Irish cotter, on the estate of the Knight of Glyn. At the age of fifteen he shouldered a musket, and joined a regiment which was ordered to Holland at the time the Duke of York was opposed to Dumourier. His only reading up to this time had been "The Seven Champions of Christendom," and "The Seven Wise Masters." With his head full of these examples of chivalry, he marched to his first battle-field, vowing to himself, that if there were a dragon to be fought, or a giant to be defied, he would be their man! - at all events, he would enact some valorous exploit, some doughty deed of arms, which should astonish the world and dub him captain on the spot. He then described with great humour and feeling his utter astonishment and mortification on finding the mechanical slaughter of a modern field of battle so widely different from the picture in his fancy; - when he found himself one of a mass in which the individual heart and arm, however generous, however strong, went for nothing - forced to stand still, to fire only by the word of command - the chill it sent to his heart, and his emotions when he saw the comrade at his side fall a quivering corse at his feet, - all this he described with a graphic liveliness and simplicity which was very amusing. He was afterwards taken prisoner, and at the time he was so overcome by the idea of the indignity he had incurred by being captured and stripped, and of the affliction and dishonour that would fall on his mother, that he was tempted to commit suicide in the old Roman fashion; but on seeing a lieutenant of his own regiment brought in prisoner, he thought better of it: a dishonour which the lieutenant endured with philosophy might, he thought, be borne by a subaltern, for by this time, at the age of eighteen, he was already sergeant.

He was soon afterwards exchanged, and ordered out to Canada with his regiment, the Forty-ninth. He obtained his commission as lieutenant in the same regiment by mere dint of bravery and talent; but as his pay was not sufficient to enable him to live like his brother officers and purchase his accoutrements, the promotion he had earned by his good conduct became, for a long time, a source of embarrassment. During the last American war he performed a most brilliant exploit, for which he received his captain's commission on the field. Immediately after receiving it, he astonished his commander by asking leave of absence, although another battle was expected in a few days. The request was, in truth, so extraordinary that General Sheaffe hesitated, and at last refused. F. said, that if his request was granted, he would be again at headquarters within three days; if refused, he would go without leave. "For," said he, "I was desperate, and the truth was, ma'am, there was a little girl that I loved, and I knew that if I could but marry her before I was killed, and I a captain, she would have the pension of a captain's widow. It was all I could leave her, and it would have been some comfort to me, though not to her, poor soul!"

Leave of absence was granted; F. mounted his horse; rode a hundred and fifty miles in an exceedingly short time, married his little girl, and returned the day following to his duties, and to fight another battle, in which, however, he was not killed, but has lived to be the father of a fine family of four brave sons and one gentle daughter.

The men who have most interested me through life were all self-educated, and what are called originals. This dear, good F. is *originalissimo*. Some time ago he amused me, and gave me at the same time a most vivid idea of the minor horrors and irremediable mischiefs of war, by a description of his being quartered in a church in Flanders. The soldiers, on taking possession of their lodging, began by breaking open the poor-boxes and ransacking the sacristy. They then broke up the chairs and benches for fires to cook their rations, and these not sufficing, the wooden saints and carved altars were soon torn down. Finding themselves incommoded by the smoke, some of the soldiers climbed up by the projecting ornaments, and smashed through the windows of rich stained glass to admit the air and let out the smoke. The next morning at sunrise they left this sanctuary of religion and art a foul defaced ruin. A century could not make good again the pollution and spoliation of those few hours.

"You must not be too hard on us poor soldiers," added F., as if answering to a look, for I did not comment aloud. "I had a sort of instinctive perception of the mischief we were doing, but I was certainly the only one; they knew no better, and the precarious life of a soldier gives him the habit of sacrificing everything to the present moment, and a certain callousness to the suffering and destruction which, besides that it ministers to the immediate want, is out of sight and forgotten the next instant. Why I was not quite so insensible as the rest, I cannot tell, unless it was through the goodness of God. When I was a boy, my first feeling, *next to my love for my mother*, was gratitude to God for having made me and called me into being out of nothing. My first thought was what I could do to please him. Now, in spite of all the priest might say, I could not perceive that fasting and praying would do *Him* any good, so I looked about in the fulness of my heart to see what I *could* do – and I fancied there was a voice which whispered continually, 'Do good to your neighbour, do good to your neighbour!'"

With so much overflowing benevolence and fearless energy of character, and all the eccentricity, and sensibility, and poetry, and headlong courage of his country, you cannot wonder that this brave and worthy man interests me; unluckily, I can see him seldom, his life being one of almost unremitting toil.

March 1.

In the different branches of art, each artist thinks his own the highest, and is filled with the idea of all its value and all its capabilities which he understands best, and has most largely studied and developed. "But," says Dr. Chalmers, "we must take the testimony of each man to the worth of that which he does know, and reject the testimony of each to the comparative worthlessness of that which he does not know."

For it is not, generally speaking, that he overrates his own particular walk of art from over-enthusiasm, (no art, when considered separately, as a means of human delight and improvement, *can* be overrated,) but such a *one-sided* artist underrates from ignorance the walks of others which diverge from his own.

Of all artists, musicians are most exclusive in devotion to their own art, and in the want of sympathy, if not absolute contempt, for other arts. A painter has more sympathies with a musician, than a musician with a painter. Vernet used to bring his easel into Pergolesi's room to paint beside his harpsichord, and used to say that he owed some of his finest skies to the inspired harmonies of his friend. Pergolesi never felt, perhaps, any harmonies but those of his own delicious art.

"Aspasia, he who loves not music is a beast of one species, and he who overloves it is a beast of another, whose brain is smaller than a nightingale's, and his heart than that of a lizard!" I refer you for the rest to a striking passage in Landor's "Pericles and Aspasia," containing a most severe philippic, not only against the professors, but the *profession*, of music, and which concludes very aptly, "Panenus said this: let us never believe a word of it!" It is too true that some excellent musicians have been ignorant, and sensual, and dissipated, but there are sufficient exceptions to the sweeping censure of Panenus to show that "imprudence, intemperance, and gluttony," do not always, or necessarily, "open their channels into the sacred stream of music." Musicians are not selfish, careless, sensual, ignorant, because they are musicians, but because, from a defective education, they are nothing else. The German musicians are generally more moral and more intellectual men than English or Italian musicians, and hence their music has taken a higher flight, is more intellectual than the music of other countries. Music as an art has not degraded them, but they have elevated music.

It is impeaching the goodness of the beneficent Creator to deem that moral evil can be inseparably connected with any of the fine arts – least of all with music – the soul of the physical, as love is of the moral, universe.

The most accomplished and intellectual musician I ever met with is Felix Mendelsohn. I do not recollect if it were himself or some one else who told me of a letter which Carl von Weber had addressed to him, warning him that he never could attain the highest honours in his profession without cultivating the virtues and the decencies of life. "A great artist," said Weber, "ought to be a good man."

While I am "i' the vein," I must give you a few more musical reminiscences before my fingers are quite frozen.

I had once some conversation with Thalberg and Felix Mendelsohn, on the unmeaning names which musicians often give to their works, as Concerto in F, Concerto in B ♭, First Symphony, Second Symphony, &c. Mendelsohn said, that though in almost every case the composer might have a leading idea, it would be often difficult, or even impossible, to give any title sufficiently comprehensive to convey the same idea or feeling to the mind of the hearer.

But music, except to musicians, can only give ideas, or rather raise images, by association; it can give the pleasure which the just accordance of musical sounds must give to sensitive ears, but the associated ideas or images, if any, must be quite accidental. Haydn, we are told, when he sat down to compose, used first to invent a story in his own fancy – a regular succession of imaginary incidents and feelings – to which he framed or suited the successive movements (motivi) of his concerto. Would it not have been an advantage if Haydn could have given to his composition such a title as would have pitched the imagination of the listener at once upon the same key? Mendelsohn himself has done this in the pieces which he has entitled "Overture to Melusina," "Overture to the Hebrides," "Meeres Stille und Glückliche Fahrt," "The Brook," and others, – which is better surely than Sonata No. 1, Sonata No. 2. Take the Melusina, for example; is there not in the sentiment of the music, all the sentiment of the beautiful old fairy tale? – first, in the flowing, intermingling harmony, we have the soft elemental delicacy of the water nymph; then, the gushing of fountains, the undulating waves; then the martial prowess of the knightly lover, and the splendour of chivalry prevailing over the softer and more ethereal nature; and then, at last, the dissolution of the charm; the ebbing, fainting, and failing away into silence of the beautiful water spirit. You will say it might answer just as well for Ondine; but this signifies little, provided we have our fancy pitched to certain poetical associations pre-existing in the composer's mind. Thus, not only poems, but pictures and statues, might be set to music. I suggested to Thalberg as a subject the Aurora of Guido. It should begin with a slow, subdued, and solemn movement, to express the slumbrous softness of that dewy hour which precedes the coming of the day, and which in the picture broods over the distant landscape, still wrapt in darkness and sleep, then the stealing upwards of the gradual dawn; the brightening, the quickening of all life; the awakening of the birds, the burst of the sunlight, the rushing of the steeds of Hyperion through the sky, the aerial dance of the Hours, and the whole concluding with a magnificent choral song of triumph and rejoicing sent up from universal nature.

And then in the same spirit – no, in his own grander spirit – I would have Mendelsohn improvise the Laocoon. There would be the pomp and procession of the sacrifice on the seashore; the flowing in of the waves; the two serpents which come gliding on their foamy crests, wreathing, and rearing, and undulating; the horror, the lamentation, the clash of confusion, the death-struggle, and, after a deep pause, the wail lamentation, the funeral march; – the whole closing with a hymn to Apollo. Can you not just imagine such a piece of music, and composed by Mendelsohn? and can you not fancy the possibility of setting to music, in the same manner, Raffaelle's Cupid and Psyche, or his Galatea, or the group of the Niobe?

Niobe would be a magnificent subject either for a concerto, or for a kind of mythological oratorio.

March 2.

Turning over Boswell to-day, I came upon this passage: Johnson says, "I do not commend a society where there is an agreement that what would not otherwise be fair shall be fair; but I maintain that an individual of any society who practises what is allowed, is not dishonest."

What say you to this reasoning of our great moralist? does it not reduce the whole moral law to something merely conventional?

In another place, Dr. Johnson asks, "What proportion does climate bear to the complex system of human life?" I shiver while I answer, "A good deal, my dear Doctor, to some individuals, and yet more to whole races of men."

He says afterwards, "I deal more in *notions* than in facts." And so do I, it seems.

He talks of "men being *held down* in conversation by the presence of women" – *held up* rather, where moral feeling is concerned; and if held down where intellect and social interests are concerned, then so much the worse for such a state of society.

Johnson knew absolutely nothing about women; witness that one assertion, among others more insulting, that it is matter of indifference to a woman whether her husband be faithful or not. He says, in another place, "If we men require more perfection from women than from ourselves, it is doing them honour."

Indeed! If, in exacting from us more perfection, you do not allow us the higher and nobler nature, you do us not honour, but gross injustice; and if you do allow us the higher nature, and yet regard us as subject and inferior, then the injustice is the greater. There, Doctor, is a dilemma for you.

Of all our modern authors, Coleridge best understood the essential nature of women, and has said the truest and most beautiful things of our sex generally; and of all our modern authors, Hazlitt was most remarkable for his utter ignorance of women, generally and individually.

Charles Lamb, of all the men I ever talked to, had the most kindly, the most compassionate, the most reverential feelings towards woman; but he did not, like Coleridge, set forth these feelings with elaborate eloquence – they came gushing out of his heart and stammering from his tongue – clothed sometimes in the quaintest disguise of ironical abuse, and sometimes in words which made the tears spring to one's eyes. He seemed to understand us not as a poet, nor yet as a man of the world; but by the unerring instinct of the most loving and benevolent of hearts.

When Coleridge said antithetically, "that it was the beauty of a woman's character to be characterless," I suppose it is as if he had said, "It is the beauty of the diamond to be colourless;" for he instances Ophelia and Desdemona; and though they are colourless in their pure, transparent simplicity, they are as far as possible from characterless, for in the very quality of being colourless consists the character.

Speaking of Coleridge reminds me that it was from Ludwig Tieck I first learned the death of this wonderful man; and as I, too, had "sat at the feet of Gamaliel and heard his words," the news struck me with a solemn sorrow. I remember that Tieck, in announcing the death of Coleridge, said, in his impressive manner, "A great spirit has passed from the world, and the world knew him not."

There are two ladies in Toronto who have conservatories, a proof of advancing wealth, and civilisation, and taste, which you will greatly admire. One of them had the kindness to send me a bouquet of hot-house flowers while I was ill this last time; and a gift of fifty times the value could not have excited the same pleasure and gratitude. I spread the flowers out on my bed, and inhaled their fragrance with emotions I dare hardly confess – even to you. I had not seen a flower since I left England. No intermediate country had been visited.

Yesterday, (March 4th,) our provincial parliament was prorogued by the governor in state, and I had the honour of *assisting*, as the French say, on that important occasion.

Now you would not ask me, nor do I feel inclined, to encumber my little note-book (consecrated to far different purposes, far different themes) with information to be obtained in every book of travels and statistics; but it is just possible that you *may* know as little of our political constitution and forms of proceeding as I did before my arrival in Upper Canada, and I wish to make the scene of yesterday as intelligible and as interesting to you as I can; so I will give you, in as few words as possible, a sketch of our state machinery.

I have mentioned to you (I believe) that the division of the province of Quebec into Upper and Lower Canada took place in 1791; at that time a chartered constitution and a separate executive and legislative government were conferred on each province: a measure well intended, doubtless, but of which the wisdom was more than doubtful, when we consider the results.

Our constitution of Upper Canada seems, at first view, that of the mother country in miniature, and identical with it. For instance, we have as the head of our executive, a governor, subject, in his military capacity, to the governor-in-chief of Lower Canada, but in all other respects dependent only on the government at home, assisted by an executive council appointed by himself; and we have a legislature composed of a legislative council, nominated by the government, and a house of assembly delegated by the people. These different branches seem to represent, not unfitly, the sovereign, the cabinet of ministers, the House of Lords, and the House of Commons, in England.

But there are some important distinctions which tend to secure the dependence of the provincial legislature on the executive government at home; for I do not know that our parliament has hitherto *legislated* for the colonies.

When Sir Francis Head arrived here, the executive council consisted of five; he added three to the number, who were noted Reformers. About three weeks afterwards this executive council addressed to the governor a document, in which they assumed as their right precisely the same powers and responsibilities as those of the cabinet ministers at home, alleging, that although nominated by the governor, they held themselves responsible to the will of the people.

To which document Sir Francis replied to this effect – "that though the constitution of the colony resembled, it was not to be considered as identical with, the constitution of the mother country: – that if the lieutenant-governor stood in place of the sovereign – if, like the sovereign, he could *do no wrong*, then it would be evident that a ministry, an executive council, or some other body of men, should be appointed, who might be responsible to the country for their conduct. But this was not the case. The lieutenant-governor was delegated by the king, not as the representative, but as the responsible minister of the sovereign, subject to impeachment for neglecting the interests of the people, and liable to immediate recal; and that under such circumstances, to render the lieutenant-governor responsible for the acts of an executive council, which was responsible only to the people, was a manifest injustice, as well as an anomaly."

All which seems to me a very clear case as thus stated. The governor also denied not only any right or power of his own to alter one letter or iota of the constitution, but all power in the united legislature of Upper Canada to alter or *improve* the political constitution of the country as by law established, this power resting only with the executive in England. From all which it appears, as far as I can understand, that the government of this province is not derived from the people who inhabit it, nor responsible to them or their delegates.

Immediately on receiving this answer, the six councillors who had presented the document or remonstrance above mentioned, resigned their seats in the council, and Sir Francis immediately appointed four others. The president of the executive council – that is, the *Premier* of our cabinet of ministers – is Mr. Sullivan.

The legislative council varies in number: at present there are, I believe, thirty members. Of these, twenty-one are Scotch and Canadians, and nine English, Irish, and Americans. They represent the aristocracy of the country, but differ from the House of Lords in not being hereditary; they are nominated for life by the governor. The speaker is the Chief Justice Robinson, a Tory in politics, and a very able and accomplished man.

The House of Assembly consists of the delegates of the people, the number increasing with the population. As soon as the number of inhabitants in a town or county amounts to a certain number fixed by law, they have the right of choosing one or two representatives in parliament. The House of Assembly consisted, in 1831, of about forty members. At present there are twenty-two counties which send each two members to parliament; three counties which send only one member; and the four ridings of York, and the four ridings of Lincoln, each one member; and seven towns each one member: in all sixty-two members. Of these, forty-four are Conservative members, and eighteen are Reformers. In the former House of Assembly, dissolved by Sir Francis Head in 1836, the majority were Radicals, or opposed to the British supremacy. The best speakers on the Conservative side are, Hagerman, the Solicitor-general,* a Tory in politics, a man of great ability and good nature, but somewhat

* Now Attorney-general.

coarse and overbearing in character and manner: Draper, the member for Toronto,* a clever, active-minded man, and a fluent speaker; M'Nab,† the member for Wentworth, also an able and influential man of large property; and Mr. Prince, member for Sandwich, a gentleman educated at the English bar, and of very superior attainments, liberal, though not revolutionary, in principle. On the Opposition side, the cleverest man and most eloquent speaker is Dr. Rolph.

The members are paid for their attendance during the session at the rate of ten shillings a day.

This slight sketch will give you some general idea of the political constitution and the state of parties in Upper Canada.

The prorogation took place yesterday at three o'clock; when we arrived in front of the government offices, the scene was very striking. The snow-expanse was all around, and, between the shore of the frozen bay and the line of building, the space was filled by sleighs of all shapes and sizes, the horses curveting and kicking up the snow, and a crowd of some hundred people, in all manner of strange defences against the piercing frost, intermingled with military costumes, and a few Indians lounging by in their blanket-coats and war-plumes.

The hall of the legislative council is a subject of great pride to the Canadians. It is certainly a spacious and lofty room, with a splendid throne and the usual superfluity of gilding and varnish; yet the interior decorations (the administration of the people here) are in the vilest possible taste – which critical observation I make in no offensive spirit; anything which is *attempted* here, beyond the putting together of a log-house, is praiseworthy. We must have time – time! "E coll' Tempo, tutto!" On the right of the throne sat Chief Justice Robinson; he has a fine head and acute features, and the most pleasing, insinuating

---

* Now Solicitor-general.

† Afterwards Speaker of the House of Assembly.

voice I ever heard. The judges and law officers of the crown sat at a table in front, and the other members of the legislative council were ranged on each side. My proper place was on the right, among the wives of the officials, the aristocracy of Toronto. The toilettes around me were gay and pretty, in the fashion of two or three years ago, and all the ladies showed a disposition to be polite and amiable; but I was too much a stranger to join in the conversation, and there were none near me to give me any necessary explanation, or to point out any remarkable or distinguished persons, if there were such. Among the spectators opposite I remarked a man with a very extraordinary head and countenance, and I was told that he was a disciple of Edward Irving, and a preacher of the "Unknown Tongues," and that several persons in Toronto, even members of the council, were converts to these wild doctrines.

The governor, as he alighted, was enthusiastically cheered by the populace – a circumstance rather unusual of late, and which caused a good deal of excitement and exultation around me. In a moment afterwards he entered and took his seat on the throne.

As an official representative, Sir Francis has not the advantage of the height, fine person, and military bearing of Sir John Colborne. He is a little man, with a neat, active figure, a small but intelligent head, grave and rather acute features; his bright blue eye is shrewd and quick, with an expression of mingled humour and benevolence, and his whole deportment in the highest degree unaffected and pleasing.

The members of the House of Assembly, being summoned, appeared below the bar, and the governor read his speech over with very distinct utterance and much quiet self-possession. He recapitulated the most important enactments of the session, thanked the gentlemen of the House of Assembly for the promptitude with which they had relieved the king's government from the embarrassment caused by the supplies having been withheld by the late House of Assembly, and ended by congratulating both Houses on the harmony, confidence, and tranquillity which prevailed generally throughout the province.

The titles of the various bills passed during the session were then read; they amounted to one hundred and forty-seven; the reading occupied about an hour and a quarter. Among them were a few which especially fixed my attention.

For instance, there was an act for making the remedy in cases of seduction more effectual, and for the provision of children born out of wedlock by the supposed fathers, &c. This bill originated in the legislative council, and it is worthy of remark that they are enacting *here*, a law, which in England has been lately repealed, and which Sir Francis Head himself has openly condemned. You remember the outcry which was raised against that provision of the new poor law act, which made women solely answerable for the consequences of their own misconduct – misconduct, into which, in nine cases out of ten, they are betrayed by the conventional license granted to the other sex; but I, as a woman, with a heart full of most compassionate tenderness for the wretched and the erring among my sister women, do still aver that the first step towards our moral emancipation is that law which shall leave us the sole responsible guardians of our own honour and chastity; it may seem at first view most pitiable that not only the ban of society, but also the legal liabilities, should fall on the least guilty; and hard indeed will be the fate of many a poor, ignorant delinquent, for the next few years, unless those women who take a generous and extended view of the whole question, be prepared to soften the horrors that will ensure by individual help and acts of mercy; but let the tendency of such an enactment, such a public acknowledgment of the moral and legal responsibility of women, be once understood, let it once be brought into action, and I am sure the result will be the general benefit and elevation of the whole sex; it brings the only remedy to this hateful mischief which can be brought; the rest remains with ourselves. The best boon we could ask of our masters and legislators is, to be left in all cases responsible for our own actions and our own debts.

Another act provided two additional judges of the Court of King's Bench, and other law improvements, by which the jail deliveries were rendered more frequent, and the long and demoralising imprisonment, previous to trial and conviction, would be shortened. This sounds well. I should observe, that by all accounts the jails in this province are in a very bad state, and require revision altogether.

Another act established a provincial court of equity, rendered necessary by the nature of the land tenures here, and to secure in the possession of their property, those whose titles, honestly acquired, were defective from mistake, ignorance, or accident; also to punish frauds and breaches of trust, beyond the reach of common law. I was rather surprised to find that this act gave to the presiding Chancellor even larger powers than those of the Lord Chancellor at home. It signifies nothing now, when there is *nothing* on which these powers can be exercised; but it will signify much, fifty or a hundred years hence, as society becomes more complex and artificial, and the rights of property more intricate.

The chancellor will have power to repeal (or, what comes to the same thing, institute proceedings to repeal) all letters patent *improvidently* granted: an indefinite and dangerous power in bad hands.

Another act was to amend the charter of the University of Upper Canada. The House of Assembly, in addressing the governor at the opening of the session, had expressed their regret, that "no useful result had hitherto attended the beneficent intentions of his majesty in granting a charter to King's College, and their hope that the province would shortly possess the means within itself of bestowing upon the young a *refined* and *liberal* education."

Next to the clergy reserves, there is no question which has been debated so long and so vehemently, as this of an

endowed university. Forty years ago, in 1797, the establishment of such an institution was recommended in an
address from the provincial legislature to the British government, but it was not till 1828 that the charter was sent
over. On this occasion, the legislative council thanked his
majesty's government humbly and gratefully for such a
munificent proof of paternal regard. The House of Assembly, on the contrary, made their gratitude conditional –
"provided that the principles upon which the charter has
been founded shall, upon inquiry, prove to be conducive
to the advancement of true learning and piety, and
friendly to the civil and religious liberty of the people."

In what might consist "the civil and religious liberty of
the people" was not so easily agreed. The first charter,
modelled after those of our English universities, was
deemed too exclusive for a young country like this, and
became a source of contention and dissatisfaction. The
bills to alter and amend the terms of the charter sent up
by the House of Assembly were always thrown out by the
legislative council, and thus matters remained until this
session. The Act just passed abolishes the necessity of any
religious test or qualification whatever in those who enter
as scholars, and places the establishment under the partial
control of the judges and legislature, instead of the exclusive direction of the clergy. The presidency of the university remains with Archdeacon Strahan, but for the future
the president shall not necessarily hold any ecclesiastical
office. Two members of the legislative council have
entered a formal protest against this Act; they objected
"that half of the lands which had been granted for the
erection of free grammar schools throughout the different
districts, amounting to two hundred and twenty-five
thousand acres, had been given up to the endowment of
the university, and that these free schools not being yet
erected, this was a misapplication of the school-lands; and
that after such two hundred and twenty-five thousand
acres had been applied to the uses of the university, the
residue of the school-lands would not suffice for the pur-

pose of erecting free seminaries, being of a bad quality; nearly eighty thousand acres of the lands originally allotted for the maintenance of schools having been exchanged for other lands of a worse quality, and less eligibly situated: that the benefits of a good education, instead of being equally diffused through the province, were confined to one large and expensive establishment – too expensive for the population and wants of the country."

Notwithstanding these objections, and the others made by the Tory and high church party, the Act has passed after vehement debates, and I presume that the erection of the new university will be commenced forthwith.

Another act was for the establishment of agricultural societies, and the encouragement of agriculture in the several districts. There are already agricultural societies in one or two districts, and whenever a certain sum of money was subscribed by the people, for a purpose, the government assisted them with a further sum of one hundred pounds and upwards.

Various bills were passed, voting sums of money for the mending of roads; the improvement of the harbours and light-houses on the lakes; the completion of the great Welland Canal, which unites Lake Ontario with Lake Erie; and the opening of a great northern and western railway to connect Lake Huron with Lake Ontario. All this is very well; but, as H. said this morning, where is the money to come from? It has become difficult to raise loans; and individuals do not willingly speculate in this country. That all these things will be done at some time or other is certain – certain as that the sun holds his course in heaven; but some changes must take place before speculation on a large scale becomes either secure or profitable.

A very important act was one introducing an improved system into the land-granting department; but the law, as explained to me, remains defective: all the arrangements of our domestic policy are such as to render it difficult and inexpedient for aliens to buy or hold land in this province, and even to British subjects the terms are not so favour-

able as in the United States. Mr. Prince brought in a bill
this session for encouraging settlers from all parts of the
world, permitting aliens to acquire and hold lands on
easier terms than at present, and to claim the rights of
citizenship after a three years' residence.

"Every one," said he, "knows well, though I am almost
afraid to mention it in this place, that countless numbers
of German, Swiss, and even British emigrants passed during the summer of 1836, through Canada to the western
parts of the United States, and that none could be prevailed on to stop and settle in this province, though the
fertility of the lands, and all other natural advantages, are
confessedly greater here, and the distance saved from five
to seven hundred miles."*

This bill was violently opposed, upon the ground that it
would introduce, as settlers, an immense number of foreigners hostile to the principles of the British constitution.
None denied that it would introduce both population and
capital, and that "men, women, and money," being the
three *wants* of the country, would tend to supply these
wants. With regard to the danger to our constitution from
the admission of aliens educated in different principles,
one member made some shrewd and pertinent observations, in a very homely style. "We profess," said he, "to
desire emigration, yet we prohibit virtually nine-tenths of
the world from setting their foot on our shores; and why?
because these foreigners, naturally republicans, would naturally overturn our institutions. Now all foreigners are not
republicans; the Swiss, Prussians and other Germans, who
pass through our country in multitudes, and cannot be
persuaded to set up their rest here, are more friendly to
our British institutions than to those of the United States;

---

* The usual route of the emigrants to the New Western States is through
the State of New York by the Erie Canal, passing the Niagara River at
Queenston, and then through the finest parts of Upper Canada to Detroit,
in Michigan. The number of the emigrants and settlers who passed
through Canada to the Western States, in 1835 and 1836, has been estimated at 200,000.

and if it were otherwise, it is a poor compliment to our government and institutions to say that they suffer from comparison, and that they who have enjoyed any other will not endure existence under ours. We are told that the Americans offer every inducement to foreigners and British subjects to settle in their new states; and we do not find that the monarchical predilections of these emigrants lead them to disturb the government of their new country," &c. &c.

This bill passed the House of Assembly, and was lost in the Legislative Council. The fate of Texas was adduced as an example of the consequences of suffering foreign capitalists to speculate in the lands of Canada; but every one agrees that something must be done to attract to the province emigrants of a higher grade than the Scotch and Irish paupers who now locate themselves on small portions of land, and who aid but little in developing the immense resources of this magnificent country. It is in the second generation that this class of people make useful and eligible settlers.

The vital question of the clergy reserves remains as yet unsettled by law; the motion for establishing fifty-seven endowed rectories within the province, exercising all powers, and privileges, and jurisdiction, which by the ecclesiastical law belongs to the Church of England, gave rise to a most violent and abusive debate in the House of Assembly, which ended in the motion being lost; but the House resolved, that "the rights acquired under the patents, by which certain rectories have already been endowed, should be considered inviolate."

An Act, for a limited time, to impose an additional duty on licenses to vend spirituous liquors can do but little good in the present state of society here. You might as well think to dam up a torrent with a bundle of reeds, or put out a conflagration with a cup of water, as attempt to put down drunkenness and vice by such trifling measures.

I was in hopes that some Act would have passed this session for the erection of a provincial lunatic asylum. At present these unfortunate persons either wander about uncared for, or are shut up in the jails. Instances are known of pauper lunatics straying into the forests, and perishing there. The fate of those confined in the prisons is not better; the malady is prolonged and aggravated by the horrid species of confinement to which, in such places, these wretched beings are *necessarily* subjected. A benevolent physician of this place (Dr. Rees) has offered a block of land a few miles from Toronto for the site of an hospital or asylum for lunatics, but at present it seems the intention of the legislature to take the penitentiary at Kingston for a lunatic asylum, and erect another penitentiary on a different plan. In the mean time this dreadful evil continues – *must* continue for two or three years longer; and think what an amount of individual suffering may be crowded into this period! When I was at Niagara there was a maniac in the jail there, who had been chained up for four years. Here was misery of the most pitiable kind suffering all the pains and penalties of crime – nay, far more, for the worst criminals had a certain degree of liberty. In the town jail of Toronto four insane persons are at this time in confinement.

It must be remembered that this state of things is not worse than that which prevailed in rich and civilised England only a few years ago.

Good night! for my spirits are wearied, and my fingers are frozen.

March 6.

As light was the eldest-born principle of the universe, so love was the eldest-born passion of humanity, though people quote Milton to prove that vanity was so – in our own sex at least: and many are the witty sayings on this favourite text; but they are wrong, and their text misinterpreted. Eve, when she looked in passionate delight on her own lovely face reflected in the stream, knew not it was her own, and had nothing else to love; the moment she found an Adam on whom to lavish the awakened sympathies, she turned from the shadow to the reality, even though "less winning soft, less amiably fair:" she did not sit upon the bank, and pine to death for her own fair face,

> "Like that too beauteous boy
>   That lost himself by loving of himself;"

– while the voice of love wooed her in vain. Vanity in this instance was but the shadow of love.

But, O me! how many women since the days of Echo and Narcissus, have pined themselves into air for the love of men who were in love only with themselves!

Where the vivacity of the intellect and the strength of the passions, exceed the developement of the moral faculties, the character is likely to be embittered or corrupted by extremes, either of adversity or prosperity. This is especially the case with women; but as far as my own observation and experience go, I should say that many more women have their heads turned by prosperity than their hearts spoiled by adversity; and, in general, the female character rises with the pressure of ill fortune. Sir James Mackintosh says somewhere, "That almost every woman is either formed in the school, or tried by the test of adversity: it may be more necessary to the greatness of the female character than that of men."

And why so? – I understand the first part of this sentence, but not the last. Why should the test of adversity be *more* necessary to the greatness of the female character than that of men? The perpetual, and painful, and struggling collision of man with man forms and tries him; woman has little compulsory collision with woman; our equals are our most severe schoolmasters, and the tyranny of circumstances supplies this *want* to women.

March 8.

Before the languid heart gasp and flutter itself to death, like a bird in an exhausted receiver, let us see what can be done, for something must be done.

This relentless winter seems to stiffen and contract every nerve, and the frost is of such fierceness and intensity, that it penetrates even to the marrow of one's bones. One of the workmen told me yesterday, that on taking hold of an iron bar it had taken the skin off his hand, as if he had grasped it red-hot: it is a favourite trick with the children to persuade each other to touch with the tongue a piece of metal which has been exposed to the open air; adhesion takes place immediately; even the metal knobs on the doors of the room I carefully avoid touching – the contact is worse than unpleasant.

Let but the spring come again, and I will take to myself wings and fly off to the west! – But will spring *ever* come? – When I look out upon the bleak, shrouded, changeless scene, there is something so awfully silent, fixed, and immutable in its aspect, that it is enough to disturb one's faith in the everlasting revolutions of the seasons. Green leaves and flowers, and streams that murmur as they flow, soft summer airs, to which we open the panting bosom – panting with too much life – shades grateful for their coolness – can such things be, or do they exist only in poetry and paradise?

If it were not for this journalising, I should fall into a lethargy – as it is, I could envy a marmot or a dormouse; and if it were not for my promise to you, I should even abandon this daily noting of daily nothings, of which I begin to be thoroughly ashamed. One day is only distinguishable from another by the degrees of the thermometer. Nor can I, while imprisoned by this relentless climate, seek the companionship and sympathy which stand aloof – for no other reason that I can guess, but because I come among them branded with notoriety. I wished to throw open my house in the evening, and break or thaw the social frost around me; but such a novel and unheard of idea would startle all the inhabitants from their propriety. There must be here, as elsewhere, kind-hearted, good people, if only they would be natural, and not afraid of each other – and of poor, solitary me. However, in the strait in which I am placed there is still a remedy.

"Books, dreams, are each a world; and books, we know,
Are a substantial world."

A world ever at hand. I must try all mechanical means to maintain the balance of my mind, and the unimpaired use of my faculties, for they will be needed. There is no rescue but in occupation – serious and useful occupation, if I can make or find it – trivial occupation, when I can *not*. The desultory reading in which I have lately indulged will never do; I must look round for something to try my strength, – and force and fix my attention. To use Lord Byron's phrase, I must get "a file for the serpent."

March 10.

I have found a *file*, or what I will use as such. I shall take to translating.

I brought from Weimar Dr. Ekermann's book,* which, as yet, I have only glanced over in parts; by this time it must be well known all over the world of literature. When I left Weimar, it was not yet published. There my attention was strongly directed to this book, not so much by the interest as by the *kind* of interest it had excited around me. I remember one of Goethe's grandsons turning over the leaves as it lay on my table, and exclaiming with animation – "Es ist der Grosspapa selbst! da lebt er! – da spricht er!" (It is grand-papa himself! – here he lives – he speaks!)

Another, habitually intimate with the domestic life of

---

* Gespräche mit Goethe. (Conversations with Goëthe.)

Goethe, said, with emotion – "Es ist das buch von liebe und wahrheit." (It is the book of love and truth.)

"Whatever may be in that book," said a dear friend of mine, when she placed it in my hands, "I would pledge myself beforehand for its truth. The mind of Ekermann, at once unsullied and unruffled by all contact with the world, is so constituted, that he could not perceive or speak other than the truth, any more than a perfectly clear and smooth mirror could reflect a false or a distorted image."

Now all this was delightful! The sort of praise one does not often hear either of a book or a writer – and so, to read I do most seriously incline.

I read the preface to-day, and part of the introduction.

In the preface, Ekermann says, very beautifully, "When I think of the fulness, the richness of those communications which for nine years formed my chief happiness, and now perceive how little of all I have been able to preserve in writing; I feel like a child, who seeks to catch in his open hands the plenteous showers of spring, and finds that the greatest part has escaped through his fingers."

A little farther on he says – "I am far from believing that I have here unveiled the whole inward being of Goethe, (der ganze innere Goethe.) One may liken this most wonderful spirit to a many-sided diamond, which in every direction reflected a different hue; and as, in his intercourse with different persons in different positions, he would himself appear different – I can only say modestly – 'This is MY Goethe!'"

This may be said with truth of every character, viewed through the mind of another; of every portrait of the same individual painted by a different artist.

And not only where we have to deal with marked and distinguished characters, but in the common intercourse of life, we should do well to take this distinction into account; and, on this principle, I would never judge a character by hearsay, nor venture further, even in my own judgment, than to admit that such a person I like, and such another I do *not* like. In the last case the fault, the deficiency, the cause, whatever it may be, is as probably on my side as on theirs; and though this may sound offensive and arbitrary, it is more just than saying such a one is worthless or disagreeable; for the first I can never know, and as for the latter, the most disagreeable people I ever met with had those who loved them, and thought them, no doubt with reason, very agreeable.

Of a very great, and at the same time complex mind, we should be careful not to trust entirely to any one portrait, even though from the life, and of undoubted truth. Johnson, as he appears in Boswell, is, I think, the only perfectly individualised portrait I remember; and hence the various and often inconsistent effect it produces. One moment he is an object of awe, the next of ridicule: we love, we venerate him on this page – on the next we despise, we abhor him. Here he gives out oracles and lessons of wisdom surpassing those of the sages of old; and there we see him grunting over his favourite dish, and "*trundling*" the meat down his throat, like a Hottentot. But, in the end, such is the influence of truth, when we *can* have the whole of it, that we dismiss Johnson like a friend to whose disagreeable habits and peculiarities we had become accustomed, while his sterling virtues had won our respect and confidence. If I had seen Johnson once, I should probably have no impression but that made on my imagination by his fame and his austere wisdom, and should remain awe-struck; at the second interview I might have disliked him. But Boswell has given me a friend, and I love the old fellow, though I cannot love his bull-dog manners, and worse than bull-dog prejudices.

Were it possible to have of Goethe as universal, many-sided, and faithful a picture, it would be something transcendent in interest; but I do not think he had a Boswell near him, nor any one, I imagine, who would be inclined to buy immortality at the same price with that worthy; – at least Ekermann does not seem such a man.*

The account of himself in the introduction is the most charming little bit of autobiography I have ever met with: it is written to account for his first introduction to, and subsequent intercourse with, Goethe, and is only too short. The perfect simplicity and modesty, yet good taste and even elegance of this little history, are quite captivating. The struggles of a poor German scholar, the secret aspirations, the feelings, the sorrows, the toils, the hardships, of [a] refined and gentle spirit, striving with obscurity and vulgar cares and poverty, are all briefly but graphically touched, – a sketch only, yet full of life and truth. Ekermann, it seems, was the son of a poor cottager and pedlar, residing, when not engaged in his ambulatory traffic, in a little village near Hamburg. Though steeped in poverty, they seem to have been above actual want, and not unhappy. For the first fourteen years of his life Ekermann was employed in taking care of their only cow, the chief support of the family; gathering wood for firing in the winter; and in summer occasionally assisting his father

---

* A lady, a near and dear relation of Goethe, who had lived for very many years in the closest communication with him, was pressed by arguments and splendid offers of emolument to give to the world the domestic life of the poet, or at least contribute some notes with regard to his private conversations and opinions. She refused at once and decidedly. "I had," said she, "several reasons for this. In the first place, I have not a good memory, and I have a very lively imagination: I could not always trust myself. What I should say would be something very near the truth, and very like the truth, but would it be *the truth*? How could I send into the world a book, of the exact truth of which I could not in my own conscience, and to my own conviction, be assured? A second reason was, that Goethe did not die young; I could not do him any justice he was unable to do himself, by telling the world what he *would* have done, what he *could* have done, or what he had intended to do, if time had been given. He lived long enough to accomplish his own fame. He told the world all he chose the world to know; and if not, is it for me – for *me!* – to fill up the vacancy, by telling what, perhaps, he never meant to be told? – what I owed to his boundless love and confidence? – *that* were too horrible!"

in carrying the package of small wares with which he travelled through the neighbouring villages. "All this time," says Ekermann, "I was so far from being tormented by any secret ambition for higher things, or any intuitive longing after science or literature, that I did not even know that they existed." In this case, as in many others, accident, as we call it, developed the latent faculties of a mind of no common order. A woodcut of a galloping horse – the excise stamp, on a paper of tobacco which his father brought from Hamburg, – first excited his admiration, and then the wish to imitate what he admired. He attempted to copy the horse with a pen and ink; succeeded, much to his own delight and the wonder of his simple parents; and then, by dint of copying some poor engravings, (lent to him by a potter in the neighbourhood, who used them to ornament his ware,) he became a tolerable draughtsman; he was then noticed and encouraged by a gentleman, who asked him if he should like to become a painter. Now the only idea of a painter which had ever occurred to his father and mother was that of a housepainter; and as they had seen house-painters at Hamburg suspended on dangerous scaffolds, when decorating the exterior of the buildings there, his tender mother begged him not to think of a trade in which he ran the risk of breaking his neck; and the offer was respectfully declined.

In the family of the gentleman who noticed him, Ekermann picked up a little French, Latin, and music; and now the thirst for information was awakened in his mind; he studied with diligence, and, as a clerk in different offices, maintained himself till the breaking out of the war of deliverance in 1813. He then, like every man who could carry a firelock, enrolled himself in the army, and made the campaigns of 1813 and 1814. The corps in which he served was marched into Flanders, and there for the first time he had the perception of what pictures are, of all that he had lost in refusing to become a painter, and could have wept, as he says, for very grief and self-approach. He passed all his leisure in wandering through the churches, gazing on the works of the great Flemish masters. At once the resolution to become an artist took possession of his mind. When his regiment was disbanded, he set to work and placed himself under the tuition of Ramberg, in Hanover. There is something very touching in this part of his history; he had himself nothing in the world – no means of subsistence; but he had a friend in tolerable circumstances at Hanover; he made his solitary way through the snow on foot to that city, and took up his residence with this friend of his youth, who shared with him his home and slender income. Anxious, however, not to be a burthen longer than was absolutely necessary, he sought employment, worked so hard as to injure his health, and brought himself to the verge of the grave, – in short, he was obliged to give up all hope of studying art as a profession, and he took to literature: here he showed the same indefatigable temper, and, conscious of his imperfect education, he put himself to school; and, that he might be enabled to pay for instruction, procured the situation of a clerk in a public office. At the age of twenty-six he became a scholar in the second class of the Gymnasium, among boys of fourteen and fifteen. Here, he says, the most advanced pupils in the school, far from turning him into ridicule, treated him with every mark of respect, and even assisted him in his studies; but between his clerk's office and his schooling there remained to him scarce one moment either for food or exercise; he who was eager to perfect himself in the classics, remained ignorant of the great laws by which he held his existence; and we are not surprised to find that the result of these excessive efforts was broken health, a constitution almost destroyed, and, in fact, permanently injured. In the midst of all this, Ekermann found time to fall deeply in love; and the wish to obtain distinction and some settled means of subsistence assumed another, a more pleasing, and a more anxious form. But ill health and a desultory education were against him. He wrote a book of poems, which was published and met with some success; the profits enabled him to go to a university, where for some time he seems to have entertained the hope of procuring an office, or a professorship, which should enable him to marry. Thus year after year passed. In the year 1822, he wrote his "Beiträge zur Poesie," (poetical essays,) and sent the MSS., with a modest letter, to Goethe; the result was, an invitation to Weimar, where he finally took up his residence. Some time afterwards he procured a permanent situation, and was enabled to marry the woman he loved. Shy by nature, and averse to society, ambitious only of literary distinction, having laid up his whole heart, and hopes, and life, in the quiet pleasures of his modest home, and in the society of the wife whom he had obtained after a protracted engagement of ten years, Ekermann during the next three years might, perhaps, be pronounced a happy man. In the third year of his marriage he lost his amiable wife, who died in giving birth to a son, and since that time he has become more shy and inaccessible than ever – shrinking nervously from the presence of strangers, and devoted to the poor little infant which has cost him so dear. The daughter-in-law and the grandsons of Goethe, who look up to him with a tender reverence, he seems to idolise, and has become in some sort the literary Mentor and aid of the young men, as Goethe had been *his,* long years ago. It is a family tie, every way sanctified, and not, I trust, to be severed in this world by aught that the world can give or take away.

The period at which these conversations commence was an interesting epoch in the personal existence of Goethe; it was about the time of his visit to Marienbad, in 1823, and was marked by the composition of one of his finest lyrical poems, the elegy in three parts, which he has entitled, "Trilogie der Leidenschaft." He was then seventy-four, but in appearance sixty: his eye still beaming with a softened fire, a cheek yet fresh with health, a well-knit figure, an upright, graceful carriage, a manner which took all hearts captive. The grand, the beautiful old man! – old, yet, alas! still young enough, it seems, in heart and frame, to feel once more, and for the last time, the touch of passion; not a mere old man's love, such as we usually see it – half disease, or half infatuation – at best a weakness – the sickly flare of a dying lamp; but genuine passion in all its effects, and under its most profound and most painful, as well as its most poetical aspect.

Ekermann merely touches on this subject with all possible, all becoming delicacy; but there seems no occasion for me to suppress here the mention of some circumstances not generally known, but which can bring nor shame, nor pain, nor regret to any human being.

The object of this love was a young person he had met at Marienbad – one of the daughters of Madame de L—— w. She has been described to me as fair and rather full-formed, intelligent, accomplished, and altogether most attractive. He began by admiring and petting her as a child – then loved her, – loved her against his will, his better sense, one might almost say, against his nature. There was a report in Germany that he had offered her marriage; this is not true; but it was feared he might do so. He returned from Marienbad changed in manner; he had lost that majestic calm, that cheerfulness, which inspired such respect as well as affection in those around him; and for some weeks all were in anxiety for the event. But Goethe was a man of the world, and a man of strong sense; he resolved to free himself from a thraldom of which he felt all the misery, and perceived all the ridicule. He struggled manfully, and conquered; but after weeks of terrible suffering and a fit of illness, during which he was seized with a kind of lethargy, a suspension of all memory, perception, feeling, from which he was with difficulty roused: but he *conquered;* and on his recovery betook himself to his usual remedy for pain and grief – hard work. He found "a file for the serpent," and was soon deep in his new theory of colours and his botanical researches. If there be any one in the world so vulgar-minded and so heartless, as to find in this story of a great poet's last love, a subject for cruel and coarse pleasantry, I must say that I pity such a being. In the elegy alluded to, we find no trace of the turbulence of youthful passion – no hopes, no wishes, no fears, no desires, no reproaches, such as lovers are wont to sing or say. It is no flowery, perfumed wreath of flattery at the feet of a mistress, but rather the funereal incense of a solemn and fated sacrifice. It breathes the profoundest, the saddest tenderness – as if in loving he took leave of love. There is nothing in these lines unbecoming to his age, nor discreditable to *her;* but all is grand, and beautiful, and decorous, and grave, in the feeling and expression. Sometimes, when I read it and think upon its truth, tears fill my eyes even to overflowing, and my very heart bows down in compassionate reverence, as if I should behold a majestic temple struck by the lightning of heaven, and trembling through its whole massy structure. In other moments of calmer reflection, I have considered the result with another kind of interest, as one of the most extraordinary poetical and psychological phenomena in the history of human genius.

The first part of this poem is addressed to the shade of Werther, and contains some of the most powerful and harmonious lines he ever wrote; to the second part he has prefixed, as a motto, those beautiful lines in his own Tasso –

> Und wenn der Mensch in seiner Qual verstummt
> Gab *mir* ein Gott zu sagen was ich leide!

Ekermann says, that when Goethe laid before him this singular poem, he found it distinguished above all the rest of his manuscripts, written with peculiar care in his own neatest handwriting, on the best paper, and fastened with a silken knot into a red morocco cover. This little piece of fanciful, sentimental dandyism will bring to your recollection the anecdote of Rousseau binding his favourite letters in the Heloise with ribbon *couleur de rose*, and using lapis-lazuli powder to dry the writing.

March 11.

Went on with Ekermann's book, and found some interesting things.

Ekermann, after he had spent some weeks at Weimar, tells his friend that he was beginning to feel the favourable influence of a more social life, and in some sort to emerge from the merely ideal and theoretical existence he had hitherto led, &c. Goethe encourages him, and says strikingly, "Hold fast to the PRESENT. Every position, (zustand,) every moment of life, is of unspeakable value as the representative of a whole eternity."

The following passage is at once very touching and very characteristic. He seems to be a little melancholy, which was not often the case. "When I look back," said Goethe, "on my early and middle life, and now in my old age reflect how few of those remain who were young with me, life seems to me like a summer residence in a watering-place. When we first arrive, we form friendships with those who have already spent some time there, and must be gone the next week. The loss is painful, but we connect ourselves with the second generation of visitors, with whom we spend some time and become dearly intimate; but these also depart, and we are left alone with a third set, who arrive just as we are preparing for our departure, in whom we feel little or no interest.

"The world has always regarded me as a peculiar favourite of fortune, nor will I complain of my existence taken as a whole; yet, in truth, it has been little else than weariness and labour; and I may say that in my five-and-seventy years I have not enjoyed four weeks of peace and comfort – it was the eternal rolling of the stone. The claims upon my time and capabilities, from within and from without, were too many. My only happiness lay on my poetic talents; yet even in this how have I been, through outward things, disturbed, limited, and hindered! Had I kept myself more apart from public business, and could I have lived more in solitude, I had been happier as a man, and as a poet I had effected much more. Thus, after the publication of my Götz and my Werther, a certain sensible friend said to me in warning, 'When a man has once done something to delight the world, the world will thenceforward take care that he shall not do it a second time.' A widespread name, a high position in society, are doubtless good things, but, with all my reputation and my rank, I could not often do more nor better than give way to the opinions of others; and this were in truth but a sorry jest, if I had not therewith so far the advantage, that I learned (erfahre) how others thought: aber sie nicht wie ich."

How solemn sounds all this from the lips of a man, who in years, in fame, in wisdom, in prosperity, exceeded so far his fellow-men!

Pointing out to Ekermann some beautiful antique gems, and comparing them with the manner in which the same subjects and ideas had been treated by modern artists, he makes the oft-repeated observation, how far in these later times we fall short of the classical models: even with the highest feeling for the pure inimitable grace, the unaffected nature of these relics, even with a conception of *how* it was all produced, we cannot repeat the results we admire. "Meyer," he added, "used often to say, 'If only it were not so difficult to think;' but the worst is, that all the *thinking* in the world will not help us to *think* – we must go direct to nature, so that beautiful ideas shall present themselves before us like God-sends, (freye kinder Gottes,) and call out to us, "*Here we are!*"*

Tiedge, in 1800, wrote a poem on the immortality of the soul, entitled "Urania," and Goethe alludes amusingly to the sensation it produced for a time. The "Urania" lay on every table – "Urania" and immortality were the subject of every conversation, and stupid, conceited women dis-

---

* He says the same thing otherwise, and better, in another place – "Alles Gescheite ist schon einmal gedacht worden; man muss nur versuchen, es noch einmal zu denken."

cussed round their tea-tables the sublimest speculations on a future life; all which seems to have excited his impatience and his derision. How truly he says somewhere, that the same things are constantly repeated in the world; that there never was anything, any fact, that had only once existed! How well I recollect when the publication of "Satan," and the "Omnipresence of the Deity," and some other poems of the same stamp, were all the rage in England, and sent our evangelical ladies, some up into the clouds, within precincts where seraphs fear to tread, and some down – never mind where, – it was Tiedge's "Urania" over again. Of course, I speak here only of the presumption and frivolity, amounting to profaneness and audacity, or worse, which I have witnessed in some women whose heated imaginations outran their reason, as different from the staid, the sober humility of real piety, as the raving Pythoness of old was unlike the meek Mary, "who sat at Jesus' feet and heard his words."

Goethe says, in the same passage, that he would not himself give up for aught in the world the belief in futurity; and he thinks with Lorenzo de' Medici, that he who lives not in the hope of a future life may be counted as already *dead*; but he exclaims against treating with vulgar and audacious familiarity the divine, the incomprehensible truths, which prophets and apostles touched upon with awe; and I think with him.

Goethe has (*has?* – I think of him as being *now!*) I should say, that out of a collection of more than seventy portfolios of engravings and original drawings, it was his general custom to have one or two laid on the table after dinner, and to turn them over in presence of his guests and the ladies of his family, discoursing most eloquently on the different subjects, or pleased to appeal to the natural sense and taste of those around him. It was a divine lecture on art.

There are in one of these portfolios some most exquisite etchings and drawings by Roos, the famous animal painter, all representing sheep or goats in every possible attitude, wonderful for their truth. "When I look at them," says Goethe, speaking in the fulness of his admiration, "I feel a certain strange uneasiness. The narrow, stupid, silly, dreamy, yawny nature of these creatures attracts me into a kind of beastly sympathy with them; I look at them till I am half afraid of becoming a sheep myself, and could almost fancy that the artist had been one; he had no vocation to paint the fiercer quadrupeds, he confined himself to the ruminating animals, and in that he did well: his sympathy with the nature of these creatures was born with him – it was innate."

What would Goethe have thought of some of Edwin Landseer's pictures – his wild deer – his dogs! – the Highland Nurse, for instance, where the colley is watching by the sleeping infant? Did Roos, or Snyders, or Rubens himself, ever give us the *morale* of animal life in the fine spirit of Edwin Landseer?

After some other things, Goethe goes on to say, that he thinks a knowledge of the universe must be *innate* with some poets. (It seems to have been so with Shakspeare.) He says he wrote "Götz von Berlichingen" when he was a young inexperienced man of two-and-twenty. "Ten years later," he adds, "I stood astonished at the truth of my own delineation; I had never beheld or experienced the like, therefore the knowledge of these multifarious aspects of human nature I must have possessed through a kind of anticipation."

Yes; the "kind of anticipation," through which Joanna Baillie conceived and wrote her noble tragedies. Where did she, whose life has been pure and "retired as noontide dew," find the dark, stern, terrible elements, out of which she framed the delinations of character and passion in De Montfort, Ethwald, Basil Constantine? – where but in her own prophetic heart and genius? – in that intuitive, almost unconscious revelation of the universal nature, which makes the poet, and not experience or knowledge. Joanna Baillie, whose most tender and refined, and womanly and christian spirit never, I believe, admitted an ungentle thought of any living being, created De Montfort, and gave us the physiology of Hatred; and might well, like Goethe, stand astonished at the truth of her own delineation.

Farther on, Goethe speaks of the perfection with which some of the German women write their own language, so as to excel in this particular some of their best authors. The same holds good in France and England; so that to understand the full force of Goethe's compliment to his countrywomen, one must recollect that it is no such easy matter to write a fine and clear German style, where there are twenty dialects and a hundred different styles. Prince Metternich once observed to me, "What I admire in your language is, that you have *one* good style in speaking and writing; and all well-bred and well-educated persons in England speak and write nearly alike. Here, in Germany, we have as many different styles as individual writers, and the difference is greater than a foreigner could easily imagine."

Yet even this kind of individuality, in point of style, may possibly have a value and a charm, and this will be felt if ever the rules of a good style be so fixed by criticism or fashion, that all Germany will write uniformly.

What he says of himself and Tieck is very interesting; he speaks of him with admiration and kind feeling, but adds, "that when the Schlegels set up Tieck as a sort of literary rival to himself, they placed him in a false position. I may say this openly," adds this great man, with a dignified and frank simplicity. "I did not make myself: and it were much the same thing as though I should even myself with Shakspeare, who also did not make himself – a being far, far above me, to whom I look up with reverence and wonder."

Driving home one day from Tiefurt, as the carriage turned, they faced the sun just as he was sinking in the west. Goethe ceased speaking, and remained for a few moments as if lost in thought; then rousing himself, he repeated from some old poet –

"Untergehend sogar ist's immer dieselbige Sonne."

He then continued, with a most cheerful and animated expression – "When a man has lived seventy-five years, he must needs think sometimes upon death. This thought brings me perfect peace, for I have the fixed conviction that the spirit is immortal, and has a never-ceasing progression from eternity to eternity; it is like the sun, which only *seems* to set to our earthly eyes, but which in reality never does set, and never ceases to shine."

Farther on, Ekermann expresses his regret that Goethe should have sacrificed so much time as director of the theatre at Weimar, and considers that many works were thus lost to the world. To which Goethe replies – "Truly, it is possible I might have written many good things during that time; yet, when I reflect, I feel no regret. All my productions, as well as endeavours, I have been accustomed to regard as merely symbolical, (that is, as I understand it, leading to something beyond, and significant of something better, than themselves,) and, in point of fact, it was with me as with a potter, to whom it is quite indifferent whether he makes pitchers or whether he makes platters of his clay."

March 13.

Idle to-day, and although I read a good deal, I translated very little, and noted less.

Yet the following passage struck me. The conversation turned on the German poetesses, and Rehbein, Goethe's physician, insisted that the poetical talent in women was "ein Art von geistigem Geschlechtstrieb."

"Hear him!" exclaimed Goethe; "hear the physician, with his 'intellectual impulse of sex!'"

Rehbein explained himself, by observing "that the

women who had distinguished themselves in literature, poetry especially, were almost universally women who had been disappointed in their best affections, and sought in this direction of the intellect a sort of compensation. When women are married, and have children to take care of, they do not often think of writing poetry."*

This is not very politely or delicately expressed; but we must not therefore shrink from it, for it involves some important considerations. It is most certain that among the women who have been distinguished in literature, three-fourths have been either by nature, or fate, or the law of society, placed in a painful or a false position; it is also most certain that in these days when society is becoming every day more artificial and more complex, and marriage, as the gentlemen assure us, more and more expensive, hazardous, and inexpedient, women *must* find means to fill up the void of existence. Men, our natural protectors, our lawgivers, our masters, throw us upon our own resources; the qualities which they pretend to admire in us, – the overflowing, the clinging affections of a warm heart, – the household devotion, – the submissive wish to please, that feels "every vanity in fondness lost," – the tender shrinking sensitiveness which Adam thought so charming in his Eve, – to cultivate these, to make them, by artificial means, the staple of the womanly character, is it not to cultivate a taste for sunshine and roses, in those we send to pass their lives in the arctic zone? We have gone away from nature, and we must, – if we can, substitute another nature. Art, literature and science remain to us. Religion, which formerly opened the doors of nunneries and convents to forlorn women, now mingling her beautiful and soothing influence with resources which the prejudices of the world have yet left open to us, teaches us another lesson, that only in utility, such as is left to us,

---

* This applies more to Germany than with us, and even up to the present time it has required a very powerful reaction of some kind to drive a German woman into the public path of literature.

only in the assiduous employment of such faculties as we are permitted to exercise, can we find health and peace, and compensation for the wasted or repressed impulses and energies more proper to our sex – more natural – perhaps more pleasing to God; but trusting in his mercy, and using the means he has given, we must do the best we can for ourselves and for our sisterhood. The cruel prejudices which would have shut us out from nobler consolation and occupations have ceased in great part, and will soon be remembered only as the rude, coarse barbarism of a by gone age. Let us then have no more caricatures of methodistical, card-playing, and acrimonious old maids. Let us hear no more of scandal, parrots, cats, and lap-dogs – or worse! – these never-failing subjects of derision with the vulgar and the frivolous, but the source of a thousand compassionate and melancholy feelings in those who can reflect! In the name of humanity and womanhood, let us have no more of them! Coleridge, who has said and written the most beautiful, the most tender, the most reverential things of women – who understands better than any man, any poet, what I will call the metaphysics of love – Coleridge, as you will remember, has asserted that the perfection of a woman's character is to be *characterless*. "Every man," said he, "would like to have an Ophelia or a Desdemona for his wife." No doubt; the sentiment is truly a masculine one: and what was *their* fate? What would now be the fate of such unresisting and confiding angels? Is this the age of Arcadia? Do we live among Paladins and Sir Charles Grandisons, and are our weakness, and our innocence, and our ignorance, safeguards – or snares? Do we indeed find our account in being

"Fine by defect, and beautifully weak?"

No, no; women need in these times *character* beyond everything else; the qualities which will enable them to endure and to resist evil; the self-governed, the cultivated, active mind, to protect and to maintain ourselves. How many wretched women marry for a maintenance! How many wretched women sell themselves to dishonour for bread! – and there is small difference, if any, in the infamy and the misery! How many unmarried women live in heart-wearing dependence; – if poor, in solitary penury, loveless, joyless, unendeared; – if rich, in aimless, pitiful trifling! How many, strange to say, marry for the independence they dare not otherwise claim! But the more paths opened to us, the less fear that we should go astray.

Surely it is dangerous, it is wicked, in these days, to follow the old saw, to bring up women to be "happy wives and mothers;" that is to say, let all her accomplishments, her sentiments, her views of life, take one direction, as if for women there existed only one destiny – one hope, one blessing, one object, one passion in existence; some people say it ought to be so, but we know that it is *not* so; we know that hundreds, that thousands of women are not happy wives and mothers – are never either wives or mothers at all. The cultivation of the moral strength and the active energies of a woman's mind, together with the intellectual faculties and tastes, will not make a woman a less good, less happy wife and mother, and will enable her to find content and independence when denied love and happiness.

March [*14*].

Got on better to-day.

Goethe speaks with great admiration of the poems, original and translated, of Talvi, (Mademoiselle Jacob, now Mrs. Robinson, and settled, I believe, in America.)

There is a great deal about Lord Byron in scattered passages. Goethe seems to have understood him astonishingly well – I mean the man as well as the poet.* At this time Lord Byron was turning all heads in Germany, and

---

* Lord Byron ist nur gross wenn er dichtet, sobald er reflectirt, ist er ein kind.

Goethe, who was flattered by the veneration and admiration of Byron, felt and acknowledged his genius. "He was," says Ekermann, "quite inexhaustible when once he began to speak of Byron," and, as a poet himself, sympathised in the transcendent poetical powers he displayed; but as a philosopher and sage, Goethe lamented the abuse, the misdirection of the talents he appreciated. He reproaches him with the negative, the gloomy tendency of his mind; he contrasts it with the healthful cheerfulness of such a spirit as Shakspeare's. Speaking of his strange attempt to defend and revive the strict law of the drama with regard to the three unities, he says pointedly, "Had he but known as well how to restrain himself within the fixed *moral* limits!"

In another place he speaks with contempt of the poets, imitators of Lord Byron, "who write as if they were all sick, and the whole bright world a lazar-house." He says, "It is a real misuse and abuse of poetry, which was given to us to console us in the struggle of life, and make man more content with the world he lives in, not less."

How entirely I sympathise with Goethe, when he breaks out in indignation against the negative and the satirical in poetry and art! He says, "When I have called the bad – *bad*, how much is gained by that? The man who would work aright must not deal in censure, must not trouble himself about what is bad, but show and do what is *good;*" and this is surely true. He says elsewhere, that when there was doubt and contradiction in his mind, he kept it within himself; he gave to the public only the assured result, (or what he considered such,) when he had arrived at it. This firmness of tone, this lofty and cheerful view of the universe and humanity, strike us particularly in many of Goethe's works. He says himself, that the origin of most of his lyrics was truth; some *real* incident, some *real* sentiment; and some of his fine moral poems – for instance, those which he has entitled "Gränzen der Menschheit" and "Das Göttliche," remind me of Wordsworth, in the pure healthful feeling, as well as the felicity and beauty of the expression through which it has found a channel of our hearts.

He says of Winckelmann, with untranslatable felicity, "Man *lernt* nichts wenn man ihn lieset, aber man *wird* etwas."

This next is amusing, and how frankly magnanimous! He says, "People talk of originality – what do they mean? As soon as we are born, the surrounding world begins to operate upon us, and so on to the end. And, after all, what *can* we truly call our own, but *energy, power, will?* Could I point out all that I myself owe to my great forerunners and cotemporaries, truly there would remain but little over!"

Goethe could afford to say this!

He speaks of Schiller so affectionately, and with such a fine, just discrimination of his powers! "All in Schiller was high and great – his deportment, his gait, the mould of his limbs, his least motion, was dignified and grand – only his eyes were soft." And, adds Goethe, "like his form was his talent. We lived together," he says, "in such close, such daily intimacy, so *in one another*, that of many thoughts which occur in the works of both, it would be a question whether they originated with the one or the other."

The two great men, thus bound together during their lives, were, after Schiller's death, placed in a kind of rivalship; and still the partisans of the different literary factions dispute where no dispute ought to exist. Coleridge says that "Schiller is a thousand times more *hearty* than Goethe, and that Goethe does not, nor ever will, command the mind of the people as Schiller does." I believe it to be true. The reason is, that Schiller has with him generally the women and the young men, i.e. those whose opinions and feelings are most loudly, most enthusiastically expressed. Goethe, in allusion to this, says playfully, "Now have the public been disputing for these twenty years which of the two is greatest, Schiller or myself! Let them go and be thankful that have two such fellows to dispute about!"

He speaks of the new school of critical historians, who have endeavoured to prove that all ancient history is fable.

"Till now," he says, "the world has believed in the heroism of a Lucretia, a Mutius Scaevola, and has been warmed and inspired by the idea. Now comes some historical critic, and assures us that these personages never had a real existence; that it is all fiction and fable, invented by the grand imagination of the old Romans. What have we to do with such pitiful truth! If the Romans were great enough to invent such things, let us at least be great enough to believe in them!"

Here I should think he was speaking more playfully and feelingly than seriously and critically; and is it not charming?

He goes on – "I used to be delighted with a certain fact in the history of the thirteenth century, where the Emperor Frederic II. being engaged against the Pope, all the north of Germany lay open to invaders. The Asiatic hordes advanced even into Silesia, where the Duke of Leignitz defeated them; they turned back to Moravia, where the Count Sternberg beat them. These gallant warriors have hitherto lived in my imagination as the saviours of the German nation. Now comes your historical critic, and he tells me that these heroes sacrificed themselves very unnecessarily, for that the Turkish army would doubtless have retired of itself – so is a grand patriotic deed lessened and maligned, and one is put horribly out of humour." It is plain that Goethe, like Johnson, did not like to have his *fagot* disturbed.

He adds, farther on, that in poetry this kind of sceptical criticism is not so mischievous. "Professor Wolf has destroyed Homer, but he could do nothing to the poem itself, for the Iliad is endued with the miraculous property of the heroes in the Valhalla, who, though hewed to pieces in the morning fight, always sit down to dinner with whole limbs."

But there is no end to this – I must stop; yet this about Shakspeare is so beautiful I must have it down.

"How inconceivably rich and great is Shakspeare! There is no *motive** in human existence which he has not represented and expressed, and with what ease and freedom! One *cannot* speak of Shakspeare, it is all insufficient. I have in the Wilhelm Meister *groped* about him, but it is mere trifling; he is no play-writer, he never thought of a stage, it was too narrow, too paltry a space for his mighty spirit: yes, even the great visible universe itself was for him in space too narrow!

"Nay, he is too rich, too mighty. A productive poet should read but one piece of his in the year, or he will wreck himself in the vain attempt to reach the *unreachable*. I did well," he adds, "that in writing my Götz and my Egmont, I shook him off my shoulders. How many excellent German poets have been destroyed through him and Calderon? for Shakspeare," he adds fancifully, "presents to us golden apples in cups of silver; through the study of his works we get hold of the cups of silver, but alas, we put potatoes into them."

I close my book, and so good night!

Where is he now, he who disappeared and could not be lost? – sitting with his Shakspeare and his Schiller up there among the stars in colloquy sublime? and Walter Scott standing by with love and thought upon his spacious brow – What a *partie carrée!*

---

* The meaning of the world *motive*, in German criticism, should perhaps be explained. It is used to signify any cause out of which the action or consequence springs. They have the verb *motiviren*, and they say of a drama, or any fiction, that it is well or ill *motivirt*.

March 15.

This last paragraph, which I wrote last evening, sent me to bed with my head full of all manner of thoughts and memories and fancies; and not being in a studious mood this miserably cold night, I draw my writing-table close to the fire, and bestow all my tediousness on you, and if it were twice as much, and you were twice as far off, I would bestow it on you *with all of my heart* – would you not accept the bargain?

I have been much busied to-day with domestic matters, for we are preparing to change our residence for a new house never yet inhabited, and now I am alone in my room. I feel tired, and have fallen into a very dismal and fantastic mood.

Whence and what are we, "that things whose sense we see not, fray us with things that be not?" If I had the heart of that wondrous bird in the Persian tales, which being pressed upon a human heart, obliged that heart to utter truth through the lips, sleeping or waking, then I think I would inquire how far in each bosom exists the belief in the supernatural? In many minds which I know, and otherwise strong minds, it certainly exists a hidden source of torment; in others, not stronger, it exists a source of absolute pleasure and excitement. I have known people most wittily ridicule, or gravely discountenance, a belief in spectral appearances, and all the time I could see in their faces that once in their lives at least they had been frightened at their own shadow. The conventional cowardice, the fear of ridicule, even the self-respect which prevents intelligent persons from revealing the exact truth of what passes through their own minds on this point, deprives us of a means to trace to its sources and develope an interesting branch of Psychology. Between vulgar credulity and exaggeration on the one hand, and the absolute scepticism and materialism of some would-be philosophers on the other, lies a vast space of debatable ground, a sort of twilight region or *limbo*, through which I do not see my way distinctly. One of the most gifted and accomplished, as well as most rational and most practical characters I ever met with, once said to me seriously, "I thank God I do not believe in the *impossibility* of anything."

How far are our perceptions confined to our outward senses? Can any one tell? – for that our perceptions are not wholly confined to impressions taken in by the outward senses seems the only one thing proved; and are such sensible impressions the only real ones? When any one asks me gaily the so common and common-place question – common even in these our rational times – "Do you now really believe in ghosts?" I generally answer as gaily – "I really don't know!" In the common, vulgar meaning of the words, I certainly do *not*; but in the reality of many things termed imaginary I certainly do.

While I was staying at Weimar, in Goethe's house, a very pretty little *soirée* was arranged for me at Madame d'Alefeldt's; there were no cards that evening; and seated round a table we became extremely talkative and confidential, and at last we took to relating ghost stories. It should seem that Germany is still like Ireland, the land of the supernatural, as well as the land of romance. There was something quite delightful in the good faith and the perfect *sérieux* of some of the narrators, as well as some of the listeners – myself included.

Baron Sternberg gave us a story of an apparition at his sister's castle in Livonia; it was admirable, and most admirably told, though, truly, it seemed the last of all apparitions that one would have expected to haunt a castle in Livonia, for it was that of Voltaire.

Then the grand Duke gave us the history of a certain Princess of Rudolstadt, whose picture is at Kochberg, and who, in the estimation of her family, had the gift of prophecy, of seeing visions, and dreaming dreams; but such visions and such dreams – so wild, so poetical, and even so grotesque – shadowing forth the former and future destinies of her family! and, in truth, the whole story, and the description of the old castle of Rudolstadt, and the old court, and the three old superannuated princesses, like gothic figures woven into tapestry – so stately, and so stiff, and so ugly, and withal so tinged with the ideal and romantic, were given with so much liveliness of detail, and so much graphic spirit, that I was beyond measure amused and interested. I thought I saw them before me, and methinks I see them now.

In return for this tale, I gave from the best authority that of Crofton Croker, the history of the Irish banshee, and particularly of that identical banshee, whose visitations as the hereditary attendant on my own family I had painful reason to remember. My banshee pleased universally; to most of the company the idea was something new, and I have even hopes that it may have inspired Sternberg with a pendant to his poem on King O'Donohue.

The conversation turned naturally upon hereditary apparitions and spectral penances, the fruit of ancestral crimes, on which superstition Grillparzer has founded his fine lyric drama of "The Ahnfrau." The castle of the W—— family, in the neighbourhood of Weimar, was mentioned as subject to this species of ghostly visitation. Two individuals present, who had been on a visit at this castle, spoke of the phantom *avec connaissance de fait*. The present Baroness W——, who had been brought up among enlightened and intelligent people, declared herself perfectly incredulous, and after her marriage went to inhabit the castle of her husband, in all the assurance that common sense and philosophy could give; but – so went the tale – it happened that, soon after the birth of her eldest child, she awoke at midnight, and beheld an unearthly being bending over the cradle of her infant – more, as it seemed, in love and benediction than with any unholy purpose; however, from this time they said that she had not willingly inhabited the castle of her husband's ancestors.

In the family of the Baron ——, whose castle is also in the neighbourhood of Weimar, there is a gold ring of marvellous power, given by some supernatural being to a former Baron, with the assurance that as long as it remained in the castle, good fortune would attend the family. Every experiment made of late by unbelieving barons to put this tradition to the test has been followed by some signal disaster, the last time by a destructive fire, which consumed nearly the whole castle. This story also was very well told.

It should seem that in these little German states there was always some ancestor, some prince with a kind of Blue-Beard renown, to serve as the hero for all tales of horror – the bug-a-boo to frighten the children. Duke Ernest August plays the *rôle du tyran* in the history of Saxe Weimar. He was not only a tyrant, but atheist, alchemist, magician, and heaven knows what besides. Now, there was a profligate adventurer, named Caumartin, who had insinuated himself into the favour of the Duke, became his chamberlain, and assisted him in his magical and chemical researches. It is a tradition, that one of the ancestors of this princely family had discovered the philosopher's stone, and had caused the receipt to be buried with him, denouncing a terrible malediction on whoever should violate, from avaricious motives, his last repose. Duke Ernest persuaded Caumartin to descend into the family vault, and pluck the mighty secret from the coffin of his ancestor. Caumartin undertook the task with gay audacity, and remained two hours in the vault. On re-ascending, he looked pale and much changed, and took solemn leave of his friends, as a man condemned to death. They mocked at him of course; but on the third day afterwards he was found dead on the floor of his room, his rapier in his hand, his clothes torn, and his features distorted, as if by a fearful struggle.

This story, so oft repeated in different ages and countries, and in every variety and form, appeared to me curious in a philosophical and historical point of view. Duke Ernest August lived at the time when a wildly superstitious credulity, a belief in magic and alchemy, rose up simultaneously with the most daring scepticism in religious matters, both becoming *fashionable* in Germany, France, and England, at the same time. It was the reign of Cagliastro and his imitators and disciples. Do you not recollect, in the Baron de Grimm's memoirs, the story of a French adventurer, who was received into the first circles of Paris as a supernatural being? He was said to possess the elixir of life, and the wandering Jew was apparently a youth to him in point of longevity. In the house of the Maréchal de Mirepoix he once sat down to the harpsichord, and played a piece of music of sublime and surpassing beauty. All inquired whether it was his own composition, or where it was to be found? To which he replied, with a pensive air – "The last time I heard it was when Alexander the Great entered Babylon!"

Many more stories were told that night of various interest, but all tinged with something poetical and characteristic. At last the party separated. I returned home, and, while still a little excited, we continued to converse for some time on the influence of fancy and its various illusions, and the superstitions of various times and countries. The thing was always there, forming, as it seemed, a part of our human nature, only modified and changed in its manifestations, sometimes by outward influences, sometimes by individual temperament; fashion, or in other words sympathy and imitation, having produced many ghosts, as well as many maniacs, and not a few suicides.

At last we bade good night. I lighted my taper, fixed in a candlestick of rather antique form, the same which had been used when Goethe was christened, and which I always took in my hand with due reverence. In coming up to my bed-room, I had to pass by the door of the apartment in which Goethe had breathed his last. It has been from that moment considered as a sanctuary; the things remain untouched and undisturbed, and the key is deposited with the librarian. In the first or anteroom there stands – at least when I was at Weimar there stood – a large house-clock, which had been presented to Goethe on

the celebration of his jubilee: it is the same which stood in
the room of his mother, and struck the hour he was born:
after passing through various hands, it was purchased by
the Grand Duke of Baden, and sent as a gift to the poet on
that memorable occasion. This clock, like the rest of the
furniture of that sacred apartment, remains untouched,
but on this very night, by some inexplicable accident, just
as I arrived at the door, the clock within began to strike –
one, two, three, four, and so on to twelve. At the first
stroke I stopped, even my breath almost stopped, as I
listened. I looked not to the left, where the door opened
into that hallowed chamber of death and immortality; – I
looked not to the right, where the dark hollow of the
staircase seemed to yawn – nor yet before me; but, with
my eyes fixed on the silver relic I held in my hand, I stood
quite still. The emotion which bound up my powers in
that moment was assuredly the farthest possibly from fear,
or aught resembling it – it was only a sound, but it was the
same sound and hour which had ushered into the world
one of the greatest and most gifted spirits whom God, in
his supreme goodness, had ever sent to enlighten the
world, and to enlarge the bounds of human delight and
improvement; it was the same sound and hour which sent
it to mingle with the great soul of nature, to be

> A voice in all her music, from the moan
> Of thunder to the song of night's sweet bird;
> To be a presence to be felt and known
> In darkness and in light.

And so in the silence and the loneliness of the night, as
those sounds fell deliberately one by one, they seemed to
fill the whole air around me, to enter in at my ears and
thrill down to my finger ends, and I saw the light tremble
which I held before me. But sense and the power of
motion returned. In the next moment I was in my room
and seated in HIS chair, with a steady pulse and a calm
spirit, glad to breathe again "queen o'er myself," – my
reasonable self; yet would I not have missed the strange,

the overpowering, deliciously awful feelings of those well-remembered moments – no – not for the universe! Short and transient as they have been, they henceforth belong to the tissue of my life: were I to live a century, I cannot forget them, nor would I dare to give them expression, – if indeed there are words which *could* express them.

March 16.

I was idle to-day, and, instead of going on regularly with my book, I turned over the leaves, and dwelt upon passages here and there, as people, when they *are* nice and are *not* hungry, capriciously pick out tit-bits.

The attempt to note down all that I would wish to retain in my memory of this delightful book, I find hopeless, quite. At first I fancied it something like Boswell: nothing can be more unlike. The difference between Dr. Johnson and Goethe is not greater than the difference between Ekermann and Boswell. Boswell's book is delicious, but the man's personal character is always in the way; we profit often by his indiscretion, but his indiscriminate trifling as often disgusts. Johnson, in his book, is the "great Colossus" bestriding this narrow world, with a Pharos in one hand, and a bundle of darts in the other; but in Ekermann's book Goethe is nothing less than the "Olympian Jupiter," seated at his table and dispensing nectar and ambrosia, while he plays child-like with his own lightnings.* Boswell's meddling coxcombry and servility sometimes place his great patron in no very dignified position; and the well-known similes of the monkey on the bear's back, and the puppy in the lion's den, seem hardly too severe. Were I to find a simile for Eker-

---

* There is now a melancholy propriety in the basso relievo over the entrance to Goethe's apartment, in his house at Weimar: it represents the empty throne of Jupiter, with the eagle cowering at its foot, and the thunderbolts lying extinguished and idle.

mann, I should say he is like a thrush singing under the wing of a great eagle, sometimes overshadowed by his mighty master, but not overdazzled, not overawed by the "terrors of his beak and lightning of his eyes," – always himself – and, as himself, always amiable, always respectable. His simplicity, his uprightness, and his gentleness, his poetical and artist-like feeling, are always delightful: one must love him for his own sake as well as Goethe's.

Yet a translation of this book would hardly please in England; it deals in "notions more than in facts," and in speculations and ideas, more than in anecdotes and personalities. It is necessary to take a strong interest in German literature and society, and in the fine arts generally, to care about a great deal of it; it is something like Coleridge's "Table Talk," which certainly few Germans would like or understand, though the criticisms and opinions are full of interest for the English reader; but it is yet more dramatic and lively in manner.

When I was first in possession of this book, and referring with delight to some few sentences which caught my attention, a friend of mine, who had known Goethe well and long, wrote me, in her own peculiar style, some very charming things of its character and intention; the meaning, and as nearly as I can, the words, I must try to render into English.

"Ekermann's book," said she, "is the purest altar that has yet been erected to the fame of Goethe. In times like these, when the feeling of reverence (Pietat) seems to be fast departing, when a young author of talent takes up the pen, as a sort of critical dissecting-knife, mangling and prying where once he trembled and adored; when his first endeavour is to fling down that heaviest burthen upon the soul of an egotist, – the burthen of admiration for the merits of another, is it not pleasant to meet with such a book as this? And when everything one reads is so artificial, so *gemacht*, so impertinent, is it not delightful to open a book where in every page we feel the pulse-throb of a warm, true heart? I do not know if I am right, but it seems to me that those who cannot admire, can have nothing in themselves to be admired; then how worthy of admiration must that man be, who thus throws down his whole heart and soul in admiration before the feet of another! the simplicity of this entire abnegation of self lends to it a certain dignity. There is nothing here but truth and love – for Goethe loved Ekermann, and O! how Ekermann loved Goethe!

"I can have no critical judgment here, and ought not to have; I can only bear witness to the general truth of the whole, – nothing can be truer. I cannot be, like you, struck and charmed by particular passages. I was too long a sort of Lady High Treasurer to be dazzled or astonished now that the caskets are opened. I greet the gems as old acquaintance!"

After this encouraging testimony, I go on with my notes and my translating.

It appears that Schiller had the notion of a theatre where pieces should be given occasionally for men only, and Goethe seems to approve of this: I do not. The two sexes are more than sufficiently separated by different duties and pursuits; what tends to separate them farther in their amusements cannot be good for either. A theatre for men only would soon become a bear-garden.

At an evening party, some of his own songs, to which Ekermann had composed beautiful music, were sung for him – he was much pleased. When all was over, he observed to Ekermann, that the songs out of the "Divan,"* seemed to have no longer any connexion with himself: "both what is Oriental and what is impassioned in those songs," said he, "have passed away from me; it is like the cast skin of a snake, which he leaves lying on his

---

* Written when he was more than seventy.

path; but the little song 'um Mitternacht'* remains with me, a living part of my own life."

After several pages on all manner of things, I find this remark on Schiller: "Through all his works," said Goethe, "we have the idea of *freedom*. And this idea changed its form as the genius and character of Schiller were progressively developed. In his early age it was physical freedom, in his latter life the ideal;" and afterwards he says finely, "*that* is not freedom where we acknowledge nothing above ourselves, but that is freedom, when we can reverence something greater than ourselves."

He says of La Grange, "he was a GOOD man, and even through that, he was truly great; for when a *good* human being is gifted with talents, he will work for the *moral* benefit of the world, whether he be artist, natural philosopher, poet, or whatever he may be." This is like what Weber wrote to Mendelsohn.

Farther on he says, "All that is great and distinguished must be in the minority. There have been ministers who had both people and sovereign against them, and yet have accomplished their own great plans; it is not to be hoped that reason will ever be popular. Passion, feeling, may be popular; but reason will be the possession of the few."

March [*17*].

I have often thought and felt, that while in England we have political liberty, we have nothing like the personal and individual freedom, the social liberty of the Germans, even under their worst governments. The passage which follows has, therefore, struck me particularly. Goethe, in speaking with approbation of Guizot, quotes his remark, that "from the old Germans we derive the idea of personal freedom, which was especially characteristic of that people, and quite unknown in the ancient republics." "Is not

---

* Written in his early youth.

this true?" said Goethe. "Is he not perfectly right? and is not the same idea prevalent among the Germans of our own time? From this source sprung the Reformation, and not less the various complexion of our literature. The continual striving after originality in our poets, so that each thinks it necessary to make or find a new path for himself, the *isolation** and eccentric habits of our learned men, where each will stand on his ground, and work his aim out of his individual mind, all come from the same cause. The French and the English, on the contrary, hold more together, and the people all imitate one another. There is something uniform in their dress and behaviour; they are afraid to swerve from a given fashion, to make themselves peculiar or ridiculous. But in Germany every man follows his humour, without troubling himself about others; each man endeavours to suffice to himself; for in each man, as Guizot has well observed, lives the idea of personal and individual freedom, from which proceeds much that is excellent, and also much that is absurd."

This appears to me very true, and must, I think, strike every one who has been in Germany, and felt the interest which this kind of individuality imparts to society; though certainly I have met with travellers who were not a little put out by it. Life, with them, having hitherto flowed on "comme une goutte d'huile sur une table de marbre," they know not how to understand the little projections and angles they have to encounter. The women appear affected, and the men quizzical, precisely because the former are natural and the latter original, and all very unlike the ladies and gentlemen they have left behind, whose minds, like their bodies, are dressed in the same fashion.

When in Germany, I was accustomed to hear Madame de Staël's "De l'Allemagne" mentioned, if mentioned at all,

---

* Verisolirung. Isolirung is solitude and separation – what the French call *isolement*. Verisolirung expresses isolation with its injurious tendency.

with something worse than contempt, either as forgotten or out of date. Her trite information, her superficial criticisms, her French prejudices, her feminine rashness, met with no quarter; but think only, what changes of opinion, what revolutions in criticism, have taken place within thirty years! Sir James Mackintosh – rich in all the lore of his age, beyond his age in most respects – writes, in 1807, (only two or three years before Madame de Staël produced her book,) of German literature and criticism, as a sort of *terra incognita*, as the navigators of the fifteenth century talked of a western continent, venturing, but with hesitation, to commend Goethe, and seeming to think his ideas on art not *quite* despicable – "rather plausible and ingenious." He mentions the *antipathy* in France and England against German literature, and speaking of distinguished modern writers, who might be considered as likely to survive their own age, he says, "I comprehend *even* Goethe and Schiller within the pale; and though I know that few, either in France or England, agree with me, I have recourse to the usual consolation of singularity, that my opinion will be more prevalent when I am myself forgotten."

Madame de Staël first made a breach through what Goethe himself called a "Chinese wall of prejudices;" and we may pass through it surely without trampling upon her who had courage to open the way for us.

The Germans understand us better than we understand them. To have a far stronger stamp of national character than most other people, yet better to comprehend and appreciate what lies in the *national nature* of other people, is one of the most interesting characteristics of the Germans. Their language lends itself with wondrous richness and flexibility to translation from every tongue, and their catholic taste embraces all literature, without insisting on any adaptation to their own canons of criticism or *bienséance*.

All that Goethe says of art and artists is admirable – worthy of him who was the greatest critic and connoisseur of his country and age; for instance, what he says of Claude Lorraine: "His pictures have the highest possible truth, and not a trace of reality; he knew the real world in its minutest details, and used these details as a means to express the fairer world within his own soul; and that is the true ideal, where real means are so used that the apparent truth shall produce an illusion, as if it were *reality*."

He calls architecture "*eine erstarrte musik,*" an expression as untranslatable as it is exquisitely felicitous. And many other passages I leave unnoted with regret.

Yet one thing I must not omit, for it has made me think much.

Goethe appears to consider our Saviour, with the twelve apostles, as presenting too much uniformity to be a good subject for sculpture. The remark may possibly refer to the famous bronzes of Peter Vischer on the tomb of St. Sibald at Nuremburg. I was struck by the variety and discrimination exhibited in these figures; yet, on recollection, the variety was in the drapery and attitude – in the external, not internal character. It were easy to distinguish in sculpture two such opposite characters as St. John and St. Paul; but how are we to distinguish St. Andrew and St. Simon, except by an external attribute, as that of giving St. Peter the keys, and St. Bartholomew his own skin over his arm, as at Milan? How make St. Thomas look incredulous? So that, on the whole, there must be something characterless in such a group.

Goethe says, that he had selected from the scriptures a cyclus of twelve figures as suited to sculpture, and presenting all together the history of our religion.

1. ADAM, as the first man and father of mankind – a type of human grandeur and perfection. He should have a spade, as the first cultivator of the earth; and to express his character of progenitor and parent, he should be accompanied by a child, looking up to him with a bold confiding glance – a kind of boyish Hercules, crushing a snake in his hand; (perhaps with reference to the promise.)

2. NOAH, the beginner of a new creation, as a vine-dresser, who, by the introduction of the grape, relieved the cares and made glad the heart of man.

3. MOSES, as the first lawgiver.

4. After him, ISAIAH, as prince and prophet.

5. DANIEL, as the harbinger of the Messiah.

6. CHRIST, as Saviour and Redeemer.

7. JOHN.

8. The CENTURION of Capernaum, as representing the believer, the Christian.

9. Next, the MARY MAGDALENE, as the symbol of humanity, reconciled to God through repentance. These two figures, Faith and Repentance, representing the spirit of Christianity.

10. Next, ST. PAUL, as promulgator of its doctrine.

11. Then ST. JAMES, as the first missionary, representing the diffusion of Christianity among strange lands.

12. Lastly, ST. PETER, as keeper of the gate of salvation. He should have an inquiring, penetrating expression, as if demanding of those who presented themselves, whether they were worthy to enter the kingdom of heaven.

"What do you think of this my cyclus?" added Goethe; "I think it would be richer in expression and contrast than the twelve apostles. The Moses and the Magdalene should be seated."

He says that he composed the witch scene in the "Faust," in the Borghese Gardens at Rome. If ever I visit those gardens again, what a strange association will now mingle itself with those antique statues, and fountains, and classical temples!

There is a great deal about his new theory of colours, which I read with interest, but dare not meddle with, because I do not quite understand all. This theory, it seems, is intended to supersede Newton's theory of light and colours: whether it will or not is another thing; but as the *savans* in France have taken it up, I suppose it will be looked into by our own philosophers; and, meantime, whichever way the question may be decided hereafter,

Goethe's own feeling on the subject will be referred to with interest, either as a curious instance of self-delusion, or a sublime anticipation of future glory.

"On what I have done as a poet," said he, "I would not presume much – I do not pique myself on it" – (hear this!) – "excellent poets have lived as my contemporaries – more excellent before me – and others will live after me; but that, in my own age, I am the only one who, in the profound science of colours, has obtained a knowledge of the *truth* – in that I do give myself some credit – in that only I have a consciousness of superiority over many."

This is something like the grand, calm, self-exultation of Milton. Is it as well founded? – Methinks I should like to know.

He speaks in various places of the unseen, imperceptible influences of all outward things in forming the genius and character. "Surely," he says, "the man who has passed all his life long beneath the lofty serious oak, will be a very different man from him who has lived beneath the shade of the myrtle and the willow."

He says, feelingly, "*It is not good for man to be alone*, and, above all, it is not good for man to work alone; he requires sympathy, encouragement, excitement, to succeed in any-thing good: in this way I may thank Schiller for some of my best ballads; and you may take the credit to yourself," he adds kindly to Ekermann, "if ever I finish the second part of Faust."

There is a great deal all through the second volume relating to the second part of the Faust, which occupied Goethe during the last years of his life, and which he finished at the age of eighty-two. On completing it he says, "Now I may consider the remainder of my existence as a free gift, and it is indifferent whether I do anything more or not;" as if he had considered his whole former life as held conditionally, binding him to execute certain objects to which he believed himself called. He survived the completion of the Faust only one year.

The purport of the second part of Faust has puzzled

many German and English scholars, and in Germany there are already treatises and commentaries on it, as on the Divina Commedia. I never read it, and, if I had, would not certainly venture an opinion "where doctors disagree;" but I recollect that Von Hammer once gave me, in his clear animated manner, a comprehensive analysis of this wonderful production – that is, according to his *own* interpretation of it. "I regard it," said he, "as being from beginning to end a grand poetical piece of irony on the whole universe, which is turned, as it were, wrong side out. In this point of view I understand it; in any other point of view it appears to me incomprehensible. It contains some of the most splendid passages he has written."

Everywhere Goethe speaks of Sir Walter Scott with the utmost enthusiasm of admiration, as the greatest writer of his time; he speaks of him as being without his *like*, as without his equal.

I remember Goethe's daughter-in-law saying to me playfully, "When my father got hold of one of Scott's romances, there was no speaking to him till he had finished the third volume: he was worse than any girl at a boarding-school with her first novel!"

I have particular pleasure in noting this, because I have seen in several English papers and reviews a passage from some book of travels in which Goethe, on what authority I know not, is represented as holding Sir Walter Scott in the utmost contempt. This is altogether false; yet the same passage I have lately seen translated into American papers, and thence into the papers of Upper and Lower Canada. Thus over the whole reading world is the belief diffused, that one great genius could either be wretchedly mistaken or enviously unjust in estimating another great genius – a belief as dishonourable to genius and human nature, as it is consolatory to the common cry of curs, to ignorant mediocrity, "for folly loves the martyrdom of fame." I held in my own hands – read with mine own eyes – a long letter addressed by Sir Walter to Goethe, giving an account of his own family, his pursuits, &c., as friend to friend, and expressive of the utmost reverence, as well as gratitude for marks of kindness and approbation received from Goethe.

"A lie," says the Chinese proverb, "has no feet, it cannot stand;" but it has wings and can fly fast and far enough. I only wish that truth may be able to follow it, and undo the mischief thus done – through some unintentional mistake perhaps, – but not the less *mischief* and *injustice*.

The following beautiful and original interpretation of Goethe's ballad of the "Erl-King" is not in Ekermann's book; but never mind, I give it to you in the words in which it was given to me.

"Goethe's 'Erl-König' is a moral allegory of deep meaning, though I am not sure he meant it as such, or intended all that it signifies.

"There are beings in the world who see, who feel, with a finer sense than that granted to other mortals. They see the spiritual, the imaginative sorrow, or danger, or terror which threatens them; and those who see not with the same eyes, talk reason and philosophy to them. The poor frightened child cries out for aid, for mercy; and Papa Wisdom – worldly wisdom – answers,

" 'Mein Sohn, es ist ein Nebelstrief!'

"Or,

" 'Es scheinen die alten Weiden so grau!'

"It is only the vapour-wreath, or the grey willows waving, and tells him to be quiet! At last the poor child of feeling is found dead in the arms of Wisdom, from causes which no one else perceived – or believed! Is it not often so?"

What Goethe says of false and true *tendencies* of mind,

and the mistaking a *tendency* for a *talent*, deserves attention; it is a mistake we often fall into, both with regard to
ourselves and others.

He says, smiling, "People think that a man must needs
grow old, in order to be wise; the truth is, that as years
increase upon us, we have enough to do to be as good and
as wise as we *have* been. . . . In certain things a man is as
likely to be in the right at twenty as at sixty."

On this point there is much more, to which I subscribe
heartily.

On the subject of religion I find this beautiful comparison, but am not sure whether it be Ekermann's or Goethe's. "A connoisseur standing before the picture of a great
master will regard it as a whole. He knows how to combine instantly the scattered parts into the general effect;
the universal, as well as the individual, is to him animated.
He has no preference for certain portions: he does not ask
why this or that face is beautiful or otherwise; why *this*
part is light, *that* dark; only he requires that all shall be in
the right place, and according to the just rules of art; but
place an ignorant person before such a picture, and you
will see that the great design of the whole will either be
overlooked by him, or confuse him utterly. Some small
portion will attract him, another will offend him, and in
the end he will dwell upon some trifling object which is
familiar to him, and praise this helmet, or that feather, as
being well executed."

"We men, before the great picture of the destinies of the
universe, play the part of such dunces, such novices in art.
Here we are attracted by a bright spot, a graceful
configuration; *there* we are repelled by a deep shadow, a
painful object; the immense WHOLE bewilders and per-
plexes us; we seek in vain to penetrate the leading idea of
that great Being, who designed the whole upon a plan
which our limited human intellect cannot comprehend."

When Goethe was more than eighty, he purchased, for the

first time, an easy chair. His indifference, and even contempt for the most ordinary comforts and luxuries of this kind, were amusing. The furniture of his study and bedroom (still preserved as he left them) is of the most homely description. A common deal table, a wooden desk, and a high stool, the very sight of which gave me a pain in my back, were the only conveniences. He used to say, that never being accustomed from his youth to luxuries and fine furniture, they took his attention from his work. But his drawing-room was elegant – I remember two very large frames, in which he was accustomed to dispose a variety of original drawings by the old masters, perhaps eight or ten in each. When they had hung some time, he changed them for another set. These were *his* luxuries: the set of drawings which he last selected, remain hanging in the room.

The anecdote related by Ekermann of the Roman cobbler, who used an antique head of one of the Caesars as a block to hammer his leather on, reminds me that the head of the Ilioneus was put to a similar use by a cobbler at Prague.

The most extraordinary thing in this book is what Goethe calls "Das Dämonische." I have (I believe) a kind of glimmering of what he means: whatever exercises a power, a fascination over the mind, whatever in intellect or nature is inexplicable, whatever seems to have a spiritual existence apart from all understood or received laws, acknowledged as irresistible, yet mocking all reason to explain it – a kind of intellectual electricity or magnetism – in short, whatever is unaccountable – he classes under the general head of "Das Dämonische;" a very convenient way, and truly a very poetical way, of getting rid of what one does not comprehend. It is, he says, as if "the curtain was drawn away from the background of existence." In *things*, he instances as examples of this Dämonische, music in itself and in its effect on the mind; poetry of the highest order; and in characters he instances Shakspeare, Napoleon, Byron, the late Grand Duke, (his friend, Karl August,) and others. But it is dangerous almost to go on playing thus with his and one's own deepest, wildest thoughts – and I cannot follow them.

There are passages scattered up and down the book, which clearly prove that Goethe never considered himself as one called upon to take a part in the revolutions and political struggles of his time; but because he stood calmly on the "shore of peace with unwet eye," and let the giddy torrent whirl past him, shall we infer that he took no heed of its course? Can we think that this great and gifted being, whose ample ken embraced a universe, had neither sympathies in the grandest interests, nor hopes in the brightest destinies, of humanity? It were a profanation to think thus:

> "Although his heart (so near allied to earth)
>   Cannot but pity the perplexed state
> Of troublous and distressed mortality,
>   That thus make way unto the ugly berth
> Of their own sorrows; and do still beget
>   Affliction upon imbecility:
> Yet seeing thus the course of things must run,
>   He looks thereon not strange, but as foredone."*

(Even while these lines were printing, Thomas Carlyle has observed, with equal truth and eloquence, "That to ask of such a mind as Goethe's, that he should mix himself up with the political turmoils of the day, was as if we should call down the moon from the firmament of heaven, and convert her into a street torch.")

Great and worthy of all gratitude and fame were those men who have devoted their best faculties, poured out their best blood, for the cause of freedom, for the land they called their own, the principles they espoused; but greater far, and more worthy of gratitude, and of purer and more enduring fame, the very few, who lived not for an age, a country, but for all ages – for all mankind; who

* Daniel.

did not live to preach up this or that theory, to sustain this or that sect or party, to insist on this or that truth, but who lived to work out the intellectual and spiritual good, and promote the progress of the whole human race – to kindle within the individual mind the light which is true freedom, or leads to it. Such was the example left by Jesus Christ – such a man was Shakspeare – such a man was Goethe.

March 18.

I have before me the list of criminals tried at the spring assizes here, and the mayor's charge to the jury.

The calendar (for Toronto only) contains forty-six.

For larcenies, twenty-seven.

Receiving stolen goods, five.

Taking up goods under false pretences, one.

Assaults, seven.

Keeping disorderly houses, six.

The mayor, in his charge to the jury, complains of the increase of crime, and of poverty, wretchedness, and disease, (the natural causes of crime,) within the bounds of the city, and particularly of the increase of street beggars and juvenile depredators, and he recommends the erection of a house of industry on a large scale.

Before we can estimate the increase in the number of criminals as the increase of crime, we must look to the increase of the population, which is enormous. The whole population of Upper Canada had doubled in about nine years, the general average increase per annum being 18,712;* that of Toronto has doubled within five years. The whole number of criminal convictions for the city of Toronto only, from the spring assizes of 1832 to the assizes of the present year, (1837,) is four hundred and twenty-four men and twenty-five women; of the former ten were

---

* In 1837, the entire population of Upper Canada was estimated at 375,000.

for murder, and twenty-three for manslaughter and other violent crimes; and among the women, two were for manslaughter, all the rest were for larcenies and petty crimes.

These are very imperfect data, and quite useless where we wish to come at results; nor can I succeed in getting copies of the yearly calendars in the various districts to compare with the yearly increase of the population; the officials are all too busy, and know nothing except in their own peculiar department; the difficulty of obtaining correct information of *any* kind is beyond what you can conceive: and this, too, where there is no want of good-nature, and the most obliging *intentions;* but labour is here the state of existence; no one has leisure apparently to interest himself about anything but what concerns his own business and subsistence.

March 28.

About a week ago we removed into a new house, and I have since been too much occupied to go on with my studies, domestic matters having "possessed me wholly." Our present residence has never yet been inhabited, and is not quite finished. It will be very pretty and pleasant, no doubt, when it is not so *very* cold and comfortless. We are surrounded by a garden of some extent – or, rather, what will be a garden at some future time; at present it is a bleak waste of snow; we are so completely blockaded by ice and mud, that to reach the house-door is a matter of some difficulty and even danger. Planks laid from one snow heap to another form the only access to the house door. The site, though now so dreary, must be charming in summer, for we command, at one glance, the entrance to the bay, the King's Pier, the lighthouse, and beyond, the whole expanse of Lake Ontario to the Niagara shore, which in some particular states of the atmosphere is distinctly visible, though distant nearly thirty miles. They say, that in the clear summer mornings, the cloud of spray rising from the Falls can be seen from this point. There is yet no indication of the approach of spring, and I find it more than ever difficult to keep myself warm. Nothing in myself or around me feels or looks like *home*. How much is comprised in that little word! May it but please God to preserve to me all that I love! But, O absence! how much is comprised in *that* word too! it is death of the heart and darkness of the soul; it is the ever-springing, ever-dying hope; the ever-craving, never-having wish; it is fear, and doubt, and sorrow, and pain; – a state in which the past swallows up the present, and the future becomes the past before it arrives!

It is now seven weeks since the date of the last letters from my dear far-distant home. The archdeacon told me, by way of comfort, that when he came to settle in this country, there was only one mail-post from England in the course of a whole year, and it was called, as if in mockery, "The Express;" now, either by way of New York or Halifax, we have a post almost every day.

March 29.

To those who see only with their eyes, the distant is always indistinct and little, becoming less and less as it recedes, till utterly lost; but to the imagination, which thus reverses the perspective of the senses, the far off is great and imposing, the magnitude increasing with the distance.

I amused myself this morning with that most charming book "The Doctor;" – it is not the second nor the third time of reading. How delicious it is wherever it opens! – how brimful of erudition and wit, and how rich in thought, and sentiment, and humour! but containing assumptions, and opinions, and prognostications, in which I would not believe; – no, not for the world!

Southey's is a mind at which I must needs admire; he stands upon a vast height, as upon a pinnacle of learning;

he commands all around an immense, a boundless prospect over whatever human intellect and capacity has
achieved or may achieve; but, from the peculiar construction of his mind, he obstinately looks but one way – back
to the past, to what has been done; if ever he looks to the
future, he merely glances at it sideways.

If I might, like Solomon, ask a gift of God, I would
profit by his mistake. I would not ask a *wise* and an
understanding heart: for what did his wisdom and his
understanding do for him? They brought him to the conclusion, that all under the sun was vanity and vexation of
spirit, and that the increase of knowledge was the increase
of sorrow, and so the end was epicurism, despair, and
idolatry. "O most lame and impotent conclusion!" No! – I
would ask, were it permitted, for a *simple* heart, that
should not deceive itself or others, but seek truth for its
own sake, and, having found truth, find also goodness and
happiness, which *must* follow to complete the moral har-
monic chord.

We are so accustomed to the artificial atmosphere
round us, that we lose sometimes the power of distinguish-
ing the false from the true, till we call in our natural
instincts to do for us what our perverted reason cannot.
They say that the Queen of Sheba once presented before
Solomon two garlands of flowers, and desired him to
pronounce which was the natural, which the artificial
wreath. The wisdom of this wisest of men did not enable
him to do this by the appearance only, so exquisitely had
art imitated nature, till on seeing a bee fluttering near, he
called it to his aid. The little creature at once settled the
question by alighting on the real flowers, and avoiding the
false ones.

We have instincts as true as those of the bee to refuse
the evil and to choose the good, if we did not smother
them up with nonsense and metaphysics.

How true what Southey says! (the Doctor I mean – I beg
his pardon,) – "We make the greater part of the evil cir-

cumstances in which we are placed, and then we fit our-selves for those circumstances by a process of degradation, the effect of which most people see in the classes below them, though they may not be conscious that it is opera-ting in a different manner, but with equal force, upon themselves."

The effect of those pre-ordained evils – if they are such – which we inherit with our mortal state; inevitable death – the separation from those we love – old age with its wants, its feebleness, its helplessness – those sufferings which are in the course of nature, are quite sufficient in the infliction, or in the fear of them, to keep the spirit chastened, and the reflecting mind humble before God. But what I *do* deprecate, is to hear people preaching resig-nation to social, self-created evils; fitting, or trying to fit, their own natures by "a process of degradation" to cir-cumstances which they ought to resist, and which they do *inwardly* resist, keeping up a constant, wearing, impotent strife between the life that is *within* and the life that is *without*. How constantly do I read this in the counte-nances of those I meet in the world! – They do not know themselves why there should be this perpetual uneasiness, this jarring and discord within; but it is the vain struggle of the soul, which God created in his own image, to fit its strong, immortal nature for the society which men have framed after their own devices. A *vain* struggle it is! succeeding only in appearance, never in reality, – so we walk about the world the masks of ourselves, pitying each other. When we meet truth we are as much astonished as I used to be at the carnival, when, in the midst of a crowd of fantastic, lifeless, painted faces, I met with some one who had plucked away his mask and stuck it in his hat, and looked out upon me with the real human smile.

Custom is a mere face, or rather a mere mask: as opinion is a mere voice – or less – the echo of a voice.

The Aurora Borealis is of almost nightly occurrence, but this evening it has been more than usually resplendent; radiating up from the north, and spreading to the east and west in form like a fan, the lower point of a pale white, then yellow, amber, orange, successively, and the extremities of a glowing crimson, intense, yet most delicate, like the heart of an unblown rose. It shifted its form and hue at every moment, flashing and waving like a banner in the breeze; and through this portentous veil, transparent as light itself, the stars shone out with a calm and steady brightness; and I thought, as I looked upon them, of a character we both know, where, like those fair stars, the intellectual powers shine serenely bright through a veil of passions, fancies, and caprices. It is most awfully beautiful! I have been standing at my window watching its evolutions, till it is no longer night, but morning.

April 1.

So, there is another month gone; and the snows are just beginning to disappear, and the flocks of snow-birds with them; and the ice is breaking up at the entrance of the bay, and one or two little vessels have ventured as far as the King's Wharf; and the wind blows strong to dry up the melting snow, and some time or other, perhaps, spring will come, and this long winter's imprisonment will be at an end. Yes; I have been spoiled during these last years – I have been existing only for, and by, the highest faculties of my being – have lived through admiration, hope, and love, "until aversion and contempt were things I only knew by name;" and now another time is come – how ill, how very ill I bear it!

This is the worst season in Canada. The roads are breaking up, and nearly impassable; lands are flooded, and in low situations there is much sickness, particularly ague. We have still sixteen square miles of ice within the bay.

The market at Toronto is not well supplied, and is at a

great distance from us. The higher class of people are supplied with provisions from their own lands and farms, or by certain persons they know and employ. With a little management and forethought, we now get on very well; but at first we had to suffer great inconvenience. Quantities of salted provisions are still imported into the country for the consumption of the soldiers and distant settlers, and at certain seasons – at present, for example – there is some difficulty in procuring anything else.

Our table, however, is pretty well supplied. Beef is tolerable, but lean; mutton bad, scarce, and dearer than beef; pork excellent and delicate, being fattened principally on Indian corn. The fish is of many various kinds, and delicious. During the whole winter we had black-bass and white-fish, caught in holes in the ice, and brought down by the Indians. Venison, game, and wild fowl are always to be had; the quails, which are caught in immense numbers near Toronto, are most delicate eating; I lived on them when I could eat nothing else. What they call partridge here is a small species of pheasant, also very good; and now we are promised snipes and woodcocks in abundance. The wild goose is also excellent eating when well cooked, but the old proverb about Heaven sending meat, &c. &c. is verified here. Those who have farms near the city, or a country establishment of their own, raise poultry and vegetables for their own table. As yet I have seen no vegetables whatever but potatoes; even in the best seasons they are not readily to be procured in the market. Every year, however, as Toronto increases in population and importance, will diminish these minor inconveniences.

The want of good servants is a more serious evil. I could amuse you with an account of the petty miseries we have been enduring from this cause, the strange characters who come to offer themselves, and the wages required. Almost all the servants are of the lower class of Irish emigrants, in general honest, warm-hearted, and willing; but never having seen anything but want, dirt, and reckless misery at home, they are not the most eligible persons to trust with the cleanliness and comfort of one's household. Yet we make as many complaints, and express as much surprise at their deficiencies, as though it were possible it could be otherwise. We give to our man-servant eight dollars a month, to the cook six dollars, and to the housemaid four; but these are lower wages than are usual for good and experienced servants, who might indeed command almost any wages here, where all labour is high priced.

A carriage of some kind is here one of the necessaries of life, but a light English-built carriage would be quite unfit for the country – absolutely useless. There is, however, an excellent coachmaker here, who has turned out some very pretty equipages – both sleighs and barouches – of the build which is calculated for the roads in the neighbourhood.

There are other good shops in the town, and one, that of the apothecary, worthy of Regent-street in its appearance. The importations of China, glass, hardware, and clothing, arrive from England in the spring and autumn, the seasons for making our purchases. All these articles are much dearer than in England, and there is little choice as to taste or fashion. Two years ago we bought our books at the same shop where we bought our shoes, our spades, our sugar, and salt pork; now we have two good booksellers' shops, and at one of these a circulating library of two or three hundred volumes of common novels. As soon as there is a demand for something better, there will be a supply of course; but, as I said before, we must have *time*. Archdeacon Strahan and Chief Justice Robinson have very pretty libraries, but in general it is about two years before a new work of any importance finds its way here; the American reprints of the English reviews and magazines, and the Albion newspaper, seem to supply amply our literary wants.

Apropos to newspapers – my table is covered with them. In the absence or scarcity of books, they are the principal medium of knowledge and communication in Upper Canada. There is no stamp-act here – no duty on paper;

and I have sometimes thought that the great number of local newspapers which do not circulate beyond their own little town or district, must, from the vulgar, narrow tone of many of them, do mischief; but on the whole, perhaps, they do more good. Paragraphs printed from English or American papers, on subjects of general interest, the summary of political events, extracts from books or magazines, are copied from one paper into another, till they have travelled round the country. It is true that a great deal of base, vulgar, inflammatory party feeling is also circulated by the same means; but, on the whole, I should not like to see the number or circulation of the district papers checked. There are about forty published in Upper Canada; of these, three are religious, viz. the "Christian Guardian," "The Wesleyan Advocate," and "The Church;" a paper in the German language is published at Berlin, in the Gore district, for the use of the German settlers; "The Correspondent and Advocate" is the leading Radical, "The Toronto Patriot" the leading Conservative paper. The newspapers of Lower Canada and the United States are circulated in great numbers; and as they pay postage, it is no inconsiderable item in the revenue of the post-office. In some of these provincial papers I have seen articles written with considerable talent; among other things, I have remarked a series of letters signed Evans, addressed to the Canadians, on the subject of an education fitted for an agricultural people, and written with infinite good sense and kindly feeling; these have been copied from one paper into another, and circulated widely: no doubt they will do good. Last year the number of newspapers circulated through the post-office, and paying postage, was,

Provincial papers 178,065
United States and foreign papers 149,502

Add 100,000 papers stamped or free, here are 427,567 papers circulated yearly among a population of 370,000, of whom, perhaps, one in fifty can read; – this is pretty well. The gross receipts of the post-office are 21,000*l.* a year. It is rather affecting to see the long lists of unclaimed letters lying at the post-office, and read the advertisements in the Canada and American journals for husbands, relatives, friends, lost or strayed.

There is a commercial news-room in the city of Toronto, and this is absolutely the only place of assembly or amusement, except the taverns and low drinking-houses. An attempt has been made to found a mechanics' institute and a literary club; but as yet they create little interest, and are very ill supported.

If the sympathy for literature and science be small, that for music is less. Owing to the exertions of an intelligent musician here, some voices have been so far drilled that the psalms and anthems at church are very tolerably performed; but this gentleman receives so little general encouragement, that he is at this moment preparing to go over to the United States. The archdeacon is collecting subscriptions to pay for an organ which is to cost a thousand pounds; if the money were expended in aid of a singing-school, it would do more good.

The interior of the episcopal church here is rather elegant, with the exception of a huge window of painted glass which cost 500*l.,* and is in a vile, tawdry taste.

Besides the episcopal church, the Presbyterians, Methodists, Roman Catholics, and Baptists have each a place of worship. There is also an African church for the negroes.

The hospital, a large brick building, is yet too small for the increasing size of the city. The public grammar-school, called the "Upper Canada College," forms a cluster of ugly brick buildings; and although the system of education there appears narrow and defective, yet it is a *beginning*, and certainly productive of good.

The physician I have mentioned to you, Dr. Rees, entertains the idea of founding a house of reception for destitute female emigrants on their arrival in Canada – a house where, without depending of *charity*, they may be boarded and lodged at the smallest possible cost, and respectably protected till they can procure employment. You may easily imagine that I take a deep interest in this design.

There you have the result of a walk I took this morning up and down our city with a very intelligent guide.

I am afraid these trifling facts will not much interest you. For me, no facts, merely as facts, are in the slightest degree interesting, except as they lead to some truth. I must combine them, and in the combination seek or find a result, before such facts excite either my curiosity or attention.

April 15.

The ice in the Bay of Toronto has been, during the winter months, from four to five feet in thickness: within the last few days it has been cracking in every direction with strange noises, and last night, during a tremendous gale from the east, it was rent, and loosened, and driven at once out of the bay. "It moveth altogether, if it move at all." The last time I drove across the bay, the ice beneath me appeared as fixed and firm as the foundations of the earth, and within twelve hours it has disappeared.

To-day the first steam-boat of the season entered our harbour. They called me to the window to see it, as, with flags and streamers flying, and amid the cheers of the people, it swept majestically into the bay. I sympathised with the general rejoicing, for I can fully understand all the animation and bustle which the opening of the navigation will bring to our torpid capital.

In former times, when people travelled into strange countries, they travelled *de bonne foi*, really to see and learn what was new to them. Now, when a traveller goes to a foreign country, it is always with a set of preconceived notions concerning it, to which he fits all he sees, and refers all he hears: and this, I suppose, is the reason that the old travellers are still safe guides; while modern travellers may be pleasant reading, but are withal the most unsafe guides any one can have.

I am inclined to distrust the judgment of those persons whom I see occupied by one subject, one idea, one object, and referring all things to that, till it assumes by degrees an undue magnitude and importance, and prevents them from feeling the true relative proportion and value of other objects: yet thus it is, perhaps, that single truths are worked out and perfected. Yet, again, I doubt whether there *be* separate and single truths – whether it be possible for one to arrive at *the truth* by any narrow path; – or is truth, like heaven, "a palace with many doors," to which we arrive by many paths, each thinking his own the right one; and it is not till we have arrived within the sanctuary that we perceive we are in a central point to which converge a thousand various paths from every point of the compass – every region of thought?

In the Pitti Palace at Florence there is a statue, standing alone in its naked beauty, in the centre of a many-sided saloon, panelled with mirrors, in which it is reflected at once in every different aspect, and in each, though differently, yet *truly*, as long as the mirror be clear and unwarped – and such is truth. We all look towards it, but each mind beholds it under a different angle of incidence; and unless we were so freed from all earthly bonds as to behold in one and the same moment the statue itself, in its pure unvarying *oneness*, and all its multiplied and ever-varying reflections imaged around, how shall we presume to settle which of these is the false, and which the true?

To reason from analogy is often dangerous, but to illustrate by a fanciful analogy is sometimes a means by which we *light* an idea, as it were, into the understanding of another.

April 24.

The King of Prussia, after seeing Othello, forbade Desdemona to be murdered for the future, and the catastrophe was altered accordingly – "by his majesty's command." This good-natured monarch, whose ideas of art are quite singular, also insisted that in the opera of Undine, Huldibrand should not die as in the tale, but become a water-spirit, and "all end happily;" but I would not advise you to laugh at this, as long as we endure the new catastrophes tacked to Shakspeare.

It was Hoffmann, so celebrated for his tales of diablerie, and in Germany not less celebrated as a musician, who composed the opera of Undine. The music, as I have been assured, was delicious, and received at Berlin with rapturous approval. After the first few representations, the opera-house was burnt down, and with it the score of the Undine perished. Hoffmann had accidentally one *partie* in his desk, but in the excess of his rage and despair he threw that also into the fire, and thus not a note of this charming opera survives.

Only the other day I was reading Hoffmann's analysis and exposition of the Don Juan. It is certainly one of the wildest, and yet one of the most beautiful, pieces of criticism I ever met with – the criticism of an inspired poet and musician. Methinks that in this opera the words and the music are as body and soul; and certainly we must judge the character and signification of the whole by the music, not by the words. Hoffmann regards Don Juan as a kind of Faust, and insists that Donna Anna was in love with him; and the music given to her expresses certainly a depth of passion and despair beyond the words, and something *different* from them. The *text* speaks the conventional woman, and the music breathes the voice of nature revealing the struggle, the tempest within.

When at New York this winter, I was introduced to a fine old Italian, with long and flowing white hair, and a most venerable and marked physiognomy; it was Lorenzo da Porta, the man who had first introduced Mozart to the Emperor Joseph, and who wrote for him the text of the Don Juan, the Figaro, and the Cosi fan Tutti: we have no such *libretti* now!

The German text of the Zauberflöte was by Schichenada, a buffoon comedian and singer in the service of Joseph II.; he was himself the original Papageno. Some people think that he meant to dramatise in this opera the mysteries of Freemasonry, and others are anxious to find in it some profound allegorical meaning; whereas I doubt whether the text has any meaning at all, while to the delicious music we may ally a thousand meanings, a thousand fairy-dreams of poetry. Schichenada was patronised by Joseph, and much attached to him; after the emperor's death, he went mad, and spent the rest of his life sitting in an armchair, with a large sheet thrown all over him, refusing to speak to his family. When any one visited him, he would lift the sheet from his head, and ask, with a fixed look, "Did you know Joseph?" If the answer were "*Yes*," he would, perhaps, condescend to exchange a few words with his visitor, – always on the same subject, his emperor and patron; but if the answer were "*No*," he immediately drew his sheet about him like a shroud, hid his face, and sank again into his arm-chair and obstinate silence; and thus he died.

April 29.

This day, after very cold weather during the whole week, the air became filled with a haze like smoke, the wind blew suddenly hot as from the mouth of a furnace, and for a few hours I suffered exceedingly from languid depression, and could scarcely breathe. It was worse than an Italian sirocco.

I cannot learn the cause of this phenomenon: the wind blew from the lake.

May 1.

Exceedingly cold, – a severe frost – a keen, boisterous wind, and a most turbulent lake. Too ill to do anything but read. I amused myself with Friedrich Rückert's poems,* which left on my imagination an impression like that which the perfume of a bouquet of hot-house flowers, or the sparkling of a casket of jewels, would leave on my senses. As an amatory lyric poet, he may be compared to Moore; – there is the same sort of *efflorescence* of wit and fancy, the same felicity of expression, the same gem-like polish, and brilliance, and epigrammatic turn in his exquisite little lyrics. I suppose there could not be a greater contrast than between his songs and those of Heine. It is greater than the difference between Moore and Burns, and the same kind of difference.

Lenau,† again, is altogether distinct; and how charming he is! Yet great as is his fame in Germany, I believe it has not reached England. He is the great pastoral poet of modern Germany – not pastoral in the old-fashioned style, for he trails no shepherd's crook, and pipes no song "to Amaryllis in the shade," nor does he deal in Fauns or Dryads, and such "cattle." He is the priest of Nature, her Druid, and the expounder of her divinest oracles. It is not the poet who describes or comments on nature; – it is Nature, with her deep mysterious voice, commenting on the passions and sorrows of humanity. His style is very difficult, but very expressive and felicitous: in one of those compound words to which the German language lends itself – like the Greek, Lenau will place a picture suddenly before the imagination, like a whole landscape revealed to

* Friedrich Rückert is professor of the Oriental languages at Erlangen. He has published three volumes of poems, partly original, and partly translated or imitated from eastern poets, and enjoys a very high reputation both as a scholar and a poet.

† Nicholaus Lenau is a noble Hungarian, a Magyar by birth: the name under which his poetry is published is not, I believe, his real name.

sight by a single flash of lightning. Some of his poems, in which he uses the commonest stuff of our daily existence as a material vehicle for the loftiest and deepest thought and sentiments, are much in the manner of Wordsworth. One of the most beautiful of these is "Der Postilion."

Lenau has lately written a dramatic poem on the subject of "Faust," the scope and intention of which I find it difficult to understand – more difficult than that of Goethe. For the present I have thrown it aside in despair.

The genius of Franz Grillparzer has always seemed to me essentially lyric, rather than dramatic: in his admirable tragedies the character, the sentiment, are always more *artistically* evolved than the situation or action.

The characters of Sappho and Medea, in his two finest dramas,* are splendid creations. We have not, I think, in the drama of the present day, anything conceived with equal power, and at the same time carried out in every part, and set forth with such glorious poetical colouring. Lord Byron's "Sardanapalus" would give perhaps a more just idea of the *manner* in which Grillparzer treats a dramatic subject, than anything else in our literature to which I could compare him.

Sappho is the type of the woman of genius. She enters crowned with the Olympic laurel, surrounded by the shouts of gratulating crowds, and shrinks within herself to find that they bring her incense, not happiness – applause, not sympathy – fame, not love. She would fain renew her youth, the golden dreams of her morning of life, before she had sounded the depths of grief and passion, before experience had thrown its shadow over her heart, in the

---

* The "Sappho" appeared after the "Ahnfrau," to which it presents a remarkable contrast in style and construction. The "Golden Fleece," in three parts, appeared in 1822. Both these tragedies have been represented on all the theatres in Germany; and Madame Wolff at Berlin, Madame Heygendorf at Weimar, Madame Schroeder at Munich and Vienna, have all excelled as Sappho and Medea.

love of the youthful, inexperienced, joyous Phaon; and it is well imagined too, that while we are filled with deepest admiration and compassion for Sappho, betrayed and raging like a Pythoness, we yet have sympathy for the boy Phaon, who leaves the love of his magnificent mistress – love rather bestowed than yielded – for that of the fair, gentle slave Melitta. His first love is the woman to whom he does homage; his second, the woman to whom he gives protection. Nothing can be more natural; it is the common course of things.

Learned and unlearned agree in admiring Grillparzer's versification of Sappho's celebrated ode –

"Golden-Thronende Aphrodite!"

– It sounds to my unlearned ears wonderfully grand and Greek, and musical and classical; and when Schroeder recites these lines in the theatre, you might hear your own heart beat in the breathless silence around.*

German critics consider the "Medea" less perfect than the "Sappho" in point of style, and, considered merely as a work of art, inferior. Of this I cannot so well judge, but I shall never forget reading it for the first time – I think of it as an era in my poetic reminiscences. It is the only conception of the character in which we understand the *necessity* for Medea's murder of her children. In the other tragedies on the same subject, we must take it for granted; but Grillparzer conducts us to the appalling catastrophe through such a linked chain of motives and feelings, that when it comes, it comes as something inevitable.

Medea is the type of the woman of instinct and passion. Contrasted with the elegant, subdued Greek females, she is a half savage, all devotion and obedience one moment,

* The translation of the same ode by Ambrose Phillips,
    "O Venus! beauty of the skies,
    To whom a thousand temples rise,"
is well known. In spite of the commendation bestowed on it by Addison, it appears very trivial and affected, compared with that of Grillparzer.

a tameless tigress in the next; first subdued by the masculine valour, then revolted by the moral cowardice of Jason. Grillparzer has wisely kept the virago and the sorceress, with whom we hardly sympathise, out of sight as much as possible; while the human being, humanly acted upon and humanly acting and feeling, is for ever before us. There is a dreadful truth and nature in the whole portrait, which is perfectly finished throughout. Placed beside the Medea of Euripides, it is the picturesque compared with the statuesque delineation.

The subject of the "Medea" has a strange fascination around it, like that of the terrible agonised beauty of the "Medusa," on which we *must* gaze though it turn us to stone. It has been treated in every possible style, in I know not how many tragedies and operas, ancient and modern. I remember, at Vienna, a representation of a singular kind given by Madame Schroëder; it was a monologue in prose, with musical symphonies, composed by George Benda, about 1755. After every two or three spoken sentences came a strain of music, which the actress accompanied by expressive pantomime. The prose text (by Gotter) appeared to me a string of adjurations, exclamations, and imprecations, without any colouring of poetry; and the music interrupted rather than aided the flow of the passion. Still it was a most striking exhibition of Schroëder's peculiar talent; her fine classical attitudes were a study for an artist, and there were bursts of pathos, and flashes of inconceivable majesty, which thrilled me. The fierceness was better expressed than the tenderness of the woman, and the adjuration to Hecate recalled for a moment Mrs. Siddons's voice and look when she read the witch-scene in "Macbeth;" yet, take her altogether, she was not so fine as Pasta in the same character. Schroëder's Lady Macbeth I remember thinking insufferable.

May 19.

After some days of rather severe indisposition from ague and fever, able to sit up.

Sat at the window drawing, or rather not drawing, but with a pencil in my hand. This beautiful Lake Ontario! – my lake – for I begin to be in love with it, and look on it as mine! – it changed its hues every moment, the shades of purple and green fleeting over it, now dark, now lustrous, now pale – like a dolphin dying; or, to use a more exact though less poetical comparison, dappled, and varying like the back of a mackarel, with every now and then a streak of silver light dividing the shades of green: magnificent, tumultuous clouds came rolling round the horizon; and the little graceful schooners, falling into every beautiful attitude, and catching every variety of light and shade, came curtseying into the bay: and flights of wild geese, and great black loons, were skimming, diving, sporting over the bosom of the lake; and beautiful little unknown birds, in gorgeous plumage of crimson and black, were fluttering about the garden: all life, and light, and beauty were abroad – the resurrection of Nature! How beautiful it was! how dearly welcome to my senses – to my heart – this spring which comes at last – so long wished for, so long waited for!

May 30.

Last night, a ball at the government-house, to which people came from a distance of fifty – a hundred – two hundred miles – which is nothing to signify *here*. There were very pretty girls, and very nice dancing; but we had all too much reason to lament the loss of the band of the 66th regiment, which left us a few weeks ago – to my sorrow.

It is to be hoped that all the governors sent here for the future may be married men, and bring their wives with them, for the presence of a female at the head of our little provincial court – particularly if she be intelligent, good-natured, and accomplished – is a greater advantage to the society here, and does more to render the government popular, than you can well imagine.

Erindale.

– A very pretty place, with a very pretty name. A kind of invitation led me hither, to seek change of air, change of scene, and every other change I most needed.

The Britannia steam-boat, which plies daily between Toronto and Hamilton, brought us to the mouth of the Credit River in an hour and a half. By the orders of Mr. M——, a spring cart or wagon, the usual vehicle of the country, was waiting by the inn, on the shore of the lake, to convey me through the woods to his house; and the master of the inn, a decent, respectable man, drove the wagon. He had left England a mere child, thirty years ago, with his father, mother, and seven brothers and sisters, and eighteen years ago had come to Canada from the United States, at the suggestion of a relation, to settle "in the bush," the common term for uncleared land; at that time they had nothing, as he said, but "health and hands." The family, now reduced to five, are all doing well. He has himself a farm of two hundred and fifty acres, his own property; his brother as much more; his sisters are well settled. "Any man," said he, "with health and a pair of hands, could get on well in this country, if it were not for *the drink; that* ruins hundreds."

They are forming a harbour at the mouth of the river – widening and deepening the channel; but, owing to the want of means and money during the present perplexities, the works are not going on. There is a clean, tidy inn, and some log and frame houses; the situation is low, swampy, and I should suppose unhealthy; but they assured me, that though still subject to ague and fever in the spring, every year diminished this inconvenience, as the draining and clearing of the lands around was proceeding rapidly.

The River Credit is so called, because in *ancient* times (*i.e.* forty or fifty years ago) the fur traders met the Indians on its banks, and delivered to them on *credit* the goods for which, the following year, they received the value, or rather ten times the value, in skins. In a country where there is no law of debtor or creditor, no bonds, stamps, bills, or bailiffs, no possibility of punishing, or even catching a refractory or fraudulent debtor, but, on the contrary, every possibility of being tomahawked by said debtor, this might seem a hazardous arrangement; yet I have been assured by those long engaged in the trade, both in the upper and lower province, that for an Indian to break his engagements is a thing unheard of: and if, by any personal accident, he should be prevented from bringing in the stipulated number of beaver skins, his relatives and friends consider their honour implicated, and make up the quantity for him.

The fur trade has long ceased upon these shores, once the scene of bloody conflicts between the Hurons and the Missassaguas. The latter were at length nearly extirpated; a wretched, degenerate remnant of the tribe still continued to skulk about their old haunts and the burial-place of their fathers, which is a high mound on the west bank of the river, and close upon the lake. These were collected by the Methodist missionaries, into a village or settlement, about two miles farther on, where an attempt has been made to civilise and convert them. The government have expended a large sum in aid of this charitable purpose, and about fifty log-huts have been constructed for the Indians, each hut being divided by a partition, and capable of lodging two or more families. There is also a chapel and a school-house. Peter Jones, otherwise Kahkequona-by, a half-cast Indian, is the second chief and religious teacher; he was in England a few years ago to raise contributions for his people, and married a young enthusiastic Englishwoman with a small property. She has recently quitted the village to return to Europe. There is, besides, a regular Methodist preacher established here, who cannot speak one word of the language of the natives, nor hold any communion with them, except through an interpreter. He complained of the mortality among the children, and the yearly diminution of numbers in the settlement. The greater number of those who remain are half-breeds, and of these, some of the young women and children are really splendid creatures; but the general appearance of the place and people struck me as gloomy. The Indians, whom I saw wandering and lounging about, and the squaws wrapped in dirty blankets, with their long black hair falling over their faces and eyes, filled me with compassion. When the tribe were first gathered together, they amounted to seven hundred men, women, and children; there are now about two hundred and twenty. The missionary and his wife looked dejected; he told me that the Conference never allowed them (the missionaries) to remain with any congregation long enough to know the people, or take a personal interest in their welfare. In general the term of their residence in any settlement or district was from two to three years, and they were then exchanged for another. Among the inhabitants a few have cultivated the portion of land allotted to them, and live in comparative comfort; three or four women (half cast) are favourably distinguished by the cleanliness of their houses, and general good conduct; and some of the children are remarkably intelligent, and can read both their own language and English; but these are exceptions, and dirt, indolence, and drunkenness, are but too general. Consumption is the prevalent disease, and carries off numbers* of these wretched people.

After passing the Indian village, we plunged again into the depth of the green forests, through a road or path which presented every now and then ruts and abysses of mud, into which we sank nearly up to the axletree, and I began to appreciate feelingly the fitness of a Canadian wagon. On each side of this forest path the eye sought in

---

* The notes thrown together here are the result of three different visits to the Credit, and information otherwise obtained.

vain to penetrate the labyrinth of foliage, and intermingled flowers of every dye, where life in myriad forms was creeping, humming, rustling in the air or on the earth, on which the morning dew still glittered under the thick shades.

From these woods we emerged, after five or six miles of travelling, and arrived at Springfield, a little village we had passed through in the depth of winter – how different its appearance now! – and diverging from the road, a beautiful path along the high banks above the river Credit, brought us to Erindale, for so Mr. M—— , in fond recollection of his native country, has named his romantic residence.

Mr. M—— is the clergyman and magistrate of the district, beside being the principal farmer and land proprietor. His wife, sprung from a noble and historical race, blended much sweetness and frankheartedness, with more of courtesy and manner than I expected to find. My reception was most cordial, though the whole house was in unusual bustle, for it was the 4th of June, parade day, when the district militia were to be turned out; and two of the young men of the family were buckling on swords and accoutrements, and furbishing up helmets, while the sister was officiating with a sister's pride at this military toilette, tying on sashes and arranging epaulettes; and certainly, when they appeared – one in the pretty green costume of a rifleman, the other all covered with embroidery as a captain of lancers – I thought I had seldom seen two finer-looking men. After taking coffee and refreshments, we drove down to the scene of action.

On a rising ground above the river which ran gurgling and sparkling through the green ravine beneath, the motley troops, about three or four hundred men, were marshalled – no, not marshalled, but scattered in a far more picturesque fashion hither and thither: a few log-houses and a saw-mill on the river-bank, and a little wooden church crowning the opposite height, formed the chief features of the scene. The boundless forest spread all around us. A few men, well mounted, and dressed as lancers, in uniforms which were, however, anything but uniform, flourished backwards on the green sward, to the manifest peril of the spectators; themselves and their horses, equally wild, disorderly, spirited, undisciplined: but this was perfection compared with the infantry. Here there was no uniformity attempted of dress, of appearance, of movement; a few had coats, others jackets; a greater number had neither coats nor jackets, but appeared in their shirt-sleeves, white or checked, or clean or dirty, in edifying variety! Some wore hats, others caps, others their own shaggy heads of hair. Some had firelocks; some had old swords, suspended in belts, or stuck in their waistbands; but the greater number shouldered sticks or umbrellas. Mrs. M—— told us that on a former parade day she had heard the word of command given thus – "Gentlemen with the umbrellas, take ground to the right! Gentlemen with the walking-sticks, take ground to the left!" Now they ran after each other, elbowed and kicked each other, straddled, stooped, chattered; and if the commanding officer turned his back for a moment, very coolly sat down on the bank to rest. Not to laugh was impossible, and defied all power of face. Charles M. made himself hoarse with shouting out orders which no one obeyed, except, perhaps, two or three men in the front; and James, with his horsemen, flourished their lances, and galloped, and capered, and curveted to admiration. James is the popular storekeeper and postmaster of the village, and when, after the show, we went into his warehouse to rest, I was not a little amused to see our captain of lancers come in, and, taking off his plumed helmet, jump over the counter to serve one customer to a "pennyworth of tobacco," and another to a "yard of check." Willy, the younger brother, a fine young man, who had been our cavalier on the field, assisted; and half in jest, half in earnest, I gravely presented myself as the purchaser of something or other, which Willy served out with a laughing gaiety and unembarrassed simplicity quite delightful. We returned to sit down to a plain, plenteous, and excellent dinner; everything on the table, the wine excepted, was the produce of their own farm. Our wine, water, and butter were iced, and everything was the best of its kind.

The parade day ended in a drunken bout and a riot, in which, as I was afterwards informed, the colonel had been knocked down, and one or two serious and even fatal accidents had occurred; but it was all taken so very lightly, so very much as a thing of course, in this half-civilised community, that I soon ceased to think about the matter.

The next morning I looked out from my window upon a scene of wild yet tranquil loveliness. The house is built on the edge of a steep bank, (what in Scotland they term a *scaur*,) perhaps a hundred feet high, and descending precipitously to the rapid river.* The banks on either side were clothed with overhanging woods of the sumach, maple, tamarask, birch, in all the rich yet delicate array of the fresh opening year. Beyond, as usual, lay the dark pine-forest; and near to the house there were several groups of lofty pines, the original giant-brood of the soil; beyond these again lay the "clearing." The sky was without a cloud, and the heat intense. I found breakfast laid in the verandah: excellent tea and coffee, rich cream, delicious hot cakes, new-laid eggs – a banquet for a king! The young men and their labourers had been out since sunrise and the younger ladies of the house were busied in domestic affairs; the rest of us sat lounging all the morning in the verandah; and in the intervals of sketching and reading, my kind host and hostess gave me an account of their emigration to this country ten years ago.

Mr. M. was a Protestant clergyman of good family, and had held a considerable living in Ireland; but such was the disturbed state of the country in which he resided, that he was not only unable to collect his tithes, but for several years neither his own life nor that of any of his family was

---

* In this river the young sportsmen of the family had speared two hundred salmon in a single night. The salmon-hunts in Canada are exactly like that described so vividly in Guy Mannering. The fish thus caught is rather a large species of trout than genuine salmon. The sport is most exciting.

safe. They never went out unarmed, and never went to rest at night without having barricadoed their house like a fortress. The health of his wife began to fail under this anxiety, and at length, after a severe struggle with old feelings and old habits, he came to the determination to convert his Irish property into ready money and emigrate to Canada, with four fine sons from seven to seventeen years old, and one little daughter. Thus you see that Canada has become an asylum, not only for those who cannot pay tithes, but for those who cannot get them.

Soon after his arrival, he purchased eight hundred acres of land along the banks of the Credit. With the assistance of his sons and a few labourers, he soon cleared a space of ground for a house, in a situation of great natural beauty, but then a perfect wilderness; and with no other aid designed and built it in very pretty taste. Being thus secure of lodging and shelter, they proceeded in their toilsome work – toilsome, most laborious, he allowed it to be, but not unrewarded; and they have now one hundred and fifty acres of land cleared and in cultivation; a noble barn, entirely constructed by his sons, measuring sixty feet long by forty in width; a carpenter's shop, a turning-lathe, in the use of which the old gentleman and one of his sons are very ingenious and effective; a forge; extensive outhouses; a farmyard well stocked; and a house comfortably furnished, much of the ornamental furniture being contrived, carved, turned, by the father and his sons. These young men, who had received in Ireland the rudiments of a classical education, had all a mechanical genius, and here, with all their energies awakened, and all their physical and mental powers in full occupation, they are a striking example of what may be done by activity and perseverance; they are their own architects, masons, smiths, carpenters, farmers, gardeners; they are, moreover, bold and keen hunters, quick in resource, intelligent, cheerful, united by strong affection, and doating on their gentle sister, who has grown up among these four tall, manly brothers, like a beautiful azalia under the towering and sheltering pines. Then I should add, that one of the young men knows something of surgery, can bleed or set a broken limb in case of necessity; while another knows as much of law as enables him to draw up an agreement, and settle the quarrels and arrange the little difficulties of their poorer neighbours, without having recourse to the "attorney."

The whole family appear to have a lively feeling for natural beauty, and a taste for natural history; they know the habits and the haunts of the wild animals which people their forest domain; they have made collections of minerals and insects, and have "traced each herb and flower that sips the silvery dew." Not only the stout servant girl, (whom I met running about with a sucking-pig in her arms, looking for its mother,) and the little black boy Alick; – but the animals in the farmyard, the old favourite mare, the fowls which come trooping round the benignant old gentleman, or are the peculiar pets of the ladies of the family, – the very dogs and cats appear to me, each and all, the most enviable of their species.

There is an atmosphere of benevolence and cheerfulness breathing round, which penetrates to my very heart. I know not when I have felt so quietly – so entirely happy – so full of sympathy – so light-hearted – so inclined to shut out the world, and its cares and vanities, and "fleet the time as they did i' the golden age."

In the evening it was very sultry, the sky was magnificently troubled, and the clouds came rolling down, mingling, as it seemed to me, with the pine tops. We walked up and down the verandah, listening to the soft melancholy cry of the whip-poor-will, and watching the evolutions of some beautiful green snakes of a perfectly harmless species, which were gliding after each other along the garden walks; by degrees a brooding silence and thick darkness fell around us; then the storm burst forth in all its might, the lightning wrapped the whole horizon round in sheets of flame, the thunder rolled over the forest, and still we lingered – lingered till the fury and tumult of the elements had subsided, and the rain began to fall in torrents; we then went into the house and had some music. Charles and Willy had good voices, and much natural taste; and we sang duets and trios till supper-time. We again assembled round the cheerful table, where there was infinite laughing – the heart's laugh – and many a jest seasoned with the true Irish gallantry, and humour; and then the good old gentleman, after discussing his sober tumbler of whisky-punch, sent us all with his blessing to our rest.

Mr. M. told me, that for the first seven or eight years they had all lived and worked together on his farm; but latterly he had reflected that though the proceeds of the farm afforded a subsistence, it did not furnish the means of independence for his sons, so as to enable them to marry and settle in the world. He has therefore established two of his sons as storekeepers, the one in Springfield, the other at Streetsville, both within a short distance of his own residence, and they have already, by their intelligence, activity, and popular manners succeeded beyond his hopes.

I could perceive that in taking this step there had been certain prejudices and feelings to be overcome, on his own part and that of his wife: the family pride of the well-born Irish gentleman, and the antipathy to anything like trade, once cherished by a certain class in the old country – these were to be conquered, before he could reconcile himself to the idea of his boys serving out groceries in a Canadian village; but they *were* overcome. Some lingering of the "old Adam" made him think it necessary to excuse – to account for this state of things. He did not know with what entire and approving sympathy I regarded, not the foolish national prejudices of my country, but the honest, generous spirit and good sense through which he had conquered them, and provided for the future independence of his children.

I inquired concerning the extent of his parish, and the morals and condition of his parishioners.

He said that on two sides the district under his charge

might be considered as without bounds, for, in fact, there
was no parish boundary line between him and the North
Pole. He has frequently ridden from sixteen to thirty miles
to officiate at a marriage or a funeral, or baptize a child, or
preach a sermon, wherever a small congregation could be
collected together; but latterly his increasing age rendered
such exertion difficult. His parish church is in Springfield.
When he first took the living, to which he was appointed
on his arrival in the country, the salary – for here there are
no tithes – was two hundred a year: some late measure,
fathered by Mr. Hume, had reduced it to one hundred. He
spoke of this without bitterness as regarded himself,
observing that he was old, and had other means of subsistence; but he considered it as a great injustice both to
himself and to his successors – "For," said he, "it is clear
that no man could take charge of this extensive district
without keeping a good horse, and a boy to rub him down.
Now, in this country, where wages are high, he could not
keep a horse and a servant, and wear a whole coat, for less
than one hundred a year. No man, therefore, who had not
other resources, could live upon this sum; and no man
who *had* other resources, and had received a fitting education, would be likely to come here. I say nothing of the
toil, the fatigue, the deep responsibility – these belong to
his vocation, in which, though a man must labour, he
need not surely starve: – yet starve he must, unless he
takes a farm or a store in addition to his clerical duties. A
clergyman in such circumstances could hardly command
the respect of his parishioners: what do *you* think,
madam?"

When the question was thus put, I could only think the
same: it seems to me that there must be something wrong
in the whole of this Canadian church system, from beginning to end.

With regard to the morals of the population around
him, he spoke of two things as especially lamentable – the
prevalence of drunkenness, and the early severing of
parental and family ties; the first, partly owing to the low
price of whisky, the latter to the high price of labour,

which rendered it the interest of the young of both sexes to leave their home, and look out and provide for themselves as soon as possible. This fact, and its consequences, struck him the more painfully, from the contrast it exhibited to the strong family affections, and respect for parental authority, which, even in the midst of squalid, reckless misery and ruin, he had been accustomed to in poor Ireland. The general morals of the women he considered infinitely superior to those of the men; and in the midst of the horrid example and temptation, and one may add, provocation, round them, their habits were generally sober. He knew himself but two females abandoned to habits of intoxication, and in both instances the cause had been the same – an unhappy home and a brutal husband.

He told me many other interesting circumstances and anecdotes, but being of a personal nature, and his permission not expressly given, I do not note them down here.

On the whole, I shall never forget the few days spent with this excellent family. We bade farewell, after many a cordial entreaty on their part, many a promise on mine, to visit them again. Charles M. drove me over to the Credit, where we met the steam-boat, and I returned to Toronto with my heart full of kindly feelings, my fancy full of delightful images, and my lap full of flowers, which Charles had gathered for me along the margin of the forest – flowers such as we transplant and nurture with care in our gardens and green-houses, most dazzling and lovely in colour, strange and new to me in their forms, and names, and uses. Unluckily I am no botanist, so will not venture to particularise farther; but one plant struck me particularly, growing everywhere in thousands: the stalk was about two feet in height, and at the top were two large fan-like leaves, one being always larger than the other; from between the two sprung a single flower, in size and shape somewhat resembling a large wild rose, the petal white, just tinted with a pale blush. The flower is succeeded by an oval-shaped fruit, which is eaten, and makes an excellent preserve. They call it here the May-apple.

Summer Rambles

Summer Rambles in Canada.

.   .   .   .   You dwell alone;
You walk, you read, you speculate alone;
Yet doth remembrance, like a sovereign prince,
For you a stately gallery maintain
Of gay or tragic pictures.

                                        Wordsworth.

Vergnügen sitzt in Blumen-kelchen, und kommt alle Jahr
einmal als Geruch heraus.

                                        Rahel.

June 8.

WE HAVE already exchanged "the bloom and ravish-
ment of spring" for all the glowing maturity of summer; we gasp with heat, we long for ices, and are planning
venetian blinds; and three weeks ago there was snow lying
beneath our garden fences, and not a leaf on the trees! In
England, when Nature wakes up from her long winter, it is
like a sluggard in the morning, – she opens one eye and
then another, and shivers and draws her snow coverlet
over her face again, and turns round to slumber more
than once, before she emerges at last, lazily and slowly,

from her winter chamber; but here, no sooner has the sun peeped through her curtains, than up she springs, like a huntress for the chase, and dons her kirtle of green, and walks abroad in full-blown life and beauty. I am basking in her smile like an insect or a bird! – Apropos to birds, we have, alas! no singing birds in Canada. There is, indeed, a little creature of the ouzel kind, which haunts my garden, and has a low, sweet warble, to which I listen with pleasure; but we have nothing like the rich, continuous song of the nightingale or lark, or even the linnet. We have no music in our groves but that of the frogs, which set up such a shrill and perpetual chorus every evening, that we can scarce hear each other speak. The regular manner in which the bass and treble voices respond to each other is perfectly ludicrous, so that in the midst of my impatience I have caught myself laughing. Then we have every possible variety of note, from the piping squeak of the tree-frog, to the deep, guttural croak, almost roar, of the bull-frog.

The other day, while walking near a piece of water, I was startled by a very loud deep croak, as like the croak of an ordinary frog, as the bellow of a bull is like the bleat of a calf; and looking round, perceived one of those enormous bull-frogs of the country seated with great dignity on the end of a plank, and staring at me. The monster was at least a foot in length, with a pair of eyes like spectacles; on shaking my parasol at him, he plunged to the bottom in a moment. They are quite harmless, I believe, though slander accuses them of attacking the young ducks and chickens.

It would be pleasant, verily, if, after all my ill-humoured and impertinent *tirades* against Toronto, I were doomed to leave it with regret; yet such is likely to be the case. There are some most kind-hearted and agreeable people here, who look upon me with more friendliness than at first, and are winning fast upon my feelings, if not on my sympathies. There is considerable beauty too around me – not that I am going to give you descriptions of scenery, which are always, however eloquent, in some respect failures. Words can no more give you a definite idea of the combination of forms and colours in scenery, than so many musical notes: music were, indeed, the better vehicle of the two. Felix Mendelsohn, when a child, used to say, "I cannot tell you how such or such a thing was – I cannot speak it – I will play it to you!" – and run to his piano: sound was then to him a more perfect vehicle than words; – so, if I were a musician, I would *play* you Lake Ontario, rather than describe it. Ontario means *the beautiful*, and the word is worthy of its signification, and the lake is worthy of its beautiful name; yet I can hardly tell you in what this fascination consists: there is no scenery around it, no high lands, no bold shores, no picture to be taken in at once by the eye; the swamp and the forest enclose it, and it is so wide and so vast that it presents all the monotony without the majesty of the ocean. Yet, like that great ocean, when I lived beside it, the expanse of this lake has become to me like the face of a friend. I have all its various *expressions* by heart. I go down upon the green bank, or along the King's Pier, which projects about two hundred yards into the bay. I sit there with my book, reading sometimes, but oftener watching untired the changeful colours as they flit over the bosom of the lake. Sometimes a thunder-squall from the west sends the little sloops and schooners sweeping and scudding into the harbour for shelter. Sometimes the sunset converts its surface into a sea of molten gold, and sometimes the young moon walks trembling in a path of silver; sometimes a purple haze floats over its bosom like a veil; sometimes the wind blows strong, and the turbid waves come rolling in like breakers, flinging themselves over the pier in wrath and foam, or dancing like spirits in their glee. Nor is the land without some charm. About four miles from Toronto the river Humber comes down between high wood-covered banks, and rushes into the lake: a more charming situation for villas and garden-houses could hardly be desired than the vicinity of this beautiful little river, and such no doubt we shall see in time.

The opposite side of the bay is formed by a long sand-bank, called "the Island," though, in fact, no island, but a very narrow promontory, about three miles in length, and forming a rampart against the main waters of the lake. At the extremity is a light-house, and a few stunted trees and underwood. This marsh, intersected by inlets and covered with reeds, is the haunt of thousands of wild fowl, and of the terapin, or small turtle of the lake; and as evening comes on, we see long rows of red lights from the fishing-boats gleaming along the surface of the water, for thus they spear the lake salmon, the bass, and the pickereen.

The only road on which it is possible to take a drive with comfort is Young-street, which is macadamised for the first twelve miles. This road leads from Toronto north-wards to Lake Simcoe, through a well-settled and fertile country. There are some commodious, and even elegant houses in this neighbourhood. Dundas-street, leading west to the London district and Lake Huron, is a very rough road for a carriage, but a most delightful ride. On this side of Toronto you are immediately in the pine forest, which extends with little interruption (except a new settlement rising here and there) for about fifty miles to Hamilton, which is the next important town. The wooded shores of the lake are very beautiful, and abounding in game. In short, a reasonable person might make himself very happy here, if it were not for some few things, among which, those Egyptian plagues, the flies and frogs in summer, and the relentless iron winter, are not the most intolerable: add, perhaps, the prevalence of sickness at certain seasons. At present many families are flying off to Niagara, for two or three days together, for change of air; and I am meditating a flight myself, of such serious extent, that some of my friends here laugh outright; others look kindly alarmed, and others civilly incredulous. Bad roads, bad inns – or rather *no* roads, no inns; – wild Indians, and white men more savage far than they; – dangers and difficulties of every kind are threatened and prognosticated, enough to make one's hair stand on end. To undertake such a jour-

ney *alone* is rash perhaps – yet alone it must be achieved,
I find, or not at all; I shall have neither companion nor
man-servant, nor *femme de chambre*, nor even a "little
foot-page" to give notice of my fate, should I be swamped
in a bog, or eaten up by a bear, or scalped, or disposed of
in some strange way; but shall I leave this fine country
without seeing anything of its great characteristic
features? – and, above all, of its aboriginal inhabitants?
Moral courage will not be wanting, but physical strength
may fail, and obstacles, which I cannot anticipate or overcome, may turn me back; yet the more I consider my
project – wild though it be – the more I feel determined to
persist. The French have a proverb which does honour to
their gallantry, and to which, from experience, I am
inclined to give full credence – "*Ce que femme veut, Dieu
veut.*" We shall see.

June 10.

Mr. Hepburne brought me yesterday the number of the
Foreign Review for February last, which contains, among
other things, a notice of Baron Sternberg's popular and
eloquent novels. It is not very well done. It is true, as far as
it goes; but it gives no sufficient idea of the general character of his works, some of which display the wildest and
most playful fancy, and others again, pictures, not very
attractive ones, of every day social life.

Sternberg, whom I knew in Germany, is a young nobleman of Livonia, handsome in person, and of quiet, elegant manners. Yet I remember that in our first interview,
even while he interested and fixed my attention, he did
not quite please me; there was in his conversation something cold, guarded, not flowing; and in the expression of
his dark, handsome features, something too invariable
and cynical; but all this thawed or brightened away, and I
became much interested in him and his works.

Sternberg, as an author, may be classed, I think, with
many other accomplished and popular authors of the day,

flourishing here, in France, and in England, simultaneously – signs of the times in which we live, taking the form
and pressure of the age, not informing it with their own
spirit. They are a set of men who have drunk deep, even
to license, of the follies, the pleasures, and the indulgences
of society, even while they struggled (some of them at
least) with its most bitter, most vulgar cares. From this
gulf the intellect rises, perhaps, in all its primeval strength,
the imagination in all its brilliance, the product of both as
luxuriant as ever; but we are told,

> "That every gift of noble origin,
>   Is breathed upon by Hope's perpetual breath!"

And a breath of a different kind has gone over the works
of these writers – a breath as from a lazar-house. A power
is gone from them which nothing can restore, – the
healthy, the clear visions, with which a fresh, pure mind
looks round upon the social and the natural world, per-
ceiving the due relations of all things one with another,
and beholding the "soul of goodness in things evil:" these
authors, if we are to believe their own account of themselves, given in broad hints, and very intelligible *mysterious* allusions, have suffered horribly from the dominion
of the passions, from the mortifications of wounded self-
love, betrayed confidence, ruined hopes, ill-directed and
ill-requited affections, and a long *etcetera* of miseries.
They wish us to believe, that in order to produce anything
true and great in art, it is necessary to have known and
gone through all this, to have been dragged through this
sink of dissipation, or this fiery furnace of suffering and
passion. I don't know. Goethe, at least, did not think so,
when he spoke of the "sort of anticipation" through which
he produced his Götz von Berlichingen and his Werther. I
hope it is not so. I hope that a knowledge of our human
and immortal nature, and the due exercise of our faculties, does not depend on this sort of limited, unhealthy,
artificial experience. It is as if a man or woman either, in
order to learn the free, natural, graceful use of the limbs,

were to take lessons of a rope-dancer; but waving this, we see in these writers, that what they call truth and experience has at least been bought rather dear; they can never again, by all the perfumes of Arabia, sweeten what has been once polluted, nor take the blistering scar from their brow. From their works we rise with admiration, with delight, with astonishment at the talent displayed; with the most excited feelings, but never with that blameless as well as vivid sense of pleasure, that unreproved delight, that grateful sense of a healing, holy influence, with which we lay down Shakspeare, Walter Scott, Wordsworth, Goethe. Yet what was hidden from these men? Did they not know all that the world, and man, and nature could unfold? They knew it by "anticipation," by soaring on the wings of untrammelled thought, far, far above the turmoil, and looking superior down, and with the ample ken of genius embraced a universe. These modern novel writers appear to me in comparison like children, whose imperfect faculties and experience induce them to touch everything they see; so they burn or soil their fingers, and the blister and the stain sticks perpetual to their pages – those pages which yet can melt or dazzle, or charm. Nothing that is, or has been, or may be, can they see but through some personal medium. What they have themselves felt, suffered, seen, is always before them, is mixed up with their fancy, is the material of their existence, and this gives certainly a degree of vigour, a palpable reality, a life, to all they do, which carries us away; but a man might as well think to view the face of universal nature, to catch the pure, unmixed, all-embracing light of day through one of the gorgeous painted windows of Westminster Abbey, as to perceive abstract moral truth through the minds of these writers; but they have their use, ay, and their beauty – like all things in the world – only I would not be one of such. I do not think them enviable either in themselves as individuals, or in the immediate effect they produce, and the sort of applause they excite; but they have their praise, their merit, their *use*, – they have their *day* – hereafter,

perhaps, to be remembered as we remember the school of
writers before the French revolution; as we think of the
wretched slave, or the rash diver, who from the pit or from
the whirlpool has snatched some gems worthy to be gathered into Truth's immortal treasury, or wreathed into her
diadem of light.

They have their day – how long it will last, how long
they will last, is another thing.

To this school of fiction-writing belong many authors of
great and various merit, and of very different character
and tendencies. Some, by true but partial portraitures of
social evils, boldly aiming at the overthrow of institutions
from which they have as individuals suffered; others,
through this medium, publicly professing opinions they
would hardly dare to promulgate in a drawing-room, and
discussing questions of a doubtful or perilous tendency;
others, only throwing off, in a manner, the impressions of
their own minds, developed in beautiful fictions, without
any ultimate object beyond that of being read with sympathy and applause – especially by women.

I think Sternberg belongs to the latter class. He has
written some most charming things. I should not exactly
know where to find his prototype: he reminds me of
Bulwer sometimes, and one or two of his tales are in Barry
St. Leger's best manner, – the eloquence, the depth of
tragic and passionate interest, are just his; then, again,
others remind me of Wilson, when he is fanciful and
unearthly; but, on the whole, his genius differs essentially
from all these.

His comic and fantastic tales are exquisite. The fancy
and the humour run into pathos and poetry, and never
into caricature, like some of Hoffmann's.

One of the first things I fell upon was his "Herr von
Mondshein," (Master Moonshine,) a little *jeu d'esprit* on
which it seems he sets small value himself, but which is an
exquisite thing for all that – so wildly, yet so playfully, so
gracefully grotesque! The effect of the whole is really like
that of moonlight on a rippled stream, now seen, now lost,

now here, now there – it is the moon we see – and then it is not; and yet it is again! and it smiles, and it shines, and it simpers, and it glitters, and it is at once in heaven and on the earth, near and distant, by our side, or peeped at through an astronomer's telescope; now helping off a pair of lovers – then yonder among the stars – and in the end we rub our eyes, and find it is just what it ought to be – *all moonshine!*

Superior and altogether different is the tale of "Molière," – the leading idea of which appears to me beautiful.

A physician of celebrity at Paris, the inventor of some famous elixir – half quack, half enthusiast, and something too of a philosopher – finds himself, by some chance, in the parterre at the representation of one of Molière's comedies, in which the whole learned faculty are so exquisitely ridiculed; the player who represents the principal character, in order to make the satire more poignant, arrays himself in the habitual dress of Tristan Dieudonné; the unfortunate doctor sees himself reproduced on the stage with every circumstance of ignominious ridicule, hears around him the loud applause, the laugh of derision – meets in every eye the mocking glance of recognition; his brain turns, and he leaves the theatre a raving maniac. (So far the tale is an "o'er true tale.") By degrees this frenzy subsides into a calmer but more hopeless, more melancholy madness; he shuts himself up from mankind, at one time sinking into a gloomy despondency, at another revelling in projects of vengeance against Molière, his enemy and destroyer. One only consolation remains to him: in this miserable, abject state, a charitable neighbour comes to visit him daily; by degrees wins upon the affections, and gains the confidence of the poor madman – soothes him, cheers him, and performs for him all tender offices of filial love; and this good Samaritan is of course the heart-stricken, remorseful poet, Molière himself.

There is a love-story interwoven of no great interest, and many discussions between the poet and the madman, on morals, medicine, philosophy: that in which the insane doctor endeavours to prove that many of his patients who appear to be living are in reality *dead*, is very striking and very true to nature: it shows how ingenious metaphysical madness can sometimes be.

Other known personages, as Boileau, Chapelain, Racine, are introduced in person, and give us their opinions on poetry, acting, the fine arts, with considerable discrimination in the characters of the speakers.

The scenes of Parisian society in this novel are not so good; rather heavy and Germanesque – certainly not French.

"Lessing" is another tale in which Sternberg has taken a real personage for his hero. He says that he has endeavoured, in these two tales, to delineate the strife which a man whose genius is in advance of the age in which he lives, must carry on with all around him. They may be called biographical novels.

"Galathée," Sternberg's last novel, had just made its appearance when I was at Weimar; all the women were reading it and commenting on it – some in anger, some in sorrow, almost all in admiration. It is allowed to be the finest thing he has done in point of style. To me it is a painful book. It is the history of the intrigues of a beautiful coquette and a Jesuit priest to gain over a young Protestant nobleman from his faith and his betrothed love. They prove but too successful. In the end he turns Roman Catholic, and forsakes his bride. The heroine, Galathée, dies quietly of a broken heart. "The more fool she!" I thought, as I closed the book, "to die for the sake of a man who was not worth living for!" but "'tis a way we have."

Sternberg's women – his virtuous women especially, (to be sure he is rather sparing of them,) – have always individual character, and are touched with a firm, a delicate, a graceful pencil; but his men are almost without exception vile, or insipid, or eccentric – and his heroes (where could he find them?) are absolutely *characterless* – as weak as they are detestable.

Sternberg possesses, with many other talents, that of being an accomplished amateur artist. He sketches charmingly, and with enviable facility and truth catches the characteristic forms both of persons and things. Then he has all the arcana of a lady's toilette at the end of his pencil, and his glance is as fastidious as it is rapid in detecting any peculiarity of dress or manner. Whenever he came to us he used to ask for some white paper, which, while he talked or listened, he covered with the prettiest sketches and fancies imaginable; but whether this was to employ his fingers, or to prevent me from looking into his eyes while he spoke, I was never quite sure.

This talent for drawing – this lively sense of the picturesque in form and colour, we trace through all his works. Some of the most striking passages – those which dwell most strongly on the memory – are pictures. Thus, the meeting of Molière and the Doctor in the church-yard at dusk of evening, the maniac seated on the grave, the other standing by, wrapped in his flowing mantle, with his hat and feather pulled over his brow, and bending over his victim with benevolent expression, is what painters call a fine "bit of effect." The scene in the half-lighted chapel, where the beautiful Countess Melicerte is doing penance, and receiving on her naked shoulders the scourge from the hand of her confessor, is a very powerful but also a very disagreeable piece of painting. The lady in crimson velvet seated on the ground *en Madelene*, with her silver crucifix on her knees and her long dark jewelled tresses flowing dishevelled, is a fine bit of colour, and the court ballet in the gardens of the Favorita Palace a perfect Watteau. Reading very fine, eloquent, and vivid descriptions of nature and natural scenery, by writers who give us licentious pictures of social life in a narrow, depraved, and satirical spirit, is very disagreeable – it always leaves on the mind an impression of discord and unfitness. And this discrepancy is of perpetual recurrence in Sternberg, and in other writers of his class.

But it is in the tale entitled Die Gebrüder Breughel (the Two Breughels) that Sternberg has abandoned himself *con amore* to all his artist-like feelings and predilections. The younger Breughel (known by the names of Höllen Breughel and the "Mad Painter," on account of the diabolical subjects in which his pencil revelled,) is the hero of this remarkable tale: forsaking the worship of beauty, he paid a kind of crazed adoration to deformity, and painted his fantastic and extravagant creations with truly demoniac skill and power. Sternberg makes the cause of this eccentric perversion of genius a love-affair, which has turned the poor painter's wits "the seamy side without," and rendered him the apostate to all that is beautiful in nature and art. This love-tale, however, occupies little of the interest. The charm of the whole consists in the lively sketches of Flemish art, and the characteristic portraits of different well-known artists: we have the gay, vivacious Teniers – the elegant and somewhat affected Poelenberg, the coarse, good-humoured Jordaens – Peter Laers, the tavern-keeper, – the grave yet splendid coxcombry of the Velvet Breughel – his eccentric, half-crazed brother, the Hero – old Peter Kock, with his colour mania, (the Turner of his day,) and presiding over all, the noble, the magnificent Peter Paul Rubens, and the dignified, benevolent Burgomaster Hubert, the patron of art: all these are brought together in groups, and admirably discriminated. In this tale Sternberg has most ingeniously transferred to his pages some celebrated and well-known pictures as actual scenes; and thus Painting pays back part of her debt to Poetry and Fiction. The Alchymist in his laboratory – the Gambling Soldiers – the Boors and Beggars at cards – the Incantation in the Witch's Tower – the Burning Mill – the Page asleep in the Ante-chamber – and the country Merrymaking – are each a Rembrandt, a Jordaens, an Ostade, a Peter Laers, a Breughel, or a Teniers, transferred from the canvass to the page, and painted in words almost as brilliant and lively as the original colours.

I doubt whether a translation of this clever tale would please generally in England; it is too discursive and argumentative. It requires a familiar knowledge of art and artists, as well as a feeling for art, to enter into it, for it is almost entirely devoid of any interest arising from incident or passion. Yet I sat up till after two o'clock this morning to finish it – wasting my eyes over the small type, like a most foolish improvident woman.

As the rolling stone gathers no moss, so the roving heart gathers no affections.

I have met with certain minds which seem never to be themselves penetrated by truth, yet have the power to demonstrate it clearly and beautifully to other minds, as there are certain substances which most brightly reflect, and only partially absorb, the rays of light.

Reading what Charles Lamb says on the "sanity of true genius," it appears to me that genius and sanity have nothing (necessarily) to do with each other. Genius may be combined with a healthy or a morbid organisation. Shakspeare, Walter Scott, Goethe, are examples of the former: Byron, Collins, Kirke White, are examples of the latter.

A man may be as much a fool from the want of sensibility as the want of sense.

How admirable what Sir James Mackintosh says of Madame de Maintenon! – that "she was as virtuous as the fear of hell and the fear of shame could make her." The same might be said of the virtue of many women I know, and of these, I believe that more are virtuous from the fear of shame than the fear of hell. – Shame is the woman's hell.

Rahel* said once of an acquaintance, "Such a one is an ignorant man. He knows nothing but what he has learned, and that is little, for a man can only learn that which man already knows." – Well, and truly, and profoundly said!

Every faculty, every impulse of our human nature, is useful, available, in proportion as it is dangerous. The greatest blessings are those which may be perverted to most pain: as fire and water are the two most murderous agents in nature, and the two things in which we can least endure to be stinted.

Who that has lived in the world, in society, and looked on both with observing eye, but has often been astonished at the fearlessness of women, and the cowardice of men, with regard to public opinion? The reverse would seem to be the natural, the necessary result of the existing order of things, but it is not always so. Exceptions occur so often, and so immediately within my own province of observation, that they have made me reflect a good deal. Perhaps this seeming discrepancy might be thus explained.

Women are brought up in the fear of opinion, but, from their ignorance of the world, they are in fact ignorant of that which they fear. They fear opinion as a child fears a spectre, as something shadowy and horrible, not defined or palpable. It is a fear based on habit, on feeling, not on principle or reason. When their passions are strongly excited, or when reason becomes matured, this exagger-

* Madame Varnhagen von Ense, whose remains were published a few years ago. The book of "Rahel" is famous from one end of Germany to the other, but remains, I believe, a sealed fountain still for English readers.

ated fear vanishes, and the probability is, that they are immediately thrown into the opposite extreme of incredulity, defiance, and rashness: but a man, even while courage is preached to him, learns from habitual intercourse with the world the immense, the terrible power of opinion. It wraps him round like despotism; it is a reality to him; to a woman a shadow, and if she can overcome the fear in her own person, all is overcome. A man fears opinion for himself, his wife, his daughter; and if the fear of opinion be brought into conflict with primary sentiments and principles, it is ten to one but the habit of fear prevails, and opinion triumphs over reason and feeling too.

The new law passed during the last session of our provincial parliament, "to render the remedy in cases of seduction more effectual," has just come into operation. What were the circumstances which gave rise to this law, and to its peculiar provisions, I cannot learn. Here it is touching on delicate and even forbidden ground to ask any questions. One person said that it was to guard against infanticide; and I recollect hearing the same sort of argument used in London against one particular clause of the new Poor Law Act, viz. that it would *encourage* infanticide. This is the most gross and unpardonable libel on our sex ever uttered. Women do not murder their children from the fear of want, but from the fear of shame. In this fear, substituted for the light and the strength of virtue and genuine self-respect, are women trained, till it becomes a second nature – not indeed stronger than the natural instincts and the passions which God gave us, but strong enough to drive to madness and delirious outrage the wretched victim who finds the struggle between these contradictory feelings too great for her conscience, her reason, her strength. Nothing, as it seems to me, but throwing the woman upon her own self-respect and added responsibility, can bring a remedy to this fearful state of things. To say that the punishment of the fault, already too great, is thereby increased, is not true; it admitted of no real increase. In entailing irremediable disgrace, and death of name and fame, upon the frail woman, the law of society had done its utmost; and to let it be supposed that the man had power to make amends by paying a nominal tax for indulgence bought at such a tremendous price, what was it but to flatter and delude both the vanity of lordly, sensual man, and the weakness of wretched, ignorant, trusting woman? As long as treachery to woman is honourable in man; as long as men *do* not, or *will* not protect us; as long as we women *cannot* protect ourselves, their protecting laws are a farce and a mockery. Opinion has ever been stronger than law. Luckily there is something stronger than either.

It was not for the forms, though fair,
Though grand they were beyond compare, –
It was not only for the forms
Of hills in sunshine or in storms,
Or only unrestrain'd to look
On wood and lake, that she forsook
    By day or night
      Her home, and far
    Wander'd by light
      Of sun or star –
It was to feel her fancy free,
    Free in a world without an end:
With ears to hear, and eyes to see,
    And heart to apprehend.

      TAYLOR'S Philip Van Artevelde.

June 13.

IN THESE latter days I have lived in friendly communion with so many excellent people, that my departure from Toronto was not what I anticipated – an escape on one side, or a riddance on the other. My projected tour to the west excited not only some interest, but much kind solicitude; and aid and counsel were tendered with a feeling which touched me deeply. The chief justice, in particular, sent me a whole sheet of instructions, and several letters of introduction to settlers along my line of route. Fitzgibbon, always benevolent, gave me sensible and cheerful encouragement as we walked leisurely down to the pier, to embark in the steam-boat which was to carry me across the lake to Niagara.

And here I might moralise on the good effects of being *too* early instead of too late on a journey: on the present occasion, having a quarter of an hour or twenty minutes to spare proved the most important and most fortunate circumstance which could have occurred at my outset.

The first bell of the steam-boat had not yet rung, when my good friend Dr. Rees came running up to tell me that the missionary from the Sault St. Marie, and his Indian wife, had arrived at Toronto, and were then at the inn, and that there was just time to introduce me to them. No sooner thought than done: in another moment we were in the hotel, and I was introduced to Mrs. MacMurray, otherwise O-ge-ne-bu-go-quay, (i.e. *the wild rose*.)

I must confess that the specimens of Indian squaws and half-cast women I had met with, had in no wise prepared me for what I found in Mrs. MacMurray. The first glance, the first sound of her voice, struck me with a pleased surprise. Her figure is tall – at least it is rather above than below the middle size, with that indescribable grace and undulation of movement which speaks the perfection of form. Her features are distinctly Indian, but softened and refined, and their expression at once bright and kindly. Her dark eyes have a sort of fawn-like shyness in their glance, but her manner, though timid, was quite free from embarrassment or restraint. She speaks English well, with a slightly foreign intonation, not the less pleasing to my ear that it reminded me of the voice and accent of some of my German friends. In two minutes I was seated by her – my hand kindly folded in hers – and we were talking over the possibility of my plans. It seems that there is some chance of my reaching the Island of Michillimackinac, but of the Sault St. Marie I dare hardly think as yet – it looms

in my imagination dimly descried in far space, a kind of
Ultima Thule; yet the sight of Mrs. MacMurray seemed to
give something definite to the vague hope which had been
floating in my mind. Her sister, she said, was married to
the Indian agent at Michillimackinac,* a man celebrated
in the United States for his scientific researches; and from
both she promised me a welcome, should I reach their
island. To her own far off home at the Sault St. Marie,
between Lake Huron and Lake Superior, she warmly
invited me – without, however, being able to point out any
conveyance or mode of travel thither that could be
depended on – only a possible chance of such. Meantime
there was *some* hope of our meeting *some*where on the
road, but it was of the faintest. She thanked me feelingly
for the interest I took in her own fated race, and gave me
excellent hints as to my manner of proceeding. We were in
the full tide of conversation when the bell of the steam-
boat rang for the last time, and I was hurried off. On the
deck of the vessel I found her husband, Mr. MacMurray,
who had only time to say, in fewest words, all that was
proper, polite, and hospitable. This rencontre, which some
would call accidental, and some providential, pleased and
encouraged me, and I felt very grateful to Dr. Rees.

Then came blessings, good wishes, kind pressures of the
hand, and last adieus, and waving of handkerchiefs from
the shore, as the paddles were set in motion, and we glided
swiftly over the mirror-like bay, while "there was a breath
the blue waves to curl."

I had not been happy enough in Toronto to regret it as a
place; and if touched, as I truly was, by the kind solicitude
of those friends who but a few weeks ago were entire
strangers to me, I yet felt no sorrow. Though no longer
young, I am quite young enough to feel all the excitement
of plunging into scenes so entirely new as were now opening before me; and this, too, with a specific object far

* Henry Schoolcraft, Esq.

beyond mere amusement and excitement – an object not unworthy.

But though the spirit was willing and cheerful, I was under the necessity of remembering that I was not all spirit, but clogged with a material frame which required some looking after. My general health had suffered during the long trying winter, and it was judiciously suggested that I should spend a fortnight at the falls of Niagara to recruit, previous to my journey. The good sense of this advice I could not appreciate at the time, any more than I could anticipate the fatigues and difficulties which awaited me; but my good angel, in the shape of a certain languid inclination for silence and repose, whispered me to listen and obey – fortunately, or providentially. Meantime I was alone – alone – and on my way to that ultimate somewhere of which I knew nothing, with forests, and plains, and successive seas intervening. The day was sultry, the air heavy and still, and a strange fog, or rather a series of dark clouds, hung resting on the bosom of the lake, which in some places was smooth and transparent as glass – in others, little eddies of wind had ruffled it into tiny waves, or welts rather – so that it presented the appearance of patchwork. The boatmen looked up, and foretold a storm; but when we came within three or four miles from the mouth of the river Niagara, the fog drew off like a curtain, and the interminable line of the dark forest came into view, stretching right and left along the whole horizon; then the white buildings of the American fort, and the spires of the town of Niagara, became visible against the rich purple-green background, and we landed after a four hours' voyage. The threatened storm came on that night. The summer storms of Canada are like those of the tropics: not in Italy, not among the Appennines, where I have in my time heard the "live thunder leaping from crag to crag," did I ever hear such terrific explosives of sound as burst over our heads this night. The silence and the darkness lent an added horror to the elemental tumult – and for the first time in my life I felt sickened and unpleasantly affected in the intervals between the thunder-claps, though I cannot say I felt fear. Meantime the rain fell as in a deluge, threatening to wash us into the lake, which reared itself up, and roared – like a monster for its prey.

Yet, the next morning, when I went down upon the shore, how beautiful it looked – the hypocrite! – there it lay rocking and sleeping in the sunshine, quiet as a cradled infant. Niagara, in its girdle of verdure and foliage, glowing with fresh life, and breathing perfume, appeared to me a far different place from what I had seen in winter. Yet I recollect, as I stood on the shore, the effect produced on my mind by the sound of the death-bell, pealing along the sunny blue waters. They said it was tolled for a young man of respectable family, who, at the age of three or four and twenty, had died from habitual drinking; his elder brother having a year or two before fallen from his horse in a state of intoxication, and perished in consequence. Yes, everything I see and hear on this subject convinces me that it should be one of the first objects of the government to put down, by all and every means, a vice which is rotting at the core of this infant society – poisoning the very sources of existence. But all their taxes, and prohibitions, and excise laws, will do little good, unless they facilitate the means of education. In society, the same evening, the appearance of a very young, very pretty, sad looking creature, with her first baby at her bosom, whose husband was staggering and talking drunken gibberish at her side, completed the impression of disgust and affright with which the continual spectacle of this vile habit strikes me since I have been in this country.

In the dockyard here, I was glad to find all in movement; a steamer was on the stocks, measuring one hundred and twenty-nine feet in length, and twenty in the beam; also a large schooner; and all the brass-work and casting is now done here, which was formerly executed at Montreal, to the manifest advantage of the province, as well as the town. And I have been assured, not only here but elsewhere, that the work turned out is excellent – of the first order.

In the jail here, a wretched maniac is confined in chains for murdering his wife. He was convicted, condemned to death, and on the point of being hung; for though the physician believed the man mad, he could not prove it in evidence: he appeared rational on every subject. At length, after his condemnation, the physician, holding his wrist, repeated the religious Orange toast – something about the Pope and the devil; and instantly as he expressed it, the man's pulse bounded like a shot under his fingers, and he was seized with a fit of frenzy. He said that his wife had been possessed by the seven deadly sins, and he had merely given her seven kicks to exorcise her – and thus he murdered the poor woman. He has been in the jail four years, and is now more mad, more furious, than when first confined. This I had from the physician himself.

Before quitting the subject of Niagara, I may as well mention an incident which occurred shortly afterwards, on my last visit to the town, which interested me much at the time, and threw the whole of this little community into a wonderful ferment.

A black man, a slave somewhere in Kentucky, having been sent on a message, mounted on a very valuable horse, seized the opportunity of escaping. He reached Buffalo after many days of hard riding, sold the horse, and escaped beyond the lines into Canada. Here, as in all the British dominions, God be praised! the slave is slave no more, but free, and protected in his freedom.* This man acknowledged that he had not been ill treated; he had received some education, and had been a favourite with his master. He gave as a reason for his flight, that he had

---

* Among the addresses presented to Sir Francis Head in 1836, was one from the coloured inhabitants of this part of the province, signed by four hundred and thirty-one individuals, most of them refugees from the United States, or their descendants.

long wished to marry, but was resolved that his children should not be born slaves. In Canada, a runaway slave is assured of legal protection; but, by an international compact between the United States and our provinces, all felons are mutually surrendered. Against this young man the jury in Kentucky had found a true bill for horse-stealing; as a felon, therefore, he was pursued, and, on the proper legal requisition, arrested; and then lodged in the jail of Niagara, to be given up to his master, who, with an American constable, was in readiness to take him into custody, as soon as the government order should arrive. His case excited a strong interest among the whites, while the coloured population, consisting of many hundreds in the districts of Gore and Niagara, chiefly refugees from the States, were half frantic with excitement. They loudly and openly declared that they would peril their lives to prevent his being carried again across the frontiers, and surrendered to the vengeance of his angry master. Meantime there was some delay about legal forms, and the mayor and several of the inhabitants of the town united in a petition to the governor in his favour. In this petition it was expressly mentioned, that the master of the slave had been heard to avow that his intention was not to give the culprit up to justice, but to make what he called an *example* of him. Now there had been lately some frightful instances of what the slave proprietors of the south called "making an example;" and the petitioners entreated the governor to interpose, and save the man from a torturing death "under the lash or at the stake." Probably the governor's own humane feelings pleaded even more strongly in behalf of the poor fellow. But it was a case in which he could not act from feeling, or, "to do a great right, do a little wrong." The law was too expressly and distinctly laid down, and his duty as governor was clear and imperative – to give up the felon, although, to have protected the slave, he would, if necessary, have armed the province.

In the mean time the coloured people assembled from the adjacent villages, and among them a great number of their women. The conduct of this black mob, animated and even directed by the females, was really admirable for its good sense, forbearance, and resolution. They were quite unarmed, and declared their intention not to commit any violence against the English law. The culprit, they said, might lie in the jail, till they could raise among them the price of the horse; but if any attempt were made to take him from the prison, and send him across to Lewiston, they would resist it at the hazard of their lives.

The fatal order *did* at length come; the sheriff with a party of constables prepared to enforce it. The blacks, still unarmed, assembled round the jail, and waited till their comrade, or their brother as they called him, was brought out and placed handcuffed in a cart. They then threw themselves simultaneously on the sheriff's party, and a dreadful scuffle ensued; the artillery men from the little fort, our only military, were called in aid of the civil authority, and ordered to fire on the assailants. Two blacks were killed, and two or three wounded. In the melée the poor slave escaped, and has not since been retaken, neither was he, I believe, pursued.

But it was the conduct of the women which, on this occasion, excited the strongest surprise and interest. By all those passionate and persuasive arguments that a woman knows so well how to use, whatever be her colour, country, or class, they had prevailed on their husbands, brothers, and lovers, to use no arms, to do no illegal violence, but to lose their lives rather than see their comrade taken by force across the lines. They had been most active in the fray, throwing themselves fearlessly between the black men and the whites, who, of course, shrank from injuring them. One woman had seized the sheriff, and held him pinioned in her arms; another, on one of the artillery-men presenting his piece, and swearing that he would shoot her if she did not get out his way, gave him only one glance of unutterable contempt, and with one hand knocking up his piece, and collaring him with the other, held him in such a manner as to prevent his firing. I was curious to see a mulatto woman who had been foremost in the fray, and whose intelligence and influence had mainly contributed to the success of her people; and young Mr. M——, under pretence of inquiring after a sick child, drove me round to the hovel in which she lived, outside the town. She came out to speak to us. She was a fine creature, apparently about five-and-twenty, with a kindly animated countenance; but the feelings of exasperation and indignation had evidently not yet subsided. She told us, in answer to my close questioning, that she had formerly been a slave in Virginia; that, so far from being ill treated, she had been regarded with especial kindness by the family on whose estate she was born. When she was about sixteen her master died, and it was said that all the slaves on the estate would be sold, and therefore she ran away. "Were you not attached to your mistress?" I asked. "Yes," said she, "I liked my mistress, but I did not like to be sold." I asked her if she was happy here in Canada? She hesitated a moment, and then replied, on my repeating the question, "Yes – that is, I was happy here – but now – I don't know – I thought we were safe *here* – I thought nothing could touch us *here*, on your British ground, but it seems I was mistaken, and if so, I won't stay here – I won't – I won't! I'll go and find some country where they cannot reach us! I'll go to the end of the world, I will!" And as she spoke, her black eyes flashing, she extended her arms, and folded them across her bosom, with an attitude and expression of resolute dignity, which a painter might have studied; and truly the fairest white face I ever looked on never beamed with more of soul and high resolve than hers at that moment.

B ETWEEN the town of Queenston and the cataract of Niagara lies the pretty village of Stamford, (close to Lundy Lane, the site of a famous battle in the last war,) and celebrated for its fine air. Near it is a beautiful house with its domain, called Stamford Park, built and laid out by a former governor (Sir Peregrine Maitland.) It is the only place I saw in Upper Canada combining our ideas of an elegant, well-furnished English villa and ornamented grounds, with some of the grandest and wildest features of the forest scene. It enchanted me altogether. From the lawn before the house, an open glade, commanding a park-like range of broken and undulating ground and wooded valleys, displayed beyond them the wide expanse of Lake Ontario, even the Toronto light-house, at a distance of thirty miles, being frequently visible to the naked eye. By the hostess of this charming seat I was conveyed in a light pony carriage to the hotel at the Falls, and left, with real kindness, to follow my own devices. The moment I was alone, I hurried down to the Table Rock. The body of water was more full and tremendous than in the winter. The spray rose, densely falling again in thick showers, and behind those rolling volumes of vapour the last gleams of the evening light shone in lurid brightness, amid amber and crimson clouds; on the other side, night was rapidly coming on, and all was black, impenetrable gloom, and "boundless contiguity of shade." It was very, very beautiful, and strangely awful too! For now it was late, and as I stood there, lost in a thousand reveries, there was no human being near, no light but that reflected from the leaping, whirling foam; and in spite of the deep-voiced continuous thunder of the cataract, there was such a stillness that I could hear my own heart's pulse throb – or did I mistake feeling for hearing? – so I strayed homewards, or housewards I should say, through the leafy, gloomy, pathways – wet with the spray, and fairly tired out.

Two or three of my Toronto friends are here, and declare against my projects of solitude. To-day we had a beautiful drive to Colonel Delatre's. We drove along the road *above* the Falls. There was the wide river spreading like a vast lake, then narrowing, then boiling, foaming along in a current of eighteen miles an hour, till it swept over the Crescent Rock in a sheet of emerald green, and threw up the silver clouds of spray into the clear blue sky. The fresh luxurious verdure of the woods, relieved against the dark pine forest, added to the beauty of the scene. I wished more than ever for those I love most! – for some one who would share all this rapture of admiration and delight, without the necessity of speaking – for, after all, what are words? They express nothing, reveal nothing, avail nothing. So it all sinks back into my own heart, there to be kept quiet. After a pleasant dinner and music, I returned to the hotel by the light of a full moon, beneath which the Falls looked magnificently mysterious, part glancing silver light, and part dark shadow, mingled with fleecy folds of spray, over which floated a soft, sleepy gleam; and in the midst of this tremendous velocity of motion and eternity of sound, there was deep, deep repose, as in a dream. It impressed me for the time like something supernatural – a vision, not a reality.

The good people, travellers, describers, poets, and others, who seem to have hunted through the dictionary for words in which to depict these cataracts under every aspect, have never said enough of the rapids above – even for which reason, perhaps, they have struck me the more; not that any words in any language would have prepared me for what I now feel in this wondrous scene. Standing to-day on the banks above the Crescent Fall, near Mr. Street's mill, gazing on the rapids, they left in my fancy two impressions which seldom meet together – that of the sublime and terrible, and that of the elegant and graceful – like a tiger at play. I could not withdraw my eyes; it was like a fascination.

The verge of the rapids is considerably above the eye; the whole mighty river comes rushing over the brow of a hill, and as you look up, it seems coming down to over-whelm you. Then meeting with the rocks, as it pours down the declivity, it boils and frets like the breakers of the ocean. Huge mounds of water, smooth, transparent, and gleaming like the emerald, or rather like the more delicate hue of the chrysopaz, rise up and bound over some unseen impediment, then break into silver foam, which leaps into the air in the most graceful fantastic forms; and so it rushes on, whirling, boiling, dancing, sparkling along, with a playful impatience, rather than overwhelming fury, rejoicing as if escaped from bondage, rather than raging in angry might – wildly, magnificently beautiful! The idea, too, of the immediate danger, the consciousness that anything caught within their verge is inevitably hurried to a swift destination, swallowed up, annihilated, thrills the blood; the immensity of the pic-ture, spreading a mile at least each way, and framed in by the interminable forests, adds to the feeling of grandeur: while the giddy, infinite motion of the headlong waters, dancing and leaping, and revelling and roaring, in their mad glee, gave me a sensation of rapturous terror, and at last caused a tension of the nerves in my head, which obliged me to turn away.

The great ocean, when thus agitated by conflicting winds or opposing rocks, is a more tremendous thing, but it is merely tremendous – it makes us think of our prayers; whereas, while I was looking on these rapids, beauty and terror, and power and joy, were blended, and so thoroughly, that even while I trembled and admired, I could have burst into a wild laugh, and joined the dancing billows in their glorious, fearful mirth –

> Leaping like Bacchanals from rock to rock,
> Flinging the frantic Thyrsus wild and high!

I shall never see again, or feel again, aught like it – never! I did not think there was an object in nature, animate or inanimate, that could thus overset me *now!*

I HAVE ONLY three books with me here, besides the *one* book needful, and find them sufficient for all purposes, – Shakspeare, Schiller, Wordsworth. One morning, being utterly disinclined for all effort, either of conversation or movement, I wandered down to a little wild bosquet beyond the Table Rock, not very accessible to dilettante hunters after the picturesque, and just where the waters, rendered smooth by their own infiniti velocity, were sweeping by, before they take their leap into the gulf below; – there I sat all the sultry noontide, – quiet, among the birds and the thick foliage, and read through Don Carlos, – one of the finest dramas in the world, I should think.

It is a proof of the profound humanity of Schiller, that in this play one must needs pity King Philip, though it is in truth the sort of pity which Saint Theresa felt for the devil, – one pities him because he is *the devil*. The pitiableness and the misery of wickedness were never so truly and so pathetically demonstrated. The unfathomable abyss of egotism in the character turns one giddy to look into.

With regard to Posa, it has been objected, I believe – for I never read any criticism on this play – that he is a mere abstraction, or rather the embodied mouthpiece of certain abstract ideas of policy and religion and morals – those of Schiller himself – and not an individual human being – in short, an impossibility. Yet why so? Perhaps such a man as Posa never did exist; – but why impossible? Can a man conceive that which a man could not by possibility be? If Schiller were great enough to invent such a character, is not humanity great enough to realise it? My belief is, that it is only a glorious anticipation – that poets, in some sort, are the prophets of perfection – that Schiller himself might have been a Posa, and, had he lived a century or two hence, would have been a Posa. Is that a mere abstraction which, while I read, makes me thrill, tremble, exult, and burn, and on the stage filled my eyes with most delicious tears? Is that a mere abstraction which excites our human sympathies in the strongest, highest degree? Every woman, methinks, would like a Posa for a lover – at least, if I could love, it would be such a man. The notion that Posa could not by possibility exist in the court of Philip II appears to me unfounded, for such a court would be just the place where such a character would be needed, and by reaction produced: extremes meet. Has not the Austrian court, in these days, produced Count Auersperg, the poet of freedom, who has devoted his whole soul, his genius, and his gift of song, to the cause of humanity and liberty? Francis the First and Metternich, and the dungeons of the Spielberg, have as naturally produced an Auersperg, as Philip and the Autos-da-Fé in Flanders might have produced a Posa.

It may be said that the moral unity and consistency of the character of Posa is violated by that lie which he tells to save the life of Carlos. Posa is living in an atmosphere of falsehood; the existence and honour of Carlos are about to be sacrificed by a lie, and Posa, by another lie, draws the vengeance of the king upon himself;

> Magnanima menzogna! or quando é il vero
> Si bello, che si possa a te preporre?

– But the effect of this "magnanimous" falsehood is like that of *all* falsehood, evil. This one deviation from the clear straight line of truth not only fails of its purpose, but plunges Carlos, the queen, and Posa himself, in the same abyss of destruction.

It was the opinion of —— , with whom I read this play in Germany, that the queen (Elizabeth of France, Philip's second wife) is a character not defined, not easily understood – that there is a mystery about her intended by the author. I do not see the character in this point of view. It does not seem to me that Schiller meant her to be anything but what she appears. There is no mask here, conscious or unconscious; in such a mind her love for Don Carlos is not a feeling combated, struggled with, but put out of her mind altogether, as a thing which ought not to be thought of, ought not to exist, and therefore ceases to exist; – a tender, perfectly pure interest in the happiness and the fate of Don Carlos remains; but this is all; she does not cheat herself nor us with verbal virtue. The cloudless, transparent, crystalline purity of the character is its greatest charm, it will be said, perhaps, that if we see *the whole* – if there be indeed nothing veiled, beyond or beneath what is visible and spoken, then it is *shallow*. Not so – but, like perfectly limpid water, it seems shallower than it is. The mind of a woman, which should be wholly pure, simple, and true, would produce this illusion: we see at once to the bottom, whether it be shining pebble or golden sands, and do not perceive the true depth till we try, and are made to feel and know it by getting beyond our own depth before we are aware. Such a character is that of Elizabeth of France. The manner in which she rebukes the passionate ravings of Carlos, – the self-confiding simplicity, – the dignity without assumption, – the virtue, so clothed in innocence as to be almost unconscious, – all is most beautiful, and would certainly lose its charm the moment we doubted its *truth* – the moment we suspected that the queen was acting a forced or a conscious part, however virtuous. The scene in which Elizabeth repels the temptation of the Duke of Alva and the monk might be well contrasted with the similar scene between Catherine of Arragon and the two cardinals in

Shakspeare. Elizabeth has a passive, graceful, uncontending pride of virtue, which does not assert itself, only guards itself. Her genuine admiration of Posa, and the manner in which, in the last scene, you see the whole soft, feminine being, made up of affections, tears, and devotion, develop itself to be caught and crushed as in an iron vice, renders this delineation, delicate as it is in the conception, and subordinate in interest, one of the finest I have met with out of Shakspeare, and comparable only to his Hermione in the beauty and singleness of the conception.

When I saw Don Carlos performed at Vienna, with a perfection and *ensemble* of which our stage affords few examples, it left, as a work of art, an impression of a moral kind, at once delightful and elevating, which I cannot easily forget. I was never more touched, more excited, by any dramatic representation that I can remember. Korn, allowed to be one of their finest actors, played Posa magnificently; and it seemed to be no slight privilege to tread the stage but for three hours, clothed in such godlike attributes – to utter, in words eloquent as music, the sentiments of a MAN – sentiments and aspirations that, in every thrilling heart, found at least a silent echo – sentiments which, if uttered or written off the stage, would have brought down upon him the surveillance of the secret police, or the ban of the censor.

Fichtner played Don Carlos with impassioned youthful sensibility; and though I heard it objected by the Princess H—— that he had not sufficiently *l'air noble*, it did not strike me. Karl La Roche, an actor formed under Goethe's tuition, in the golden age of the Weimar theatre, played Philip II, and looked, and dressed, and acted the character with terrible and artist-like fidelity. Mademoiselle Fournier, one of the most beautiful women I ever beheld, and a clever actress, was admirable in the Princess Eboli. Mademoiselle Peche, also a good actress, failed in the queen, as at the time I felt rather than thought, for I had not well considered the character. She embodied too for-

mally, perhaps intentionally, the idea of something
repressed and concealed with effort, which I do not find in
Schiller's Elizabeth. On this representation occurred an
incident worth noting. The old Emperor Francis was present in his box, looking, as usual, very heavy-headed and
attentive; it was about a month or six weeks before his
death. In the scene where Posa expostulates with King
Philip, pleads eloquently for toleration and liberty, and at
length, throwing himself at his feet, exclaims, "Geben Sie
uns Gedankenfreiheit!" the audience, that is, the parterre,
applauded; and there were around me cries, not loud but
deep, of "Bravo, Schiller!" After this the performance of
Don Carlos was forbidden, and it was not given again
while I was at Vienna.

This I write for your edification before I go to rest, after a
day of much quiet enjoyment and luxurious indolence.
The orb of the moon new risen is now suspended upon
the very verge of the American fall, just opposite to my
balcony; the foam of the rapids shines beneath her in
dazzling, shifting, fantastic figures of frosted silver, while
the downward perpendicular leap of the waters is almost
lost to view – all mysterious tumult and shadow.

Accompanied the family of Colonel Delatre to the American side, and dined on Goat Island. Though the various
views of the two cataracts be here wonderfully grand and
beautiful, and the bridge across the rapids a sort of mira-
cle, as they say, still it is not altogether to be compared to
the Canadian shore for picturesque scenery. The Americans have disfigured their share of the rapids with mills
and manufactories, and horrid red brick houses, and other
unacceptable, unseasonable sights and signs of sordid
industry. Worse than all is the round tower, which some
profane wretch has erected on the Crescent Fall; it stands
there so detestably impudent and *mal-à-propos* – it is such
a signal yet puny monument of bad taste – so miserably

mesquin, and so presumptuous, that I do hope the violated majesty of nature will take the matter in hand, and overwhelm or cast it down the precipice one of these fine days, though indeed a barrel of gunpowder were a shorter if not a surer method. Can you not send us out some Guy Faux, heroically ready to be victimised in the great cause of insulted nature, and no less insulted art? – But not to tire you with descriptions of precipices, caves, rocks, woods, and rushing waters, which I can buy here ready made for sixpence, I will only tell you that our party was very pleasant.

Colonel Delatre is a veteran officer, who has purchased a fine lot of land in the neighbourhood, has settled on it with a very interesting family, and is cultivating it with great enthusiasm and success. He served for twenty years in India, chiefly in the island of Ceylon, and was present at the capture of that amiable despot, the king of Candy – he who had such a penchant for pounding his subjects in a mortar. He gave me some anecdotes of this savage war, and of Oriental life, which were very amusing. After answering some questions relative to the condition of the European women in Ceylon, and the manners and morals of the native women, Colonel Delatre said, with unaffected warmth, "I have seen much hard service in different climates, much of human nature in savage and civilised life, in the east and in the west, and all I have seen has raised your sex generally in my estimation. It is no idle compliment – I speak from my heart. I have the very highest idea of the worth and capabilities of women, founded on experience, but, I must say, the highest pity too! You are all in a false position; in England, in Ceylon, in America – everywhere I have found women alike in essentials, and alike ill treated, in one way or in another!"

The people who have spoken or written of these Falls of Niagara, have surely never done justice to their loveliness, their inexpressible, inconceivable beauty. The feeling of their beauty has become with me a deeper feeling than that of their sublimity. What a scene this evening! What splendour of colour! The emerald and chrysopaz of the transparent waters, the dazzling gleam of the foam, and the snow-white vapour on which was displayed the most perfect and gigantic iris I ever beheld – forming not a half, but at least two-thirds of an entire circle, one extremity resting on the lesser (or American) Fall, the other in the very lap of the Crescent Fall, spanning perhaps half a mile, perfectly resplendent in hue – so gorgeous, so vivid, and yet so ethereally delicate, and apparently within a few feet of the eye; the vapours rising into the blue heavens at least four hundred feet, three times the height of the Falls, and tinted rose and amber with the evening sun; and over the woods around every possible variety of the richest foliage – no, nothing was ever so transcendently lovely! The effect, too, was so grandly uniform in its eternal sound and movement, it was quite different from that of those wild, impatient, tumultuous rapids. It soothed, it melted, it composed, rather than excited.

There are no water-fowl now as in the winter – when driven from the ice-bound shores and shallows of the lake, they came up here to seek their food, and sported and wheeled amid the showers of spray. They have returned to their old quiet haunts; sometimes I miss them: they were a beautiful variety in the picture.

How I wish for those I love to enjoy all this with me! I am not enough in myself to feel it all. I cannot suffice for it all, without some sympathy to carry off this "superflu d'ame et de vie;" it overwhelms, it pains me. Why should I not go down *now* to the Table Rock or to the river's brink below the Falls – now when all is still and solitary, and the rich moonlight is blending heaven and earth, and vapours, and woods, and waters, in shadowy splendour? All else in nature sleeps – all but those ever-bounding and rejoicing waters, still holding on their way, ceaseless, exhaustless, without pause or rest. I look out with longing and wakeful eye, but it is midnight, and I am alone; and if I do not feel fear, I feel at least the want of a supporting arm, the want of a sustaining heart. So to bed, to be hushed to slumber by that tremendous lullaby.

A DREAM.

Very significant, poetical, allegorical dreams have often been invented or dreamt with open eyes; but once I had a singular dream, which was a real dream of sleep – such a one as, if I had lived in the days of Pharaoh or Nebuchadnezzar, I should have sent for the nearest magician or prophet to interpret. I remember no vision of the night which ever left on my waking fancy so strong, so vivid an impression; but unfortunately the beginning and the end of the vision faded before I could collect the whole in my remembrance.

I had been reading over, late in the evening, Sternberg's *Herr von Mondshein*, and in sleep the impression continued. I dreamed I was reading a volume of German tales, and as I read, it seemed as if, by a strange, dream-like, double power of perception, not only the words before me, but the forms and feelings they expressed, became visible and palpable to sense. What I read seemed to act itself before my eyes. It was a long history, full of fantastic shapes and perplexing changes, and things that seemed and were not; but, finally, one image predominated and dwelt on my memory clearly and distinctly, even long after I waked. It was that of a Being, I know not of what nature or sex, which went up and down upon our world lamenting, – for it loved all things, suffered with all things, sympathised with all things; and a crowd of all sentient creatures followed – men, women, and children, and animals – a mournful throng.

And the Being I have mentioned looked round upon them, and feeling in itself all their miseries, desire, and wants, wept and wrung its hands.

And at length a wish arose in the heart of that Being to escape from the sight of sorrow and suffering which it could share and not alleviate; and with this wish it looked up for a moment towards heaven, and a cup was held forth by a heavenly hand – a charmed cup, by which the secret wish was fulfilled, and the Being drank of this cup.

And then, I know not how, all things changed. And I saw the same Being standing upon a high altar, in an illuminated temple. The garments were floating in light. The arms were extended towards heaven; the eyes ever upwards turned; but there was no hope or rapture in those eyes; on the contrary, they were melancholy, and swimming in tears. And around the altar was the same crowd of all human and sentient beings, and they looked up constantly with clasped hands, and with a sad and anxious gaze, imploring one of those looks of sympathy and tenderness to which they had been accustomed – but in vain.

And I looked into the heart of that Being which stood alone upon the altar, and it was also sad, and full of regret and love towards the earth, and vain longing to look down once more on those creatures: but the consecrating spell was too strong; the eyes remained ever directed towards heaven, and the arms were extended upwards; and the bond which had united the sympathising with the suffering heart was broken for ever.

I do not mean to tell you that I dreamed all this to the sound of the Falls of Niagara; but I do aver that it was a real *bonâ fide* dream. Send me now the interpretation thereof – or look to be sphinx-devoured.

R ETURNED FROM Stamford Park, where I spent a few
days rather agreeably, for there were books, music
and mirth within, though a perpetual storm raged without.

The distance from the Falls is four miles, and the hollow
roar of the cataract not only sounded all night in my ears,
but violently shook doors and windows. The very walls
seemed to vibrate to the sound.

I came back to the Clifton Hotel, to find my beautiful
Falls quite spoiled and discoloured. Instead of the soft
aquamarine hue, relieved with purest white, a dull dirty
brown now imbued the waters. This is owing to the shallowness of Lake Erie, where every storm turns up the
muddy bed from the bottom, and discolours the whole
river. The spray, instead of hovering in light clouds round
and above the cataracts, was beaten down, and rolled in
volumes round their base; then by the gusty winds driven
along the surface of the river hither and thither, covering
everything in the neighbourhood with a small rain. I sat

down to draw, and in a moment the paper was wet through. It is as if all had been metamorphosed during my absence – and I feel very disconsolate.

There are, certainly, two ways of contemplating the sublime and beautiful. I remember one day as I was standing on the Table Rock, feeling very poetical, an Irishman behind me suddenly exclaimed, in a most cordial brogue, and an accent of genuine admiration – "Faith, then, that's a pretty dacent dhrop o' water that's coming over there!"

T HAT YOU may have some understanding of my whereabouts, my outgoings, and my incomings, I intend
this to be a chapter on localities; and putting poetry and
description far from me, I now write you a common
sensible lecture on topography and geography. It is no
unpardonable offence, I hope, to suppose you as ignorant
as I was myself, till I came here.

Perhaps even for my sake you may now and then look
upon a map of Canada, and there, as in the maps of
Russia in Catherine the Second's time, you will find not a
few towns and cities laid down by name which you might
in vain look for within the precincts of the province,
seeing that they are non-extant, as yet at least, though full
surely *to be*, some time or other, somewhere or other,
when this fair country shall have fair play, and its fair
quota of population. But from this anticipation I would
willingly except a certain CITY OF THE FALLS which I have
seen marked on so many maps, and mentioned in so
many books, as already laid out and commenced, that I
had no doubt of its existence till I came here for the first
time last winter. But here it is not – *Grazie a Dio!* – nor
likely to be, as far as I can judge, for a century to come.
Were a city to rise here, it would necessarily become a

manufacturing place, because of the "water powers and privileges," below and above the cataract, which would then be turned to account. Fancy, if you can, a range of cotton factories, iron foundries, grist mills, saw mills, where now the mighty waters rush along in glee and liberty – where the maple and the pine woods now bend and wave along the heights. Surely they have done enough already with their wooden hotels, museums, and curiosity stalls: neither in such a case were red brick tenements, gaslights, and smoky chimneys, the worst abomination to be feared. There would be a moral pollution brought into this majestic scene, far more degrading; – more than all those rushing waters, with their "thirteen millions of tons per minute," could wash away.

Let us pray against such a desecration. In the mean time can you tell me who was the first white man whose eyes beheld this wonder of the earth? He was a Frenchman, but nowhere do I find record of his name, nor of the impressions which such a discovery would make on any, even the most vulgar and insensible nature.

In former seasons, the two hotels have been full to overflowing. They tell me here that last summer one hundred and fifty persons sat down almost daily to dinner; the far greater number were travellers and visiters from the United States. This year, owing to the commercial embarrassments of that country, there are so few visiters, that one hotel (Forsyth's) is closed, and the other (Clifton House) is nearly empty, to the serious loss, I fear, of the poor people, but to myself individually an unspeakable comfort – for thus I wander about and drive about in full liberty and loneliness.

The whole of this district between the two great lakes is superlatively beautiful, and was the first settled district in Upper Canada; it is now the best cultivated. The population is larger in proportion to its extent than that of any other district. In Niagara, and in the neighbouring district of Gore, many fruits come to perfection, which are not found to thrive in other parts of the province, and cargoes of fruit are sent yearly to the cities of Lower Canada, where the climate is much more severe and the winter longer than with us.

On the other side the country is far less beautiful, and they say less fertile, but rich in activity and in population; and there are within the same space at least half a dozen flourishing towns. Our speculating energetic Yankee neighbours, not satisfied with their Manchester, their manufactories, and their furnaces, and their mill "privileges," have opened a railroad from Lewiston to Buffalo, thus connecting Lake Erie with the Erie Canal. On our side, we have the Welland Canal, a magnificent work, of which the province is justly proud; it unites Lake Erie with Lake Ontario.

Yet from the Falls all along the shores of the Lake Erie to the Grand River and far beyond it, the only place we have approaching to a town is Chippewa, just above the rapids, as yet a small village, but lying immediately in the road from the Western States to the Falls. From Buffalo to this place the Americans run a steam-boat daily; they have also planned a suspension bridge across the Niagara river, between Lewiston and Queenston. Another village, Dunn-ville, on the Grand River, is likely to be the commercial depôt of that part of the province; it is situated where the Welland Canal joins Lake Erie.

As the weather continued damp and gloomy, without hope of change, a sudden whim seized me to go to Buffalo for a day or two; so I crossed the turbulent ferry to Man-chester, and thence an engine, snorting, shrieking like fifty tortured animals, conveyed to us to Tonawando,* once a little village of Seneca Indians, now rising into a town of some size and importance; and there to my great delight I encountered once more my new friends, Mr. and Mrs. MacMurray, who were on their return from Toronto to the Sault Ste. Marie. We proceeded on to Buffalo together,

---

* Near this place lived and died the chief Redjacket, one of the last and greatest specimens of the Indian patriot and warrior.

and during the rest of the day had some pleasant opportunities of improving our acquaintance.

Buffalo, as all travel-books will tell you, is a very fine young city, about ten years old, and containing already about twenty thousand inhabitants. There is here the largest and most splendid hotel I have ever seen except at Frankfort. Long rows of magnificent houses – not of painted wood, but of brick and stone – are rising on every side.

The season is unusually dull and dead, and I hear nothing but complaints around me; but compared to our sleepy Canadian shore, where a lethargic spell seems to bind up the energies of the people, all here is bustle, animation, activity. In the port I counted about fifty vessels, sloops, schooners and steam-boats; the crowds of people buying, selling, talking, bawling; the Indians lounging by in their blankets, the men looking so dark, and indifferent, and lazy; the women so busy, care-worn, and eager; and the quantities of sturdy children, squalling, frisking among the feet of busy sailors, – formed altogether a strange and amusing scene.

On board the Michigan steamer, then lying ready for her voyage up the lakes to Chicago, I found all the arrangements magnificent to a degree I could not have anticipated. This is one of three great steam-boats navigating the Upper Lakes, which are from five to seven hundred tons burthen, and there are nearly forty smaller ones coasting Lake Erie, between Buffalo and Detroit, besides schooners. We have (in 1837) on this lake two little ill-constructed steamers, which go puffing up and down like two little tea-kettles, in proportion to the gigantic American boats; and unfortunately, till our side of the lake is better peopled and cultivated, we have no want of them. When they are required, they will exist, as on Lake Ontario, where we have, I believe, eight or ten steamers.

I found here several good booksellers' shops, the counters and shelves loaded with cheap American editions of English publications, generally of a trashy kind, but some good ones; and it is not a pleasing fact that our two booksellers at Toronto are principally supplied from this place. When I wanted a book at Toronto which was not forthcoming, the usual answer was, "that it would be sent for from Buffalo." The clothing and millinery shops were the best and gayest in appearance. In the window of one of the largest of these I saw written up in large letters, "Walk in, and name your price!" Over the door of another was inscribed, "Book and bandbox store." I marvelled what could bring these apparently heterogeneous articles into such close emulation and juxtaposition, till I remembered – that both are made of paper.

The MacMurrays, with their beautiful infant and his Indian nurse, embarked on board the Michigan, and I parted from them with regret, for Mrs. MacMurray had won upon me more and more with her soft voice and her benign eyes, and her maternal anxieties.

I was now again alone, in a vast inn swarming with dirty, lazy, smoking men – the rain was falling in a deluge, and no books – no companions. As I walked disconsolately up and down a great room they call in American hotels the ladies' parlour, a young girl, very pretty and well dressed, who was swinging herself in a rocking-chair and reading Mrs. Hemans, rose from her seat, left the room without saying a word, and returned with a handful of books and several numbers of an excellent literary periodical, "The Knickerbocker of New York," which she most courteously placed before me. A cup of water in a desert could hardly have been more welcome, or excited warmer thanks and gratitude. Thus charitably furnished with amusement, the gloomy wet morning did at last glide away, for time and the hour will creep through the dullest, as they "run through" the roughest day. In the evening I went to the theatre, to a private box, a luxury which I had not expected to find in this most democratical of cities. The theatre is small of course, but very neat and prettily decorated. They had an actress from New York *starring* it here for a few nights – the tallest, handsomest woman I ever saw on the stage, who looked over the head of her diminutive Romeo, or down upon him – the said Romeo being dressed in the costume of Othello, turban and all. When in the balcony, the rail did not reach up to Juliet's knees, and I was in perpetual horror lest she should topple down headlong. This would have been the more fatal, as she was the only one who knew anything of her part. The other actors and actresses favoured us with a sort of gabble, in which not only Shakspeare, but numbers, sense, and grammar, were equally put to confusion. Mercutio was an enormously corpulent man with a red nose, who swaggered about and filled up every hiatus of memory with a good round oath. The whole exhibition was so inexpressibly ludicrous, that I was forced to give way to fits of uncontrollable laughter – whereat my companions looked not well pleased. Nor was the audience less amusing than the dramatis personæ: the pit was filled by artisans of the lowest grade, and lake mariners sitting in their straw hats and shirt-sleeves – for few had either coats or waistcoats. They were most devoutly attentive to the story in their own way, eating cakes and drinking whisky between the acts, and whenever anything especially pleased them, they uttered a loud whoop and halloo, which reverberated through the theatre, at the same time slapping their thighs and snapping their fingers. In their eyes, Peter and the nurse were evidently the hero and heroine of the piece, and never appeared without calling forth the most boisterous applause. The actor and actress had enriched the humour of Shakspeare by adding several Yankee witticisms and allusions, the exact import of which I could not comprehend; but they gave unqualified delight to the merry parterre. I did not wait for the second entertainment, having some fear that as the tragedy had proved a farce, the farce might prove a tragedy.

The next morning I returned to the Falls, which are still sullen and turbid, owing to the stormy weather on Lake Erie.

> How divine
> The liberty for frail, for mortal man
> To roam at large among unpeopl'd glens;
> And mountainous retirements, only trod
> By devious footsteps – regions consecrate
> To oldest time!

WORDSWORTH.

June 27.

I N A strange country much is to be learned by travelling in the public carriages: in Germany and elsewhere I have preferred this mode of conveyance, even when the alternative lay within my choice, and I never had reason to regret it.

The Canadian stage-coaches* are like those of the United States, heavy lumbering vehicles, well calculated to live in roads where any decent carriage must needs founder. In one of these I embarked to return to the town

---

* That is, the better class of them. In some parts of Upper Canada, the stage-coaches conveying the mail were large oblong wooden boxes, formed of a few planks nailed together and placed on wheels, into which you entered by the windows, there being no doors to open and shut, and no springs. Two or three seats were suspended inside on leather straps. The travellers provided their own buffalo-skins or cushions to sit on.

of Niagara, thence to pursue my journey westward: a much easier and shorter course had been by the lake steamers; but my object was not haste, nor to see merely sky and water, but to see the country.

In the stage-coach two persons were already seated – an English emigrant and his wife, with whom I quickly made acquaintance after my usual fashion. The circumstances and the story of this man I thought worth noting – not because there was anything uncommon or peculiarly interesting in his case, but simply because his case is that of so many others; while the direct good sense, honesty, and intelligence of the man pleased me exceedingly.

He told me that he had come to America in his own behalf and that of several others of his own class – men who had each a large family and a small capital, who found it difficult to *get on* and settle their children in England. In his own case, he had been some years ago the only one of his trade in a flourishing country town, where he had now fourteen competitors. Six families, in a similar position, had delegated him on a voyage of discovery: it was left to him to decide whether they should settle in the United States or in the Canadas; so leaving his children at school in Long Island, "he was just," to use his own phrase, "taking a turn through the two countries, to look about him and gather information before he decided, and had brought his little wife to see the grand Falls of Niagara, of which he had heard so much in the old country."

As we proceeded, my companion mingled with his acute questions, and his learned calculations on crops and prices of land, certain observations on the beauty of the scenery, and talked of lights and shades, and foregrounds, and effects, in very homely, plebeian English, but with so much of real taste and feeling that I was rather astonished, till I found he had been a print-seller and frame-maker, which last branch of trade had brought him into contact with artists and amateurs; and he told me, with no little exultation, that among his stock of movables he had brought out with him several fine drawings of Prout, Hunt, and even Turner, acquired in his business. He said he had no wish at present to part with these, for it was his intention, wherever he settled, to hang them up in his house, though that house were a log-hut, that his children might have the pleasure of looking at them, and learn to distinguish what is excellent in its kind.

The next day, on going on from Niagara to Hamilton in a storm of rain, I found, to my no small gratification, the English emigrant and his quiet, silent little wife, already seated in the stage, and my only *compagnons de voyage*. In the deportment of this man there was that deferential courtesy which you see in the manners of respectable tradesmen, who are brought much into intercourse with their superiors in rank, without, however, a tinge of servility; and his conversation amused and interested me more and more. He told me he had been born on a farm, and had first worked as a farmer's boy, then as a house-carpenter, lastly, as a decorative carver and gilder, so that there was no kind of business to which he could not readily turn his hand. His wife was a good sempstress, and he had brought up all his six children to be useful, giving them such opportunities of acquiring knowledge as he could. He regretted his own ignorance, but, as he said, he had been all his life too busy to find time for reading much. He was, however, resolved that his boys and girls should read, because, as he well observed, "every sort of knowledge, be it much or little, was sure to turn to account some time or other." His notions on education, his objections to the common routine of common schools, and his views for his children, were all marked by the same originality and good sense. Altogether he appeared to be, in every respect, just the kind of settler we want in Upper Canada. I was therefore pleased to hear that hitherto he was better satisfied with the little he had seen of this province than with those States of the Union through which he had journeyed; he said, truly, it was more "home-like, more English-like." I did my best to encourage him in this favourable opinion, promising myself that the little I might be able to do to promote his views, that I *would* do.*

While the conversation was thus kept up with wonderful pertinacity, considering that our vehicle was reeling and tumbling along the detestable road, pitching like a scow among the breakers in a lake-storm, our driver stopped before a vile little log-hut, over the door of which hung crooked-wise a board, setting forth that "wiskey and tabacky" were to be had there. The windows were broken, and the loud voice of some intoxicated wretch was heard from within, in one uninterrupted torrent of oaths and blasphemies, so shocking in their variety, and so new to my ears, that I was really horror-struck.

After leaving the hut, the coach stopped again. I called to the driver in some terror, "You are not surely going to admit that drunken man into the coach?" He replied, coolly, "O no, I an't; don't you be afeard!" In the next moment he opened the door, and the very wretch I stood in fear of was tumbled in head foremost, smelling of spirits, and looking – O most horrible! Expostulation was in vain. Without even listening, the driver shut the door, and drove on at a gallop. The rain was at this time falling in torrents, the road knee-deep in mud, the wild forest on either side of us dark, grim, impenetrable. Help there was none, nor remedy, nor redress, nor hope, but in patience. Here then was one of those inflictions to which speculative travellers are exposed now and then, appearing, *for the time*, to outweigh all the possible advantages of experience or knowledge bought at such a price.

I had never before in my whole life been obliged to

* And I *did* my best, in referring him by letter to Dr. Dunlop; for, though personally unknown to him, I knew that my emigrant was exactly the man to deserve and obtain his notice. I also wrote to Chief-Justice Robinson in his favour, and invited him to come to us on his arrival in Toronto, promising him the Chancellor's good-will and assistance. But I never heard of the man again, nor could I find, before I left Canada, that his name was registered as a purchaser of land.

endure the presence or proximity of such an object for two minutes together, and the astonishment, horror, disgust, even to sickness and loathing, which it now inspired, are really unspeakable. The Englishman, placing himself in the middle seat, in front of his wife and myself, did his best to protect us from all possibility of contact with the object of our abomination; while the wretched being, aware of our adverse feeling, put on at one moment an air of chuckling self-complacency, and the next glared on us with ferocious defiance. When I had recovered myself sufficiently to observe, I saw, with added horror, that he was not more than five-and-twenty, probably much younger, with a face and figure which must have been by nature not only fine, but uncommonly fine, though now deformed, degraded, haggard and inflamed with filth and inebriety – a dreadful and humiliating spectacle. Some glimmering remains of sense and decency prevented him from swearing and blaspheming when once in the coach; but he abused us horribly: his nasal accent, and his drunken objurgations against the old country, and all who came from it, betrayed his own birth and breeding to have been on the other side of the Niagara, or "down east." Once he addressed some words to me, and, offended by my resolute silence, he exclaimed, with a scowl, and a hiccup of abomination at every word, "I should like – to know – madam – how – I came under your diabolical influence?" Here my friend the emigrant, seeing my alarm, interposed, and a scene ensued, which, in spite of the horrors of this horrible propinquity, was irresistibly comic, and not without its pathetic significance too, now I come to think of it. The Englishman, forgetting that the condition of the man placed him for the time beyond the influence of reasoning or sympathy, began with grave and benevolent earnestness to lecture him on his profligate habits, expressing his amazement and his pity at seeing such a fine young man fallen into such evil ways, and exhorting him to amend, – the fellow, meanwhile, rolling himself from side to side with laughter. But suddenly his countenance changed, and he said, with a wistful expression, and the tears in his eyes, "Friend, do you believe in the devil?"

"Yes, I do," replied the Englishman with solemnity.

"Then it's your opinion, I guess, that a man may be tempted by the devil?"

"Yes, and I should suppose as how that has been your case, friend; though," added he, looking at him from head to foot with no equivocal expression, "I think the devil himself might have more charity than to put a man in such a pickle."

"What do you mean by that?" exclaimed the wretch fiercely, and for the first time uttering a horrid oath. The emigrant only replied by shaking his head significantly; and the other, after pouring forth a volley of abuse against the insolence of the "old country folk," stretched himself on his back, and kicking up his legs on high, and setting his feet against the roof of the coach, fell asleep in this attitude, and snored, till, at the end of a long hour, he was tumbled out at the door of another drinking hovel as he had tumbled in, and we saw him no more.

The distance from the town of Niagara to Hamilton is about forty miles. We had left the former place at ten in the morning, yet it was nearly midnight before we arrived, having had no refreshment during the whole day. It was market-day, and the time of the assizes, and not a bed to be had at the only tolerable hotel, which, I should add, is large and commodious. The people were civil beyond measure, and a bed was made up for me in a back parlour, into which I sank half starved, and very completely tired.

The next day rose bright and beautiful, and I amused myself walking up and down the pretty town for two or three hours.

Hamilton is the capital of the Gore district, and one of the most flourishing places in Upper Canada. It is situated at the extreme point of Burlington Bay, at the head of Lake Ontario, with a population, annually increasing, of about three thousand. The town is about a mile from the lake shore, a space which, in the course of time, will probably be covered with buildings. I understand that seventeen thousand bushels of wheat were shipped here in one month. There is a bank here; a court-house and jail looking unfinished, and the commencement of a public reading-room and literary society, of which I cannot speak from my own knowledge, and which appears as yet in embryo. Some of the linendrapers' shops, called here clothing stores, and the grocery stores, or shops for all descriptions of imported merchandise, made a very good appearance; and there was an air of business, and bustle, and animation about the place which pleased me. I saw no bookseller's shop, but a few books on the shelves of a grocery store, of the most common and coarse description.

Allan M'Nab, the present speaker of the house of assembly, has a very beautiful house here, and is a principal merchant and proprietor in the town; but he was at this time absent. I had heard much of Mr. Cattermole, the author of a very clever little book addressed to emigrants, and also a distinguished inhabitant of the place. I wished to see this gentleman, but there were some difficulties in finding him, and, after waiting some time, I was obliged to take my departure, a long day's journey being before me.

I hope you have a map of Canada before you, or at hand, that what I am now going to tell you may be intelligible.

They have projected a railroad from Hamilton westward through the London and Western districts – certainly one of the grandest and most useful undertakings in the world, – in *this* world, I mean. The want of a line of road, of an accessible market for agricultural produce, keeps this magnificent country poor and ignorant in the midst of unequalled capabilities. If the formation of the Rideau Canal, in the eastern districts, (connecting Lake Ontario with the Ottawa river,) has, in spite of many disadvantages in the soil and locality, brought that part of the province so far in advance of the rest in population, wealth, and intelligence – what would not a railroad do for them here, where the need is at least as great – the resources, natural and *accidental*, much superior – and the prospect of advantage, in every point of view, infinitely more promising?

Under all disadvantages, this part of the province has been the usual route of emigrants to the Western States of the Union; for, as you will perceive by a glance at the map, it is the shortest road to Michigan and the Illinois by some hundreds of miles. If there were but a railroad, opening a direct communication through the principal settlements between Hamilton on Lake Ontario, and Sandwich at the head of Lake Erie, there is no calculating the advantages that must arise from it – even immediate advantage; but "want of capital," as I hear all around me – and they might add want of energy, want of enterprise, want of everything needful, besides money – the one thing most needful – are likely to defer the completion of this magnificent plan for many years. I wonder some of our great speculators and monied men in England do not speculate here, instead of sending their money to the United States; – or rather I do *not* wonder, seeing what I see. But I wish that the government would do something to remove the almost universal impression, that this province is regarded by the powers at home with distrust and indifference – something to produce more confidence in public men and public measures, without which there can be no enterprise, no prosperity, no railroads. What that something is, being no politician nor political economist like Harriet Martineau, I cannot point out, nor even conjecture. I have just sense enough to see, to feel, that something *must* be done – that the necessity speaks in every form all around me.

I should not forget to mention, that in the Niagara and Gore districts there is a vast number of Dutch and German settlers, favourably distinguished by their industrious, sober, and thriving habits. They are always to be distinguished in person and dress from the British settlers;

and their houses and churches, and, above all, their burial-places, have a distinct and characteristic look. At Berlin, the Germans have a printing-press, and publish a newspaper in their own language, which is circulated among their countrymen through the whole province.

At Hamilton I hired a light *wagon*, as they call it, a sort of gig perched in the middle of a wooden tray, wherein my baggage was stowed; and a man to drive me over to Brandtford, the distance being about five-and-twenty miles, and the charge five dollars. The country all the way was rich, and beautiful, and fertile beyond description – the roads abominable as could be imagined to exist. So I then thought, but have learned since that there are degrees of badness in this respect, to which the human imagination has not yet descended. I remember a space of about three miles on this road, bordered entirely on each side by dead trees, which had been artificially blasted by fire, or by girdling. It was a ghastly forest of tall white spectres, strangely contrasting with the glowing luxurious foliage all around.

The pity I have for the trees in Canada, shows how far I am yet from being a true Canadian. How do we know that trees do not feel their downfall? We know nothing about it. The line which divides animal from vegetable sensibility is as undefined as the line which divides animal from human intelligence. And if it be true "that nothing dies on earth but nature mourns," how must she mourn for these the mighty children of her bosom – her pride, her glory, her garment? Without exactly believing the assertion of the old philosopher,* that a tree *feels* the first stroke of the axe, I know I never witness nor hear that first stroke without a shudder; and as yet I cannot look on with indifference, far less share the Canadian's exultation, when these huge oaks, these umbrageous elms and stately pines, are lying prostrate, lopped of all their honours, and piled in heaps with the brushwood, to be fired, – or burned

* Quoted by Evelyn.

down to a charred and blackened fragment, – or standing, leafless, sapless, seared, ghastly, having been "girdled," and left to perish. The "Fool i' the Forest,"* moralised not more quaintly over the wounded deer, than I could sometimes over those prostrate and mangled trees. I remember, in one of the clearings to-day, one particular tree which had been burned and blasted; only a blackened stump of mouldering bark – a mere shell remained; and from the centre of this, as from some hidden source of vitality, sprang up a young green shoot, tall and flourishing, and fresh and leafy. I looked and thought of hope! Why, indeed, should we ever despair? Can Heaven do for the blasted tree what it cannot do for the human heart?

The largest place we passed was Ancaster, very prettily situated among pastures and rich woods, and rapidly improving.

Before sunset I arrived at Brandtford, and took a walk about the town and its environs. The situation of this place is most beautiful – on a hill above the left bank of the Grand River. And as I stood and traced this noble stream, winding through richly-wooded flats, with green meadows and cultivated fields, I was involuntarily reminded of the Thames near Richmond; the scenery has the same character of tranquil and luxuriant beauty.

In Canada the traveller can enjoy little of the interest derived from association, either historical or poetical. Yet the memory of General Brock, and some anecdotes of the last war, lend something of this kind of interest to the Niagara frontier; and this place, or rather the name of this place, has certain recollections connected with it, which might well make an idle contemplative wayfarer a little pensive.

Brandt was the chief of that band of Mohawk warriors which served on the British side during the American War of Independence. After the termination of the contest, the

* As You Like It.

"Six Nations" left their ancient seats to the south of Lake Ontario, and having received from the English government a grant of land along the banks of the Grand River, and the adjacent shore of Lake Erie, they settled here under their chief, Brandt, in 1783. Great part of this land, some of the finest in the province, has lately been purchased back from them by the government, and settled by thriving English farmers.

Brandt, who had intelligence enough to perceive and acknowledge the superiority of the whites in all the arts of life, was at first anxious for the conversion and civilisation of his nation; but I was told by a gentleman who had known him, that after a visit he paid to England, this wish no longer existed. He returned to his own people with no very sublime idea either of our morals or manners, and died in 1807.

He is the Brandt whom Campbell has handed down to most undeserved execration as the leader in the massacre at Wyoming. The poet indeed tells us, in the notes to Gertrude of Wyoming, that all he has said against Brandt must be considered as pure fiction, "for that he was remarkable for his humanity, and not even present at the massacre;" but the name stands in the text as heretofore, apostrophised as the "accursed Brandt," the "monster Brandt;" and is not this most unfair, to be hitched into elegant and popular rhyme as an assassin by wholesale, and justice done in a little fag-end of prose?

His son, John Brandt, received a good education, and was member of the house of assembly for his district. He too died in a short time before my arrival in this country; and the son of his sister, Mrs. Kerr, is at present the hereditary chief of the Six Nations.

They consist at present of two thousand five hundred, out of the seven or eight thousand who first settled here. Here, as everywhere else, the decrease of the Indian population settled on the reserved lands is uniform. The white population throughout America is supposed to double itself on an average in twenty-three years; in about the same proportion do the Indians perish before them.

The interests and property of these Indians are at present managed by the government. The revenue arising from the sale of their lands is in the hands of commissioners, and much is done for their conversion and civilisation. It will, however, be the affair of two, or three, or more generations; and by that time not many, I am afraid, will be left. Consumption makes dreadful havoc among them. At present they have churches, schools, and an able missionary who has studied their language, besides several resident Methodist preachers. Of the two thousand five hundred already mentioned, the far greater part retain their old faith and customs, having borrowed from the whites only those habits which certainly "were more honoured in the breach than in the observance." I saw many of these people, and spoke to some, who replied with a quiet, self-possessed courtesy, and in very intelligible English. One group which I met outside the town, consisting of two young men in blanket coats and leggings, one haggard old woman, with a man's hat on her head, a blue blanket and deer-skin moccasins, and a very beautiful girl, apparently not more than fifteen, similarly dressed, with long black hair hanging loose over her face and shoulders, and a little baby, many shades fairer than herself, peeping from the folds of her blanket behind, – altogether reminded me of a group of gipsies, such as I have seen on the borders of Sherwood Forest many years ago.

The Grand River is navigable for steam-boats from Lake Erie up to the landing-place, about two miles below Brandtford, and from thence a canal is to be cut, some time or other, to the town. The present site of Brandtford was chosen on account of those very rapids which do indeed obstruct the navigation, but turn a number of mills, here of the first importance. The usual progress of a Canadian village is this: first, on some running stream, the erection of a saw-mill and grist-mill for the convenience of the neighbouring scattered settlers; then a few shanties or log-houses for the workpeople; then a grocery-store; then a tavern – a chapel – perchance a school-house – *und so weiter*, as the Germans say.*

Not having been properly forewarned, I unfortunately allowed the driver to take me to a wrong inn. I ought to have put up at the Mansion-house, well kept by a retired half-pay British officer; instead of which I was brought to the Commercial Hotel, newly undertaken by an American. I sent to the landlord to say I wished to speak to him about proceeding on my journey next day. The next moment the man walked into my bed-room without hesitation or apology. I was too much accustomed to foreign manners to be greatly discomfited; but when he proceeded to fling his hat down on my bed, and throw himself into the only arm-chair in the room, while I was standing, I must own I did look at him with some surprise. To those who have been accustomed to the servile courtesy of English innkeepers, the manners of the innkeepers in the United States are not pleasant. I cannot say they ever discomposed me: I always met with civility and attention; but the manners of the country innkeepers in Canada are worse than anything you can meet with in the United States, being generally kept by refugee Americans of the lowest class, or by Canadians who, in affecting American manners and phraseology, grossly exaggerate both.

In the present case I saw at once that no incivility was intended; my landlord was ready at a fair price to drive me

* The erection of a church or chapel generally precedes that of a school-house in Upper Canada, but the mill and the tavern invariably precede both. "In the United States," says Mr. Schoolcraft, "the first public edifice is a court-house; then a jail; then a school-house – perhaps an academy, where religious exercises may be occasionally held; but a house of public worship is the result of a more mature state of the settlement. If," he adds, "we have sometimes been branded as litigious, it is not altogether without foundation; and, notwithstanding the very humble estimate which foreign reviewers have been pleased to make of our literary character and attainments, there is more likelihood of our obtaining the reputation of a learned than a pious people." – *Schoolcraft's Travels*.

over himself, in his own "wagon," to Woodstock; and after this was settled, finding, after a few questions, that the man was really a most stupid, ignorant fellow, I turned to the window, and took up a book, as a hint for him to be gone. He continued, however to lounge in the chair, rocking himself in silence to and fro, till at last he *did* condescend to take my hint, and to take his departure.

Though tired beyond expression, I was for some time prevented from going to rest by one of those disgraceful scenes which meet me at every turn. A man in the dress of a gentleman, but in a state of brutal intoxication, was staggering, swearing, vociferating, beneath my window, while a party of men, also respectably dressed, who were smoking and drinking before the door, regarded him with amusement or indifference; some children and a few Indians were looking on. This person, as the maid-servant informed me, was by birth a gentleman, and had good practice in the law. "Three years ago there wasn't a smarter (cleverer) man in the district;" now he was ruined utterly in health, fortune, and character. His wife's relations had taken her and her children away, and had since clothed him, and allowed him something for a subsistence. He continued to disturb the whole neighbourhood for two hours, and I was really surprised by the forbearance with which he was treated.

Next morning I took another walk. There are several good shops and many houses in progress, some of them of brick and stone. I met two or three well-dressed women walking down Colborne-street; and the people were bustling about with animated faces – a strong contrast to the melancholy, indolent-looking Indians. I understand that there are now about twelve hundred inhabitants, the population having tripled in three years: and they have a newspaper, an agricultural society, a post-office; a Congregational, a Baptist, and Methodist church, a large chair manufactory, and other mills and manufactories which I had no time to visit.

At ten o'clock, a little vehicle, like that which brought me from Hamilton, was at the door; and I set off for Woodstock, driven by my American landlord, who showed himself as good-natured and civil as he was impenetrably stupid.

No one who has a single atom of imagination, can travel through these forest roads of Canada without being strongly impressed and excited. The seemingly interminable line of trees before you; the boundless wilderness around; the mysterious depths amid the multitudinous foliage, where foot of man hath never penetrated, – and which partial gleams of the noontide sun, now seen, now lost, lit up with a changeful, magical beauty – the wondrous splendour and novelty of the flowers, – the silence, unbroken but by the low cry of a bird, or hum of insect, or the splash and croak of some huge bull-frog, – the solitude in which we proceeded mile after mile, no human being, no human dwelling within sight, – are all either exciting to the fancy, or oppressive to the spirits, according to the mood one may be in. Their effect on myself I can hardly describe in words.

I observed some birds of a species new to me; there was the lovely blue-bird, with its brilliant violet plumage; and a most gorgeous species of woodpecker, with a black head, white breast, and back and wings of the brightest scarlet; hence it is called by some the field-officer, and more generally the cock of the woods. I should have called it the coxcomb of the woods, for it came flitting across our road, clinging to the trees before us, and remaining pertinaciously in sight, as if conscious of its own splendid array, and pleased to be admired.

There was also the Canadian robin, a bird as large as a thrush, but in plumage and shape resembling the sweet bird at home "that wears the scarlet stomacher." There were great numbers of small birds of a bright yellow, like canaries, and I believe of the same genus. Sometimes, when I looked up from the depth of foliage to the blue firmament above, I saw an eagle sailing through the air on apparently motionless wings. Nor let me forget the splendour of the flowers which carpeted the woods on either side. I might have exclaimed with Eichendorff,

> "O Welt! Du schöne welt, Du!
> Mann sieht Dich vor Blümen kaum!"

for thus in some places did a rich embroidered pall of flowers literally *hide* the earth. There those beautiful plants, which we cultivate with such care in our gardens, azalias, rhododendrons, all the gorgeous family of the lobelia, were flourishing in wild luxuriance. Festoons of creeping and parasitical plants hung from branch to branch. The purple and scarlet iris, blue larkspur, and the elegant Canadian columbine with its bright pink flowers; the scarlet lychnis, a species of orchis of the most dazzling geranium-colour, and the white and yellow and purple cyprepedium,* bordered the path, and a thousand others of most resplendent hues, for which I knew no names. I could not pass them with forbearance, and my Yankee driver, alighting, gathered for me a superb bouquet from the swampy margin of the forest. I contrived to fasten my flowers in a wreath along the front of the wagon, that I might enjoy at leisure their novelty and beauty. How lavish, how carelessly profuse, is Nature in her handiwork! In the interior of the cyprepedium, which I tore open, there was variety of configuration and colour, and gem-like richness of ornament, enough to fashion twenty different flowers; and for the little fly, in jewelled cuirass, which I found couched within its recesses, what a palace! that of Aladdin could not have been more splendid!

But I spare you these fantastic speculations and cogitations, and many more that came flitting across my fancy. I

---

* From its resemblance in form to a shoe, this splendid flower bears everywhere the same name. The English call it lady's-slipper; the Indians know it as the moccasin flower.

am afraid that, old as I am, my youth has been yokefellow with my years, and that I am yet a child in some things.

From Brandtford we came to Paris, a new settlement, beautifully situated, and thence to Woodstock, a distance of eighteen miles. There is no village, only isolated inns, far removed from each other. In one of these, kept by a Frenchman, I dined on milk and eggs and excellent bread. Here I found every appearance of prosperity and plenty. The landlady, an American woman, told me they had come into this wilderness twenty years ago, when there was not another farmhouse within fifty miles. She had brought up and settled in comfort several sons and daughters. An Irish farmer came in, who had refreshments spread for him in the porch, and with whom I had some amusing conversation. He, too, was prospering with a large farm and a large family – here a blessing and a means of wealth, too often in the old country a curse and a burthen. The good-natured fellow was extremely scandalised by my homely and temperate fare, which he besought me to mend by accepting a glass of whisky out of his own travelling-store, genuine potheen, which he swore deeply, and not unpoetically, "had never seen God's beautiful world, nor the blessed light of day, since it had been bottled in ould Ireland." He told me, boastingly, that at Hamilton he had made eight hundred dollars by the present extraordinary rise in the price of wheat. In the early part of the year wheat had been selling for three or four dollars a bushel, and rose this summer to twelve and fourteen dollars a bushel, owing to the immense quantities exported during the winter to the back settlements of Michigan and the Illinois.

The whole drive would have been productive of unmixed enjoyment, but for one almost intolerable drawback. The roads were throughout so execrably bad, that no words can give you an idea of them. We often sank into mud-holes above the axletree; then over trunks of trees laid across swamps, called here corduroy roads, were my poor bones dislocated. A wheel here and there, or broken shaft lying by the wayside, told of former wrecks and disasters. In some places they had, in desperation, flung huge boughs of oak into the mud abyss, and covered them with clay and sod, the rich green foliage projecting on either side. This sort of illusive contrivance would sometimes give way, and we were nearly precipitated in the midst. By the time we arrived at Blandford, my hands were swelled and blistered by continually grasping with all my strength an iron bar in front of my vehicle, to prevent myself from being flung out, and my limbs ached wofully. I never beheld or imagined such roads. It is clear that the people do not apply any, even the commonest, principles of roadmaking; no drains are cut, no attempt is made at levelling or preparing a foundation. The settlers around are too much engrossed by the necessary toil for a daily subsistence to give a moment of their time to road-making, without compulsion or good payment. The statute labour does not appear to be duly enforced by the commissioners and magistrates, and there are no labourers, and no spare money; specie, never very plentiful in these parts, is not to be had at present, and the 500,000*l.* voted during the last session of the provincial parliament for the repair of the roads is not yet even raised, I believe.

Nor is this all: the vile state of the roads, the very little communication between places not far distant from each other, leave it in the power of ill-disposed persons to sow mischief among the ignorant, isolated people.

On emerging from a forest road seven miles in length, we stopped at a little inn to refresh the poor jaded horses. Several labourers were lounging about the door, and I spoke to them of the horrible state of the roads. They agreed, one and all, that it was entirely the fault of the government; that their welfare was not cared for; that it was true that money had been voted for the roads, but that before anything could be done, or a shilling of it expended, it was always necessary to write to the old country to ask the king's permission – which might be sent or not – who could tell? And meantime they were ruined for want of roads, which it was nobody's business to reclaim.

It was in vain that I attempted to point out to the orator of the party the falsehood and absurdity of this notion. He only shook his head, and said he knew better.

One man observed, that as the team of Admiral V—— (one of the largest proprietors in the district) had lately broken down in a mud-hole there was some hope that the roads about here might be looked to.

About sunset I arrived at Blandford, dreadfully weary, and fevered, and bruised, having been more than nine hours travelling twenty-five miles; and I must needs own that not all my *savoir faire* could prevent me from feeling rather dejected and shy, as I drove up to the residence of a gentleman, to whom, indeed, I had not a letter, but whose family, as I had been assured, were prepared to receive me. It was rather formidable to arrive thus, at fall of night, a wayfaring lonely woman, spiritless, half-dead with fatigue, among entire strangers; but my reception set me at ease in a moment. The words "We have been long expecting you!" uttered in a kind, cordial voice, sounded "like sweetest music to attending ears." A handsome, elegant-looking woman, blending French ease and politeness with English cordiality, and a whole brood of lively children of all sizes and ages stood beneath the porch to welcome me with smiles and outstretched hands. Can you imagine my bliss, my gratitude? – no! – impossible, unless you had travelled for three days through the wilds of Canada. In a few hours I felt quite at home, and my day of rest was insensibly prolonged to a week, spent with this amiable and interesting family – a week, ever while I live, to be remembered with pleasurable and grateful feelings.

The region of Canada in which I now find myself, is called the London District; you will see its situation at once by a glance on the map. It lies between the Gore District and the Western District, having to the south a large extent of the coast of Lake Erie; and on the north the Indian territories, and part of the southern shore of Lake Huron. It is watered by rivers flowing into both lakes, but chiefly by the river Thames, which is here (about one hundred miles from its mouth) a small but most beautiful stream, winding like the Isis at Oxford. Woodstock, the nearest *village*, as I suppose I must in modesty call it, is fast rising into an important town, and the whole district is, for its scenery, fertility, and advantages of every kind, perhaps the finest in Upper Canada.*

The society in this immediate neighbourhood is particularly good; several gentlemen of family, superior education, and large capital, (among whom is the brother of an English and the son of an Irish peer, a colonel and a major in the army,) have made very extensive purchases of land, and their estates are in flourishing progress.

One day we drove over to the settlement of one of these magnificos, Admiral V——, who has already expended upwards of twenty thousand pounds in purchases and improvements. His house is really a curiosity, and at the first glance reminded me of an African village – a sort of Timbuctoo set down in the woods; it is two or three miles from the high road, in the midst of the forest, and looked as if a number of log-huts had jostled against each other by accident, and there stuck fast.

The admiral had begun, I imagine, by erecting, as is usual, a log-house, while the woods were clearing; then, being in want of space, he added another, then another and another, and so on, all of different shapes and sizes, and full of a seaman's contrivances – odd galleries, passages, porticos, corridors, saloons, cabins and cupboards; so that if the outside reminded me of an African village, the interior was no less like that of a man-of-war.

The drawing-room, which occupies an entire building,

---

* The average produce of an acre of land is greater throughout Canada than in England; in these western districts greater than in the rest of Canada.

is really a noble room, with a chimney, in which they pile twenty oak logs at once. Around this room runs a gallery, well lighted with windows from without, through which there is a constant circulation of air, keeping the room warm in winter and cool in summer. The admiral has, besides, so many ingenious and inexplicable contrivances for warming and airing his house, that no insurance office will insure him upon any terms. Altogether it was the most strangely picturesque sort of dwelling I ever beheld, and could boast not only of luxuries and comforts, such as are seldom found so far inland, but "cosa altra più *cara*," or at least "più *rara*." The admiral's sister, an accomplished woman of independent fortune, has lately arrived from Europe, to take up her residence in the wilds. Having recently spent some years in Italy, she has brought out with her all those pretty objects of virtù, with which English travellers load themselves in that country. Here, ranged round the room, I found views of Rome and Naples; tazzi, and marbles, and sculpture in lava, or alabaster; miniature copies of the eternal Sibyl and Cenci, Raffaelle's Vatican, &c. – things not wonderful nor rare in themselves – the wonder was to see them here.

The woods are yet close up to the house; but there is a fine well-cultivated garden, and the process of clearing and log-burning proceeds all around with great animation.

The good admiral, who is no longer young – *au contraire* – has recently astonished the whole neighbourhood – nay, the whole province – by taking to himself a young, very young wife, of a station very inferior to his own. There have been considerable doubts in the neighbourhood as to the propriety of visiting the young lady – doubts which appear to me neither reasonable nor goodnatured, and which will, no doubt, give way before the common sense and kind feeling of the people. Selden might well say, that of all the actions of a man's life his marriage was that in which others had the least concern, and were sure to meddle the most! If this gentleman be unhappy, he has committed a folly, and will be punished for it sufficiently without the interference of his friends and neighbours. If he be happy, and they say he is, then he has committed no folly, and may laugh at them all round. His good sister has come out to countenance him and his ménage – a proof equally of her affection and her understanding. I can now only wish her a continuance of the same cheerfulness, fortitude, and perseverance she has hitherto shown – virtues very necessary in this new province.

On Sunday we attended the pretty little church at Woodstock, which was filled by the neighbouring settlers of all classes: the service was well read, and the hymns were sung by the ladies of the congregation. The sermon, which treated of some abstract and speculative point of theology, seemed to me not well adapted to the sort of congregation assembled. The situation of those who had here met together to seek a new existence in a new world, might have afforded topics of instruction, praise, and gratitude, far more practical, more congenial, more intelligible, than a mere controversial essay on a disputed text, which elicited no remark nor sympathy that I could perceive. After the service, the congregation remained some time assembled before the church-door, in various and interesting groups – the well-dressed families of settlers who had come from many miles' distance in vehicles well suited to the roads – that is to say, carts, or, as they call them here, teams or wagons; the belles and the beaux of "the Bush," in Sunday trim – and innumerable children. Many were the greetings and inquiries; the news and gossip of all the neighbourhood had to be exchanged. The conversation among the ladies was of marriages and births – lamentations on the want of servants, and the state of the roads – the last arrival of letters from England – and speculations upon the character of a new neighbour come to settle in the Bush: among the gentlemen, it was of crops and clearings, lumber, price of wheat, road-mending, deer-shooting, log-burning, and so forth –

subjects in which I felt a lively interest and curiosity; and if I could not take a very brilliant and prominent part in the discourse, I could at least listen, like the Irish corn-field, "with all my ears."

I think it was this day at dinner that a gentleman described to me a family of Mohawk Indians, consisting of seven individuals, who had encamped upon some of his uncleared land in two wigwams. They had made their first appearance in the early spring, and had since subsisted by hunting, selling their venison for whisky or tobacco; their appearance and situation were, he said, most wretched, and their indolence extreme. Within three months, five out of the seven were dead of consumption; two only were left – languid, squalid, helpless, hopeless, heartless.

A FTER SEVERAL pleasant and interesting visits to the neighbouring settlers, I took leave of my hospitable friends at Blandford with deep and real regret; and, in the best and only vehicle which could be procured – videlicet, a baker's cart – set out for London, the chief town of the district; the distance being about thirty miles – a long day's journey; the cost seven dollars.

The man who drove me proved a very intelligent and civilised person. He had come out to Canada in the capacity of a gentleman's servant; he now owned some land – I forget how many acres – and was besides baker-general for a large neighbourhood, rarely receiving money in pay, but wheat and other farm produce. He had served as constable of the district for two years, and gave me some interesting accounts of his thief-taking expeditions through the wild forests in the deep winter nights. He considered himself, on the whole, a prosperous man. He said he should be quite happy here, were it not for his wife, who fretted and pined continually after her "home."

"But," said I, "surely wherever you are is her *home*, and she ought to be happy where she sees you getting on better, and enjoying more of comfort and independence than you could have hoped to obtain in the old country."

"Well, yes," said he hesitatingly; "and I can't say but that my wife is a good woman: I've no particular fault to find with her; and it's very natural she should mope, for she has no friend or acquaintance, you see, and she doesn't take to the people and the ways here; and at home she had her mother and her sister to talk to; they lived with us, you see. Then, I'm out all day long, looking after my business, and she feels quite lonely like, and she's a crying when I come back – and I'm sure I don't know what to do!"

The case of this poor fellow with his discontented wife is of no unfrequent occurrence in Canada, and among the better class of settlers the matter is worse still, the suffering more acute, and of graver consequences.

I have not often in my life met with contented and cheerful-minded women, but I never met with so many repining and discontented women as in Canada. I never met with *one* woman recently settled here, who considered herself happy in her new home and country: I *heard* of one, and doubtless there are others, but they are exceptions to the general rule. Those born here, or brought here early by their parents and relations, seemed to me very happy, and many of them had adopted a sort of pride in their new country, which I liked much. There was always a great desire to visit England, and some little airs of self-complacency and superiority in those who had been there, though for a few months only; but all, without a single exception, returned with pleasure, unable to forego the early habitual influences of their native land.

I like patriotism and nationality in women. Among the German women both these feelings give a strong tincture to the character, and seldom disunited, they blend with peculiar grace in our sex; but with a great statesman they should stand well distinguished. Nationality is not always patriotism, and patriotism is not, necessarily, nationality. The English are more patriotic than national; the Americans generally more national than patriotic; the Germans both national and patriotic.

I have observed that really accomplished women, accustomed to what is called the best society, have more resources here, and manage better, than some women who have no pretensions of any kind, and whose claims to social distinction could not have been great anywhere, but whom I found lamenting over themselves, as if they had been so many exiled princesses.

Can you imagine the position of a fretful, frivolous woman, strong neither in mind nor frame, abandoned to her own resources in the wilds of Upper Canada? I do not believe you *can* imagine anything so pitiable, so ridiculous, and, to borrow the Canadian word, "so shiftless."

My new friend and kind hostess was a being of quite a different stamp, and though I believe she was far from thinking that she had found in Canada a terrestrial paradise, and the want of servants, and the difficulty of educating her family as she wished, were subjects of great annoyance to her, yet these and other evils she had met with a cheerful spirit. Here, amid these forest wilds, she had recently given birth to a lovely baby, the tenth, or indeed I believe the twelfth, of a flock of manly boys and blooming girls. Her eldest daughter meantime, a fair and elegant girl, was acquiring, at the age of fifteen, qualities and habits which might well make ample amends for the possession of mere accomplishments. She acted as manager in chief, and glided about in her household avocations with a serene and quiet grace which was quite charming.

The road, after leaving Woodstock, pursued the course of the winding Thames. We passed by the house of Colonel Light, in a situation of superlative natural beauty, on a rising-ground above the river. A lawn, tolerably cleared, sloped down to the margin, while the opposite shore rose clothed in varied woods which had been managed with great taste, and a feeling for the picturesque not common here; but the colonel being himself an accomplished artist accounts for this. We also passed Beechville, a small but beautiful village, round which the soil is reckoned very fine and fertile; a number of most respectable settlers have recently bought land and erected houses here. The next place we came to was Oxford, or rather Ingersol, where we stopped to dine and rest previous to plunging into an extensive forest, called the Pine Woods.

Oxford is a little village, presenting the usual saw-mill, grocery-store, and tavern, with a dozen shanties congregated on the bank of the stream, which is here rapid and confined by high banks. Two back-woodsmen were in deep consultation over a wagon which had broken down in the midst of that very forest road we were about to traverse, and which they described as most execrable – in some parts even dangerous. As it was necessary to gird up my strength for the undertaking, I laid in a good dinner, consisting of slices of dried venison, broiled; hot cakes of Indian corn, eggs, butter, and a bowl of milk. Of this good fare I partook in company with the two back-woodsmen, who appeared to me perfect specimens of their class – tall and strong, and bronzed and brawny, and shaggy and unshaven – very much like two bears set on their hind legs; rude but not uncivil, and spare of speech, as men who had lived long at a distance from their kind. They were too busy, however, and so was I, to feel or express any mutual curiosity; time was valuable, appetite urgent – so we discussed our venison steaks in silence, and after dinner I proceeded.

The forest land through which I had lately passed, was principally covered with *hard timber*, as oak, walnut, elm, basswood. We were now in a forest of pines, rising tall and dark, and monotonous on either side. The road, worse certainly "than fancy ever feigned or fear conceived," put my neck in perpetual jeopardy. The driver had often to dismount, and partly fill up some tremendous hole with boughs before we could pass – or drag or lift the wagon over trunks of trees – or we sometimes sank into abysses, from which it is a wonder to me that we *ever* emerged. A natural question were – why did you not get out and walk? – Yes indeed! I only wish it had been possible. Immediately on the border of the road so called was the wild, tangled, untrodden thicket, as impervious to the foot as the road was impassable, rich with vegetation, variegated verdure, and flowers of loveliest dye, but the haunt of the rattlesnake and all manner of creeping and living things not pleasant to encounter, or even to think of.

The mosquitoes, too, began to be troublesome; but not being yet in full force, I contrived to defend myself pretty well by waving a green branch before me whenever my two hands were not employed in forcible endeavours to keep my seat. These seven miles of pine forest we traversed in three hours and a half, and then succeeded some miles of open flat country, called the Oak Plains, and so called because covered with thickets and groups of oak, dispersed with a park-like and beautiful effect; and still flowers, flowers everywhere. The soil appeared sandy, and not so rich as in other parts.* The road was comparatively good, and as we approached London, clearings and new settlements appeared on every side.

The sun had set amid a tumultuous mass of lurid threatening clouds, and a tempest was brooding in the air, when I reached the town, and found very tolerable accommodations in the principal inn. I was so terribly bruised and beaten with fatigue, that to move was impossible, and even to speak, too great an effort. I cast my weary aching limbs upon the bed, and requested of the very civil and obliging young lady who attended, to bring me some books and newspapers. She brought me thereupon an old compendium of geography, published at Philadelphia forty years ago, and three newspapers. Two of these, the London Gazette and the Freeman's Journal, are printed and published within the district; the third, the New York Albion, I have already mentioned to you as having been my delight and consolation at Toronto. This paper, an

---

* It is not the most open land which is most desirable for a settler. "The land," says Dr. Dunlop in his admirable little book, "is rich and lasting, just in proportion to the size and quantity of the timber which it bears, and therefore the more trouble he is put to in clearing his land, the better will it repay him the labour he has expended on it."

extensive double folio, is compiled for the use of the British settlers in the United States, and also in Canada, where it is widely circulated. It contains all the interesting public news in extracts from the leading English journals, with tales, essays, reviews, &c., from the best periodicals. Think, now, if I had not reason to bless newspapers and civilisation! Imagine me alone in the very centre of this vast wild country, a storm raging without, as if heaven and earth had come in collision – lodged and cared for, reclining on a neat comfortable bed, and reading by the light of one tallow candle, (for there was a scarcity either of candles or of candlesticks,) Serjeant Talfourd's speech in the Commons for the alteration of the law of copyright, given at full length; and if I had been worse than "kilt entirely," his noble eulogy of Wordsworth, responded to by the cheers of the whole house, would have brought me to life; so did it make my very heart glow with approving sympathy.

In the same paper, and in the two provincial papers, I found whole columns extracted from Miss Martineau's long-expected book on America. What I now read, fulfilled the highest expectations I had previously formed. There will, of course, be diversity of opinion on many points; but one thing is clear, that she is a good woman, and a lover of truth for truth's sake; and that she has written in a good and womanly spirit, candid and kind; – stern sometimes, never sharp, never satirical. There is, in these passages at least, an even tone of good-nature and good temper – of high principle and high feeling of every kind, which has added to my admiration of her, and makes me long more than ever to see the book itself. There are things in it, apparently, which will not yet be appreciated – but all in good time.

With regard to the law of copyright, I see in another part of the paper that the publishers have taken the alarm, and are beginning to bestir themselves against it. We shall have them crying out like the French actresses, "C'est une chose étonnante qu'on ne trouve pas un moyen de se passer d'auteurs!" Perhaps the best thing at this moment for all parties would be an international law, which should protect both authors and publishers; for if they have no respect for the property which is the mere produce of the brain, perhaps they will respect and acknowledge the existence of property for which a man can prove he has paid hard money.

T HE NEXT morning the weather continued very lowering and stormy. I wrote out my little journal for you carefully thus far, and then I received several visiters, who, hearing of my arrival, had come with kind offers of hospitality and attention, such as are most grateful to a solitary stranger. I had also much conversation relative to the place and people, and the settlements around, and then I took a long walk about the town, of which I here give you the results.

When Governor Simcoe was planning the foundation of a capital for the whole province, he fixed at first upon the present site of London, struck by its many and obvious advantages. Its central position, in the midst of these great lakes, being at an equal distance from Huron, Erie, and Ontario, in the finest and most fertile district of the whole province, on the bank of a beautiful stream, and at a safe distance from the frontier, all pointed it out as the most eligible site for a metropolis; but there was the want of land and water communication – a want which still remains the only drawback to its rising prosperity. A canal or railroad, running from Toronto and Hamilton to London, then branching off on the right to the harbour of Goderich on Lake Huron, and to Sandwich on Lake Erie, were a glorious thing! – the one thing needful to make this fine country the granary and storehouse of the west; for here all grain, all fruits which flourish in the south of Europe, might be cultivated with success – the finest wheat and rice, and hemp and flax, and tobacco. Yet, in spite of this want, soon, I trust, to be supplied, the town of London has sprung up and become within ten years a place of great importance. In size and population it exceeds every town I have yet visited, except Toronto and Hamilton. The first house was erected in 1827; it now contains more than two hundred frame or brick houses, and there are many more building. The population may be about thirteen hundred people. The jail and court-house, comprised in one large and stately edifice, seemed the glory of the towns-people. As for the style of architecture, I may not attempt to name or describe it; but a gentleman informed me, in rather equivocal phrase, that it was "*somewhat gothic.*" There are five places of worship, for the Episcopalians, Presbyterians, Methodists, Roman Catholics, and Baptists. The church is handsome. There are also three or four schools, and seven taverns. The Thames is very beautiful here, and navigable for boats and barges. I saw to-day a large timber raft floating down the stream, containing many thousand feet of timber. On the whole, I have nowhere seen such evident signs of progress and prosperity.

The population consists principally of artisans – as blacksmiths, carpenters, builders, all flourishing. There is, I fear, a good deal of drunkenness and profligacy; for though the people have work and wealth, they have neither education nor amusements.* Besides the seven

---

* Hear Dr. Channing, the wise and the good: – "People," he says, "should be guarded against temptation to unlawful pleasures by furnishing the means of innocent ones. In every community there *must* be pleasures, relaxations, and means of agreeable excitement; and if innocent are not furnished, resort will be had to criminal. – Man was made to enjoy as well as to labour; and the state of society should be adapted to this principle of

taverns, there is a number of little grocery stores, which are, in fact, drinking-houses. And though a law exists which forbids the sale of spirituous liquors in small quantities by any but licensed publicans, they easily contrive to elude the law; as thus: – a customer enters the shop, and asks for two or three pennyworth of nuts, or cakes, and he receives a few nuts, and a large glass of whisky. The whisky, you observe, is given, not sold, and no one can swear to the contrary. In the same manner the severe law against selling intoxicating liquors to the poor Indians, is continually eluded or violated, and there is no redress for the injured, no punishment to reach the guilty. It appears to me that the government should be more careful in the choice of the district magistrates. While I was in London, a person who had acted in this capacity was carried from the pavement dead drunk.

Here, as everywhere else, I find the women of the better class lamenting over the want of all society, except of the lowest grade in manners and morals. For those who have recently emigrated, and are settled more in the interior, there is absolutely no social intercourse whatever; it is quite out of the question. They seem to me perishing of ennui, or from the want of sympathy which they cannot obtain, and, what is worse, which they cannot feel: for being in general unfitted for out-door occupations, unable to comprehend or enter into the interests around them, and all their earliest prejudices and ideas of the fitness of things continually outraged in a manner exceedingly unpleasant, they may be said to live in a perpetual state of inward passive discord and fretful endurance –

---

human nature." – "Men drink to excess very often to shake off depression, or to satisfy the restless thirst for agreeable excitement, and these motives are excluded in a cheerful community."

When I was in Upper Canada, I found no means whatever of social amusement for any class, except that which the tavern afforded: taverns consequently abounded everywhere.

"All too timid and reserved
For onset, for resistance too inert –
Too weak for suffering, and for hope too tame."

A gentleman well known to me by name, who was not a resident in London, but passing through it on his way from a far western settlement up by Lake Huron, was one of my morning visiters. He had been settled in the bush for five years, had a beautiful farm, well cleared, well stocked. He was pleased with his prospects, his existence, his occupations: all he wanted was a wife, and on this subject he poured forth a most eloquent appeal.

"Where," said he, "shall I find such a wife as I could, with a safe conscience, bring into these wilds, to share a settler's fate, a settler's home? You, who know your own sex so well, point me out such a one, or tell me at least where to seek her. I am perishing and deteriorating, head and heart, for want of a companion – a wife, in short. I am becoming as rude and coarse as my own labourers, and as hard as my own axe. If I wait five years longer, no woman will be able to endure such a fellow as I shall be by that time – no woman, I mean, whom I could marry – for in this lies my utter unreasonableness. Habituated to seek in woman those graces and refinements which I have always associated with her idea, I must have them here in the forest, or dispense with all female society whatever. With some one to sympathise with me – to talk to – to embellish the home I return to at night – such a life as I now lead, with all the cares and frivolities of a too artificial society cast behind us, security and plenty all around us, and nothing but hope before us, a life of 'cheerful yesterdays and confident to-morrows' – were it not delicious? I want for myself nothing more, nothing better; but – perhaps it is a weakness, an inconsistency! – I could not love a woman who was inferior to all my preconceived notions of feminine elegance and refinement – inferior to my own mother and sisters. You know I was in England two years ago; – well, I have a vision of a beautiful creature, with the figure of a sylph and the head of a sibyl, bending over her harp, and singing *A te, O cara*; and when I am logging in the woods with my men, I catch myself meditating on that vision, and humming *A te, O cara,* which somehow or other runs strangely in my head. Now, what is to be done? What could I do with that fair vision here? Without coxcombry may I not say, that I need not entirely despair of winning the affections of an amiable, elegant woman, and might even persuade her to confront, for my sake, worse than all this? For what will not your sex do and dare for the sake of us men creatures, savages that we are? But even for that reason shall I take advantage of such sentiments? You know what this life is – this isolated life in the bush – and so do I; but by what words could I make it comprehensible to a fine lady? Certainly I might draw such a picture of it as should delight by its novelty and romance, and deceive even while it does not deviate from the truth. A cottage in the wild woods – solitude and love – the world forgetting, by the world forgot – the deer come skipping by – the red Indian brings game, and lays it at her feet – how pretty and how romantic! And for the first few months, perhaps the first year, all goes well; but how goes it the next, and the next? I have observed with regard to the women who come out, that they do well enough the first year, and some even the second; but the third is generally fatal: and the worst with you women – or the best shall I not say? – is, that you cannot, and do not, forget domestic ties left behind. We men go out upon our land, or to the chase, and the women, poor souls, sit, and sew, and *think*. You have seen Mrs. A. and Mrs. B., who came out here, as I well remember, full of health and bloom – what are they now? premature old women, sickly, care-worn, without nerve or cheerfulness: – and as for C—— , who brought his wife to his place by Lake Simcoe only three years ago, I hear the poor fellow must sell all off, or see his wife perish before his eyes. Would you have me risk the alternative? Or perhaps you will say, marry one of the women of the country – one of the daughters *of the bush*. No, I cannot; I must have something different. I may not have been particularly fortunate, but the women I have seen are in general coarse and narrow-minded, with no education whatever, or with an education which apes all I most dislike, and omits all I could admire in the fashionable education of the old country. What could I do with such women? In the former I might find an upper servant, but no companion – in the other, neither companionship nor help!"

To this discontented and fastidious gentleman I ventured to recommend two or three very amiable girls I had known at Toronto and Niagara; and I told him, too, that among the beautiful and spirited girls of New England he might also find what would answer his purpose. But with regard to Englishwomen of that grade in station and education, and personal attraction, which would content him, I could not well speak; not because I knew of none who united grace of person and lively talents with capabilities of strong affection, ay, and sufficient energy of character to meet trials and endure privations; but in women, as now educated, there is a strength of local habits and attachments, a want of cheerful self-dependence, a cherished physical delicacy, a weakness of temperament, – deemed, and falsely deemed, in deference to the pride of man, essential to feminine grace and refinement, – altogether unfitting them for a life which were otherwise delightful: – the active out-of-door life in which she must share and sympathise, and the in-door occupations which in England are considered servile; for a woman who cannot perform for herself and others all household offices, has no business here. But when I hear some men declare that they cannot endure to see women eat, and others speak of brilliant health and strength in young girls as being rude and vulgar, with various notions of the same kind too grossly absurd and perverted even for ridicule, I cannot wonder at any nonsensical affectations I meet with in my own sex; nor do otherwise than pity the mistakes and deficiencies of those who are sagely brought up with the one end and aim – to get married. As you always used to say, "Let there be a demand for a better article, and a better article will be supplied."

A woman blessed with good health, a cheerful spirit, larger sympathies, larger capabilities of reflection and action, some knowledge of herself, her own nature, and the common lot of humanity, with a plain understanding, which has been allowed to throw itself out unwarped by sickly fancies and prejudices, – such a woman would be as happy in Canada as anywhere in the world. A weak, frivolous, half-educated, or ill-educated woman may be as miserable in the heart of London as in the heart of the forest. But there her deficiencies are not so injurious, and are supplied to herself and others by the circumstances and advantages around her.

I have heard (and seen) it laid down as a principle, that the purpose – one purpose at least – of education is to fit us for the circumstances in which we are likely to be placed. I deny it absolutely. Even if it could be exactly known (which it cannot) what those circumstances may be, I should still deny it. Education has a far higher object. I remember to have read of some Russian prince (was it not Potemkin?) who, when he travelled, was preceded by a gardener, who around his marquee scattered an artificial soil, and stuck into it shrubs and bouquets of flowers, which, while assiduously watered, looked pretty for twenty-four hours perhaps, then withered or were plucked up. What shallow barbarism to take pleasure in such a mockery of a garden! Better the wilderness, better the waste! that forest, that rock yonder, with creeping weeds around it! An education that is to fit us for circumstances, seems to me like that Russian garden. No; the true purpose of education is to cherish and unfold the seed of immortality already sown within us; to develope, to their fullest extent, the capacities of every kind with which the God who made us has endowed us. Then we shall be fitted for all circumstances, or know how to fit circumstances to ourselves. Fit us for circumstances! Base and mechanical!

Why not set up at once a "*fabrique d'education*," and educate us by steam? The human soul, be it man's or woman's, is not, I suppose, an empty bottle, into which you shall pour and cram just what you like, and as you like; nor a plot of waste soil, in which you shall sow what you like; but a divine, a living germ planted by an almighty hand, which you may indeed render more or less productive, or train to this or that form – no more. And when you have taken the oak sapling, and dwarfed it, and pruned it, and twisted it, into an ornament for the jardinière in your drawing-room, much have you gained truly; and a pretty figure your specimen is like to make in the broad plain, and under the free air of heaven!

THE PLAN of travel I had laid down for myself did not permit of my making any long stay in London. I was anxious to push on to the Talbot Settlement, or, as it is called here, the Talbot *Country* – a name not ill applied to a vast tract of land stretching from east to west along the shore of Lake Erie, and of which Colonel Talbot is the sovereign *de facto*, if not *de jure* – be it spoken without any derogation to the rights of our lord the king. This immense settlement, the circumstances to which it owed its existence, and the character of the eccentric man who founded it on such principles as have insured its success and prosperity, altogether inspired me with the strongest interest and curiosity.

To the residence of this "big chief," as an Indian styled him – a solitary mansion on a cliff above Lake Erie, where he lived alone in his glory – was I now bound, without exactly knowing what reception I was to meet there; for that was a point which the despotic habits and eccentricities of this hermit-lord of the forest rendered a little doubtful. The reports I had heard of his singular manners, of his being a sort of woman-hater, who had not for thirty years allowed a female to appear in his sight, I had partly discredited, yet enough remained to make me feel a little nervous. However, my resolution was taken, and the colonel had been apprised of my intended visit, though of his gracious acquiescence I was yet to learn; so, putting my trust in Providence as heretofore, I prepared to encounter the old buffalo in his lair.

From the master of the inn at London I hired a vehicle and a driver for eight dollars. The distance was about thirty miles; the road, as my Irish informant assured me, was quite "iligant!" but hilly, and so broken by the recent storms, that it was thought I could not reach my destination before nightfall, and I was advised to sleep at the little town of St. Thomas, about twelve or fifteen miles on this side of Port Talbot. However, I was resolute to try, and, with a pair of stout horses and a willing driver, did not despair. My conveyance from Blandford had been a baker's cart on springs; but springs were a luxury I was in future to dispense with. My present vehicle, the best to be procured, was a common cart, with straw at the bottom; in the midst a seat was suspended on straps, and furnished with a cushion, not of the softest. A board nailed across the front served for the driver, a quiet, demure-looking boy of fifteen or sixteen, with a round straw hat and a fustian jacket. Such was the elegant and appropriate equipage in which the "chancellor's lady," as they call me here, paid her first visit of state to the "great Colonel Talbot."

On leaving the town, we crossed the Thames on a wooden bridge, and turned to the south through a very beautiful valley, with cultivated farms and extensive clearings on every side. I was now in the Talbot country, and had the advantage of travelling on part of the road constructed under the colonel's direction, which, compared with those I had recently travelled, was better than tolerable. While we were slowly ascending an eminence, I took the opportunity of entering into some discourse with my driver, whose very demure and thoughtful though boyish face, and very brief but pithy and intelligent replies to some of my questions on the road, had excited my attention. Though perfectly civil, and remarkably self-possessed, he was not communicative or talkative; I had to pluck out the information blade by blade, as it were. And here you have my catechism, with question and response, word for word, as nearly as possible.

"Were you born in this country?"

"No; I'm from the old country."

"From what part of it?"

"From about Glasgow."

"What is your name?"

"Sholto —— ."

"Sholto! – that is rather an uncommon name, is it not?"

"I was called Sholto after a son of Lord Douglas. My father was Lord Douglas's gardener."

"How long have you been here?"

"I came over with my father about five years ago." (In 1832.)

"How came your father to emigrate?"

"My father was one of the commuted pensioners, as they call them.* He was an old soldier in the veteran battalion, and he sold his pension of fivepence a day for four years and a grant of land, and came out here. Many did the like."

"But if he was gardener to Lord Douglas, he could not have suffered from want?"

"Why, he was not a gardener *then;* he was a weaver; he worked hard enough for us. I remember often waking in the middle of the night, and seeing my father working still at his loom, as if he would never give over, while my mother and all of us were asleep."

"All of us! – how many of you?"

"There were six of us; but my eldest brother and myself could do something."

"And you all emigrated with your father?"

"Why, you see, at last he couldn't get no work, and trade was dull, and we were nigh starving. I remember I was always hungry then – always."

---

* Of the commuted pensioners, and their fate in Canada, more will be said hereafter.

"And you all came out?"

"All but my eldest brother. When we were on the way to the ship, he got frightened and turned back, and wouldn't come. My poor mother cried very much, and begged him hard. Now the last we hear of him is, that he is very badly off, and can't get no work at all."

"Is your father yet alive?"

"Yes, he has land up in Adelaide."

"Is your mother alive?"

"No; she died of the cholera, coming over. You see the cholera broke out in the ship, and fifty-three people died, one after t'other, and were thrown into the sea. My mother died, and they threw her into the sea. And then my little sister, only nine months old, died, because there was nobody to take care of her, and they threw *her* into the sea – poor little thing!"

"Was it not dreadful to see the people dying around you? Did you not feel frightened for yourself?"

"Well – I don't know – one got used to it – it was nothing but splash, splash, all day long – first one, then another. There was one Martin on board, I remember, with a wife and nine children – one of those as sold his pension: he had fought in Spain with the Duke of Wellington. Well, first his wife died, and they threw her into the sea; and then *he* died, and they threw *him* into the sea; and then the children, one after t'other, till only two were left alive; the eldest, a girl about thirteen, who had nursed them all, one after another, and seen them die – well, *she* died, and then there was only the little fellow left."

"And what became of him?"

"He went back, as I heard, in the same ship with the captain."

"And did you not think sometimes it might be your turn next?"

"No – I didn't; and then I was down with the fever."

"What do you mean by *the fever?*"

"Why, you see, I was looking at some fish that was going by the ship in shoals, as they call it. It was very pretty, and

I never saw anything like it, and I stood watching over the ship's side all day long. It poured rain, and I was wet through and through, and felt very cold, and I went into my berth and pulled the blanket round me, and fell asleep. After that I had the fever very bad. I didn't know when we landed at Quebec, and after that I didn't know where we were for five weeks, nor nothing."

I assured him that this was only a natural and necessary consequence of his own conduct, and took the opportunity to explain to him some of those simple laws by which he held both health and existence, to all which he listened with an intelligent look, and thanked me cordially, adding, –

"Then I wonder I didn't die! and it was a great mercy I didn't."

"I hope you will live to think so, and be thankful to Heaven. And so you were detained at Quebec?"

"Yes; my father had some money to receive of his pension, but what with my illness and the expense of living, it soon went; and then he sold his silver watch, and that brought us on to York – that's Toronto now. And then there was a schooner provided by government to take us on board, and we had rations provided, and that brought us on to Port Stanley, far below Port Talbot; and then they put us ashore, and we had to find our way, and pay our way, to Delaware, where our lot of land was; that cost eight dollars; and then we had nothing left – nothing at all. There were nine hundred emigrants encamped about Delaware, no better off than ourselves."

"What did you do then? Had you not to build a house?"

"No; the government built each family a house, that is to say, a log-hut, eighteen feet long, with a hole for the chimney; no glass in the windows, and empty of course; not a bit of furniture – not even a table or a chair."

"And how did you live?"

"Why, the first year, my father and us, we cleared a couple of acres, and sowed wheat enough for next year."

"But meantime you must have existed – and without food or money – ?"

"O, why we worked meantime on the roads, and got half a dollar a day and rations."

"It must have been rather a hard life?"

"*Hard!* yes, I believe it was; why, many of them couldn't stand it no ways. Some died; and then there were the poor children and the women – it was very bad for them. Some wouldn't sit down on their land at all; they lost all heart to see everywhere trees, and trees, and nothing beside. And then they didn't know nothing of farming – how should they, being soldiers by trade? There was one Jim Grey, of father's regiment – he didn't know how to handle his axe, but he could handle his gun well; so he went and shot deer, and sold them to the others; but one day we missed him, and he never came back; and we thought the bears had got him, or maybe he cleared off to Michigan – there's no knowing."

"And your father?"

"O, *he* stuck to his land, and he has now five acres cleared: and he's planted a bit of a garden, and he has two cows and a calf, and two pigs; and he's got his house comfortable – and stopped up the holes, and built himself a chimney."

"That's well; but why are you not with him?"

"O, he married again, and he's got two children, and I didn't like my stepmother, because she didn't use my sisters well, and so I came away."

"Where are your sisters now?"

"Both out at service, and they get good wages; one gets four, and the other gets five dollars a month. Then I've a brother younger than myself, and he's gone to work with a shoemaker at London. But the man drinks hard, like a great many here – and I'm afeard my brother will learn to drink, and that frets me; and he won't come away, though I could get him a good place any day – no want of places here, and good wages too."

"What wages do you receive?"

"Seven dollars a month and my board. Next month I shall have eight."

"I hope you put by some of your wages?"

"Why, I bought a yoke of steers for my father last fall, as cost me thirty dollars, but they won't be fit for ploughing these two years."

(I should inform you, perhaps, that a yoke of oxen fit for ploughing costs about eighty dollars.)

I pointed out to him the advantages of his present situation, compared with what might have been his fate in the old country; and urged him to avoid all temptations to drink, which he promised.

"You can read, I suppose?"

He hesitated, and looked down. "I can read in the Testament a little. I never had no other book. But this winter," looking up brightly, "I intend to give myself some schooling. A man who has reading and writing, and a pair of hands, and keeps sober, may make a fortune here – and so will I, with God's blessing!"

Here he gave his whip a very expressive flourish. We were now near the summit of a hill, which he called Bear Hill; the people, he said, gave it that name because of the number of bears which used to be found here. Nothing could exceed the beauty and variety of the timber trees, intermingled with most luxuriant underwood, and festooned with the wild grape and flowering creepers. It was some time, he said, since a bear had been shot in these woods; but only last spring one of his comrades had found a bear's cub, which he had fed and taken care of, and had sold within the last few weeks to a travelling menagerie of wild beasts for five dollars.

On reaching the summit of this hill, I found myself on the highest land I had yet stood upon in Canada, with the exception of Queenston heights. I stopped the horses and looked around, and on every side, far and near – east, west, north, and south, it was all forest – a boundless sea of forest, within whose leafy recesses lay hidden as infinite a variety of life and movement as within the depths of the ocean; and it reposed in the noontide so still and so vast! *Here* the bright sunshine rested on it in floods of golden light; *there* cloud-shadows sped over its bosom, just like the effects I remember to have seen on the Atlantic; and here and there rose wreaths of white smoke from the new clearings, which collected into little silver clouds, and hung suspended in the quiet air.

I gazed and meditated till, by a process like that of the Arabian sorcerer of old, the present fell like a film from my eyes: the future was before me, with its towns and cities, fields of waving grain, green lawns and villas, and churches and temples turret-crowned; and meadows tracked by the frequent footpath; and railroads, with trains of rich merchandise steaming along: – for all this *will* be! Will be? *It is* already in the sight of Him who hath ordained it, and for whom there is no past nor future: though I cannot behold it with my bodily vision, even *now* it is.

But is *that* NOW better than *this* present NOW? When these forests, with all their solemn depth of shade and multitudinous life, have fallen beneath the axe – when the wolf, and bear, and deer are driven from their native coverts, and all this infinitude of animal and vegetable being has made way for restless, erring, suffering humanity, – will it then be better? *Better* – I know not; but surely it will be *well* and right in His eyes who has ordained that thus the course of things shall run. Those who see nothing in civilised life but its complicated cares, mistakes, vanities, and miseries, may doubt this – or despair. For myself and you too, my friend, we are of those who believe and hope; who behold in progressive civilisation progressive happiness, progressive approximation to nature and to nature's God; for are we not in his hand? – and all that He does is good.

Contemplations such as these were in my mind as we descended the Hill of Bears, and proceeded through a beautiful plain, sometimes richly wooded, sometimes opening into clearings and cultivated farms, on which were usually compact farm-houses, each flanked by a barn three times as large as the house, till we came to a place called Five Stakes, where I found two or three tidy cottages, and procured some bread and milk. The road here was no longer so good, and we travelled slowly and with difficulty for some miles. About five o'clock we reached St. Thomas, one of the prettiest places I had yet seen. Here I found two or three inns, and at one of them, styled the "Mansion House Hotel," I ordered tea for myself and good entertainment for my young driver and his horses, and then walked out.

St. Thomas is situated on a high eminence, to which the ascent is rather abrupt. The view from it, over a fertile, well-settled country, is very beautiful and cheering. The place bears the christian name of Colonel Talbot, who styles it his capital, and, from a combination of advantages, it is rising fast into importance. The climate, from its high position, is delicious and healthful; and the winters in this part of the province are milder by several degrees than elsewhere. At the foot of the cliff or eminence runs a deep rapid stream, called the Kettle Creek,* (I wish they had given it a prettier name,) which, after a course of eight miles, and turning a variety of saw-mills, grist-mills, &c., flows into Lake Erie at Port Stanley, one of the best harbours on this side of the lake. Here steam-boats and schooners land passengers and merchandise, or load with grain, flour, lumber. The roads are good all round; and the Talbot road, carried directly through the town, is the finest in the province. This road runs nearly parallel with Lake Erie, from thirty miles below Port Stanley, westward as far as Delaware. The population of St. Thomas is at present rated at seven hundred, and it has doubled within two years. There are three churches, one of which is very neat;

---

* When I remonstrated against this name for so beautiful a stream, Colonel Talbot told me that his first settlers had found a kettle on the bank, left by some Indians, and had given the river, from this slight circumstance, a name which he had not thought it worth while to alter.

and three taverns. Two newspapers are published here, one violently tory, the other as violently radical. I found several houses building, and, in those I entered, a general air of cheerfulness and well-being very pleasing to contemplate. There is here an excellent manufacture of cabinet ware and furniture: some articles of the black walnut, a tree abounding here, appeared to me more beautiful in colour and grain than the finest mahogany; and the elegant veining of the maplewood cannot be surpassed. I wish they were sufficiently the fashion in England to make the transport worth while. Here I have seen whole piles, nay, whole forests of such trees, burning together.

I was very much struck with this beautiful and cheerful little town, more, I think, than with any place I have yet seen.

By the time my horses were refreshed, it was near seven o'clock. The distance from Port Talbot is about twelve miles, but hearing the road was good, I resolved to venture. The sky looked turbulent and stormy, but luckily the storm was moving one way while I was moving another; and, except a little sprinkling from the tail of a cloud, we escaped very well.

The road presented on either side a succession of farmhouses and well-cultivated farms. Near the houses there was generally a patch of ground planted with Indian corn and pumpkins, and sometimes a few cabbages and potatoes. I do not recollect to have seen one garden, or the least attempt to cultivate flowers.

The goodness of the road is owing to the systematic regulations of Colonel Talbot. Throughout the whole "country" none can obtain land without first applying to him, and the price and conditions are uniform and absolute. The lands are divided into lots of two hundred acres, and to each settler fifty acres are given gratis, and one hundred and fifty at three dollars an acre. Each settler must clear and sow ten acres of land, build a house, (a loghut of eighteen feet in length,) and construct one chain of road in front of his house, within three years; failing in this, he forfeits his deed.

Colonel Talbot does not like gentlemen settlers, nor will he have any settlements within a certain distance of his own domain. He never associates with the people except on one grand occasion, the anniversary of the foundation of his settlement. This is celebrated at St. Thomas by a festive meeting of the most respectable settlers, and the colonel himself opens the ball with one of the ladies, generally showing his taste by selecting the youngest and prettiest.

The evening now began to close in; night came on, with the stars and the fair young moon in her train. I felt much fatigued, and my young driver appeared to be out in his reckoning – that is, with regard to distance – for luckily he could not miss the *way*, there being but one. I stopped a man who was trudging along with an axe on his shoulder, "How far to Colonel Talbot's?" "About three miles and a half." This was encouraging; but a quarter of an hour afterwards, on asking the same question of another, he replied, "About seven miles." A third informed me that it was about three miles beyond Major Burwell's. The next person I met advised me to put up at "Waters's," and not think of going any farther to-night; however, on arriving at Mr. Waters's hotel, I was not particularly charmed with the prospect of a night's rest within its precincts. It was a long-shaped wooden house, comfortless in appearance; a number of men were drinking at the bar, and sounds of revelry issued from the open door. I requested my driver to proceed, which he did with all willingness.

We had travelled nearly the whole day through open well-cleared land, more densely peopled than any part of the province I had seen since I left the Niagara district. Suddenly we came upon a thick wood, through which the road ran due west, in a straight line. The shadows fell deeper and deeper from the depth of foliage on either side, and I could not see a yard around, but exactly before me the last gleams of twilight lingered where the moon was setting. Once or twice I was startled by seeing a deer bound across the path, his large antlers being for one instant defined, *pencilled*, as it were, against the sky, then lost. The darkness fell deeper every moment, the silence more solemn. The whip-poor-will began his melancholy cry, and an owl sent forth a prolonged shriek, which, if I had not heard it before, would have frightened me. After a while my driver stopped and listened, and I could plainly hear the tinkling of cow-bells. I thought this a good sign, till the boy reminded me that it was the custom of the settlers to turn their cattle loose in the summer to seek their own food, and that they often strayed miles from the clearing.

We were proceeding along our dark path very slowly, for fear of accidents, when I heard the approaching tread of a horse, and the welcome sound of a man whistling. The boy hailed him with some impatience in his voice, – "I say, mister! whereabouts *is* Colonel Talbot's?"

"The Colonel's? why, straight afore you; – follow your nose, you buzzard!"

Here I interposed. "Be so good, friend, as to inform me how far we are yet from Colonel Talbot's house."

"Who have you got here?" cried the man in surprise.

"A lady, comed over the sea to visit the Colonel."

"Then," said the man, approaching my carriage – my cart, I should say, – with much respect, "I guess you're the lady that the Colonel has been looking out for this week past. Why, I've been three times to St. Thomas's with the team after you!"

"I'm very sorry you've had that trouble."

"O no trouble at all – shall I ride back and tell him you're coming?"

This I declined, for the poor man was evidently going home to his supper.

To hear that the formidable Colonel was anxiously expecting me was very encouraging, and, from the man's description, I supposed that we were close to the house. Not so; the road, mocking my impatience, took so many bends, and sweeps, and windings, up hill and down hill, that it was an eternity before we arrived. The Colonel piques himself exceedingly on this graceful and picturesque approach to his residence, and not without reason; but on the present occasion I could have preferred a line more direct to the line of beauty. The darkness, which concealed its charms, left me sensible only to its length.

On ascending some high ground, a group of buildings was dimly descried; and after oversetting part of a snakefence before we found an entrance, we drove up to the door. Lights were gleaming in the windows, and the Colonel sallied forth with prompt gallantry to receive me.

My welcome was not only cordial, but courtly. The Colonel, taking me under his arm, and ordering the boy and his horses to be well taken care of, handed me into the hall or vestibule, where sacks of wheat and piles of sheepskins lay heaped in primitive fashion; thence into a room, the walls of which were formed of naked logs. Here no fauteuil, spring-cushioned, extended its comfortable arms – no sofa here "insidiously stretched out its lazy length;" Colonel Talbot held all such luxuries in sovereign contempt. In front of a capacious chimney stood a long wooden table, flanked with two wooden chairs, cut from the forest in the midst of which they now stood. To one of these the Colonel handed me with the air of a courtier, and took the other himself. Like all men who live out of the world, he retained a lively curiosity as to what was passing in it, and I was pressed with a profusion of questions as well as hospitable attentions; but wearied, exhausted, aching in every nerve, the spirit with which I had at first met him in his own style was fast ebbing. I could neither speak nor eat, and was soon dismissed to repose.

With courteous solicitude he ushered me himself to the door of a comfortable, well furnished bed room, where a fire blazed cheerfully, where female hands had evidently presided to arrange my toilet, and where female aid awaited me; – so much had the good Colonel been calumniated!

—— You shall
Go forth upon your arduous task alone,
None shall assist you, none partake your toil,
None share your triumph! still you must retain
Some one to trust your glory to – to share
Your rapture with.

PARACELSUS.

Port Talbot, July 10.

"MAN IS, properly speaking, based upon hope. He has no other possession but hope. This world of his is emphatically the place of hope:"* and more emphatically than of any other spot on the face of the globe it is true of this new world of ours, in which I am now a traveller and a sojourner. This is the land of hope, of faith, ay, and of charity, for a man who hath not all three had better not come here; with them he may, by strength of his own right hand and trusting heart, achieve miracles: witness Colonel Talbot.

Of the four days in which I have gone wandering and wondering up and down, let me now tell you something – *all* I cannot tell you; for the information I have gained,

---

* Vide Sartor Resartus.

and the reflections and feelings which have passed through
my mind would fill a volume – and I have little time for
scribbling.

And first of Colonel Talbot himself. This remarkable
man is now about sixty-five, perhaps more, but he does
not look so much. In spite of his rustic dress, his good-
humoured, jovial, weather-beaten face, and the primitive
simplicity, not to say rudeness, of his dwelling, he has in
his features, air, and deportment, that *something* which
stamps him gentleman. And that *something* which thirty-
four years of solitude has not effaced, he derives, I suppose, from blood and birth – things of more consequence,
when philosophically and philanthropically considered,
than we are apt to allow. He must have been very handsome when young; his resemblance now to our royal family, particularly to the King, (William the Fourth,) is so
very striking as to be something next to identity. Good-
natured people have set themselves to account for this
wonderful likeness in various ways, possible and impossible; but after a rigid comparison of dates and ages, and
assuming all that latitude which scandal usually allows
herself in these matters, it remains unaccountable, unless
we suppose that the Talbots have, *par la grâce de Dieu*, a
family knack at resembling kings. You may remember
that the extraordinary resemblance which his ancestor
Dick Talbot (Duke of Tyrconnel) bore to Louis the Four-
teenth, gave occasion to the happiest and most memorable repartee ever recorded in the chronicle of wit.*

Colonel Talbot came out to Upper Canada as aide-de-
camp to Governor Simcoe in 1793, and accompanied the
governor on the first expedition he made to survey the

---

* As it is just possible that the reader may not have met with this
anecdote, it is here repeated – perhaps for the thousandth time.

When Richard Talbot was sent ambassador to France, the king, struck
by that likeness to himself which had excited the attention of his courtiers,
addressed him on some occasion, "M. l'Ambassadeur, est-ce que madame
votre mère a jamais été dans la cour du Roi mon père?" Talbot replied
with a low bow, "Non, sire – mais mon père y était!"

western district, in search (as it was said) of an eligible site
for the new capital he was then projecting. At this time the
whole of the beautiful and fertile region situated between
the lakes was a vast wilderness. It contained not one white
settler, except along the borders, and on the coast opposite
to Detroit: a few wandering tribes of Hurons and Chippewas, and the Six Nations settled on Grand River, were
its only inhabitants.

It was then that the idea of founding a colony took
possession of Colonel Talbot's mind, and became the rul-
ing passion and sole interest of his future life. For this
singular project, wise people have set themselves to
account much in the same manner as for his likeness to
William the Fourth. That a man of noble birth, high in
the army, young and handsome, and eminently qualified
to shine in society, should voluntarily banish himself from
all intercourse with the civilised world, and submit, not
for a temporary frolic, but for long tedious years, to the
most horrible privations of every kind, appeared too
incomprehensible to be attributed to any of the ordinary
motives and feelings of a reasonable human being; so they
charitably set it down to motives and feelings very
extraordinary indeed, – and then "they looked the lie they
dared not speak." Others went no farther than to insinu-
ate or assert that early in life he had met with a disappointment in love, which had turned his brain. I had
always heard and read of him as the "eccentric" Colonel
Talbot. Of his eccentricity I heard much more than of his
benevolence, his invincible courage, his enthusiasm, his
perseverance; but perhaps, according to the worldly
nomenclature, these qualities come under the general
head of "eccentricity," when devotion to a favourite object
cannot possibly be referred to self-interest.

On his return to England, he asked and obtained a grant
of 100,000 acres of land along the shores of Lake Erie, on
condition of placing a settler on every two hundred acres.
He came out again in 1802, and took possession of his
domain, in the heart of the wilderness. Of the life he led

for the first sixteen years, and the difficulties and obstacles he encountered, he drew, in his discourse with me, a strong, I might say a *terrible* picture: and observe that it was not a life of wild wandering freedom – the life of an Indian hunter, which is said to be so fascinating that "no man who has ever followed it for any length of time, *ever* voluntarily returns to civilised society!"* Colonel Talbot's life has been one of persevering, heroic self-devotion to the completion of a magnificent plan, laid down in the first instance, and followed up with unflinching tenacity of purpose. For sixteen years he saw scarce a human being, except the few boors and blacks employed in clearing and logging his land: he himself assumed the blanket-coat and axe, slept upon the bare earth, cooked three meals a day for twenty woodsmen, cleaned his own boots, washed his own linen, milked his cows, churned the butter, and made and baked the bread. In this latter branch of household economy he became very expert, and still piques himself on it.

To all these heterogeneous functions of sowing and reaping, felling and planting, frying, boiling, washing, wringing, brewing, and baking, he added another even more extraordinary; – for many years he solemnised all the marriages in his district!

While Europe was converted into a vast battlefield, an arena

> "Where distract ambition compassed
> And was encompass'd,"

and his brothers in arms, the young men who had begun the career of life with him, were reaping bloody laurels, to be gazetted in the list of killed and wounded, as heroes – then forgotten; – Colonel Talbot, a true hero after another fashion, was encountering, amid the forest solitude, uncheered by sympathy, unbribed by fame, enemies far

* Dr. Dunlop.

more formidable, and earning a far purer as well as a more real and lasting immortality.

Besides natural obstacles, he met with others far more trying to his temper and patience. His continual quarrels with the successive governors, who were jealous of the independent power he exercised in his own territory, are humorously alluded to by Dr. Dunlop.

"After fifteen years of unremitting labour and privation," says the Doctor, "it became so notorious in the province, that even the executive government at Toronto became aware that there was such a place as the Talbot Settlement, where roads were cut and farms in progress; and hereupon they rejoiced, for it held out to them just what they had long felt the want of – a well-settled, opened, and cultivated country, wherein to obtain estates for themselves, their children, born and unborn, and their whole kith, kin, and allies. When this idea, so creditable to the paternal feelings of these worthy gentlemen, was intimated to the Colonel, he could not be brought to see the fitness of things in an arrangement which would confer on the next generation, or the next again, the fruits of the labour of the present; and accordingly, though his answer to the proposal was not couched in terms quite so diplomatic as might have been wished, it was brief, soldier-like, and not easily capable of misconstruction; it was in these words – 'I'll be be d–d if you get one foot of land here;' and thereupon the parties joined issue."

"On this, war was declared against him by his Excellency in council, and every means were used to annoy him here, and misrepresent his proceedings at home; but he stood firm, and by an occasional visit to the colonial office in England, he opened the eyes of ministers to the proceedings of both parties, and for a while averted the danger. At length, some five years ago, finding the enemy was getting too strong for him, he repaired once more to England, and returned in triumph with an order from the Colonial Office, that nobody was in any way to interfere with his proceedings; and he has now the pleasure of contemplating some hundreds of miles of the best roads in the province, closely settled on each side by the most prosperous farmers within its bounds, who owe all they possess to his judgment, enthusiasm, and perseverance, and who are grateful to him in proportion to the benefits he has bestowed upon them, though in many instances sorely against their will at the time."

The original grant must have been much extended, for the territory now under Colonel Talbot's management, and bearing the general name of the Talbot Country, contains, according to the list I have in his own handwriting, twenty-eight townships, and about 650,000 acres of land, of which 98,700 are cleared and cultivated. The inhabitants, including the population of the towns, amount to about 50,000. "You see," said he gaily, "I may boast, like the Irishman in the farce, of having peopled a whole country with my own hands."

He has built his house, like the eagle his eyry, on a bold high cliff overhanging the lake. On the east there is a precipitous descent into a wild woody ravine, along the bottom of which winds a gentle stream, till it steals into the lake: this stream is in winter a raging torrent. The storms and the gradual action of the waves have detached large portions of the cliff in front of the house, and with them huge trees. Along the lake-shore I found trunks and roots of trees half buried in the sand, or half overflowed with water, which I often mistook for rocks. I remember one large tree, which, in falling headlong, still remained suspended by its long and strong fibres to the cliff above; its position was now reversed – the top hung downwards, shivered and denuded: the large spread root, upturned, formed a platform, on which new earth had accumulated, and a new vegetation sprung forth, of flowers, and bushes, and sucklings. Altogether it was a most picturesque and curious object.

Lake Erie, as the geography book says, is two hundred and eighty miles long, and here, at Port Talbot, which is near the centre, about seventy miles across. The Colonel tells me that it has been more than once frozen over from side to side, but I do not see how this fact could be ascertained, as no one has been known to cross to the opposite shore on the ice. It is true that more ice accumulates in this lake than in any other of the great lakes, by reason of its shallowness; it can be sounded through its whole extent, while the other lakes are found in some parts unfathomable.

But to return to the château: It is a long wooden building, chiefly of rough logs, with a covered porch running along the south side. Here I found suspended, among sundry implements of husbandry, one of those ferocious animals of the feline kind, called here the cat-a-mountain, and by some the American tiger, or panther, which it more resembles. This one, which had been killed in its attack on the fold or poultry-yard, was at least four feet in length, and glared on me from the rafters above, ghastly and horrible. The interior of the house contains several comfortable lodging-rooms; and one really handsome one, the dining-room. There is a large kitchen with a tremendously hospitable chimney, and underground are cellars for storing wine, milk, and provisions. Around the house stands a vast variety of out-buildings, of all imaginable shapes and sizes, and disposed without the slightest regard to order or symmetry. One of these is the very log-hut which the Colonel erected for shelter when he first "sat down in the bush," four-and-thirty years ago, and which he is naturally unwilling to remove. Many of these outbuildings are to shelter the geese and poultry, of which he rears an innumerable quantity. Beyond these is the cliff, looking over the wide blue lake, on which I have counted six schooners at a time with their white sails; on the left is Port Stanley. Behind the house lies an open tract of land, prettily broken and varied, where large flocks of sheep and cattle were feeding – the whole enclosed by beautiful and luxuriant woods, through which runs the little creek or river above mentioned.

The farm consists of six hundred acres: but as the Colonel is not quite so active as he used to be, and does not employ a bailiff or overseer, the management is said to be slovenly, and not so productive as it might be.

He has sixteen acres of orchard-ground, in which he has planted and reared with success all the common European fruits, as apples, pears, plums, cherries, in abundance; but what delighted me beyond everything else, was a garden of more than two acres, very neatly laid out and enclosed, and in which he evidently took exceeding pride and pleasure; it was the first thing he showed me after my arrival. It abounds in roses of different kinds, the cuttings of which he had brought himself from England in the few visits he had made there. Of these he gathered the most beautiful buds, and presented them to me with such an air as might have become Dick Talbot presenting a bouquet to Miss Jennings.* We then sat down on a pretty seat under a tree, where he told me he often came to meditate. He described the appearance of the spot when he first came here, as contrasted with its present appearance, or we discussed the exploits of some of his celebrated and gallant ancestors, with whom my acquaintance was (luckily) almost as intimate as his own. Family and aristocratic pride I found a prominent feature in the character of this remarkable man. A Talbot of Malahide, of a family representing the same barony from father to son for six hundred years, he set, not unreasonably, a high value on his noble and unstained lineage; and, in his lonely position, the simplicity of his life and manners lent to these lofty and not unreal pretensions a kind of poetical dignity.

I told him of the surmises of the people relative to his early life and his motives for emigrating, at which he laughed.

"Charlevoix," said he, "was, I believe, the true cause of

---

* Dick Talbot married Frances Jennings – la belle Jennings of De Grammont's Memoirs, and elder sister of the celebrated Duchess of Marlborough.

my coming to this place. You know he calls this the 'Paradise of the Hurons.' Now I was resolved to get to paradise by hook or by crook, and so I came here."

He added more seriously, "I have accomplished what I resolved to do – it is done. But I would not, if any one was to offer me the universe, go through again the *horrors* I have undergone in forming this settlement. But do not imagine I repent it; I like my retirement."

He then broke out against the follies and falsehoods and restrictions of artificial life, in bitter and scornful terms; no ascetic monk or *radical* philosopher could have been more eloquently indignant.

I said it was granted to few to live a life of such complete retirement, and at the same time such general utility; in flying from the world he had benefited it: and I added, that I was glad to see him so happy.

"Why, yes, I'm very happy here" – and then the old man sighed.

I understood that sigh, and in my heart echoed it. No, "it is not good for man to be alone;" and this law, which the Father of all life pronounced himself at man's creation, was never yet violated with impunity. Never yet was the human being withdrawn from, or elevated above, the social wants and sympathies of his human nature, without paying a tremendous price for such isolated independence.

With all my admiration for what this extraordinary man has achieved, and the means, the powers, through which he has achieved it, there mingles a feeling of commiseration, which has more than once brought the tears to my eyes while listening to him. He has passed his life in worse than solitude. He will admit no equal in his vicinity. His only intercourse has been with inferiors and dependents, whose servility he despised, and whose resistance enraged him – men whose interests rested on his favour – on his will, from which there was no appeal. Hence despotic habits, and contempt even for those whom he benefited: hence, with much natural benevolence and generosity, a total disregard, or rather total ignorance, of the feelings of others; – all the disadvantages, in short, of royalty, only on a smaller scale. Now, in his old age, where is to him the solace of age? He has honour, power, obedience; but where are the love, the troops of friends, which also should accompany old age? He is alone – a lonely man. His constitution has suffered by the dreadful toils and privations of his earlier life. His sympathies have had no natural outlet, his affections have wanted their natural food. He suffers, I think; and not being given to general or philosophical reasoning, causes and effects are felt, not known. But he is a great man who has done great things, and the good which he has done will live after him. He has planted, at a terrible sacrifice, an enduring name and fame, and will be commemorated in this "brave new world," this land of hope, as Triptolemus among the Greeks.

For his indifference or dislike to female society, and his determination to have no settler within a certain distance of his own residence, I could easily account when I knew the man; both seemed to me the natural result of certain habits of life acting upon a certain organisation. He has a favourite servant, Jeffrey by name, who has served him faithfully for more than five-and-twenty years, ever since he left off cleaning his own shoes and mending his own coat. This honest fellow, not having forsworn female companionship, began to sigh after a wife –

> "A wife! ah! Saint Marie Benedicité,
>   How might a man have any adversité
>   That hath a wife?"

And, like the good knight in Chaucer, he did

> "Upon his bare knees pray God him to send
>   A wife to last unto his life's end."

So one morning he went and took unto himself the woman nearest at hand – one, of whom we must needs suppose that he chose her for her virtues, for most certainly it was not for her attractions. The Colonel swore at him for a fool; but, after a while, Jeffrey, who is a favourite, smuggled his wife into the house; and the Colonel, whose increasing age renders him rather more dependent on household help, seems to endure very patiently this addition to his family, and even the presence of a white-headed chubby little thing, which I found running about without let or hindrance.

The room into which I first introduced you, with its rough log-walls, is Colonel Talbot's library and hall of audience. On leaving my apartment in the morning, I used to find groups of strange figures lounging round the door, ragged, black-bearded, gaunt, travel-worn and toil-worn emigrants, Irish, Scotch, and American, come to offer themselves as settlers. These he used to call his land-pirates; and curious, and characteristic, and dramatic beyond description, were the scenes which used to take place between this grand bashaw of the wilderness and his hungry, importunate clients and petitioners.

Another thing which gave a singular interest to my conversations with Colonel Talbot, was the sort of indifference with which he regarded all the stirring events of the last thirty years. Dynasties rose and disappeared; kingdoms were passed from hand to hand like wine decanters; battles were lost and won; – he neither knew, nor heard, nor cared. No post, no newspaper brought to his forest-hut the tidings of victory and defeat, of revolutions of empires, "or rumours of unsuccessful and successful war."

When he first took to the bush, Napoleon was consul; when he emerged from his solitude, the tremendous game of ambition had been played out, and Napoleon and his deeds and his dynasty were numbered with the things o'erpast. With the stream of events had flowed by equally unmarked the stream of mind, thought, literature – the progress of social improvement – the changes in public opinion. Conceive what a gulf between us! but though I

could go to him, he could not come to me – my sympathies had the wider range of the two.

The principal foreign and domestic events of his *reign*
are the last American war, in which he narrowly escaped
being taken prisoner by a detachment of the enemy, who
ransacked his house, and drove off his horses and cattle;
and a visit which he received some years ago from three
young Englishmen of rank and fortune, Lord Stanley, Mr.
Stuart Wortley, and Mr. Labouchere, who spent some
weeks with him. These events, and his voyages to
England, seemed to be the epochs from which he dated.
His last trip to England was about three years ago. From
these occasional flights he returns like an old eagle to his
perch on the cliff, whence he looks down upon the world
he has quitted with supreme contempt and indifference,
and around on what which he has created, with much self-
applause and self-gratulation.

"Alles was Du siehst und so wie Du's siehst, – was Dir das Liebste, das Schrecklichste, das Peinlichste, das Heimlichste, das Verführerischeste ist, das kehre hervor – "

RAHEL.

IT WAS not till the sixth day of my sojourn at Port Talbot that the good colonel could be persuaded to allow of my departure.

He told me, with good-humoured peremptoriness, that he was the grand autocrat of the forest, and that to presume to order horses, or take any step towards departing, without his express permission, was against "his laws." At last he was so good as to issue his commands – with flattering reluctance, however – that a vehicle should be prepared, and a trusty guide provided; and I bade farewell to this extraordinary man with a mixture of delighted, and grateful, and melancholy feelings not easily to be described, nor ever forgotten.

My next journey was from Port Talbot to Chatham on the river Thames, whence it was my intention to cross Lake St. Clair to Detroit, and there take my chance of a vessel going up Lake Huron to Michillinachinac. I should, however, advise any future traveller, not limited to any particular time or plan of observation, to take the road along the shore of the Lake to Amherstberg and Sandwich, instead of turning off to Chatham. During the first day's journey I was promised a good road, as it lay through the Talbot settlements; what was to become of me the second day seemed a very doubtful matter.

The best vehicle which the hospitality and influence of Colonel Talbot could provide was a farmer's cart, or team, with two stout horses. The bottom of the cart was well filled with clean soft straw, on which my luggage was deposited. A seat was slung for me on straps, and another in front for the driver, who had been selected from among the most respectable settlers in the neighbourhood as a fit guide and protector for a lone woman. The charge for the two days' journey was to be twelve dollars.

As soon as I had a little recovered from the many thoughts and feelings which came over me as we drove down the path from Colonel Talbot's house, I turned to take a survey of my driver, and from his physiognomy, his deportment, and the tone of his voice, to divine, if I could, what chance I had of comfort during the next two days. The survey was on the whole encouraging, though presenting some inconsistencies I could by no means reconcile. His dress and figure were remarkably neat, though plain and homely; his broad-brimmed straw hat, encircled with a green ribbon, was pulled over his brow, and from beneath it peered two sparkling, intelligent eyes. His accent was decidedly Irish. It was indeed a brogue as "nate and complate" as ever was sent forth from Cork or Kerry; but then his face was not an Irish face; its expression had nothing of the Irish character; the cut of his features and his manner and figure altogether in no respect harmonised with his voice and accent.

After proceeding about three miles, we stopped in front of a neat farmhouse, surrounded with a garden and spacious outbuildings, and forth came a very pretty and modest-looking young woman, with a lovely child in her arms, and leading another by the hand. It was the wife of my driver; and I must confess she did not seem well pleased to have him taken away from her. They evidently parted with reluctance. She gave him many special charges to take care of himself, and commissions to execute by the way. The children were then held up to be kissed heartily by their father, and we drove off. This little family scene interested me, and augured well, I thought, for my own chances of comfort and protection.

When we had jogged and jolted on at a reasonable pace for some time, and I had felt my way sufficiently, I began to make some inquiries into the position and circumstances of my companion. The first few words explained those discrepancies in his features, voice, and appearance, which had struck me.

His grandfather was a Frenchman. His father had married an Irishwoman, and settled in consequence in the south of Ireland. He became, after some changes of fortune, a grazier and cattle-dealer; and having realised a small capital which could not be safely or easily invested in the old country, he had brought out his whole family, and settled his sons on farms in this neighbourhood. Many of the first settlers about this place, generally emigrants of the poorest and lowest description, after clearing a certain portion of the land, gladly disposed of their farms at an advanced price; and thus it is that a considerable improvement has taken place within these few years by the introduction of settlers of a higher grade, who have purchased half-cleared farms, rather than waste toil and time on the wild land.

My new friend, John B——, had a farm of one hundred and sixty acres, for which, with a log-house and barn upon it, he had paid 800 dollars, (about 200*l.*); he has now one hundred acres of land cleared and laid down in pasture. This is the first instance I have met with in these parts of a grazing farm, the land being almost uniformly arable, and the staple produce of the country, wheat. He told me that he and his brother had applied most advantageously their knowledge of the management and rearing of live stock; he had now thirty cows and eighty sheep. His wife being clever in the dairy, he was enabled to sell a good deal of butter and cheese off his farm, which the neighbourhood of Port Stanley enabled him to ship with advantage. The wolves, he said, were his greatest annoyance; during the last winter they had carried off eight of his sheep and thirteen of his brother's flock, in spite of all their precautions.

The Canadian wolf is about the size of a mastiff, in colour of a dirty yellowish brown, with a black stripe along his back, and a bushy tail of about a foot in length. His habits are those of the European wolf; they are equally bold, "hungry, and gaunt, and grim," equally destructive, ferocious, and troublesome to the farmer. The Canadian wolves hunt in packs, and their perpetual howling during the winter nights has often been described to me as frightful. The reward given by the magistracy for their destruction (six dollars for each wolf's head) is not enough. In the United States the reward is fifteen and twenty dollars a head, and from their new settlements the wolves are quickly extirpated. *Here*, if they would extend the reward to the Indians, it would be of some advantage; for at present they never think it worth while to expend their powder and shot on an animal whose flesh is uneatable, and the skin of little value; and there can be no doubt that it is the interest of the settlers to get rid of the wolves by all and any means. I have never heard of their destroying a man, but they are the terror of the sheepfold – as the wild cats are of the poultry yard. Bears become scarcer in proportion as the country is cleared, but there are still a great number in the vast tracts of forest land which afford them shelter. These, in the severe winters, advance to the borders of the settlements, and carry off the pigs and young cattle. Deer still abound, and venison is common food in the cottages and farmhouses.

My guide concluded his account of himself by an eloquent and heartfelt eulogium on his wife, to whom, as he assured me, "he owed all his *peace of mind* from the hour he was married!" Few men, I thought, could say the same.

She, at least, is not to be numbered among the drooping and repining women of Upper Canada; but then she has left no family – no home on the other side of the Atlantic – all her near relations are settled here in the neighbourhood.

The road continued very tolerable during the greater part of this day, running due west, at a distance of about six or ten miles from the shore of Lake Erie. On either side I met a constant succession of farms partially cleared, and in cultivation, but no village, town, or hamlet. One part of the country through which I passed to-day is settled chiefly by Highlanders, who bring hither all their clannish attachments, and their thrifty, dirty habits – add also their pride and their honesty. We stopped about noon at one of these Highland settlements, to rest the horses and procure refreshments. The house was called Campbell's Inn, and consisted of a log-hut and a cattle-shed. A long pole, stuck into the decayed stump of a tree in front of the hut, served for a sign. The family spoke nothing but Gaelic; a brood of children, ragged, dirty and without shoes or stockings, (which latter I found hanging against the wall of the best room, as if for a show,) were running about – and all stared upon me with a sort of half-scared, uncouth curiosity, which was quite savage. With some difficulty I made my wants understood, and procured some milk and Indian corn cakes. This family, notwithstanding their wretched appearance, might be considered prosperous. They have a property of two hundred acres of excellent land, of which sixty acres are cleared, and in cultivation: five cows and forty sheep. They have been settled here sixteen years, – had come out destitute, and obtained their land gratis. For them, what a change from abject poverty and want to independence and plenty! But the advantages are all outward; if there be any inward change, it is apparently retrogradation, not advancement.

I know it has been laid down as a principle, that the more and the closer men are congregated together, the more prevalent is vice of every kind; and that an isolated or scattered population is favourable to virtue and simplicity. It may be so, if you are satisfied with negative virtues and the simplicity of ignorance. But here, where a small population is scattered over a wide extent of fruitful country, where there is not a village or a hamlet for twenty or thirty or forty miles together – where there are no manufactories – where there is almost entire equality of condition – where the means of subsistence are abundant – where there is no landed aristocracy – no poor laws, nor poor rates, to grind the souls and the substance of the people between them, till nothing remains but chaff, – to what shall we attribute the gross vices, the profligacy, the stupidity, and basely vulgar habits of a great part of the people, who know not even how to enjoy or to turn to profit the inestimable advantages around them? – And, alas for them! there seems to be no one as yet to take an interest about them, or at least infuse a new spirit into the next generation. In one log-hut in the very heart of the wilderness, where I might well have expected primitive manners and simplicity, I found vulgar finery, vanity, affectation, under the most absurd and disgusting forms, combined with a want of the commonest physical comforts of life, and the total absence of even elementary knowledge. In another I have seen drunkenness, profligacy, stolid indifference to all religion; and in another, the most senseless fanaticism. There are people, I know, who think – who fear, that the advancement of knowledge and civilisation must be the increase of vice and insubordination; who deem that a scattered agricultural population, where there is a sufficiency of daily food for the body; where no schoolmaster interferes to infuse ambition and discontent into the abject, self-satisfied mind; where the labourer reads not, writes not, thinks not – only loves, hates, prays, and toils – that such a state must be a sort of Arcadia. Let them come here! – there is no march of intellect here! – there is no "schoolmaster abroad" here! And what are the consequences? Not the most agreeable to contemplate, believe me.

I passed in these journeys some school-houses built by the wayside: of these several were shut up for want of schoolmasters; and who that could earn a subsistence in any other way, would be a schoolmaster in the wilds of Upper Canada? Ill fed, ill clothed, ill paid, or not paid at all – boarded at the houses of the different farmers in turn, I found indeed some few men, poor creatures! always either Scotch or Americans, and totally unfit for the office they had undertaken. Of female teachers I found none whatever, except in the towns. Among all the excellent societies in London for the advancement of religion and education, are there none to send missionaries here? – such missionaries as we want, be it understood – not sectarian fanatics. Here, without means of instruction, of social amusement, of healthy and innocent excitements – can we wonder that whisky and camp-meetings assume their place, and "season toil" which is unseasoned by anything better?

Nothing, believe me, that you may have heard or read of the frantic disorders of these Methodist love-feasts and camp-meetings in Upper Canada can exceed the truth; and yet it is no less a truth that the Methodists are in most parts the only religious teachers, and that without them the people were utterly abandoned. What then are our church and our government about?* Here, as in the old country, they are quarrelling about the tenets to be inculcated, the means to be used: and so, while the shepherds are disputing whether the sheep are to be fed on old hay or fresh grass – out of the fold or in the fold – the poor sheep starve, or go astray.

---

* "When we consider the prevalent want of missionary spirit in that branch of the Church of England which has been transplanted to this colony, we doubt whether its members will not be regarded rather as novices in their religion, mistrustful of their qualifications to become the instructors of the ignorant; or, which is worse, *in the light of men half persuaded themselves, and therefore hesitating to attempt the conversion of others*." – Vide Report of the Church Society for converting and civilising the Indians, and propagating the gospel among destitute settlers.

This night I met with a bed and supper at the house of Mrs. Wheatly, the widow of an officer in the commissariat. She keeps the post-office of the Howard township. She told me, as a proof of the increasing population of the district, that the receipts of the post-office, which six years ago had been below ten dollars a quarter, now exceed forty dollars.

The poor emigrants who have not been long from the old country, round whose hearts tender remembrances of parents, and home, and home friends, yet cling in all the strength of fresh regret and unsubdued longing, sometimes present themselves at the post-offices, and on finding that their letters cost three shillings and four pence, or perhaps five or six shillings, turn away in despair. I have seen such letters not here only, but often and in greater numbers at the larger post-offices,* and have thought with pain how many fond, longing hearts must have bled over them. The torture of Tantalus was surely nothing to this.

I supped here on eggs and radishes, and milk and bread. On going to my room, (Mrs. Wheatly had given me up her own,) I found that the door, which had merely a latch, opened into the road. I expressed a wish to fasten it, on which the good lady brought a long nail, and thrust it lengthways over the latch, saying, "That's the way we lock doors in Canada!" The want of a more secure defence did not trouble my rest, for I slept well till morning. After breakfast, my guide, who had found what he called "a

---

* At Brandtford I saw forty-eight such letters, and an advertisement from the postmaster, setting forth that these letters, if not claimed and paid for by such a time, would be sent to the dead-letter office.

The management of the post-office in Upper Canada will be found among the "grievances" enumerated by the discontented party; and without meaning to attach any blame to the functionaries, I have said enough to show that the letter-post of Canada does not fulfil its purpose of contributing to the solace and advantage of the people, whatever profit it may bring to the revenue.

shake-down" at a neighbouring farm, made his appearance, and we proceeded.

For the first five or six miles the road continued good, but at length we reached a point where we had to diverge from the Talbot road, and turn into what they call a "town line," a road dividing the Howard from the Harwich township. My companion stopped the team to speak to a young man who was mixing lime, and as he stood talking to us, I thought I had never seen a better figure and countenance: his accent was Irish; his language and manner infinitely superior to his dress, which was that of a common workman. I soon understood that he was a member of one of the richest and most respectable families in the whole district, connected by marriage with my driver, who had been boasting to me of their station, education, and various attainments. There were many and kind greetings and inquiries after wives, sisters, brothers, and children. Towards the conclusion of this family conference, the following dialogue ensued.

"I say, how are the roads before us?"

"Pretty bad!" (with an ominous shake of the head.)

"Would we get on at all, do you think?"

"Well, I don't know but you may."

"If only we a'n't *mired down* in that big hole up by Harris's, plaze God, we'll do finely! Have they done anything up there?"

"No, I don't know that they have; but (with a glance and a good-humoured smile at me) don't be frightened! you have a good stout team there. I dare say you'll get along – first or last!"

"How are the mosquitos?"

"Pretty bad too; it is cloudy, and then they are always worse; but there is some wind, and that's in your favour again. However, you've a long and a hard day's work, and I wish you well through it; if you cannot manage, come back to *us* – that's all! Good-bye!" And lifting the gay handkerchief knotted round his head, he bowed us off with the air of a nobleman.

Thus encouraged, we proceeded; and though I was not *mired down*, nor yet absolutely eaten up, I suffered from both the threatened plagues, and that most severely. The road was scarcely passable; there were no longer cheerful farms and clearings, but the dark pine forest, and the rank swamp, crossed by those terrific corduroy paths, (my bones ache at the mere recollection!) and deep holes and pools of rotted vegetable matter, mixed with water, black, bottomless sloughs of despond! The very horses paused on the brink of some of these mud-gulfs, and trembled ere they made the plunge downwards. I set my teeth, screwed myself to my seat, and commended myself to Heaven—but I was well nigh dislocated! At length I abandoned my seat altogether, and made an attempt to recline on the straw at the bottom of the cart, disposing my cloaks, carpet bags, and pillow, so as to afford some support – but all in vain; myself and all my well-contrived edifice of comfort were pitched hither and thither, and I expected at every moment to be thrown over headlong; while to walk, or to escape by any means from my disagreeable situation, was as impossible as if I had been in a ship's cabin in the midst of a rolling sea.

But the worst was yet to come. At the entrance of a road through the woods,

> If road that might be called where road was none
> Distinguishable,

we stopped a short time to gain breath and courage, and refresh the poor horses before plunging into a forest of about twenty miles in extent.

The inn – the only one within a circuit of more than five-and-thirty miles, presented the usual aspect of these forest inns; that is, a rude log-hut, with one window and one room, answering all purposes, a lodging or sleeping place being divided off at one end by a few planks; outside, a shed of bark and boughs for the horses, and a hollow trunk of a tree disposed as a trough. Some of the trees around it were in full and luxuriant foliage; others, which had been girdled, stood bare and ghastly in the sunshine. To understand the full force of the scripture phrase, "desolate as a lodge in a wilderness," you should come here! The inmates, from whom I could not obtain a direct or intelligible answer to any question, continued during the whole time to stare upon me with stupid wonder. I took out a card to make a sketch of the place. A man stood near me, looking on, whose appearance was revolting beyond description – hideous, haggard, and worn, sinewy, and fierce, and squalid. He led in one hand a wild-looking urchin of three or four years old; in the other he was crushing a beautiful young pigeon, which panted and struggled within his bony grasp in agony and terror. I looked on it, pitying.

"Don't hurt it!"

He replied with a grin, and giving the wretched bird another squeeze, "No, no, I won't hurt it."

"Do you live here?"

"Yes, I have a farm hard by – in the bush here."

"How large is it?"

"One hundred and forty acres."

"How much cleared?"

"Five or six acres – thereabout."

"How long have you been on it?"

"Five years."

"And only five acres cleared? That is very little in five years. I have seen people who had cleared twice that quantity of land in half the time."

He replied, almost with fierceness, "Then they had money, or friends, or hands to help them; I have neither. I have in this wide world only myself! and set a man with only a pair of hands at one of them big trees there! – see what he'll make of it! You may swing the axe here from morning to night for a week before you let the daylight in upon you."

"You are right!" I said, in compassion and self-reproach, "and I was wrong! pray excuse me!"

"No offence."

"Are you from the old country?"

"No, I was *raised* here."

"What will you do with your pigeon there?"

"O, it will do for the boy's supper, or may be he may like it best to play with."

I offered to redeem its life at the price of a shilling, which I held out. He stretched forth immediately one of his huge hands and eagerly clutched the shilling, at the same moment opening the other, and releasing his captive; it fluttered for a moment helplessly, but soon recovering its wings, wheeled round our heads, and then settled in the topmost boughs of a sugar-maple. The man turned away with an exulting laugh, thinking, no doubt, that he had the best of the bargain – but upon this point we differed.

Turning the horses' heads again westward, we plunged at once into the deep forest, where there was absolutely no road, no path, except that which is called a *blazed* path, where the trees marked on either side are the only direction to the traveller. How savagely, how solemnly wild it was! So thick was the overhanging foliage, that it not only shut out the sunshine, but almost the daylight; and we travelled on through a perpetual gloom of vaulted boughs and intermingled shade. There were no flowers here – no herbage. The earth beneath us was a black, rich vegetable mould, into which the cart-wheels sank a foot deep; a rank, reedy grass grew round the roots of the trees, and sheltered rattlesnakes and reptiles. The timber was all hard timber, walnut, beech, and bass-wood, and oak and maple of most luxuriant growth; here and there the lightning had struck and shivered one of the loftiest of these trees, riving the great trunk in two, and flinging it horizontally upon its companions. There it lay, in strangely picturesque fashion, clasping with its huge boughs their outstretched arms as if for support. Those which had been hewn to open a path lay where they fell, and over their stumps and roots the cart had to be lifted or dragged. Sometimes a swamp or morass lay in our road, partly filled up or laid over with trunks of fallen trees, by way of bridge.

As we neared the limits of the forest, some new clearings broke in upon the solemn twilight monotony of our path: the aspect of these was almost uniform, presenting an opening of felled trees of about an acre or two; the commencement of a log-house; a patch of ground surrounded by a snake-fence, enclosing the first crop of wheat, and perhaps a little Indian corn; great heaps of timber-trees and brushwood laid together and burning; a couple of oxen, dragging along another enormous trunk to add to the pile. These were the general features of the picture, framed in, as it were, by the dark mysterious woods. Here and there I saw a few cows, but no sheep. I remember particularly one of these clearings, which looked more desolate than the rest; there was an unfinished log-house, only one half roofed in and habitable, and this presented some attempt at taste, having a small rustic porch or portico, and the windows on either side framed. No ground was fenced in, and the newly-felled timber lay piled in heaps ready to burn; around lay the forest, its shadows darkening, deepening as the day declined. But what rivetted my attention was the light figure of a female, arrayed in a silk gown and a handsome shawl, who was pacing up and down in front of the house, with a slow step and pensive air. She had an infant lying on her arm, and in the other hand she waved a green bough, to keep off the mosquitos. I wished to stop – to speak, though at the hazard of appearing impertinent; but my driver represented so strongly the danger of being benighted within the verge of the forest, that I reluctantly suffered him to proceed,

"And oft look'd back upon that vision fair,
  And wondering ask'd, whence and how came it there?"

At length we emerged from the forest-path into a plain, through which ran a beautiful river (my old acquaintance the Thames,) "winding at his own sweet will," and farmhouses with white walls and green shutters were scattered along its banks, and cheerful voices were heard, shouts of boys at play, sounds of labour and of life; and over all lay the last glow of the sinking sun. How I blessed the whole scene in my heart! Yes, I can well conceive what the exulting and joyous life of the hunter may be, roaming at large and independent through these boundless forests; but, believe me, that to be dragged along in a heavy cart through their impervious shades, tormented by mosquitos, shut in on every side from the light and from the free air of heaven, is quite another thing; and its effect upon me, at least, was to bring down the tone of the mind and reflections to a gloomy, inert, vague resignation, or rather dejection, which made it difficult at last to speak. The first view of the beautiful little town of Chatham made my sinking spirits bound like the sight of a friend. There was, besides, the hope of a good inn; for my driver had cheered me on during the last few miles by a description of "Freeman's Hotel," which he said was one of the best in the whole district. Judge then of my disappointment to learn that Mr. Freeman, in consequence of the "high price of wheat," could no longer afford to take in hungry travellers, and had "no accommodation." I was driven to take refuge in a miserable little place, where I fared as ill as possible. I was shown to a bedroom without chair or table; but I was too utterly beaten down by fatigue and dejection, too sore in body and spirit, to remonstrate, or even to stir hand or foot. Wrapping my cloak round me, I flung myself on the bed, and was soon in a state of forgetfulness of all discomforts and miseries. Next morning I rose refreshed and able to bestir myself; and by dint of bribing, and bawling, and scolding, and cajoling, I at length procured plenty of hot and cold water, and then a good breakfast of eggs, tea, and corn-cakes; – and then I set forth to reconnoitre.

So westward tow'r'd the unviolated woods
I bent my way –
But that pure archetype of human greatness
I found him not. There in his stead appeared
A creature squalid, vengeful, and impure,
Remorseless, and submissive to no law,
But superstitious fear or abject sloth.

WORDSWORTH.

At Chatham, in the Western District, and on board the steam-boat, between Chatham and Detroit. July 12, 13.

I CAN hardly imagine a more beautiful or more fortunate position for a new city than this of Chatham; (you will find it on the map just upon that neck of land between Lake St. Clair and Lake Erie.) It is sufficiently inland to be safe, or easily secured against the sudden attacks of a foreign enemy; the river Thames is navigable from the mouth up to the town, a distance of sixteen miles, for all kinds of lake craft, including steamers and schooners of the largest class. Lake St. Clair, into which the Thames discharges itself, is between Lake Erie and Lake Huron;

the banks are formed of extensive prairies of exhaustless fertility, where thousands of cattle might roam and feed at will. As a port and depôt for commerce, its position and capabilities can hardly be surpassed, while as an agricultural country it may be said literally to flow with milk and honey. A rich soil, abundant pasture, no rent, no taxes – what here is wanting but more intelligence and a better employment of capital to prevent the people from sinking into brutified laziness, and stimulate to something like mental activity and improvement? The profuse gifts of nature are here running to waste, while hundreds and thousands in the old country are trampling over each other in the eager, hungry conflict for daily food.

This land of Upper Canada is in truth the very paradise of hope. In spite of all I see and hear, which might well move to censure, to regret, to pity, – how much there is in which the trustful spirit may reasonably rejoice! It would be possible, looking at things under one aspect, to draw such a picture of the mistakes of the government, the corruption of its petty agents, the social backwardness and moral destitution of the people, as would shock you, and tempt you to regard Canada as a place of exile for convicts. On the other hand, I could, without deviating from the sober and literal truth, give you such vivid pictures of the beauty and fertility of this land of the west, of its glorious capabilities for agriculture and commerce, of the goodness and kindliness and resources of poor, much-abused human nature, as developed amid all the crushing influences of oppression, ignorance, and prejudice; and of the gratitude and self-complacency of those who have exchanged want, servitude, and hopeless toil at home, for plenty and independence and liberty here, – as would transport you in fancy into an earthly elysium. Thus, as I travel on, I am disgusted, or I am enchanted; I despair or I exult by turns; and these inconsistent and apparently contradictory emotions and impressions I set down as they arise, leaving you to reconcile them as well as you can, and make out the result for yourself.

It is seldom that in this country the mind is ever carried backward by associations or recollections of any kind. Horace Walpole said of Italy, that it was "a land in which the memory saw more than the eye," and in Canada hope must play the part of memory. It is all the difference between seed-time and harvest. We are rich in anticipation, but poor in possession – more poor in memorials. Some vague and general traditions, of no interest whatever to the ignorant settlers, do indeed exist, of horrid conflicts between the Hurons and the Iroquois, all along these shores, in the time and before the time of the French dominion; of the enterprise and daring of the early fur traders; above all, of the unrequited labours and sacrifices of the missionaries, whether Jesuits or Moravians, or Methodists, some of whom perished in tortures; others devoted themselves to the most horrible privations – each for what he believed to be the cause of truth, and for the diffusion of the light of salvation; none near to applaud the fortitude with which they died, or to gain hope and courage from their example. During the last war between Great Britain and the United States* – that war, in its commencement dishonourable to the Americans, in its conclusion shameful to the British, and in its progress disgraceful and demoralising to both; – that war, which began and was continued in the worst passions of our nature, cupidity and vengeance; – which brought no advantage to any one human being – not even the foolish noise and empty glory which wait oftentimes on human conflicts; a war scarce heard of in Europe, even by the mother country, who paid its cost in millions, and in the blood of some of her best subjects; a war obscure, fratricidal, and barbarous, which has left behind no effect but a mutual exasperation and distress along the frontiers of both nations; and a hatred which, like hatred between near kinsmen, is more bitter and irreconcilable than any

* In 1813.

hostility between the mercenary armies of rival nations; for here, not only the two governments quarrelled – but the people, their institutions, feelings, opinions, prejudices, local and personal interests, were brought into collision; – during this vile, profitless, and unnatural war, a battle was fought near Chatham, called by some the battle of the Thames, and by others the battle of the Moravian towns, in which the Americans, under General Harrison, beat General Proctor with considerable loss. But it is chiefly worthy of notice, as the last scene of the life of Técumseh, a Shawanee chief, of whom it is possible you may not have heard, but who is the historical hero of these wild regions. Some American writers call him the "Indian Napoleon;" both began their plans of policy and conquest about the same time, and both about the same time terminated their career, the one by captivity, the other by death. But the genius of the Indian warrior and his exploits were limited to a narrow field along the confines of civilisation, and their record is necessarily imperfect. It is clear that he had entertained the daring and really magnificent plan formerly embraced by Pontiac – that of uniting all the Indian tribes and nations in a league against the whites. That he became the ally of the British was not from friendship to us, but hatred to the Americans, whom it was his first object to repel from any further encroachments on the rights and territories of the Red men – in vain! These attempts of a noble and a fated race, to oppose, or even to delay for a time, the rolling westward of the great tide of civilisation, are like efforts to dam up the rapids of Niagara. The moral world has its laws, fixed as those of physical nature. The hunter must make way before the agriculturist, and the Indian must learn to take the bit between his teeth, and set his hand to the ploughshare, or *perish*. As yet I am inclined to think that the idea of the Indians becoming what *we* call a civilised people seems quite hopeless; those who entertain such benevolent anticipations should come here, and behold the effect which three centuries of contact with the whites have produced on the nature and habits of the Indian. The benevolent theorists in England should come and see with their own eyes that there is a bar to the civilisation of the Indians, and the increase or even preservation of their numbers, which no power can overleap. Their own principle, that "the Great Spirit did indeed create both the red man and the white man, but created them essentially different in nature and manners," is not perhaps far from the truth.

There is a large settlement of Moravian Indians located above Chatham, on the river Thames. They are a tribe of Delawares, and have been for a number of years congregated under the care of Moravian Missionaries, and living on the lands reserved for them by the British government; a fertile and beautiful region, comprehending about one hundred thousand acres of the richest soil of the province. Part of this district has been purchased from them by the present Lieutenant-governor; a measure for which he has been severely censured, for the tribe were by no means unanimous in consenting to part with their possessions. About one hundred and fifty refused to agree, but they were in the minority, and twenty-five thousand acres of rich land have been ceded to the government, and are already lotted out in townships.*

The Moravian missionary from whom I had these particulars, seemed an honest, commonplace man, pious, conscientious, but very simple, and very ignorant on every subject but that of his mission. He told me further, that the Moravians had resided among these Delawares from generation to generation, since the first establishment of the mission in the Southern States, in 1735; from that period to 1772, seven hundred and twenty Indians

---

* The terms are 150*l.* a year for ever – a sum which the governor truly calls "trifling." The "for ever" is like to be of short duration, for the tribe will soon be lost beyond the Missouri, or extinct, or amalgamated: these pensions also are seldom paid in dollars, but in goods, on which there is always a profit.

had been baptized. The War of the Revolution, in all its results, had fallen heavily on them; they had been driven northwards from one settlement to another, from the banks of the Delaware to that of the Ohio – from the Ohio beyond the lakes – and now they were driven from this last refuge. His assistant, Brother Vogler, was about to emigrate west with the one hundred and fifty families who objected to the sale of their lands. They were going to join a remnant of their nation beyond the Missouri, and he added that he himself would probably soon follow with the rest, for he did not expect that they would be able to retain the residue of their lands; no doubt they would be required for the use of the white settlers, and if government urged on the purchase, they had no means of resisting. He admitted that only a small portion of the tribe under his care and tuition could be called Christians; there were about two hundred and thirty baptized out of seven hundred, principally women and children, and yet the mission has been established and supported for more than a century. Their only chance, he said, was with the children; and on my putting the question to him in a direct form, he replied decidedly, that he considered the civilisation and conversion of the Indians, *to any great extent*, a hopeless task.

He admitted the reasonableness and the truth of those motives and facts, which had induced the Lieutenant-governor to purchase so large a portion of the Delaware hunting-grounds: that they lay in the midst of the white settlements, and were continually exposed to the illegal encroachments as well as the contagious example of the whites: that numbers of the tribe were half-cast – that nearly the whole were in a frightful state of degeneration, addicted to the use of ardent spirits, which they found it easy to procure; and, from the gradual diminution of the wild animals, and their own depravity and indolence, miserably poor and wretched; and that such was the diminution of their numbers from year to year, there seemed no hope for them but in removing them as far as possible from the influence of the whites. All this he allowed, and it certainly excuses the Governor, if you consider only the expediency and the benevolence, independent of the justice, of the measure.

God forbid that I should attempt to make light of the zeal and the labours of the missionaries in this land. *They* only stand between the Indian and his oppressors, and by their generous self-devotion in some measure atone for the injuries and soften the mischiefs which have been inflicted by their countrymen and fellow Christians; but while speaking with this worthy, simple-minded man, I could not help wishing that he had united more knowledge and judgment with his conscientious piety – more ability with good-will – more discretion with faith and zeal. The spirit was willing, but it was weak. The ignorance and intolerance of some of these enthusiastic, well-meaning men, have done as much injury to the good cause for which they suffered and preached, as their devotion and self-sacrifices have done honour to the same cause and to human nature. Take, for instance, the following scene, as described with great naïveté by one of these very Moravians. After a conference with some of the Delaware chief men, in which they were informed that the missionaries had come to teach them a better and purer religion, of which the one fundamental principle, leading to eternal salvation, was belief in the Redeemer, and atonement through his blood for the sins of all mankind – all which was contained in the book which he held in his hand, – "Wangoman, a great chief and medicine-man among them, rose to reply. He began by tracing two lines on the ground, and endeavoured to explain that there were two ways which led alike to God and to happiness, the way of the Red man, and the way of the White man, but the way of the Red man, he said, was the straighter and the shorter of the two."

The missionary here interposed, and represented that God himself had descended on earth to teach men the *true* way. Wangoman declared that "he had been intimately acquainted with God for many years, and had never heard that God became a man and shed his blood, and therefore the God of whom Brother Zeisberger preached could not be the true God, or he, Wangoman, would have been made acquainted with the circumstance."

The missionary then declared, "in the power of the spirit, that the God in whom Wangoman and his Indians believed was no other than the devil, the father of lies." Wangoman replied in a very moderate tone, "I cannot understand your doctrine; it is quite new and strange to me. If it be true," he added, "that the Great Spirit came down into the world, became a man and suffered so much, I assure you the Indians are not in fault, but the white men alone. God has given us the beasts of the forest for food, and our employment is to hunt them. We know nothing of your book – we cannot learn it; it is much too difficult for an Indian to comprehend."

Brother Zeisberger replied, "I will tell you the reason of it. Satan is the prince of darkness: where he reigns all is dark, and he dwells in you – therefore you can comprehend nothing of God and his word; but when you return from the evil of your ways, and come as a wretched lost sinner to Jesus Christ, it may be that he will have mercy upon you. Do not delay therefore; make haste and save your poor souls!" &c.*

I forbear to repeat the rest, because it would seem as if I intended to turn it into ridicule, which Heaven knows I do not; for it is of far too serious import. But if it be in this style that the simple and sublime precepts of Christianity are first presented to the understanding of the Indians, can we wonder at the little progress hitherto made in converting them to the truth? And with regard to all attempts to civilise them, what should the red man see in the civilisation of the white man which should move him to envy or

* History of the Missions of the United Brethren among the Indians of North America, translated from the German.

emulation, or raise in his mind a wish to exchange his "own unshackled life and his innate capacities of soul," for our artificial social habits, our morals, which are contradicted by our opinions, and our religion, which is violated both in our laws and our lives? When the good missionary said, with emphasis, that there was no hope for the conversion of the Indians but in removing them as far as possible from all intercourse with Europeans, he spoke a terrible truth, confirmed by all I see and hear – by the opinion of every one I have spoken to, who has ever had any intercourse with these people. It will be said, as it has often been said, that *here* it is the selfishness of the white man which speaks; that it is for his interest, and for his worldly advantage, that the red man should be removed out of his way, and be thrust back from the extending limits of civilisation – even like these forests, which fall before us, and vanish from the earth, leaving for a while some decaying stumps and roots over which the plough goes in time, and no vestige remains to say that here they *have been*. True; it *is* for the advantage of the European agriculturist or artisan, that the hunter of the woods, who requires the range of many hundred square miles of land for the adequate support of a single family, should make way for populous towns, and fields teeming with the means of subsistence for thousands. There is no denying this; and if there be those who think that in the present state of things the interests of the red man and the white man can ever be blended, and their natures and habits brought to harmonise, then I repeat, let them come here, and behold and see the heathen and the so-called Christian placed in near neighbourhood and comparison, and judge what are the chances for both! Wherever the Christian comes, he brings the Bible in one hand, disease, corruption, and the accursed fire-water, in the other; or flinging down the book of peace, he boldly and openly proclaims that might gives right, and substitutes the sabre and the rifle for the slower desolation of starvation and whisky.

Every means hitherto provided by the Canadian government for the protection of the Indians against the whites has failed. Every prohibition of the use or sale of ardent spirits among them has proved a mere mockery. The refuse of the white population along the back settlements have no perception of the genuine virtues of the Indian character. They see only their inferiority in the commonest arts of life; their subjection to our power; they contemn them, oppress them, cheat them, corrupt their women, and deprave them by the means and example of drunkenness. The missionaries alone have occasionally succeeded in averting or alleviating these evils, at least in some degree; but their influence is very, very limited. The chiefs and warriors of the different tribes are perfectly aware of the monstrous evils introduced by the use of ardent spirits. They have held councils, and made resolutions for themselves and their people to abstain from their use; but the very first temptation generally oversets all these good resolves. My Moravian friend described this intense passion for intoxicating liquors with a sort of awe and affright, and attributed it to the direct agency of the devil. Another missionary relates that soon after the Delaware Indians had agreed among themselves to reject every temptation of the kind, and punish those who yielded to it, a white dealer in rum came among them, and placing himself in the midst of one of their villages, with a barrel of spirits beside him, he introduced a straw into it, and with many professions of civility and friendship to his Indian friends, he invited every one to come and take a suck through the straw *gratis*. A young Indian approached with a grave and pensive air and slow step, but suddenly turning round, he ran off precipitately as one terrified. Soon after he returned, he approached yet nearer, but again ran off in the same manner as before. The third time he suffered himself to be persuaded by the white man to put his lips to the straw. No sooner had he tasted of the fiery drink, than he offered all his wampum for a dram;

and subsequently parted with everything he possessed, even his rifle and his blanket, for more.

I have another illustrative anecdote for you, which I found among a number of documents, submitted to the society established at Toronto, for converting and civilising the Indians. There can be no doubt of its truth, and it is very graphically told. The narrator is a travelling schoolmaster, who has since been taken into the service of the society, but whose name I have forgotten.

"In the winter of 1832, I was led, partly by business and partly by the novelty of the enterprise, to walk from the Indian Establishment of Coldwater, to the Sault Ste. Marie, a distance of nearly four hundred miles.

"The lake was well frozen, and the ice moderately covered with snow; with the assistance of snow-shoes, we were enabled to travel a distance of fifty miles in a day; but my business not requiring any expedition, I was tempted to linger among the thousand isles of Lake Huron. I hoped to ascertain some facts with regard to the real mode of life of the Indians frequenting the north side of the lake. With this view, I made a point of visiting every wigwam that we approached, and could, if it were my present purpose, detail many interesting pictures of extreme misery and destitution. Hunger, filth, and ignorance, with an entire absence of all knowledge of a Supreme Being, here reign triumphant.*

"Near the close of a long and fatiguing day, my Indian guide came on the recent track of a single Indian, and, anxious to please me, pursued it to the head of a very deep bay. We passed two of those holes in the ice which the Indians use for fishing, and at one of them noticed, from

---

* We should perhaps read, "An entire absence of all knowledge of a Supreme Being, as revealed to us in the gospel of Christ;" for I never heard of any tribe of north-west Indians, however barbarous, who had not the notion of a God, (the Great Spirit,) and of a future life.

the quantity of blood on the snow, that the spear had lately done considerable execution. At a very short distance from the shore, the track led up past the remains of a wigwam, adjoining to which we observed a large canoe and a small hunting canoe, both carefully laid up for the winter. After a considerable ascent, a narrow winding path brought us into a deep hollow, about four hundred yards from the bay. Here, surrounded on every side by hills, on the margin of one of the smallest inland lakes, we came to a wigwam, the smoke from which showed us that it was occupied. The path for a considerable distance was lined on both sides by billets of firewood, and a blanket cleaner than usual, suspended before the entrance, gave me at the very first a favourable opinion of the inmates. I noticed on the right hand a dog-train, and on the left, two pair of snow-shoes, and two barrels of salt-fish. The wigwam was of the square form, and so large, that I was surprised to find it occupied by two Indians only – a young man and his wife.

"We were soon made welcome, and I had leisure to look round me in admiration of the comfort displayed in the arrangement of the interior. A covering of fresh branches of the young hemlock-pine was neatly spread all round. In the centre of the right hand side, as we entered, the master of the lodge was seated on a large mat; his wife occupied the station at his left hand; good and clean mats were spread for myself and my guide – my own being opposite the entrance, and my guide occupying the remaining side of the wigwam. Three dogs, well conditioned, and of a large breed, lay before the fire. – So much for the live stock. At the back of the wife, I saw, suspended near the door, a tin can full of water, with a small tin cup; next to it, a mat bag filled with tin dishes, and wooden spoons of Indian manufacture; above that were several portions of female dress – ornamented leggings, two showy shawls, &c. A small chest and bag were behind her on the ground. At the back of the Indian were suspended two spear heads, of three prongs each; an American rifle, an English fowling-piece, and an Indian chief piece, with shot and bullet pouches, and two powder horns; there were also a highly ornamented capuchin, and a pair of new blanket leggings. The corner was occupied by a small red-painted chest; a mokkuk of sugar was placed in the corner on my right hand, and a barrel of flour, half empty, on the right hand of my Indian; and between that and the door were hanging three large salmon trout, and several pieces of dried deer flesh. In the centre, as usual, we had a bright blazing fire, over which three kettles gave promise of one of the comforts of weary travellers. Our host had arrived but a few minutes before us, and was busied in pulling off his moccasins and blankets when we entered. We had scarcely time to remove our leggings and change our moccasins, preparatory to a full enjoyment of the fire, when the Indian's wife was prepared to set before us a plentiful mess of boiled fish; this was followed in a short space by soup made of deer flesh and Indian corn, and our repast terminated with hot cakes baked in the ashes, in addition to the tea supplied from my own stores.

"Before daylight on the following morning we were about to set out, but could not be allowed to depart without again partaking of refreshment. Boiled and broiled fish were set before us, and to my surprise, the young Indian, before partaking of it, knelt to pray aloud. His prayer was short and fervent, and without that whining tone in which I had been accustomed to hear the Indians address the Deity. It appeared to combine the manliness and humility which one would naturally expect to find in an address spoken from the heart, and not got up for theatrical effect.

"On taking our departure, I tried to scan the countenance of our host, and I flatter myself I could not mistake the marks of unfeigned pleasure at having exercised the feelings of hospitality, mixed with a little pride in the display of the riches of his wigwam.

"You may be sure I did not omit the opportunity of diving into the secret of all his comfort and prosperity. It could not escape observation that here was real civilisation, and I anxiously sought for some explanation of the difference between the habits of this Indian and his neighbours. The story was soon told: – He had been brought up at the British Settlement on Drummond Island, where, when a child, he had, in frequent conversations, but in no studied form, heard the principles of religion explained, and he had been told to observe the sabbath, and to pray to the Almighty. Industry and prudence had been frequently enjoined, and, above all things, an abhorrence of ardent spirits. Under the influence of this wholesome advice, his hunting, fishing, and sugar-making had succeeded to such an extent, as to provide him with every necessary and many luxuries. He already had abundance, and still retained some few skins, which he hoped, during the winter, to increase to an amount sufficient to purchase him the indulgence of a barrel of pork, and additional clothing for himself and his wife.

"Further explanation was unnecessary, and the wearisomeness of this day's journey was pleasingly beguiled by reflections on the simple means by which a mind, yet in a state of nature, may be saved from degradation, and elevated to the best feelings of humanity.

"Shall I lift the same blanket after the lapse of eighteen months? – The second summer has arrived since my last visit; the wigwam on the Lake shore, the fit residence of summer, is unoccupied – the fire is still burning in the wigwam of winter: but the situation, which has warmth and quiet to recommend it at that season when cold is our greatest enemy, is now gloomy and dark. – Wondering what could have induced my friends to put up with the melancholy of the deep forest, instead of the sparkling of the sun-lit wave, I hastened to enter. How dreadful the change! There was, indeed, the same Indian girl that I had left healthy, cheerful, contented, and happy; but whisky, hunger, and distress of mind had marked her countenance with the furrows of premature old age. An infant, whose aspect was little better than its mother's, was hanging at

her breast, half dressed and filthy. Every part of the wigwam was ruinous and dirty, and, with the exception of
one kettle, entirely empty. Not one single article of furniture, clothing, or provision remained. Her husband had
left in the morning to go out to fish, and she had not
moved from the spot; this I thought strange, as his canoe
and spear were on the beach. In a short time he returned,
but without any food. He had, indeed, set out to fish, but
had lain down to sleep in the bush, and had been awakened by his dog barking on our arrival. He appeared worn
down and helpless both in body and mind, and seated
himself in listless silence in his place in the wigwam.

"Producing pork and flour from my travelling stores, I
requested his wife to cook them. They were prepared, and
I looked anxiously at the Indian, expecting to hear his
accustomed prayer. He did not move. I therefore commenced asking a blessing, and was astonished to observe
him immediately rise and walk out of the wigwam.

"However, his wife and child joined us in partaking of
the food, which they ate voraciously. In a little time the
Indian returned and lay down. My curiosity was excited,
and although anxious not to distress his feelings, I could
not avoid seeking some explanation of the change I
observed. It was with difficulty I ascertained the following
facts: –

"On the opening of the spring of 1833, the Indian having got a sufficiency of furs for his purpose, set off to a
distant trading post to make his purchase. The trader
presented him with a plug of tobacco and a pipe on his
entrance, and offered him a glass of whisky, which he
declined; the trader was then occupied with other customers, but soon noticed the respectable collection of furs in
the pack of the poor Indian. He was marked as his victim,
and not expecting to be able to impose upon him unless
he made him drunk, he determined to accomplished this
by indirect means.

"As soon as the store was clear of other customers, he
entered into conversation with the Indian, and invited

him to join him in drinking a glass of cider, which he unhesitatingly accepted; the cider was mixed with brandy, and soon began to affect the mind of the Indian; a second and a third glass were taken, and he became completely intoxicated. In this state the trader dealt with him; but it was not at first that even the draught he had taken could overcome his lessons of prudence. He parted with only one skin; the trader was, therefore, obliged to continue his contrivances, which he did with such effect, that for three weeks the Indian remained eating, drinking, and sleeping in his store. At length all the fur was sold, and the Indian returned home with only a few ribbons and beads, and a bottle of whisky. The evil example of the husband, added to vexation of mind, broke the resolution of the wife, and she, too, partook of the accursed liquor. From this time there was no change. The resolution of the Indian once broken, his pride of spirit, and consequently his firmness, were gone; he became a confirmed drinker – his wife's and his own ornamented dresses and at length all the furniture of his wigwam, even the guns and traps on which his hunting depended, were all sold to the store for whisky. When I arrived, they had been two days without food, and the Indian had not energy to save himself and his family from starvation.

"All the arguments that occurred to me I made use of to convince the Indian of his folly, and to induce him even now to begin life again, and redeem his character. He heard me in silence. I felt that I should be distressing them by remaining all night, and prepared to set out again, first giving to the Indian a dollar, desiring him to purchase food with it at the nearest store, and promising shortly to see him again.

"I had not proceeded far on my journey, when it appeared to me, that by remaining with them for the night, and in the morning renewing my solicitations to them, I might assist still more to effect a change. I therefore turned back, and in about two hours arrived again at the wigwam. The Indian had set off for the store, but had not returned. His wife still remained seated where I left her, and during the whole night (the Indian never coming back) neither moved nor raised her head. Morning came; I quickly despatched breakfast, and leaving my baggage, with the assistance of my guide set out for the trader's store. It was distant about two miles. I inquired for the Indian. He came there the evening before with a dollar: he purchased a pint of whisky, for which he paid half a dollar, and with the remainder bought six pounds of flour. He remained until he had drunk the whisky, and then requested to have the flour exchanged for another pint of whisky. This was done, and having consumed that also, he was so "stupidly drunk," (to use the words of the trader,) that it was necessary to shut him out of the store on closing it for the night. Search was immediately made for him, and at the distance of a few yards he was found lying on his face dead."

THAT THE poor Indians to whom reserved lands have been granted, and who, on the faith of treaties, have made their homes and gathered themselves into villages on such lands, should, whenever it is deemed expedient, be driven out of their possessions, either by purchase, or by persuasion, or by force, or by measures which include all three, and sent to seek a livelihood in distant and strange regions – as in the case of these Delawares – is horrible, and bears cruelty and injustice on the face of it. To say that they cannot exist in amicable relation with the whites, without depravation of their morals, is a fearful imputation on us as Christians; – but thus it is. And I do wish that those excellent and benevolent people who have taken the cause of the aborigines to heart, and are making appeals in their behalf to the justice of the government and the compassion of the public, would, instead of theorising in England, come out here and behold the actual state of things with their own eyes – and having seen all, let them say *what* is to be done, and what chances exist, for the independence, and happiness, and morality of a small remnant of Indians residing on a block of land, six miles square, surrounded on every side by a white population. To insure the accomplishment of those benevolent and earnest aspirations, in which so many good people indulge, what is required? what is expected? Of the white men such a pitch of lofty and self-sacrificing virtue, of humane philosophy and christian benevolence, that the future welfare of the wronged people they have supplanted shall be preferred above their own immediate interest – nay, their own immediate existence: of the red man, that he shall forget the wild hunter blood flowing through his veins, and take the plough in hand, and wield the axe and the spade instead of the rifle and the fish-spear! Truly they know not what they ask, who ask this; and among all those with whom I have conversed – persons familiar from thirty to forty years together with the Indians and their mode of life – I never heard but one opinion on the subject. Without casting the slightest imputation on the general honesty of intention of the missionaries and others delegated and well paid by various societies to teach and protect the Indians, still I will say that the enthusiasm of some, the self-interest of others, and an unconscious mixture of pious enthusiasm and self-interest in many more, render it necessary to take their testimony with some reservation; for often with them "the wish is father to the thought" set down; and feeling no lack of faith in their cause or in themselves, they look for miracles, such as waited on the missions of the apostles of old. But in the mean time, and by human agency, what is to be done? Nothing so easy as to point out evils and injuries, resulting from foregone events, or deep-seated in natural and necessary causes, and lament over them with resistless eloquence in verse and prose, or hold them up to the sympathy and indignation of the universe; but let the real friends of religion, humanity, and the poor Indians, set down a probable and feasible remedy for their wrongs and miseries; and follow it up, as the advocates for the abolition of the slave-trade followed up their just and glorious purpose. With a definite object and plan, much might be done; but mere declamation against the evil does little good. The people who propose remedies, forget that there are two parties concerned. I remember to have read in some of the early missionary histories, that one of the Jesuit fathers, (Father le Jeune,) full of sympathy and admiration for the noble qualities and lofty independence of the converted Indians, who could not and would not work, suggested the propriety of sending out some of the French peasantry to work and till the ground for them, as the only means of keeping them from running off to the woods. A doubtful sort of philanthropy, methinks! but it shows how *one-sided* a life's devotion to one particular object will make even a benevolent and a just man.

Higher up, on the river Thames, and above the Moravian settlements, a small tribe of the Chippewa nation has been for some time located. They have apparently attained a certain degree of civilisation, live in log-huts instead of bark wigwams, and have, from necessity, turned their attention to agriculture. I have now in my pocket-book an original document sent up from these Indians to the Indian agency at Toronto. It runs thus:

"We, the undersigned chiefs of the Chippewa Indians of Colborne on the Thames, hereby request Mr. Superintendent Clench to procure for us –

"One yoke of working oxen.

"Six ploughs.

"Thirty-three tons of hay.

"One hundred bushels of oats.

"The price of the above to be deducted from our land-payments."

Signed by ten chiefs, or, more properly, chief men, of the tribe, of whom one, the Beaver, signs his name in legible characters; the others, as is usual with the Indians, affix each their *totem*, (crest or sign-manual,) being a rude scratch of a bird, fish, deer, &c. Another of these papers, similarly signed, contains a requisition for working tools and mechanical instruments of various kinds. This looks well, and it *is* well; but what are the present state and probable progress of this Chippewa settlement? Why, one half the number at least are half cast, and as the whole population closes and thickens around them, we shall see in another generation or two none of entire Indian blood; they will become, at length, almost wholly amalgamated

with the white people. Is this *civilising the Indians?** I
should observe, that when an Indian woman gives herself
to a white man, she considers herself as his wife to all
intents and purposes. If forsaken by him, she considers
herself as injured, not disgraced. There are great numbers
of white settlers and traders along the borders living thus
with Indian women. Some of these have been persuaded
by the missionaries or magistrates to go through the ceremony of marriage; but the number is few in proportion.

You must not imagine, after all I have said, that I consider the Indians as an inferior race, merely because they
have no literature, no luxuries, no steam-engines; nor yet,
because they regard our superiority in the arts with a sort
of lofty indifference, which is neither contempt nor stupidity, look upon them as cast beyond the pale of our
sympathies. It is possible I may, on a nearer acquaintance,
change my opinion, but they do strike me as an *untamable* race. I can no more conceive a city filled with industrious Mohawks and Chippewas, than I can imagine a
flock of panthers browsing in a penfold.

The dirty, careless habits of the Indians, while sheltered
only by the bark-covered wigwam, matter very little. Living almost constantly in the open air, and moving their
dwellings perpetually from place to place, the worst effects
of dirt and negligence are neither perceived nor experienced. But I have never heard of any attempt to make
them stationary and congregate in houses, that has not
been followed by disease and mortality, particularly
among the children; a natural result of close air,

---

* The Indian village of Lorette, near Quebec, which I visited subsequently, is a case in point. Seven hundred Indians, a wretched remnant of
the Huron tribe, had once been congregated here under the protection of
the Jesuits, and had always been cited as examples of what might be
accomplished in the task of conversion and civilisation. When I was there,
the number was under two hundred; many of the huts deserted, the
inhabitants having fled to the woods and taken up the hunter's life again;
in those who remained, there was scarce a trace of native Indian blood.

confinement, heat, and filth. In our endeavours to civilise the Indians, we have not only to convince the mind and change the habits, but to overcome a certain physical organisation to which labour and constraint and confinement appear to be fatal. This cannot be done in less than three generations, if at all, in the unmixed race; and meantime – they perish!

I T IS time, however, that I should introduce you to our party on board the little steam-boat, which is now puffing, and snorting, and gliding at no rapid rate over the blue tranquil waters of Lake St. Clair.* First, then, there are the captain, and his mate or steersman, two young men of good manners and appearance; one English – the other Irish; one a military, the other a naval officer; both have land, and are near neighbours up somewhere by Lake Simcoe; but both being wearied out by three years solitary life in the bush, they have taken the steam-boat for this season on speculation, and it seems likely to answer. The boat was built to navigate the ports of Lake Huron from Penetanguishene, to Goderich and St. Joseph's Island, but there it utterly failed. It is a wretched little boat, dirty and ill contrived. The upper deck, to which I have fled from the close hot cabin, is an open platform, with no defence or railing around it, and I have here my establishment – a chair, a little table, with pencil and paper, and a great umbrella; a gust of wind or a pitch of the vessel would inevitably send me sliding overboard. The passengers consist of my acquaintance, the Moravian missionary, with a family of women and children, (his

* Most of the small steam-boats on the American lakes have high-pressure engines, which make a horrible and perpetual snorting like the engine on a railroad.

own wife and the relatives of his assistant Vogler,) who are about to emigrate with the Indians beyond the Missouri. These people speak a dialect of German among themselves, being descended from the early German Moravians. I find them civil, but neither prepossessing nor intelligent; in short, I can make nothing of them; I cannot extract an idea beyond eating, drinking, dressing, and praying; nor can I make out with what feelings, whether of regret, or hope, or indifference, they contemplate their intended exile to the far, far west. Meantime the children squeal, and the women chatter incessantly.

We took in at Chatham a large cargo of the usual articles of exportation from Canada to the United States, viz. barrels of flour, sacks of grain, and emigrants proceeding to Michigan and the Illinois. There are on board, in the steerage, a great number of poor Scotch and Irish of the lowest grade, and also one large family of American emigrants, who have taken up their station on the deck, and whose operations amuse me exceedingly. I wish I could place before you this very original ménage, even as it is before me now while I write. Such a group could be encountered nowhere on earth, methinks, but here in the west, or among the migratory Tartar hordes of the east.

They are from Vermont, and on their way to the Illinois, having been already eleven weeks travelling through New York and Upper Canada. They have two wagons covered in with canvass, a yoke of oxen, and a pair of horses. The chief or patriarch of the set is an old Vermont farmer, upwards of sixty at least, whose thin shrewd face has been burnt to a deep brickdust colour by the sun and travel, and wrinkled by age or care into a texture like that of tanned sail-canvass, – (the simile nearest to me at this moment.) The sinews of his neck and hands are like knotted whipcord; his turned-up nose, with large nostrils, snuffs the wind, and his small light blue eyes have a most keen, cunning expression. He wears a smock-frock over a flannel shirt, blue woollen stockings, and a broken pipe stuck in his straw hat, and all day long he smokes or chews tobacco. He has with him fifteen children of different ages by three wives. The present wife, a delicate, intelligent, care-worn looking woman, seems about thirty years younger than her helpmate. She sits on the shaft of one of the wagons I have mentioned, a baby in her lap, and two of the three younger children crawling about her feet. Her time and attention are completely taken up in dispensing to the whole brood, young and old, rations of food, consisting of lard, bread of Indian corn, and pieces of sassafras root. The appearance of all (except of the poor anxious mother) is equally robust and cheerful, half-civilised, coarse, and by no means clean; all are barefooted except the two eldest girls, who are uncommonly handsome, with fine dark eyes. The eldest son, a very young man, has been recently married to a very young wife, and these two recline together all day, hand in hand, under the shade of a sail, neither noticing the rest nor conversing with each other, but, as it seems to me, in silent contentment with their lot. I found these people, most unlike others of their class I have met with before, neither curious nor communicative, answering to all my questions and advances with cautious monosyllables, and the old man with even laconic rudeness. The contrast which the gentle anxious wife and her baby presented to all the others, interested me; but she looked so overpowered by fatigue, and so disinclined to converse, that I found no opportunity to satisfy my curiosity without being impertinently intrusive; so, after one or two ineffectual advances to the shy, wild children, I withdrew, and contented myself with observing the group at a distance.

The banks of the Thames are studded with a succession of farms, cultivated by the descendants of the early French settlers – precisely the same class of people as the *Habitants* in Lower Canada. They go on exactly as their ancestors did a century ago, raising on their rich fertile lands just sufficient for a subsistence, wholly uneducated, speaking only a French patois, without an idea of advance or improvement of any kind; submissive to their priests, gay, contented, courteous, and apparently retaining their ancestral tastes for dancing, singing, and flowers.

In the midst of half-dilapidated, old-fashioned farm-houses, you could always distinguish the priest's dwelling, with a flower-garden in front, and the little chapel or church surmounted by a cross, – both being generally neat, clean, fresh-painted, and forming a strange contrast with the neglect and slovenliness around.

Ague prevails very much at certain seasons along the banks of the river, and I could see by the manner in which the houses are built, that it overflows its banks annually; it abounds in the small fresh-water turtle (the Terrapin:) every log floating on the water, or muddy islet, was covered with them.

We stopped half way down the river to take in wood. Opposite to the landing-place stood an extensive farm-house, in better condition than any I had yet seen: and under the boughs of an enormous tree, which threw an ample and grateful shade around, our boat was moored. Two Indian boys, about seven or eight years old, were shooting with bow and arrows at a mark stuck up against the huge trunk of the tree. They wore cotton shirts, with a crimson belt round the waist ornamented with beads, such as is commonly worn by the Canadian Indians; one had a gay handkerchief knotted round his head, from beneath which his long black hair hung in matted elf locks on his shoulders. The elegant forms, free movements, and haughty indifference of these Indian boys, were contrasted with the figures of some little dirty, ragged Canadians, who stood staring upon us with their hands in their pockets, or importunately begging for cents. An Indian hunter and his wife, the father and mother of the boys, were standing by, and at the feet of the man a dead deer lay on the grass. The steward of the boat was bargaining with the squaw for some venison, while the hunter stood leaning on his rifle, haughty and silent. At the window of the farmhouse sat a well-dressed female, engaged in needlework. After looking up at me once or twice as I stood upon the deck gazing on this picture – just such a one as Edwin Landseer would have delighted to paint – the lady invited me into her house; an invitation I most gladly accepted. Everything within it and around it spoke riches and substantial plenty; she showed me her garden, abounding in roses, and an extensive orchard, in which stood two Indian wigwams. She told me that every year families of Chippewa hunters came down from the shore of Lake Huron, and encamped in her orchard, and those of her neighbours, without asking permission. They were perfectly inoffensive, and had never been known to meddle with her poultry, or injure her trees. "They are," said she, "an honest, excellent people; but I must shut the gates of my orchard upon them to-night – for this bargain with your steward will not conclude without whisky, and I shall have them all *ivres mort* before to-morrow morning."

Detroit, at night.

I passed half an hour in pleasant conversation with this lady, who had been born, educated, and married in the very house in which she now resided. She spoke English well and fluently, but with a foreign accent, and her deportment was frank and easy, with that sort of graceful courtesy which seems inherent in the French manner, or used to be so. On parting, she presented me with a large bouquet of roses, which has proved a great delight, and served all the purposes of a fan. Nor should I forget that in her garden I saw the only humming-birds I have yet seen in Canada: there were two lovely little gem-like creatures disporting among the blossoms of the scarlet-bean. They have been this year less numerous than usual, owing to the lateness and severity of the spring.

The day has been most intolerably hot; even on the lake there was not a breath of air. But as the sun went down in his glory, the breeze freshened, and the spires and towers of the city of Detroit were seen against the western sky. The schooners at anchor, or dropping into the river – the little canoes flitting across from side to side – the lofty buildings, – the enormous steamers – the noisy port, and busy streets, all bathed in the light of a sunset such as I had never seen, not even in Italy – almost turned me giddy with excitement. I have emerged from the solitary forests of Canada to be thrown suddenly into the midst of crowded civilised life; and the effect for the present is a nervous flutter of the spirits which banishes sleep and rest; though I have got into a good hotel, (the American,) and have at last, after some trouble, obtained good accommodation.

To them was life a simple art
    Of duties to be done;
A game where each man took his part –
    A race where all must run –
A battle whose great scheme and scope
    They little cared to know;
Content as men at arms to cope
    Each with his fronting foe.

MILNES.

Detroit, [*July* –].

THE ROADS by which I have at length reached this
beautiful little city were not certainly the smoothest
and the easiest in the world; nor can it be said of Upper
Canada as of wisdom, "that all her ways are ways of
pleasantness, and her paths are paths of peace." On the
contrary, one might have fancied oneself in the road to
paradise for that matter. It was difficult, and narrow, and
foul, and steep enough to have led to seventh heaven; but
in heaven I am not yet –

Since my arrival at Detroit, some malignant planet reigns in place of that favourable and guiding star which has hitherto led me so deftly on my way,

> "Through brake, through brier,
> Through mud, through mire."

Here, where I expected all would go so well, everything goes wrong, and cross, and contrary.

A severe attack of illness, the combined effect of heat, fatigue, and some deleterious properties in the water at Detroit, against which travellers should be warned, has confined me to my room for the last three days. This *malàpropos* indisposition has prevented me from taking my passage in the great steamer which has just gone up Lake Huron; and I must now wait here six days longer, till the next boat, bound for Mackinaw and Chicago, comes up Lake Erie from Buffalo. What is far worse, I have lost, for the time being, the advantage of seeing and knowing Daniel Webster, and of hearing a display of that wonderful eloquence which they say takes captive all ears, hearts, and souls. He has been making public speeches here, appealing to the people against the money transactions of the government; and the whole city has been in a ferment. He left Detroit two days after my arrival, to my no small mortification. I had letters for him; and it so happens that several others to whom I had also letters have fled from the city on summer tours, or to escape the heat. Some have gone east, some west, some up the lakes, some down the lakes; so I am abandoned to my own resources in a miserable state of languor, lassitude, and weakness.

It is not, however, the first time I have had to endure sickness and solitude together in a strange land; and the worst being over, we must needs make the best of it, and send the time away as well as we can.

Of all the places I have yet seen in these far western regions, Detroit is the most interesting. It is, moreover, a most ancient and venerable place, dating back to the dark immemorial ages, *i.e.* almost a century and a quarter ago! and having its history and antiquities, and traditions and heroes, and epochs of peace and war. "No place in the United States presents such a series of events interesting in themselves, and permanently affecting, as they occurred, both its progress and prosperity. Five times its flag has changed; three different sovereignties have claimed its allegiance; and since it has been held by the United States, its government has been thrice transferred: twice it has been besieged by the Indians, once captured in war, and once burned to the ground:" – truly, a long list of events for a young city of a century old! Detroit may almost rival her old grandam Quebec, who sits bristling defiance on the summit of her rocky height, in warlike and tragic experience.

Can you tell me why we gave up this fine and important place to the Americans, without leaving ourselves even a fort on the opposite shore? Dolts and blockheads as we have been in all that concerns the partition and management of these magnificent regions, now that we have ignorantly and blindly ceded whole countries, and millions and millions of square miles of land and water to our neighbours, they say we are likely to quarrel and go to war about a partition line through the barren tracts of the east! Well, this is not your affair nor mine – let our legislators look to it. Colonel Talbot told me that when he took a map, and pointed out to one of the English commissioners the foolish bargain they had made, the real extent, value, and resources of the countries ceded to the United States, the man covered his eyes with his clenched hands, and burst into tears.

The position of Detroit is one of the finest imaginable. It is on a strait between Lake Erie and Lake St. Clair, commanding the whole internal commerce of these great "successive seas." Michigan, of which it is the capital, being now received into the Union, its importance, both as a frontier town and a place of trade, increases every day.

The origin of the city was a little palisadoed fort, erected here in 1702 by the French under La Motte Cadillac, to defend their fur-trade. It was then called Fort Portchartrain. From this time till 1760 it remained in possession of the French, and continued to increase slowly. So late as 1721, Charlevoix speaks of the vast herds of buffalos ranging the plains west of the city. Meantime, under the protection of the fort, the settlement and cultivation of the neighbouring districts went on in spite of the attacks of some of the neighbouring tribes of Indians, particularly the Ottagamies, who, with the Iroquois, seem to have been the only decided and irreconcilable enemies whom the French found in this province. The capture of Quebec and the death of Wolfe being followed by the cession of the whole of the French territory in North America to the power of Great Britain, Detroit, with all the other trading posts in the west, was given up to the English. It is curious that the French submitted to this change of masters more easily than the Indians, who were by no means inclined to exchange the French for the English alliance. "Whatever may have been the cause," says Governor Cass, "the fact is certain, that there is in the French character a peculiar adaptation to the habits and feelings of the Indians, and to this day the period of French domination is the era of all that is happy in Indian reminiscences."

The conciliating manners of the French towards the Indians, and the judgment with which they managed all their intercourse with them, has had a permanent effect on the minds of those tribes who were in friendship with them. At this day, if the British are generally preferred to the Americans, the French are always preferred to either. A Chippewa chief addressing the American agent, at the Sault Ste. Marie, so late at 1826, thus fondly referred to the period of the French dominion: – "When the Frenchmen arrived at these Falls, they came and kissed us. They called us children, and we found them fathers. We lived like brethren in the same lodge, and we had always wherewithal to clothe us. They never mocked at our ceremonies, and they never molested the places of our dead.

Seven generations of men have passed away, but we have not forgotten it. Just, very just, were they towards us!"*

The discontent of the Indian tribes upon the transfer of the forts and trading posts into the possession of the British, showed itself early, and at length gave rise to one of the most prolonged and savage of all the Indian wars, that of Pontiac, in 1763.

Of this Pontiac you have read, no doubt, in various books of travels and anecdotes of Indian chiefs.† But it is *one* thing to read of these events by an English fireside, where the features of the scene – the forest wilds echoing to the war-whoop – the painted warriors – the very words scalping, tomahawking, bring no definite meaning to the mind, only a vague horror; – and quite *another* thing to recal them here on the spot, arrayed in all their dread yet picturesque reality. Pontiac is the hero *par excellence* of all these regions; and in all the histories of Detroit, when Detroit becomes a great capital of the west, he will figure like Caractacus or Arminius in the Roman history. The English contemporaries call him king and emperor of the Indians; but there is absolutely no sovereignty among these people. Pontiac was merely a war chief, chosen in the usual way, but exercising a more than usual influence, not by mere bravery – the universal savage virtue – but by talents of a rarer kind;† a power of reflection and combination rarely met with in the character of the red warrior. Pontiac was a man of genius, and would have ruled his fellow-men under any circumstances, and in any country. He formed a project similar to that which Tecumseh entertained fifty years later. He united all the north-western tribes of Ottawas, Chippewas, and Pottowattomies, in one great confederacy against the British, "the dogs in red coats;" and had very nearly caused the overthrow, at least the temporary overthrow, of our power. He had planned a simultaneous attack on all the trading posts in the posses-

* Vide Historical Sketches of Michigan.

† There is a Life of Pontiac in Thatcher's Indian Biography.

sion of the English, and so far succeeded that ten of these forts were surprised about the same time, and all the English soldiers and traders massacred, while the French were spared. Before any tidings of these horrors and outrages could reach Detroit, Pontiac was here in friendly guise, and all his measures admirably arranged for taking this fort also by stratagem, and murdering every Englishman within it. All had been lost, if a poor Indian woman, who had received much kindness from the family of the commandant, (Major Gladwyn,) had not revealed the danger. I do not yet quite understand why Major Gladwyn, on the discovery of Pontiac's treachery, and having him in his power, did not make him and his whole band prisoners; such a stroke would have ended, or rather it would have prevented, the war. But it must be remembered that Major Gladwyn was ignorant of the systematic plan of extermination adopted by Pontiac; the news of the massacres at the upper forts had not reached him; he knew of nothing but the attempt on himself, and from motives of humanity or magnanimity he suffered them to leave the fort and go free. No sooner were they on the outside of the palisades, than they set up the war-yell "like so many devils," as a bystander expressed it, and turned and discharged their rifles on the garrison. The war, thus savagely declared, was accompanied by all those atrocious barbarities, and turns of fate, and traits of heroism, and hair-breadth escapes, which render these Indian conflicts so exciting, so terrific, so picturesque.*

---

* The following extract from a contemporary letter given in the life of Pontiac is at least very graphic.

"Detroit, July 9, 1763.

"You have heard long ago of our pleasant situation, but the storm is blown over. Was it not very agreeable to hear every day of their cutting, carving, boiling, and eating our companions? to see every day dead bodies floating down the river, mangled and disfigured? But Britons, you know, never shrink; we always appeared gay, to spite the rascals. They boiled and ate Sir Robert Devers, and we are informed by Mr. Pauly, who escaped the other day from one of the stations surprised at

Detroit was in a state of siege by the Indians for twelve months, and gallantly and successfully defended by Major Gladwyn, till relieved by General Bradstreet.

The first time I was able to go out, my good-natured landlord drove me himself in his wagon, (*Anglicè*, gig,) with as much attention and care for my comfort, as if I had been his near relation. The evening was glorious; the sky perfectly Italian – a genuine Claude Lorraine sky, that beautiful intense amber light reaching to the very zenith, while the purity and transparent loveliness of the atmospheric effects carried me back to Italy and times long past. I felt it all, as people feel things after a sharp fit of indisposition, when the nervous system, languid at once and sensitive, thrills and trembles to every breath of air. As we drove slowly and silently along, we came to a sluggish, melancholy looking rivulet, to which the man pointed with his whip. "I expect," said he, "you know all about the battle of Bloody Run?"

I was obliged to confess my ignorance, not without a slight shudder at the hateful, ominous name which sounded in my ear like an epitome of all imaginable horrors.

This was the scene of a night attack made by three hundred British upon the camp of the Indians, who were then besieging Detroit. The Indians had notice of their intention, and prepared an ambush to receive them. They had just reached the bank of this rivulet, when the Indian foe fell upon them suddenly. They fought hand to hand, bayonet and tomahawk, in the darkness of the night. Before the English could extricate themselves, seventy men and most of the officers fell and were scalped on the spot. "Them Indians," said my informant, "fought like brutes and devils," (as most do, I thought, who fight for revenge and existence,) "and they say the creek here,

the breaking out of the war, and commanded by himself, that he had seen an Indian have the skin of Captain Robertson's arm for a tobacco pouch."

when morning came, ran red with blood; and so they call it the Bloody Run."

There certainly *is* much in a name, whatever Juliet may say, and how much in fame! Do you remember the brook Sanguinetto, which flows into Lake Thrasymene? The meaning and the derivation are the same, but what a difference in sound! The Sanguinetto! 'tis a word one might set to music. – *The Bloody Run!* pah! the very utterance pollutes one's fancy!

And in associations, too, how different, though the circumstances were not unlike! This Indian Fabius, this Pontiac, wary and brave, and unbroken by defeat, fighting for his own land against a swarm of invaders, has had no poet, no historian to immortalise him, else all this ground over which I now tread had been as *classical* as the shores of Thrasymene.

As they have called Tecumseh the Indian Napoleon, they might style Pontiac the Indian Alexander – I do not mean him of Russia, but the Greek. Here, for instance, is a touch of magnanimity quite in the *Alexander-the-great* style. Pontiac, before the commencement of the war, had provided for the safety of a British officer, Major Rogers by name, who was afterwards employed to relieve Detroit, when besieged by the Indians. On this occasion he sent Pontiac a present of a bottle of brandy, to show he had not forgotten his former obligations to him. Those who were around the Indian warrior when the present arrived, particularly some Frenchmen, warned him not to taste it, as it might be poisoned. Pontiac instantly took a draught from it, saying, as he put the bottle to his lips, that "it was not *in the power* of Major Rogers to hurt him who had so lately saved his life." I think this story is no unworthy pendant to that of Alexander and his physician.

But what avails it all! who knows or cares about Pontiac and his Ottawas?

"Vain was the chief's, the warrior's pride!
He had no poet – and he died!"

If I dwell on these horrid and obscure conflicts, it is partly to amuse the languid idle hours of convalescence, partly to inspire you with some interest for the localities around me: – and I may as well, while the pen is in my hand, give you the conclusion of the story.

Pontiac carried on the war with so much talent, courage, and resources, that the British government found it necessary to send a considerable force against him. General Bradstreet came up here with three thousand men, wasting the lands of the Miami and Wyandot Indians, "burning their villages, and destroying their corn-fields;" and I pray you to observe that in all the accounts of our expeditions against the Indians, as well as those of the Americans under General Wayne and General Harrison, mention is made of the destruction of corn-fields (plantations of Indian corn) to a great extent, which show that *some* attention must have been paid to agriculture, even by these wild hunting tribes.* I find mention also of a very interesting and beautiful tradition connected with these regions. To the east of the Detroit territory, there was settled from ancient times a band of Wyandots or Hurons, who were called the neutral nation; they never took part in the wars and conflicts of the other tribes. They had two principal villages, which were like the cities of refuge

---

* I believe it is a prevalent notion, that the Indians of the north-west never cultivated grain to any extent until under the influence of the whites. This apparently is a mistake. When General Wayne (in 1794) destroyed the settlements of the Wyandots and Miamis along the Miami river, and on the south shores of Lake Erie, he wrote thus in this official despatch: – "The very extensive and cultivated *fields* and *gardens* show the work of many hands. The margins of those beautiful rivers, the Miami of the lake and Au Glaize, appear like one continued village for a number of miles, both above and below this place. *Nor have I ever beheld such immense fields of corn in any part of America, from Canada to Florida.*" And all this fair scene was devastated and laid waste! and we complain that the Indians make no advance in civilisation!

among the Israelites; whoever fled there from an enemy found a secure and inviolable sanctuary. If two enemies from tribes long at deadly variance met there, they were friends while standing on that consecrated ground. To what circumstances this extraordinary institution owed its existence is not known. It was destroyed after the arrival of the French in the country – not by them, but by some national and internal feud.

But to return to Pontiac. With all his talents, he could not maintain a standing or permanent army, such a thing being contrary to all the Indian usages, and quite incompatible with their mode of life. His warriors fell away from him every season, and departed to their hunting grounds to provide food for their families. The British pressed forward, took possession of their whole country, and the tribes were obliged to beg for peace. Pontiac disdained to take any part in these negociations, and retired to the Illinois, where he was murdered, from some motive of private animosity, by a Peoria Indian. The Ottawas, Chippewas, and Pottowattomies, who had been allied under his command, thought it incumbent on them to avenge his death, and nearly exterminated the whole nation of the Peorias – and this was the life and the fall of Pontiac.

The name of this great chief is commemorated in that of a flourishing village, or rising town, about twenty miles west of Detroit, which is called *Pontiac*, as one of the townships in Upper Canada is styled *Tecumseh:* thus literally illustrating those beautiful lines in Mrs. Sigourney's poem on Indian names: –

> "Their memory liveth on your hills,
> *Their baptism on your shore;*
> Your everlasting rivers speak
> Their dialect of yore!"

For rivers, bearing their old Indian names, we have here the Miami, (or Maumee,) the Huron, the Sandusky: but most of the points of land, rivers, islands, &c, bear the

French appellations, as Point Pelée, River au Glaize, River des Canards, Gros-Isle, &c.

The *mélange* of proper names in this immediate neighbourhood is sufficiently curious. Here we have Pontiac, Romeo, Ypsilanti, and Byron, all within no great distance of each other.

Long after the time of Pontiac, Detroit and all the country round it became the scene of even more horrid and unnatural conflicts between the Americans and British, during the war of the revolution, in which the Indians were engaged against the Americans. When peace was proclaimed, and the independence of the United States recognized by Great Britain, this savage war on the frontiers still continued, and mutual aggressions and injuries have left bitter feelings rankling on both sides. Let us hope that in another generation they may be effaced. For myself, I cannot contemplate the possibility of another war between the English and the Americans without a mingled disgust and terror, as something cruel, unnatural, fratricidal. Have we not the same ancestry, the same father-land, the same language? "Though to drain our blood from out their being were an aim," they cannot do it!

The ruffian refuse of the two nations – the most ignorant, common-minded, and vulgar among them, may hate each other, and give each other nicknames – but every year diminishes the number of such; and while the two governments are shaking hands across the Atlantic, it were indeed supremely ridiculous if they were to go to cuffs across the Detroit and Niagara!

"In vain sedate reflections we would make
  When half our knowledge we must snatch, not take."

                                                    POPE.

Detroit.

WHEN THE intolerable heat of the day has subsided, I
sometimes take a languid stroll through the streets
of the city, not unamused, not altogether unobserving,
though unable to profit much by what I see and hear.
There are many new houses building, and many new
streets laid out. In the principal street, called the Jefferson
Avenue, there are rows of large and handsome brick
houses; the others are generally of wood, painted white,
with bright green doors and windows. The footway in
many of the streets is, like that of Toronto, of planks,
which for my own part I like better than the burning brick
or stone *pavé*. The crowd of emigrants constantly pouring
through this little city on their way to the back settlements
of the west, and the number of steamers, brigs, and
schooners always passing up and down the lakes, occasion
a perpetual bustle, variety, and animation on the shore
and in the streets. Forty-two steamers touch at the port. In
one of the Detroit papers (there are five or six published
here either daily or weekly) I found a long column, headed

MARINE INTELLIGENCE, giving an account of the arrival and departure of the shipping. Last year the profits of the steam-boats averaged seventy or eighty per cent., one with another: this year it is supposed that many will lose. There are several boats which ply regularly between Detroit and some of the new-born cities on the south shore of Lake Erie – Sandusky, Cleveland, Port Clinton, Monroe, &c. The navigation of the Detroit river is generally open from the beginning of April to the end of November. In the depth of winter they pass and repass from the British to the American shore on the ice.

There are some excellent shops in the town, a theatre, and a great number of taverns and gaming-houses. There is also a great number of booksellers' shops; and I read in the papers long lists of books, newly arrived and unpacked, which the public are invited to inspect.

Wishing to borrow some books, to while away the long solitary hours in which I am *obliged* to rest, I asked for a circulating library, and was directed to the only one in the place. I had to ascend a steep staircase – so disgustingly dirty, that it was necessary to draw my drapery carefully round me to escape pollution. On entering a large room, unfurnished except with bookshelves, I found several men sitting or rather sprawling upon chairs, and reading the newspapers. The collection of books was small; but they were not of a common or vulgar description. I found some of the best modern publications in French and English. The man – gentleman I should say, for all are gentlemen here – who stood behind the counter, neither moved his hat from his head, nor bowed on my entrance, nor showed any officious anxiety to serve or oblige; but, with this want of what *we* English consider due courtesy, there was no deficiency of real civility – far from it. When I inquired on what terms I might have some books to read, this gentleman desired I would take any books I pleased, and not think about payment or deposit. I remonstrated, and represented that I was a stranger at an inn – that my stay was uncertain, &c.; and the reply was, that from a lady and a stranger he could not think of receiving remuneration: and then gave himself some trouble to look out the books I wished for, which I took away with me. He did not even ask the name of the hotel at which I was staying; and when I returned the books, persisted in declining all payment from "a lady and a stranger."

Whatever attention and politeness may be tendered to me, in either character, as a lady or as a stranger, I am always glad to receive from any one, in any shape. In the present instance, I could indeed have dispensed with the *form:* a pecuniary obligation, small or large, not being much to my taste; but what was meant for courtesy, I accepted courteously – and so the matter ended.

Nations differ in their idea of good manners, as they do on the subject of beauty – a far less conventional thing. But there exists luckily a standard for each, in reference to which we cannot err, and to which the progress of civilisation will, it is to be hoped, bring us all nearer and nearer still. For the type of perfection in physical beauty we go to Greece, and for that of politeness we go to the gospel. As it is written in a charming little book I have just bought here, – "He who should embody and manifest the virtues taught in Christ's sermon on the Mount, would, though he had never seen a drawing-room, nor ever heard of the artificial usages of society, commend himself to all nations, the most refined as well as the most simple."*

If you look upon the map, you will find that the Detroit River, so called, is rather a strait or channel about thirty miles in length, and in breadth from one to two or three miles, dividing the British from the American shore. Through this channel all the waters of the upper lakes, Michigan, Superior, and Huron, come pouring down on their way to the ocean. Here, at Detroit, the breadth of the river does not exceed a mile. A pretty little steamer, gaily painted, with streamers flying, and shaded by an awning, is continually passing and repassing from shore to shore. I have sometimes sat in this ferry-boat for a couple of hours together, pleased to remain still, and enjoy, without exer-

* "HOME," by Miss Sedgwick.

tion, the cool air, the sparkling redundant waters, and green islands: – amused, meantime, by the variety and conversation of the passengers, English emigrants, and French Canadians; brisk Americans; dark, sad-looking Indians folded in their blankets; farmers, storekeepers, speculators in wheat; artisans; trim girls with black eyes and short petticoats, speaking a Norman patois, and bringing baskets of fruit to the Detroit market; over-dressed, long-waisted, damsels of the city, attended by their beaux, going to make merry on the opposite shore. The passage is not of more than ten minutes duration, yet there is a tavern bar on the lower deck, and a constant demand for cigars, liquors, and mint julep – by the *men* only, I pray you to observe, and the Americans chiefly; I never saw the French peasants ask for drink.

Yesterday and to-day, feeling better, I have passed some hours straying or driving about on the British shore.

I hardly know how to convey to you an idea of the difference between the two shores; it will appear to you as incredible as it is to me incomprehensible. Our shore is said to be the most fertile, and has been the longest settled; but to float between them (as I did to-day in a little canoe made of a hollow tree, and paddled by a half-breed imp of a boy) – to behold on one side a city, with its towers and spires and animated population, with villas and handsome houses stretching along the shore, and a hundred vessels or more, gigantic steamers, brigs, schooners, crowding the port, loading and unloading; all the bustle, in short, of prosperity and commerce; – and, on the other side, a little straggling hamlet, one schooner, one little wretched steam-boat, some windmills, a catholic chapel or two, a supine ignorant peasantry, all the symptoms of apathy, indolence, mistrust, hopelessness! – can I, can any one, help wondering at the difference, and asking whence it arises? There must be a cause for it surely – but what is it? Does it lie in past or in present – in natural or accidental circumstances? – in the institutions of the government, or the character of the people? Is it remediable? is it a necessity? is it a mystery? what and whence is it? – Can you tell? or can you send some of our colonial officials across the Atlantic to behold and solve the difficulty?

The little hamlet opposite to Detroit is called Richmond. I was sitting there to-day on the grassy bank above the river, resting in the shade of a tree, and speculating on all these things, when an old French Canadian stopped near me to arrange something about his cart. We entered forthwith into conversation; and though I had some difficulty in making out his *patois* he understood my French, and we got on very well. If you would see the two extremes of manner brought into near comparison, you should turn from a Yankee storekeeper to a French Canadian! It was quite curious to find in this remote region such a perfect specimen of an old-fashioned Norman peasant – all bows, courtesy, and good-humour. He was carrying a cart-load of cherries to Sandwich, and when I begged for a ride, the little old man bowed and smiled, and poured forth a voluble speech, in which the words *enchanté! honneur!* and *madame!* were all I could understand; but these were enough. I mounted the cart, seated myself in an old chair surrounded with baskets heaped with ripe cherries, lovely as those of Shenstone –

> "Scattering like blooming maid their glances round,
> And must be bought, though penury betide!"

No occasion, however, to risk penury here; for after permission asked, and granted with a pleasant smile and a hundredth removal of the ragged hat, I failed not to profit by my situation, and dipped my hand pretty frequently into these tempting baskets. When the French penetrated into these regions a century ago, they brought with them not only their national courtesy, but some of their finest national fruits, – plums, cherries, apples, pears, of the best quality – excellent grapes, too, I am told – and all these are now grown in such abundance as to be almost valueless. For his cart-load of cherries my old man expected a sum not exceeding two shillings.

Sandwich is about two miles below Detroit. It is the chief place in the Western District, the county town; yet the population does not much exceed four hundred.

I had to regret much the absence of Mr. Prince, the great proprietor of the place, and a distinguished member of our house of assembly, both for ability and eloquence; but I saw sufficient to convince me that Sandwich makes no progress. The appearance of the place and people, so different from all I had left on the opposite side of the river, made me melancholy, or rather thoughtful. What can be the reason that all flourishes *there*, and all languishes *here*?

Amherstberg, another village about ten miles farther, contains about six hundred inhabitants, has a good harbour, and all natural capabilities; but here also no progress in making. There is a wretched little useless fort, commanding, or rather *not* commanding, the entrance to the Detroit river on our side, and memorable in the history of the last American war as Fort Malden. There are here a few idle soldiers, detached from the garrison at Toronto; and it is said that even these will be removed. In case of an attack or sudden outbreak, all this exposed and important line of shore is absolutely without defence.*

Near Amherstberg there is a block of reserved land, about seven miles square, the property of a tribe of Huron or Wyandot Indians: it extends along the banks of the Detroit river, and is one of the finest regions for climate, soil, and advantages of every kind, in the whole province; of great importance too, as lying opposite to the American shore, and literally a stumbling-*block* in the way of the white settlements, diminishing very considerably the value and eligibility of the lands around. Our government has been frequently in negociation with these Indians to induce them to dispose of their lands, and I understood that fifteen thousand acres have lately been purchased

---

* This was written on the spot. Since the late troubles in Upper Canada, it is understood to be the intention of Sir John Colborne to fortify this coast.

from them. It is most certain, however, that in all these transactions they consider themselves aggrieved.

I have in my possession an original petition of these Wyandot Indians, addressed to Sir John Colborne. It appears that in 1829, the other lake tribes, the Chippewas, Pottowattomies, and Ottawas, claimed an equal right to these lands, and offered to dispose of them to our government. The Hurons resisted this claim, and were most unwilling to relinquish their right to keep and reside on their "own little piece of land." The petition, which has been translated by one of their missionaries in a style rather too ambitious and flowery, contains some very touching and beautiful passages. They open their statement of grievances thus: –

"FATHER!

"Your Red children the Hurons approach you under "the gathering clouds of affliction. Father, we visit you to "tell you the sorrows of our hearts. We have learned at a "council that the three nations of Ottawas, Chippewas, "and Pottowattomies, claim our lands. We understand, "with grief and surprise, that they proposed at that council "to traffic with you for our Huron reserve."

They then allude to their ancient contests with the Iroquois, by which they were driven up the lakes, as far as beyond Lake Michigan; and their return to their former hunting-grounds when these contests ceased.

"Our fires were quenched, and their ashes scattered; "but, Father, we collected them again, removed to our "present homes, and there rekindled the embers."

They allude to their services in the late war, as giving them a peculiar claim to protection.

"Father, when the war-hatchet was sent by our great "Father to the Americans, we too raised it against them. "Father, we fought your enemies on the very spot we now "inherit. The pathway to our doors is red with our blood. "Every track to our homes reminds us, 'here fell a "brother' – fell, Father! in the hour of strife for you. But, "Father, we mourn not for them. The memory of their "exploits lives sacred in our breasts. We mourn not for

"them; we mourn for ourselves and our children. We
"would not recal them to the pains and sufferings through
"which the steps of the living Huron must pass. Theirs is
"the morning of stillness after the tempest: the day of peace
"after the fury of the battle! Father, their brave spirits
"look down upon you. By their blood we implore you to
"stretch your protecting arm over us. The war-club has
"been glutted with the havoc of our nation. We look
"round for our young men, our warriors, our chiefs:
"where is now the Huron? gone, Father, laid low in the
"earth; nerveless are now the hands that grasped the
"Huron tomahawk. Father, in our might we aided you: let
"us not lament in our weakness that our vigour has
"been wasted."

They then attempt to substantiate their claim by pointing out the places which bear their name, as the ancient
inhabitants of the soil; and it is certain that in the time of
Charlevoix all these regions were in possession of the
Huron tribes.

"The great lake is called the *Huron* Lake. There are
"no less than three rivers in our vicinity which bear the
"name of the Huron: the Huron river on the north side
"of Lake St. Clair – the Huron river on the north side
"of Lake Erie – and the Huron river on the south side of
"Lake Erie. Upper and Lower Sandusky* owe their names
"to our language. Father, what is the soil in dispute every-
"where termed? The Ottawa or Chippewa Reserve? –
"no, Father; but simply the Huron Reserve. Thus your
"maps designate it. We had a village at Big Rock, in the
"entrance to the westerly channel of the river Detroit,
"called Brown's Town, from one of our chiefs. Another at
"Maguaga, in the same channel. But Amherstberg now
"covers the space where were once our principal town
"and settlement, extending to the mouth of the river
"Des Canards, our present abode."

"Yet, Father, the Ottawas ask our lands as their
"property; they offer to you the sale of crops they have

* Two rising towns on the American shore of Lake Erie.

"not tilled – of barns they have not raised – of houses they
"have not built – of homes wherein they never slept.
"Father, they would reap where the ancient Huron only
"has sown."

"Father, we have had the strongest declarations that we
"should not be molested, from Governor Simcoe, on the
"behalf of our great Father; also from the Governor-
"general, Lord Dorchester; from Governor Gore, and
"from every other Governor to the present day. The same
"has been repeated to us by your commanding officers
"stationed at Amherstberg. Father, on the faith of these
"repeated promises, we retained our habitations among
"you. Deeming your protection certain, we have cleared
"our fields and cultivated them, raised barns for our
"grain, and houses for our families. We have taught our
"children to smoke the pipe of peace, and follow the
"precepts of the gospel. Our feet are unaccustomed to the
"chase – their swiftness is no more; our hands unfamiliar
"with the bow, and the sureness of the arrow is lost."

They attribute these new claims to their lands to the
devices of their white neighbours, and they allude to their
fallen state and diminished numbers as pleas for the white
man's forbearance.

"We conjure you not to expel us from our homes,
"rendered dear to us by many recollections. The morning
"and the noon-day of our nation has passed away – the
"evening is fast settling in darkness round us. It is hardly
"worth an effort to hasten the close of night," &c.

"Father, the dejected Huron throws himself upon your
"clemency and justice."

This petition is signed by their principal chief Split-Log,
and nine other chiefs, of whom three sign their names in
rude but legible manuscript; the others affix their mark
only.

Is there not much reason as well as eloquence in this
appeal? Apparently it was successful, as I find the Wyandots still on their land, and no question at present of the

rights of the other tribes. Warrow and Split-Log, two of the chiefs who sign this petition, were distinguished in the last war; they were present at the council at Fort Malden, and fought in the battle in which Tecumseh was slain.

Split-Log is still living, and has been baptized a Christian, by the name of Thomas.

This same Huron reserve has been more lately (in 1836) the subject of dispute between the Lieutenant-governor and the house of assembly. The Indians petitioned the house against the encroachments of the whites and half-breeds, and the conduct of the superintendent; and complained that the territory of their fathers was taken from them without their acquiescence.

Hereupon the house of assembly sent up an address, requesting that the subject of this petition, and the proceedings of the government thereon, should be laid before the house. Sir Francis Head declined acceding to this request, and gave his reasons at length, arguing that the management of the Indian affairs belonged to the Executive alone, and that the interference of the provincial legislature was an undue invasion of the king's prerogative.*

---

* The following is part of his Excellency's answer to the address of the house of assembly.

"Without reverting to the anomalous history of the aborigines of this land, I will merely observe that in Upper Canada the Indians have hitherto been under the exclusive care of his Majesty, the territories they inhabit being tracts of crown lands devoted to their sole use as his allies. Over these lands his Majesty has never exercised his paramount right, except at their request and for their *manifest advantage*," – (this is doubtful, I presume.) "Within their own communities they have hitherto governed themselves by their own unwritten laws and customs; their lands and properties have never been subjected to tax or assessment, or themselves liable to personal service. As they are not subject to such liabilities, neither do they yet possess the political privileges of his Majesty's subjects generally. The superintendents, missionaries, schoolmasters and others who reside among them for their protection and civilisation, are appointed and paid by the King. To his representative all appeals have until now been made, and with him all responsibility has rested. In every respect they appear to be most constitutionally within the jurisdiction and prerogative of the Crown; and as I declare myself not only ready but

I am hardly competent to give an opinion either way, but it seemeth to me, in my simple wit, that this is a case in which the government of the Crown, always supposing it to be wisely and paternally administered, must be preferable to the interposition of the colonial legislature, seeing that the interests of the colonists and settlers, and those of the Indians, are brought into perpetual collision, and that the colonists can scarcely be trusted to decide in

desirous to attend to every complaint they may offer me, I consider it would be highly impolitic (especially for the object of redressing a trifling grievance) to sanction the adoption of a new course for their internal government."

I believe that Sir Francis Head entertained an enthusiastic admiration for the Indian character, and was sincerely interested in the welfare of this fated people. It was his deliberate conviction that there was no salvation for them but in their removal as far as possible from the influence and dominion of the white settlers; and in this I agree with his Excellency; but seeing that the Indians are not virtually British subjects, no measure should be adopted, even for their supposed benefit, without their acquiescence. They are quite capable of judging for themselves in every case in which their interests are concerned. The fault of our executive is, that we acknowledge the Indians our *allies* yet treat them, as well as call them, our *children*. They acknowledge in our government a *father*; they never acknowledged any master but the "Great Master of Life," and the rooted idea, or rather instinct of personal and political independence in which every Indian is born or reared, no earthly power can obliterate from his soul. One of the early missionaries expresses himself on this point with great *naïvete*. "The Indians," he says, "are convinced that every man is born free; that no one has a right to make any attempt upon his personal liberty, and that nothing can make him amends for its loss." He proceeds – "We have even had much pains to undeceive those converted to Christianity on this head, and to make them understand that in consequence of the corruption of our nature, which is the effect of sin, an unrestrained liberty of doing evil differs little from the necessity of doing it, considering the strength of the inclination which carries us to it; and that the law which restrains us brings us nearer to our first liberty in seeming to deprive us of it."

That a man, because he has the free use of his will and his limbs, must therefore necessarily do evil, is a doctrine which the Indian can never be brought to understand. He is too polite to contradict us, but he insists that it was made for the pale-faces, who, it may be, are naturally inclined to all evil; but has nothing to do with the red skins, whom the Great Spirit created free. "Where the spirit of the Lord is, there is liberty;" – but about liberty there may be as many differing notions as about charity.

their own case. As it is, the poor Indian seems hardly destined to meet with *justice*, either from the legislative or executive power.

Of the number here I can form no exact idea; they say there are about two hundred. At present they are busied in preparations for their voyage up Lake Huron to the Great Manitoolin Island to receive their annual presents, and one fleet of canoes has already departed.

Fort Malden and the whole of this coast (on both sides of the river) were the scene of various vicissitudes during the last war of 1813. The shameful retreat of the American General Hull, and his surrender with his whole army to General Brock; the equally shameful retreat of the British General Proctor, and his defeat by General Harrison, are fresh in the recollection of all people; and these national disgraces, with mutual wrongs and injuries, have left, I fear, much mutual animosity along both shores. Here it was that Tecumseh attempted in vain to prevent the retreat or rather flight of General Proctor from Fort Malden. "We are astonished," exclaimed the Indian chief, "to see our Father tying up everything and preparing to run away, without letting his red children know what his intentions are. You always told us you would never draw your foot off British ground. But now, Father, we see you are drawing back, and we are sorry to see our Father doing so without seeing the enemy. We must compare our Father's conduct to a fat dog that carries its tail upon its back, but when affrighted, it drops it between its legs and runs off. Father! you have got the arms and ammunition which our great Father sent for his red children. If you have an idea of going away, give them to us, and you may go and welcome. Our lives are in the hands of the Great Spirit. We are determined to defend our lands, and, if it be his will, we wish to leave our bones upon them."

You may find the whole of this famous speech in Thatcher's Indian Biography. Neither Tecumseh's reasoning, nor his ludicrous and scornful simile of the fat dog, had any effect on General Proctor, who continued his retreat. It is not generally known that Tecumseh, exasperated by the faint-heartedness of the British general, threatened (before the battle of the Moravian Towns) to tomahawk him if he would not fight. This fact I had from one who served most honourably in this very war – Colonel Fitzgibbon.

As yet, these bloody and obscure conflicts are little known beyond the locality, and excite but little interest when read cursorily in the dry chronicles of the time. But let some eloquent historian arise to throw over these events the light of a philosophical mind, and all the picturesque and romantic interest of which they are capable; to trace the results which have already arisen, and must in future arise, from this collision between two great nations, though fought out on a remote and half barbarous stage, with little sympathy and less applause: – we shall then have these far-off shores converted into classic ground, and the names of Pontiac, Tecumseh, Isaac Brock, become classic names familiar on all lips as household words – such at least they will become *here*.*

---

* The events of our wars with America, both the war of independence and the last war of 1813, are not a popular study in England, and imperfectly known except to those who make this part of modern history a particular study for a particular object. We cannot be surprised that exactly the reverse is the case in America, where, I remember, I got myself into irretrievable disgrace by not recollecting the battle of New Orleans.

Sunday Evening.

M Y BUSINESS here is to observe, as well as lassitude and sickness will let me; but – I must needs confess it – I never spent six fine sunshiny summer days, though in solitude, with less of profit or of pleasure. Two summers ago I was lingering thus alone, and convalescent, on the banks of the Traun-See in Upper Austria. O that I could convey to you in intelligible words all the difference between *there* and *here!* – between *then* and *now!* – between *that* solitude and *this* solitude! There I was alone with nature and my own heart, bathed in mountain torrents, and floated for hours together on the bosom of that delicious lake, not thinking, not observing, only enjoying and dreaming! As on that lake I have seen a bird hang hovering, poised on almost motionless wing, as if contemplating the reflection of its own form, suspended between two heavens, that above and that beneath it; so my mind seemed lost to earth and earth's objects, and beheld only itself and heaven! What a contrast between that still, sublime loneliness, that vague, tender, tranquil, blessed mood, and the noisy excitement of this restless yet idle existence, where attention is continually fatigued and never satisfied! and the nerves, unstrung and languid, are fretted out of all repose! What a contrast between my pretty Tyrolean *batelière* singing as she slowly pulled her oar, and my wild Indian boy flourishing his paddle! – between the cloud-capped Traunstein and gleaming glaciers, and these flat marshy shores – and *that* little cupful of water not twenty miles in circumference, and *these* inland oceans covering thousands of leagues!

But it is well to have known and seen both. Nothing so soon passes away from the mind as the recollection of physical inconvenience and pain – nothing is so permanent as the picture once impressed on the fancy; and *this* picture will be to me a pleasure and an inalienable property, like that of the Traun-See, when this irksome languor of the sinking spirit will be quite forgotten and effaced.

So, as I have said, my business here being not to dream, but to observe, and this morning being Sunday morning, I crept forth to attend the different church services merely as a spectator. I went first to the Roman Catholic church, called the Cathedral, and the largest and oldest in the place. The catholic congregation is by far the most numerous here, and is composed chiefly of the lower classes and the descendants of the French settlers. On entering the porch, I found a board suspended with written regulations, to the effect that all Christians, of whatever denomination, were welcome to enter; but it was requested that all would observe the outward ceremonial, and that all gentlemen (*tous les messieurs*) would lay aside their pipes and cigars, take off their hats, and wipe their shoes. The interior of the church was similar to that of many other provincial Roman Catholic churches, exhibiting the usual assortment of wax tapers, gilding, artificial flowers, and daubed Madonnas. The music and singing were not good. In the course of the service, the officiating priest walked up and down the aisles, flinging about the holy water on either side with a silver-handled brush. I had my share, though unworthy, of this sprinkling, and then left the church, where the heat and the smell of incense *et cetera* were too overpowering. On the steps, and in the open space before the door, there was a crowd of peasants, all talking French – laughing, smoking, tobacco-chewing, *et cetera, et cetera*. One or two were kneeling in the porch. Thence I went to the Methodist chapel, where I found a small congregation of the lower classes. A very ill-looking man, in comparison to whom Liston's Mawworm were no caricature, was holding forth in a most whining and lugu-brious tone; the poor people around joined in sobs and ejaculations, which soon became howling, raving, and crying. In the midst of this woful assembly I observed a little boy who was grinning furtively, kicking his heels, and sliding bits of apple from his pocket into his mouth. Not being able to endure this long with proper seriousness, I left the place.

I then went into the Baptist church, on the opposite side of the road. It is one of the largest in the town, plain in appearance, but the interior handsome, and in good taste. The congregation was not crowded, but composed of most respectable, serious, well-dressed people. As I entered, the preacher was holding forth on the unpardonable sin, very incoherently and unintelligibly; but, on closing his ser-mon, he commenced a prayer, and I have seldom listened to one more eloquently fervent. Both the sermon and prayer were extemporaneous. He prayed for all people, nations, orders and conditions of men throughout the world, including the king of Great Britain: but the prayer for the president of the United States seemed to me a little original, and admirably calculated to suit the two parties who are at present divided on the merits of that gentle-man. The suppliant besought the Almighty, that "if Mr. Van Buren were a good man, he might be made better, and if a bad man, he might be speedily regenerated."

I was still in time for the Episcopal church, a very spacious and handsome building, though "somewhat Gothic." On entering, I perceived at one glance that the Episcopal church is here, as at New York, the *fashionable* church of the place. It was crowded in every part: the women well dressed – but, as at New York, too much dressed, too fine for good taste and real fashion. I was handed immediately to the "strangers' pew," a book put into my hand, and it was whispered to me that the bishop would preach. Our English idea of the exterior of a bishop is an old gentleman in a wig and lawn sleeves, both equally *de rigueur;* I was therefore childishly surprised to find in the Bishop of Michigan a young man of very elegant appearance, wearing his own fine hair, and in a plain black silk gown. The sermon was on the well-worn subject of charity as it consists in *giving* – the least and lowest it may be of all the branches of charity, though indeed that depends on what we give, and how we give it. We may give our heart, our soul, our time, our health, our life, as well as our money; and the greatest of these, as well as the least, is still but charity. At home I have often thought that when people gave money they gave counters; here, when people give money they are really charitable – they give a portion of their time and their existence, both of which are devoted to money-making.

On closing his sermon, which was short and unexceptionable, the bishop leaned forward over the pulpit, and commenced an extemporaneous address to his congregation. I have often had occasion in the United States to admire the ready, graceful fluency of their extemporaneous speakers and preachers, and I have never heard anything more eloquent and more elegant than this address; it was in perfect good taste, besides being very much to the purpose. He spoke in behalf of the domestic missions of his diocese. I understood that the missions hitherto supported in the back settlements are, in consequence of the extreme pressure of the times, likely to be withdrawn, and the new, thinly-peopled districts thus left without any ministry whatever. He called on the people to give their aid towards sustaining these domestic missionaries, at least for a time, and said, among other things, that if each individual of the Episcopal Church in the United States subscribed one cent per week for a year, it would amount to more than 300,000 dollars. This address was responded to by a subscription on the spot, of above 400 dollars – a large sum for a small town, suffering, like all other places, from the present commercial difficulties.

With keen eye'd hope, with memory at her side,
And the glad muse at liberty to note
All that to each is precious as we float
Gently along: regardless who shall chide –
If the heavens smile –

WORDSWORTH.

July 18.

THIS EVENING the Thomas Jefferson arrived in the river from Buffalo, and starts early to-morrow morning for Chicago. I hastened to secure a passage as far as the island of Mackinaw: when once there, I must trust to Providence for some opportunity of going up Lake Huron to the Sault Ste. Marie to visit my friends the MacMurrays; or down the lake to the Great Manitoolin Island, where the annual distribution of presents to the Indians is to take place under the auspices of the governor. If both these plans – wild plans they are, I am told – should fail, I have only to retrace my way and come down the lake, as I went up, in a steamer; but this were horridly tedious and prosaic, and I *hope* better things. So *evviva la speranza!* and Westward Ho!

On board the Jefferson, River St. Clair, July 19.

This morning I came down early to the steam-boat, attended by a *cortège* of amiable people, who had heard of my sojourn at Detroit too late to be of any solace or service to me, but had seized this last and only opportunity of showing politeness and good-will. General Schwarz and his family, the sister of the governor, two other ladies and a gentleman, came on board with me at that early hour, and remained on deck till the paddles were in motion. The talk was so pleasant, I could not but regret that I had not seen some of these kind people earlier, or might hope to see more of them; but it was too late. Time and steam wait neither for man nor woman: all expressions of hope and regret on both sides were cut short by the parting signal, which the great bell swung out from on high; all compliments and questions "fumbled up into a loose adieu;" and these new friendly faces – seen but for a moment, then to be lost, yet not quite forgotten – were soon left far behind.

The morning was most lovely and auspicious; blazing hot though, and scarce a breath of air; and the magnificent machine, admirably appointed in all respects, gaily painted and gilt, with flags waving, glided over the dazzling waters with an easy, stately motion.

I had suffered so much at Detroit, that as it disappeared and melted away in the bright southern haze like a vision, I turned from it with a sense of relief, put the past out of my mind, and resigned myself to the present – like a wise woman – or wiser child.

The captain told me that last season he had never gone up the lakes with less than four or five hundred passengers. This year, fortunately for my individual comfort, the case is greatly altered: we have not more than one hundred and eighty passengers, consequently an abundance of accommodation, and air, and space – inestimable blessings in this sultry weather, and in the enjoyment of which I did not sympathise in the lamentations of the good-natured captain as much as I ought to have done.

We passed a large and beautifully green island, formerly called Snake Island, from the immense number of rattlesnakes which infested it. These were destroyed by turning large herds of swine upon it, and it is now, in compliment to its last conquerors and possessors, the swinish multitude, called Hog Island. This was the scene of some most horrid Indian atrocities during the Pontiac war. A large party of British prisoners, surprised while they were coming up to relieve Detroit, were brought over here, and, almost within sight of their friends in the fort, put to death with all the unutterable accompaniments of savage ferocity.

I have been told that since this war the custom of torturing persons to death has fallen gradually into disuse among the Indian tribes of these regions, and even along the whole frontier of the States an instance has not been known within these forty years.*

Leaving the channel of the river and the cluster of islands at its entrance, we stretched northwards across Lake St. Clair. This beautiful lake, though three times the size of the Lake of Geneva, is a mere pond compared with the enormous seas in its neighbourhood. About one o'clock we entered the river St. Clair, (which, like the Detroit, is rather a strait or channel than a river,) forming the communication between Lake St. Clair and Lake Huron. Ascending this beautiful river, we had, on the right, part of the western district of Upper Canada, and on the left the Michigan territory. The shores on either side, though low and bounded always by the line of forest, were broken into bays and little promontories, or diversified by islands, richly wooded, and of every variety of form. The bateaux of the Canadians, or the canoes of the Indians, were perpetually seen gliding among these winding chan-

* This was subsequently confirmed by Mr. Schoolcraft.

nels, or shooting across the river from side to side, as if playing at hide-and-seek among the leafy recesses. Now and then a beautiful schooner, with white sails relieved against the green masses of foliage, passed us, gracefully curtseying and sidling along. Innumerable flocks of wild fowl were disporting among the reedy islets, and here and there the great black loon was seen diving and dipping, or skimming over the waters. As usual, the British coast is here the most beautiful and fertile, and the American coast the best settled and cleared. Along the former I see a few isolated log-shanties, and groups of Indian lodges; along the latter, several extensive clearings, and some hamlets and rising villages. The facility afforded by the American steam-boats for the transport of goods and sale of produce, &c., is one reason of this. There is a boat, for instance, which leaves Detroit every morning for Fort Gratiot, stopping at the intermediate "landings." We are now moored at a place called "Palmer's Landing," for the purpose of taking in wood for the Lake voyage. This process has already occupied two hours, and is to detain us two more, though there are fourteen men employed in flinging logs into the wood-hold. Meantime I have been sketching and lounging about the little hamlet, where there is a good grocery-store, a sawing-mill worked by steam, and about twenty houses. Now I rest, and scribble this for you.

I was amused at Detroit to find the phraseology of the people imbued with metaphors taken from the most familiar mode of locomotion. "Will you take in wood?" signifies, will you take refreshment? "Is your steam up?" means, are you ready? The common phrase, "go ahead," has, I suppose, the same derivation. A witty friend of mine once wrote to me not to be lightly alarmed at the political and social ferments in America, nor mistake the *whizzing of the safety-valves for the bursting of the boilers!*

But all this time I have not yet introduced you to my companions on board; and one of these great American steamers is really a little world, a little social system in itself, where a near observer of faces and manners may find endless subjects of observation, amusement, and interest. At the other end of the vessel we have about one hundred emigrants on their way to the Illinois and the settlements to the west of Lake Michigan. Among them I find a large party of Germans and Norwegians, with their wives and families, a very respectable, orderly community, consisting of some farmers and some artisans, having with them a large quantity of stock and utensils – just the sort of people best calculated to improve and enrich their adopted country, wherever that may be. Then we have twenty or thirty poor ragged Irish emigrants, with good-natured potato-faces, and strong arms and willing hearts. Men are smoking, women nursing, washing, sewing; children squalling and rolling about.

The ladies' saloon and upper deck exhibit a very different scene: there are about twenty ladies and children in the cabin and state-rooms, which are beautifully furnished and carpeted, with draperies of blue silk, &c. On the upper deck, shaded by an awning, we have sofas, rocking-chairs, and people lounging up and down; some reading, some chattering, some sleeping; there are missionaries and missionaries' wives, and officers on their way to the garrisons on the Indian frontier; and settlers, and traders, and some few nondescripts – like myself.

Also among the passengers I find the Bishop of Michigan, whose preaching so delighted me on Sunday last. The governor's sister, Miss Mason, introduced us at starting, and bespoke his good offices for me. His conversation has been a great resource and interest for me during the long day. He is still a young man, who began life as a lawyer, and afterwards from a real vocation adopted his present profession: his talents and popularity have placed him in the rank he now holds. He is on his way to visit the missions and churches in the back settlements, and at Green Bay. His diocese, he tells me, extends about eight hundred miles in length and four hundred in breadth. And then if you think of the scattered population, the *sort* of population, the immensity of this spiritual charge and the amount of labour and responsibility it necessarily brings with it are enough to astound one. The amount of power is great in proportion; and the extensive moral influence exercised by such a man as this Bishop of Michigan struck me very much. In conversing with him and the missionaries on the spiritual and moral condition of his diocese, and these newly settled regions in general, I learned many things which interested me very much; and there was one thing discussed which especially surprised me. It was said that two thirds of the misery which came under the immediate notice of a popular clergyman, and to which he was called to minister, arose from the infelicity of the conjugal relations; there was no question here of open immorality and discord, but simply of infelicity and unfitness. The same thing has been brought before me in every country, every society in which I have been a sojourner and an observer; but I did not look to find it so broadly placed before me here in America, where the state of morals, as regards the two sexes, is comparatively pure; where the marriages are early, where conditions are equal, where the means of subsistence are abundant, where the women are much petted and considered by the men – too much so.

For a result then so universal, there must be a cause or causes as universal, not depending on any particular customs, manners, or religion, or political institutions. And what are these causes? Many things do puzzle me in this strange world of ours – many things in which the new world and the old world are equally incomprehensible. I cannot understand why an evil everywhere acknowledged and felt is not remedied somewhere, or discussed by some one, with a view to a remedy; – but no, it is like putting one's hand into the fire, only to touch upon it; it is the universal bruise, the putrefying sore, on which you must not lay a finger, or your patient (that is, society) cries out and resists, and, like a sick baby, scratches and kicks its physician.

Strange, and passing strange, that the relation between the two sexes, the passion of love in short, should not be taken into deeper consideration by our teachers and our legislators. People educate and legislate as if there was no such thing in the world; but ask the priest, ask the physician – let *them* reveal the amount of moral and physical results from this one cause. Must love be always discussed in blank verse, as if it were a thing to be played in tragedies or sung in songs – a subject for pretty poems and wicked novels, and had nothing to do with the prosaic current of our every-day existence, our moral welfare and eternal salvation? Must love be ever treated with profaneness, as a mere illusion? or with coarseness, as a mere impulse? or with fear, as a mere disease? or with shame, as a mere weakness? or with levity, as a mere accident? Whereas, it is a great mystery and a great necessity, lying at the foundation of human existence, morality, and happiness; mysterious, universal, inevitable as death. Why then should love be treated less seriously than death? It is as serious a thing. Love and Death, the alpha and omega of human life, the author and finisher of existence, the two points on which God's universe turns; which He, our Father and Creator, has placed beyond our arbitration – beyond the reach of that election and free will which He has left us in all other things!

Death must come, and love must come – but the state in which they find us? – whether blinded, astonished, and frightened, and ignorant, or, like reasonable creatures, guarded, prepared, and fit to manage our own feelings? – *this*, I suppose, depends on ourselves; and for want of such self-management and self-knowledge, look at the evils that ensue! – hasty, improvident, unsuitable marriages; repining, diseased, or vicious celibacy; irretrievable infamy; cureless insanity: – the death that comes early, and the love that comes late, reversing the primal laws of our nature.

It is of little consequence how unequal the conventional difference of rank, as in Germany – how equal the condition, station, and means, as in America, – if there be inequality between the sexes; and if the sentiment which attracts and unites them to each other, and the contracts and relations springing out of this sentiment, be not equally well understood by both, equally sacred with both, equally binding on both.

Another of my deck companions is a son of the celebrated Daniel Webster, with whom I began an acquaintance over Philip van Artevelde. He was reading that most charming book for the first time – a pleasure that I half envied him: but as I have it well nigh by heart, I could at least help him to admire. I know nothing prettier than this sort of sympathy over a favourite book – and then there was no end to the talk it gave rise to, for Philip van Artevelde is *àpropos* to everything – war, love, politics, religion. Mr. Webster was naturally anxious to know something of an author who had so much interested him, and I was sorry I could not better satisfy the curiosity and interest he expressed.

There is yet another person on board who has attracted my attention, and to whom I was especially introduced. This is General Brady, an officer of high distinction in the American army. He has taken a conspicuous part in all the Indian wars on the frontiers since Wayne's war in 1794, in which he served as lieutenant; and was not only present, but also a distinguished actor in most of the scenes I have alluded to. I did certainly long to ask him a thousand things; and here was a good opportunity of setting myself right on doubtful points. But General Brady, like many men who are especially men of action and daring, and whose lives have been passed amid scenes of terrific adventure, seems of a silent and modest temper; and I did not conceive that any longing or curiosity on my part gave me a right to tax his politeness, or engross his attention, or torment him with intrusive questions. So, after admiring for some time his fine military bearing, as he paced up and down the deck alone, and as if in deep thought, – I turned to my books, and the corner of my sofa.

At Detroit I had purchased Miss Sedgwick's tale of "The Rich Poor Man and the Poor Rich Man," and this sent away two hours delightfully, as we were gliding over the expanse of Lake St. Clair. Those who glanced on my book while I was reading always smiled – a significant sympathising smile, very expressive of that unenvious, affectionate homage and admiration which this genuine American writer inspires among her countrymen. I do not think I ever mentioned her name to any of them, that the countenance did not light up with pleasure and gratified pride. I have also a sensible little book, called "Three Experiments in Living," attributed to Miss Sedgwick – but I should think not hers* – it must be popular, and *true* to life and nature, for the edition I bought is the tenth. I have also another book to which I must introduce you more particularly – "The Travels and Adventures of Alexander Henry." Did you ever hear of such a man? No. Listen then, and perpend.

This Mr. Henry was a fur-trader who journeyed over these lake regions about seventy years ago, and is quoted as first-rate authority in more recent books of travels. His book, which was lent to me at Toronto, struck me so much as to have had some influence in directing the course of my present tour. Plain, unaffected, telling what he has to tell in few and simple words, and without comment – the internal evidence of truth – the natural sensibility and power of fancy, betrayed rather than displayed – render not only the narrative, but the man himself, his personal character, unspeakably interesting. Wild as are the tales of his hairbreadth escapes, I never heard the slightest impeachment of his veracity. He was living at Montreal so late as 1810 or 1811, when a friend of mine

---

* It is written by Mrs. Lee of Boston.

saw him, and described him to me as a very old man past eighty, with white hair, and still hale-looking and cheerful, so that his hard and adventurous life, and the horrors he had witnessed and suffered had in no respect impaired his spirits or his constitution. His book has been long out of print. I had the greatest difficulty in procuring the loan of a copy, after sending to Montreal, Quebec, and New York, in vain. Mr. Henry is to be my travelling companion, or rather *our* travelling companion, for I always fancy *you* of the party. I do not know how he might have figured as a squire of dames when living, but I assure you that being dead he makes a very respectable hero of epic or romance. He is the Ulysses of these parts, and to cruise among the shores, rocks, and islands of Lake Huron without Henry's travels, were like coasting Calabria and Sicily without the Odyssey in your head or hand, – only here you have the island of Mackinaw instead of the island of Circe; the land of the Ottawas instead of the shores of the Lotophagi; cannibal Chippewas, instead of man-eating Laestrygons; Pontiac figures as Polypheme; and Wa,wa,tam plays the part of good king Alcinous. I can find no type for the women, as Henry does not tell us his adventures among the squaws, but no doubt he might have found both Calypsos and Nausicaas, and even a Penelope, among them.

[*July*] 20.

Before I went down to my rest yesterday evening, I beheld a strange and beautiful scene. The night was coming on, the moon had risen round and full like an enormous globe of fire, we were still in the channel of the river, when to the right I saw a crowd of Indians on a projecting point of land – the very Hurons from near Amherstberg, already mentioned. They were encamping for the night, some hauling up their canoes, some building up their wigwams; there were numerous fires blazing amid the thick foliage, and the dusky figures of the Indians were seen glancing to and fro, and I heard loud laughs and shouts as our huge steamer swept past them. In another moment we turned a point, and all was dark; the whole had vanished like a scene in a melodrama. I rubbed my eyes, and began to think I was already dreaming.

At the entrance of the river St. Clair the Americans have a fort and garrison, (Fort Gratiot,) and a lighthouse, which we passed in the night. On the opposite side we have no station; so that, in case of any misunderstanding between the two nations, it would be in the power of the Americans to shut the entrance of Lake Huron upon us. (Pray have a map before you when you read all this!)

At seven this morning, when I went on deck, we had advanced about one hundred miles into Lake Huron; we were coasting along the south shore about four miles from the land, while, on the other side, we had about two hundred miles of open *sea*, and the same expanse before us: soon after, we had to pass the entrance of Sagginaw Bay. Here we lost sight of land for the first time. Sagginaw Bay, I should suppose, is as large as the Gulf of Genoa; it runs seventy or eighty miles up into the land, and is as famous for storms as the Bay of Biscay. Here, if there be a capful of wind or a cupful of sea, one is sure to have the benefit of it, for even in the finest weather there is a considerable swell. We were about three hours crossing from the Pointe Aux Barques to Cape Thunder, and during this time a number of my companions were put *hors de combat*. The rest is silence. After a vain struggle against the fates and the destinies I fainted away, and was consigned to my berth – a very wretch.

All this part of Michigan is unsettled, and is said to be sandy and barren. Along the whole horizon was nothing visible but the dark omnipresent pine-forest. The Sagginaw Indians, whose hunting-grounds extend along the shore, are, I believe, a tribe of Ottawas. I should add, that the Americans have built a lighthouse on a little island near Thunder Bay. A situation more terrific in its solitude you cannot imagine than that of the keeper of this lonely tower, among rocks, tempests, and savages. All their provisions come from a distance of at least one hundred miles, and a long course of stormy weather, which sometimes occurs, would place them in danger in starvation.

Doth the bright sun from the high arch of heaven,
In all his beauteous robes of flecker'd clouds,
And ruddy vapours, and deep glowing flames,
And softly varied shades, look gloriously?
Do the green woods dance to the wind? the lakes
Cast up their sparkling waters to the light?

JOANNA BAILLIE.

THE NEXT morning, at earliest dawn, I was wakened by an unusual noise and movement on board, and putting out my head to inquire the cause, was informed that we were arrived at the island of Mackinaw, and that the captain being most anxious to proceed on his voyage, only half an hour was allowed to make all my arrangements, take out my luggage, and so forth. I dressed in all haste and ran up to the deck, and there a scene burst at once on my enchanted gaze, such as I never had imagined, such as I wish I could place before you in words, – but I despair, unless words were of light, and lustrous hues, and breathing music. However, here is the picture as well as I can paint it. We were lying in a tiny bay, crescent-shaped, of which the two horns or extremities were formed by long narrow promontories projecting into the lake. On the east, the whole sky was flushed with a deep amber glow, fleck-ered with softest shades of rose-colour – the same intense splendour being reflected in the lake; and upon the extremity of the point, between the glory above and the glory below, stood the little Missionary church, its light spire and belfry defined against the sky. On the opposite side of the heavens hung the moon, waxing paler and paler, and melting away, as it seemed, before the splendour of the rising day. Immediately in front rose the abrupt and picturesque heights of the island, robed in richest foliage, and crowned by the lines of the little fortress, snow-white, and gleaming in the morning light. At the base of these cliffs, all along the shore, immediately on the edge of the lake, which, transparent and unruffled, reflected every form as in a mirror, an encampment of Indian wigwams extended far as my eye could reach on either side. Even while I looked, the inmates were beginning to bestir themselves, and dusky figures were seen emerging into sight from their picturesque dormitories, and stood gazing on us with folded arms, or were busied about their canoes, of which some hundreds lay along the beach.

There was not a breath of air; and while heaven and earth were glowing with light, and colour, and life, and elysian stillness – a delicious balmy serenity, wrapt and interfused the whole. O how passing lovely it was! how wondrously beautiful and strange! I cannot tell how long I may have stood, lost – absolutely lost, and fearing even to wink my eyes, lest the spell should dissolve, and all should vanish away like some air-wrought phantasy, some dream out of fairy land, – when the good Bishop of Michigan came up to me, and with a smiling benevolence waked me out of my ecstatic trance; and reminding me that I had but two minutes left, seized upon some of my packages himself, and hurried me on to the little wooden pier just in time. We were then conducted to a little inn, or boarding-house, kept by a very fat half-cast Indian woman, who spoke Indian, bad French, and worse English, and who was addressed as *Madame*. Here I was able to arrange my hasty toilette, and we, that is, General Brady, his aide-de-camp, the bishop, two Indian traders, myself, and some others, sat down to an excellent breakfast of white-fish, eggs, tea and coffee, for which the charge was twice what I should have given at the first hotel in the United States, and yet not unreasonable, considering that European luxuries were placed before us in this remote spot. By the time breakfast was discussed it was past six o'clock, and taking my sketch-book in my hand, I sauntered forth alone to the beach till it should be a fitting hour to present myself at the door of the American agent, Mr. Schoolcraft.

The first object which caught my eye was the immense steamer gliding swiftly away towards the straits of Michilimackinac, already far, far to the west. Suddenly the thought of my extreme loneliness came over me – a momentary wonder and alarm to find myself so far from any human being who took the least interest about my fate. I had no letter to Mr. Schoolcraft, and if Mr. and Mrs. MacMurray had not passed this way, or had forgotten to mention me, what would be my reception? what should I do? Here I must stay for some days at least. All the accommodation that could be afforded by the half French, half Indian "Madame," had been already secured, and, without turning out the bishop, there was not even a room for me. These thoughts and many others, some natural doubts, and fears, came across my mind, but I cannot say that they remained there long, or that they had the effect of rendering me uneasy and anxious for more than half a minute. With a sense of enjoyment keen and unanticipative as that of a child – looking neither before nor after – I soon abandoned myself to the present, and all its delicious exciting novelty, leaving the future to take care of itself, – which I am more and more convinced is the truest wisdom, the most real philosophy, after all.

The sun had now risen in cloudless glory – all was life and movement. I strayed and loitered for full three hours along the shore, I hardly knew whither, sitting down occasionally under the shadow of a cliff or cedar fence to rest, and watching the operations of the Indian families. It were endless to tell you of each individual group or picture as successively presented before me. But there were some general features of the scene which struck me at once. There were more than one hundred wigwams, and round each of these lurked several ill-looking, half-starved, yelping dogs. The women were busied about their children, or making fires and cooking, or pounding Indian corn, in a primitive sort of mortar, formed of part of a tree hollowed out, with a heavy rude pestle which they moved up and down as if churning. The dress of the men was very various – the cotton shirt, blue or scarlet leggings, and deerskin moccasins and blanket coat, were most general; but many had no shirt nor vest, merely the cloth leggings, and a blanket thrown round them as drapery: the faces of several being most grotesquely painted. The dress of the women was more uniform; a cotton shirt, and cloth leggings and moccasins, and a dark blue blanket. Necklaces, silver armlets, silver earrings, and circular plates of silver fastened on the breast, were the usual ornaments of both sexes. There may be a general equality of rank among the Indians; but there is evidently all that inequality of condition which difference of character and intellect might naturally produce; there were rich wigwams and poor wigwams; whole families ragged, meagre, and squalid, and others gay with dress and ornaments, fat and well-favoured: on the whole, these were beings quite distinct from any Indians I had yet seen, and realised all my ideas of the wild and lordly savage. I remember I came upon a family group, consisting of a fine tall young man and two squaws; one had a child swaddled in one of their curious bark cradles, which she composedly hung up against the side of the wigwam. They were then busied launching a canoe, and in a moment it was dancing upon the rippling waves: one woman guided the canoe, the other paddled; the young man stood in the prow in a striking and graceful attitude, poising his fish-spear in his hand. When they were about a hundred yards from the shore, suddenly I saw the fish-spear darted down into the water, and disappear beneath it; as it sprang up again to the surface, it was rapidly seized, and a large fish was sticking to the prongs; the same process was repeated with unerring success, and then the canoe was paddled back to the land. The young man flung his spear into the bottom of the canoe, and, drawing his blanket round him, leapt on shore, and lounged away without troubling himself farther; the women drew up the canoe, kindled a fire, and suspended the fish over it, to be cooked *à la mode Indienne*.

There was another group which amused me exceedingly: it was a large family, and, compared with some others, they were certainly people of distinction and substance, rich in beads, blankets and brass kettles, with "all things handsome about them;" they had two wigwams and two canoes. But I must begin by making you understand the construction of a wigwam, – such, at least, as those which now crowded the shore.

Eight or twelve long poles are stuck in the ground in a circle, meeting at a point at the top, where they are all fastened together. The skeleton thus erected is covered over, thatched in some sort with mats, or large pieces of birch bark, beginning at the bottom, and leaving an opening at top for the emission of smoke: there is a door about four feet high, before which a skin or blanket is suspended; and as it is summer time, they do not seem particular about closing the chinks and apertures.* As to the canoes, they are uniformly of birch bark, exceedingly light, flat-bottomed, and most elegant in shape, varying in size from eighteen to thirty-six feet in length, and from a foot and a half to four feet in width. The family I have mentioned were preparing to embark, and were disman-

* I learned subsequently, that the cone-like form of the wigwam is proper to the Ottawas and Pottowottomies, and that the oblong form, in which the branches or poles are bent over at top in an arch, is proper to the Chippewa tribe. But as this latter is more troublesome to erect, the former construction is usually adopted by the Chippewas also in their temporary encampments.

tling their wigwams and packing up their goods, not at all discomposed by my vicinity, as I sat on a bank watching the whole process with no little interest. The most striking personage in this group was a very old man, seated on a log of wood, close upon the edge of the water; his head was quite bald, excepting a few gray hairs which were gathered in a tuft at the top, and decorated with a single feather – I think an eagle's feather; his blanket of scarlet cloth was so arranged as to fall round his limbs in graceful folds, leaving his chest and shoulders exposed; he held a green umbrella over his head, (a gift of purchase from some white trader,) and in the other hand a long pipe – and he smoked away, never stirring, nor taking the slightest interest in anything which was going on. Then there were two fine young men, and three women, one old and hideous, with matted grizzled hair, the youngest really a beautiful girl about fifteen. There were also three children; the eldest had on a cotton shirt, the breast of which was covered with silver ornaments. The men were examining the canoes, and preparing to launch them; the women were taking down their wigwams, and as they uncovered them, I had an opportunity of observing the whole interior economy of their dwellings.

The ground within was spread over with mats, two or three deep, and skins and blankets, so as to form a general couch: then all around the internal circle of the wigwam were ranged their goods and chattels in very tidy order; I observed wooden chests, of European make, bags of woven grass, baskets and cases of birch bark (called *mokkuks*,) also brass kettles, pans, and, to my surprise, a large coffee-pot of queen's metal.

When all was arranged, and the canoes afloat, the poles of the wigwams were first placed at the bottom, then the mats and bundles, which served apparently to sit on, and the kettles and chests were stowed in the middle; the old man was assisted by the others into the largest canoe; women, children, and dogs followed; the young men stood in the stern with their paddles as steersmen; the

women and boys squatted down, each with a paddle; –
with all this weight, the elegant buoyant little canoes
scarcely sank an inch deeper in the water – and in this
guise away they glided with surprising swiftness over the
sparkling waves, directing their course eastwards for the
Manitoolin Islands, where I hope to see them again. The
whole process of preparation and embarkation did not
occupy an hour.

About ten o'clock I ventured to call on Mr. Schoolcraft,
and was received by him with grave and quiet politeness.
They were prepared, he said, for my arrival, and then he
apologised for whatever might be deficient in my reception, and for the absence of his wife, by informing me that
she was ill, and had not left her room for some days.

I leave you to imagine how much I was discomposed –
how shocked to find myself an intruder under such circumstances. I said so, and begged that they would not
think of me – that I could easily provide for myself – and
so I could and would. I would have laid myself down in
one of the Indian lodges rather than have been *de trop*.
But Mr. Schoolcraft said, with much kindness, that they
knew already of my arrival by one of my fellow-
passengers – that a room was prepared for me, a servant
already sent down for my goods, and Mrs. Schoolcraft,
who was a little better that morning, hoped to see me.
Here, then, I am installed for the next few days – and I
know not how many more – so completely am I at the
mercy of "fates, destinies, and such branches of learning!"

I am charmed with Mrs. Schoolcraft. When able to
appear, she received me with true lady-like simplicity. The
damp, tremulous hand, the soft, plaintive voice, the
touching expression of her countenance, told too painfully
of resigned and habitual suffering. Mrs. Schoolcraft's
features are more decidedly Indian than those of her sister

Mrs. MacMurray. Her accent is slightly foreign – her choice of language pure and remarkably elegant. In the course of an hour's talk, all my sympathies were enlisted in her behalf, and I thought that I perceived that she, on her part, was inclined to return these benignant feelings. I promised myself to repay her hospitality by all the attention and gratitude in my power. I am here a lonely stranger, thrown upon her sufferance; but she is good, gentle, and in most delicate health, and there are a thousand quiet ways in which woman may be kind and useful to her sister woman. Then she has two sweet children about eight or nine years old – no fear, you see, that we shall soon be the best friends in the world!

This day, however, I took care not to be *à charge*, so I ran about along the lovely shore, and among the Indians, inexpressibly amused, and occupied, and excited by all I saw and heard. At last I returned – O so wearied out – so spent in body and mind! I was fain to go to rest soon after sunset. A nice little room had been prepared for me, and a *wide* comfortable bed, into which I sank with such a feeling of peace, security, and thankfulness, as could only be conceived by one who had been living in comfortless inns and close steam-boats for the last fortnight.

Mackinaw

"Un pezzo del cielo caduto in terra."

O N A little platform not quite half way up the wooded height which overlooks the bay, embowered in foliage, and sheltered from the tyrannous breathing of the north by the precipitous cliff, rising almost perpendicularly behind, stands the house in which I find myself at present a grateful and contented inmate. The ground in front sloping down to the shore, is laid out in a garden, with an avenue of fruit trees, the gate at the end opening on the very edge of the lake. From the porch I look down upon the scene I have endeavoured – how inadequately! – to describe to you: the little crescent bay; the village of Mackinaw; the beach thickly studded with Indian lodges; canoes, fishing, or darting hither and thither, light and buoyant as sea-birds; a tall graceful schooner swinging at anchor. Opposite rises the Island of Bois-blanc, with its tufted and most luxuriant foliage. To the east we see the open lake, and in the far western distance the promontory of Michilimackinac, and the strait of that name, the portal of Lake Michigan. The exceeding beauty of this little paradise of an island, the attention which has been excited by its enchanting scenery, and the salubrity of its summer climate, the facility of communication lately afforded by the lake steamers, and its situation half-way between

Detroit and the newly-settled regions of the west, are likely to render Mackinaw a sort of watering-place for the Michigan and Wisconsin fashionables, or, as the bishop expressed it, the "Rockaway of the west;" so at least it is anticipated.

How far such an accession of fashion and reputation may be desirable, I know not; I am only glad it has not yet taken place, and that I have beheld this lovely island in all its wild beauty. I am told that last year there were several strangers staying here, in spite of the want of all endurable accommodation. This year there is only one *permanent* visiter – if I may so express myself – a most agreeable little Irish-woman, with all the Irish warmth of heart and ease of manner, who emigrated with her husband some years ago, and settled near St. Joseph's, in Michigan. She has brought her children here for the summer, and has her piano, her music, her French and Italian books, and we have begun an acquaintance which is likely to prove very pleasant.

When I left my room this morning, I remained for some time in the parlour, looking over the Wisconsin Gazette, a good sized, well printed newspaper, published on the west shore of Lake Michigan. I was reading a most pathetic and serious address from the new settlers in Wisconsin to *the down-east girls*, (*i.e.* the women of the eastern states,) who are invited to go to the relief of these hapless hard-working bachelors in the backwoods. They are promised affluence and love, – the "picking and choosing among a set of the finest young fellows in the world," who were ready to fall at their feet, and make the most adoring and the most obedient of husbands! Can you fancy what a pretty thing a Wisconsin pastoral might be? Only imagine one of these despairing backwoodsmen inditing an Ovidian epistle to his unknown mistress – "*down east*," – wooing her to come and be wooed! Well, I was enjoying this comical effusion, and thinking that women must certainly be at a premium in these parts, when suddenly the windows were darkened, and looking up, I beheld a crowd of faces,

dusky, painted, wild, grotesque – with flashing eyes and
white teeth, staring in upon me. I quickly threw down the
paper and hastened out. The porch, the little lawn, the
garden walks, were crowded with Indians, the elder chiefs
and warriors sitting on the ground, or leaning silently
against the pillars; the young men, women, and boys
lounging and peeping about, with eager and animated
looks, but all perfectly well conducted, and their voices
low and pleasing to the ear. They were chiefly Ottawas and
Pottowottomies, two tribes which "call brother," that is,
claim relationship, and are usually in alliance, but widely
different. The Ottawas are the most civilised, the Pottowottomies the least so of all the lake tribes. The Ottawa
I soon distinguished by the decency of his dress, and the
handkerchief knotted round the head – a custom borrowed from the early French settlers, with whom they
have had much intercourse: the Pottowattomie by the
more savage finery of his costume, his tall figure, and a
sort of swagger in his gait. The dandyism of some of these
Pottowottomie warriors is inexpressibly amusing and grotesque; I defy all Regent Street and Bond Street to go
beyond them in the exhibition of self-decoration and self-
complacency. One of these exquisites, whom I distinguished as Beau Brummel, was not indeed much
indebted to a tailor, seeing he had neither a coat nor any
thing else that gentlemen are accustomed to wear; but
then his face was most artistically painted, the upper half
of it being vermilion, with a black circle round one eye,
and a white circle round the other; the lower half of a
bright green, except the tip of his nose, which was also
vermilion. His leggings of scarlet cloth were embroidered
down the sides, and decorated with tufts of hair. The
band, or garter, which confines the leggings, is always an
especial bit of finery; and his were gorgeous, all embroidered with gay beads, and strings and tassels of the liveliest
colours hanging down to his ankle. His moccasins were
also beautifully worked with porcupine quills; he had
armlets and bracelets of silver, and round his head a silver

band stuck with tufts of moose-hair, dyed blue and red; and conspicuous above all, the eagle feather in his hair, showing he was a warrior, and had taken a scalp – *i.e.* killed his man.

Over his shoulders hung a blanket of scarlet cloth, very long and ample, which he had thrown back a little, so as to display his chest, on which a large outspread hand was painted in white. It is impossible to describe the air of perfect self-complacency with which this youth strutted about. Seeing my attention fixed upon him, he came up and shook hands with me, repeating "Bojou! bojou!"* Others immediately pressed forward also to shake hands, or rather take my hand, for they do not *shake* it; and I was soon in the midst of a crowd of perhaps thirty or forty Indians, all holding out their hands to me, or snatching mine, and repeating "bojou" with every expression of delight and good-humour.

This must suffice in the way of description, for I cannot further particularise dresses; they were very various, and few so fine as my young Pottowottomie. I remember another young man, who had a common black beaver hat, all round which, in several silver bands, he had stuck a profusion of feathers, and long tufts of dyed hair, so that it formed a most gorgeous helmet. Some wore the hair hanging loose and wild in elf-locks, but others again had combed and arranged it with much care and pains.

The men seemed to engross the finery; none of the women that I saw were painted. Their blankets were mostly dark blue; some had strings of beads round their necks, and silver armlets. The hair of some of the young women was very prettily arranged, being parted smooth upon the forehead, and twisted in a knot behind, very much *à la Grecque*. There is, I imagine, a very general and hearty aversion to cold water.

---

* This universal Indian salutation is merely a corruption of *bon jour*.

This morning there was a "talk" held in Mr. Schoolcraft's office, and he kindly invited me to witness the proceedings. About twenty of their principal men, including a venerable old chief, were present; the rest stood outside, crowding the doors and windows, but never attempting to enter, nor causing the slightest interruption. The old chief wore a quantity of wampum, but was otherwise undistinguished, except by his fine head and acute features. His gray hair was drawn back, and tied on the top of his head with a single feather. All, as they entered, took me by the hand with a quiet smile and a "bojou," to which I replied, as I had been instructed, "Bojou, neeje!" (good-day, friend!) They then sat down upon the floor, all around the room. Mr. Johnston, Mrs. Schoolcraft's brother, acted as interpreter, and the business proceeded with the utmost gravity.

After some whispering among themselves, an orator of the party addressed Mr. Schoolcraft with great emphasis. Extending his hand and raising his voice, he began: "Father, I am come to tell you a piece of my mind." But when he had uttered a few sentences, Mr. Schoolcraft desired the interpreter to tell him that it was useless to speak farther on *that* subject, (I understood it to relate to some land-payments.) The orator stopped immediately, and then, after a pause, he went up and took Mr. Schoolcraft's hand with a friendly air, as if to show he was not offended. Another orator then arose, and proceeded to the object of the visit, which was to ask an allowance of corn, salt, and tobacco, while they remained on the island – a request which I presume was granted, as they departed with much apparent satisfaction.

There was not a figure among them that was not a study for a painter; and how I wished that my hand had been readier with the pencil to snatch some of those picturesque heads and attitudes! But it was all so new – I was so lost in gazing, listening, observing, and trying to comprehend, that I could not make a single sketch for you, except the above, in most poor and inadequate words.

The Indians here – and fresh parties are constantly arriving – are chiefly Ottawas, from Arbre Croche, on the east of Lake Michigan; Pottowottomies; and Winnebagos from the west of the lake; a few Menomonies and Chippewas from the shores north-west of us; – the occasion of this assemblage being the same with all. They are on the way to the Manitoolin Islands, to receive the presents annually distributed by the British government to all those Indian tribes who were friendly to us during the wars with America, and call themselves our allies and our children, though living within the bounds of another state. Some of them make a voyage of five hundred miles to receive a few blankets and kettles; coasting along the shores, encamping at night, and paddling all day from sunrise to sunset, living on the fish or game they may meet, and the little provision they can carry with them, which consists chiefly of parched Indian corn and bear's fat. Some are out on this excursion during six weeks, or more, every year; returning to their hunting-grounds by the end of September, when the great hunting season begins, which continues through October and November; they then return to their villages and wintering-grounds. This applies generally to the tribes I find here, except the Ottawas of Arbre Croche, who have a good deal of land in cultivation, and are more stationary and civilised than the other Lake Indians. They have been for nearly a century under the care of the French jesuit missions, but do not seem to have made much advance since Henry's time, and the days when they were organised under Pontiac; they were even then considered superior in humanity and intelligence to the Chippewas and Pottowottomies, and more inclined to agriculture.

After some most sultry weather, we have had a grand storm. The wind shifted to the northeast, and rose to a hurricane. I was then sitting with my Irish friend in the mission-house; and while the little bay lay almost tranquil, gleam and shadow floating over its bosom, the expanse of the main lake was like the ocean lashed to fury. On the east side of the island the billows came "rolling with might," flinging themselves in wrath and foam far up the land. It was a magnificent spectacle. Returning home, I was anxious to see how the wigwam establishments had stood out the storm, and was surprised to find that little or no damage had been done. I peeped into several, with a nod and a *bojou*, and found the inmates very snug. Here and there a mat was blown away, but none of the poles were displaced or blown down, which I had firmly expected.

Though all these lodges seem nearly alike to a casual observer, I was soon aware of differences and gradations in the particular arrangements, which are amusingly characteristic of the various inhabitants. There is one lodge, a little to the east of us, which I call the Château. It is rather larger and loftier than the others: the mats which cover it are whiter and of a neater texture than usual. The blanket which hangs before the opening is new and clean. The inmates, ten in number, are well and handsomely dressed; even the women and children have abundance of ornaments; and as for the gay cradle of the baby, I quite covet it – it is so gorgeously elegant. I supposed at first that this must be the lodge of a chief; but I have since understood that the chief is seldom either so well lodged or so well dressed as the others, it being a part of his policy to avoid everything like ostentation, or rather to be ostentatiously poor and plain in his apparel and possessions. This wigwam belongs to an Ottawa, remarkable for his skill in hunting, and for his habitual abstinence from the "firewater." He is a baptized Roman Catholic, belonging to the mission at Arbre Croche, and is reputed a rich man.

Not far from this, and almost immediately in front of our house, stands another wigwam, a most wretched concern. The owners have not mats enough to screen them from the weather; and the bare poles are exposed through the "looped and windowed raggedness" on every side. The woman, with her long neglected hair, is always seen cowering despondingly over the embers of her fire, as if lost in sad reveries. Two naked children are scrambling among the pebbles on the shore. The man wrapt in a dirty ragged blanket, without a single ornament, looks the image of savage inebriety and ferocity. Observe that these are the two extremes, and that between them are many gradations of comfort, order, and respectability. An Indian is *respectable* in his own community, in proportion as his wife and children look fat and well fed; this being a proof of his prowess and success as a hunter, and his consequent riches.

I was loitering by the garden gate this evening, about sunset, looking at the beautiful effects which the storm of the morning had left in the sky and on the lake. I heard the sound of the Indian drum, mingled with the shouts and yells and shrieks of the intoxicated savages, who were drinking in front of the village whisky-store; – when at this moment a man came slowly up, whom I recognised as one of the Ottawa chiefs, who had often attracted my attention. His name is Kim,e,wun, which signifies the Rain, or rather "it rains." He now stood before me, one of the noblest figures I ever beheld, above six feet high, erect as a forest pine. A red and green handkerchief was twined round his head with much elegance, and knotted in front, with the two ends projecting; his black hair fell from beneath it, and his small black piercing eyes glittered from among its masses, like stars glancing through the thunder clouds. His ample blanket was thrown over his left shoulder, and brought under his right arm, so as to leave it free and exposed; and a sculptor might have envied the disposition of the whole drapery – it was so felicitous, so richly graceful.* He stood in a contemplative attitude, evidently undecided whether he should join his drunken companions in their night revel, or return, like a wise man, to his lodge and his mat. He advanced a few steps, then turned, then paused and listened – then turned back again. I retired a little within the gate, to watch, unseen, the issue of the conflict. Alas! it was soon decided – the fatal temptation prevailed over better thoughts. He suddenly drew his blanket round him, and strided onwards in the direction of the village, treading the earth with an air of defiance, and a step which would have become a prince.On returning home, I mentioned this scene to Mr. and Mrs. Schoolcraft, as I do everything which strikes me, that I may profit by their remarks and explanations. Mr. S. told me a laughable anecdote.

A distinguished Pottowottomie warrior presented himself to the Indian agent at Chicago, and observing that he was a very good man, very good indeed – and a good friend to the Long-knives, (the Americans,) requested a dram of whisky. The agent replied, that he never gave whisky to *good* men, – good men never asked for whisky; and never drank it. It was only *bad* Indians who asked for whisky, or liked to drink it. 'Then,' replied the Indian quickly in his broken English, 'me damn rascal!'

The revel continued far through the night, for I heard the wild yelling and whooping of the savages long after I had gone to rest. I can now conceive what it must be to hear that shrill prolonged cry (unlike any sound I ever heard in

* While among the Indians, I often had occasion to observe that what we call the *antique* and the *ideal* are merely free, unstudied nature. Since my return from Canada, I have seen some sketches made by Mr. Harvey when in Ireland – figures of the Cork and Kerry girls, folded in their large blue cloaks; and I remember, on opening the book, I took them for drawings after the antique – figures brought from Herculaneum or Pompeii, or some newly-discovered Greek temple.

my life before) in the solitude of the forest, and when it is the certain harbinger of death.

It is surprising to me, considering the number of savages congregated together, and the excess of drunkenness, that no mischief is done; that there has been no fighting, no robberies committed, and that there is a feeling of perfect security around me. The women, they tell me, have taken away their husband's knives and tomahawks, and hidden them – wisely enough. At this time there are about twelve hundred Indians here. The fort is empty – the garrison having been withdrawn as useless; and perhaps there are not a hundred white men in the island, – rather unequal odds! And then that fearful Michilimackinac in full view, with all its horrid, murderous associations!* But do not for a moment imagine that I feel *fear*, or the slightest doubt of security; only a sort of thrill which enhances the enjoyment I have in these wild scenes – a thrill such as one feels in the presence of danger when most safe from it – such as I felt when bending over the rapids of Niagara.

The Indians, apparently, have no idea of correcting or restraining their children; personal chastisement is unheard of. They say that before a child has any understanding there is no use in correcting it; and when old enough to understand, no one has a right to correct it. Thus the fixed, inherent sentiment of personal independence grows up with the Indians from earliest infancy. The will of an Indian child is not forced; he has nothing to learn but what he sees done around him, and he learns by imitation. I hear no scolding, no tones of command or reproof; but I see no evil results from this mild system, for the general reverence and affection of children for parents is delightful: where there is no obedience exacted, there

---

* Michilimachinac was one of the forts surprised by the Indians at the breaking out of the Pontiac war, when seventy British soldiers with their officers were murdered and scalped. Henry gives a most vivid description of this scene of horror in few words. He was present, and escaped through the friendship of an Indian (Wa,wa,tam) who, in consequence of a dream in early youth, had adopted him as his brother.

can be no rebellion; they dream not of either, and all live in peace under the same wigwam.

I observe, while loitering among them, that they seldom raise their voices, and they pronounce several words much more softly than we write them. Wigwam, a house, they pronounce *wee-ga-waum*; moccasin, a shoe, *muck-a-zeen*; manito, spirit, *mo-nee-do*, – lengthening the vowels, and softening the aspirates. *Chippewa* is properly *O-jĭb-wày; ab,bin,no,jee* is a little child. The accent of the women is particularly soft, with a sort of plaintive modulation, reminding me of recitative. Their low laugh is quite musical, and has something infantine in it. I sometimes hear them sing, and the strain is generally in a minor key; but I cannot succeed in detecting or retaining an entire or distinct tune. I am, however, bent on bringing you an Indian song, if I can catch one.

There was a mission established on this island in 1823, for the conversion of the Indians, and the education of the Indian and half-breed children.* A large mission and school house was erected, and a neat little church. Those who were interested about the Indians entertained the most sanguine expectations of the success of the undertaking. But at present the extensive buildings of the mission-house are used merely as storehouses, or as lodgings; and if Mackinaw should become a place of resort, they will probably be converted into fashionable hotel.† The mission itself is established farther west, somewhere near Green Bay, on Lake Michigan; and when overtaken by the

* In 1828, Major Anderson, our Indian agent, computed the number of Canadians and mixed breed married to Indian women, and residing on the north shores of Lake Huron, and in the neighbourhood of Michillimackinac, at nine hundred. This he called the *lowest* estimate.

† I have before me a copy of certain queries proposed by Bishop M'Donell (of Upper Canada) in 1828, with the answers of our Indian agent, Major Anderson, who has been employed in the Indian department for many years, and passed the last thirty years of his life in

advancing stream of white civilisation, and the contagion which it carries with it, no doubt it must retire yet farther.

As for the little missionary church, it has been for some time disused, the French Canadians and half-breeds on the island being mostly Roman Catholics. To-day, however, divine service was performed in it by the Bishop of Michigan, to a congregation of about twenty persons. Around the open doors of the church, a crowd of Indians, principally women, had assembled, and a few came in, and stood leaning against the pews, with their blankets folded round them, mute and still, and respectfully attentive.

Immediately before me sat a man who at once attracted my attention. He was an Indian, evidently of unmixed blood, though wearing a long blanket coat and a decent but worn hat. His eyes, during the whole service, were fixed on those of the Bishop with a passionate, eager gaze; not for a moment were they withdrawn: he seemed to devour every word both of the office and the sermon, and, by the working of his features, I supposed him to be strongly impressed – it was the very enthusiasm of devotion: and yet, strange to say, not one word did he understand. When I inquired how it was that his attention was so fixed, and that he seemed thus moved by what he could not possibly comprehend, I was told, "it was by the power

---

communication with the tribes round Lake Huron. Speaking of this missionary establishment at Mackinaw, he says, that "it has caused great excitement in the minds of the Indians, that one hundred and twenty half breeds and Indians are actually receiving instruction; and that if a similar establishment were promoted at Drummond's Island," (then in possession of the English,) "he believes the Indians would swarm to it." He adds, "that the mission-house built at Mackinaw was supposed to be sufficient space to contain all that would present themselves for instruction for many years to come; *but such is the thirst for knowledge* that the house is full and at least fifty from Prairie du Chien, Green Bay, and Lake Superior, have prayed for admittance this season, without being able to obtain it from want of room." The house thus described is now empty.

of faith." I have the story of this man (whom I see frequently) from Mr. Schoolcraft. His name is Chusco. He was formerly a distinguished man in his tribe as professor of the *Meta* and the *Wabeno*, – that is, physician and conjuror; and no less as a professor of whisky-drinking. His wife, who had been converted by one of the missionaries, converted her husband. He had long resisted her preaching and persuasion, but at last one day, as they were making maple sugar together on an island, "he was suddenly thrown into an agony as if an evil spirit haunted him, and from that moment had no peace till he had been baptized and received into the christian church." From this time he avoided drunkenness, and surrendered his medicine bag, manitos, and implements of sorcery, into the hands of Mr. Schoolcraft. Subsequently he showed no indisposition to speak of the power and arts he had exercised. He would not allow that it was all mere trick and deception, but insisted that he had been enabled to perform certain cures, or extraordinary magical operations, by the direct agency of the evil spirit, *i.e.* the devil, who, now that he was become a Christian, had forsaken him, and left him in peace. I was a little surprised to find, in the course of this explanation, that there were educated and intelligent people who had no more doubt of this direct satanic agency than the poor Indian himself.

Chusco has not touched ardent spirits for the last seven years, and, ever since his conversion in the sugar-camp, he has firmly adhered to his christian profession. He is now between sixty and seventy years old, with a countenance indicating more of mildness and simplicity than intellect. Generally speaking, the men who practise medicine among the Indians make a great mystery of their art, and of the herbs and nostrums they are in the habit of using; and it were to be wished that one of these converted medicine-men could be prevailed on to disclose some of their medical arcana; for of the efficacy of some of their prescriptions, apart from the mummery with which they are accompanied, there can be no doubt.

We have taken several delicious drives over this lovely little island, and traversed it in different directions. It is not more than three miles in length, and wonderfully beautiful. There is no large or lofty timber upon it, but a perpetual succession of low, rich groves, "alleys green, dingles, and bosky dells." There is on the eastern coast a natural arch or bridge, where the waters of the Lake have undermined the rock, and left a fragment thrown across a chasm two hundred feet high. Strawberries, raspberries, whortleberries, and cherries, were growing everywhere wild, and in abundance. The whole island, when seen from a distance, has the form of a turtle sleeping on the water: hence its Indian appellation, Michilimackinac, which signifies the great turtle. The same name is given to a spirit of great power and might, "a spirit who never lies," whom the Indians invoke and consult before undertaking any important or dangerous enterprise;* and this island, as I apprehend, has been peculiarly dedicated to him; at all events, it has been from time immemorial a place of note and sanctity among the Indians. Its history, as far as the Europeans are connected with it, may be told in few words.

After the destruction of the fort at Michilimackinac, and the massacre of the garrison in 1763, the English removed the fort and the trading post to this island, and it continued for a long time a station of great importance. In 1796 it was ceded, with the whole of the Michigan territory, to the United States. The fort was then strengthened, and garrisoned by a detachment of General Wayne's army.

In the war of 1813 it was taken and garrisoned by the British, who added to the strength of the fortifications.

* See Henry's Travels, p. 117.

The Americans were so sensible of its importance, that they fitted out an expensive expedition in 1814 for the purpose of retaking it, but were repulsed with the loss of one of their bravest commanders and a great number of men, and forced to retreat to their vessels. After this, Michilimackinac remained in possession of the British, till at the peace it was again quietly ceded, one hardly knows why, to the Americans, and in their possession it now remains. The garrison, not being required in time of profound peace, has been withdrawn. The pretty little fort remains.

We drove to-day to visit a spot of romantic interest in the life of Henry; the cave in which he was secreted after the massacre at Michilimackinac by his adopted brother, Wa,wa,tam, lest he should be made into a "mess of English broth," like some of his hapless companions. He describes the manner in which he was brought here at eventide; how he crept into its farthest recesses and fell asleep; – and waking in the morning, found himself lying upon a heap of human skulls! Henry's opinion is, that the cave was an ancient receptacle for the bones of prisoners, sacrificed and devoured at war-feasts. "I have always observed," he adds, "that the Indians pay particular attention to the bones of sacrifices, preserving them unbroken, and depositing them in some place kept exclusively for the purpose." The cave is admirably contrived for a place of concealment, the opening being in the rock, high above the level of the ground, and almost entirely concealed by the rich foliage of bushes and underwood. It is still called the "cave of skulls," but all the bones have been removed and interred in a desolate, picturesque little cemetery hard by. This rock is upon the highest point of the island, from which the view over the neighbouring islands, the main land, the two capes of Michilimackinac and St. Ignace, and the straits between them, as seen beneath the glow of an evening sun, formed a panorama of surpassing beauty.

In short, this is a *bijou* of an island! – a little bit of fairy ground, just such a thing as some of our amateur travellers would like to pocket and run away with (if they could) – and set down in the midst of one of their fish-ponds – cave of skulls, wigwams, Indians, and all.

It might indeed be an objection to *some people*, that several luxuries, and some things usually considered as necessaries of life, seldom find their way here; meat is very scarce, not often seen; but poultry, wild-fowl, the most exquisite fish – as the white-fish, bass, sturgeon, lake trout – abound. These, dressed in different ways, with corn-cakes and buck-wheat cakes, form the usual food; no better can be desired. As to the white-fish, I have never tasted anything like it, either for delicacy or flavour.

The most delightful as well as most profitable hours I spend here, are those passed in the society of Mrs. Schoolcraft. Her genuine refinement and simplicity, and native taste for literature, are charming; and the exceeding delicacy of her health, and the trials to which it is exposed, interest all my womanly sympathies. While in conversation with her, new ideas of the Indian character suggest themselves; new sources of information are opened to me, such as are granted to few, and such as I gratefully appreciate. She is proud of her Indian origin; she takes an enthusiastic and enlightened interest in the welfare of her people, and in their conversion to Christianity, being herself most unaffectedly pious. But there is a melancholy and pity in her voice, when speaking of them, as if she did indeed consider them a doomed race. We were conversing to-day of her grandfather, Waub-Ojeeg, (the White-fisher,) a distinguished Chippewa chief and warrior, of whose life and exploits she has promised to give me some connected particulars. Of her mother, O,shah,gush,ko,da,wa,qua, she speaks with fond and even longing affection, as if the very sight of this beloved mother would be sufficient to restore her to health and strength. "I should be well if I could see my mother," seems the predominant feeling. Nowhere is the instinctive affection between parent and child so strong, so deep, so sacred, as among these people.

I recollect, some years ago, meeting with a strange story of a north-west Indian hunter, who, on the sudden death of his wife in childbirth, had suckled his surviving infant. I asked Mrs. Schoolcraft if this could possibly be true? She said that the man belonged to her people, and that the fact was not doubted among them. Her mother recollects to have seen the man some years after the circumstance occurred. At that time his bosom retained something of the full feminine form. This is very curious evidence. I cannot remember by whom the anecdote was first brought to Europe, but it excited so much attention and disputation among our scientific and medical people, that you will probably recollect it.

Celibacy in either sex is almost unknown among the Indians; equally rare is all profligate excess. One instance I heard of a woman who had remained unmarried from choice, not from accident or necessity. In consequence of a dream in early youth, (the Indians are great dreamers,) she not only regarded the sun as her manito or tutelary spirit, (this had been a common case,) but considered herself especially dedicated, or in fact married, to the luminary. She lived alone; she had built a wigwam for herself, which was remarkably neat and commodious; she could use a rifle, hunt, and provided herself with food and clothing. She had carved a rude image of the sun, and set it up in her lodge; the husband's place, the best mat, and a portion of food, were always appropriated to this image. She lived to a great age, and no one ever interfered with her mode of life, for that would have been contrary to all their ideas of individual freedom. Suppose that, according to our most approved European notions, the poor woman had been burnt at the stake, corporeally or metaphorically, or hunted beyond the pale of the village, for deviating from the law of custom, no doubt there would have been directly a new female sect in the nation of the Chippewas, an order of *wives of the sun*, and Chippewa vestal virgins; but these wise people trusted to nature and common sense. The vocation apparently was not generally admired, and found no imitators.

Their laws, or rather their customs, command certain virtues and practices, as truth, abstinence, courage, hospitality; but they have no prohibitory laws whatever that I could hear of. In this respect their moral code has something of the spirit of Christianity, as contrasted with the Hebrew dispensation. Polygamy is allowed, but it is not common; the second wife is considered as subject to the first, who remains mistress of the household, even though the younger wife should be the favourite. Jealousy, however, is a strong passion among them: not only has a man been known to murder a woman whose fidelity he suspected, but Mr. Schoolcraft mentioned to me an instance of a woman, who, in a transport of jealousy, had stabbed her husband. But these extremes are very rare.

Some time ago, a young Chippewa girl conceived a violent passion for a hunter of a different tribe, and followed him from his winter hunting-ground to his own village. He was already married, and the wife, not being inclined to admit a rival, drove this love-sick damsel away, and treated her with the utmost indignity. The girl, in desperation, offered herself as a slave to the wife, to carry wood and water, and lie at her feet – anything to be admitted within the same lodge and only look upon the object of her affection. She prevailed at length. Now, the mere circumstance of her residing within the same wigwam made her also the wife of the man, according to the Indian custom; but apparently she was content to forego all the privileges and honours of a wife. She endured, for several months, with uncomplaining resignation, every species of ill usage and cruelty on the part of the first wife, till at length this woman, unable any longer to suffer even the presence of a rival, watched an opportunity as the other entered the wigwam with a load of fire-wood, and cleft her skull with the husband's tomahawk.

"And did the man permit all this?" was the natural question.

The answer was remarkable. "What could *he* do? he could not help it: a woman is always absolute mistress in her own wigwam!"

In the end, the murder was not punished. The poor victim having fled from a distant tribe, there were no relatives to take vengeance, or do justice, and it concerned no one else. She lies buried at a short distance from the Sault Ste. Marie, where the murderess and her husband yet live.

Women sometimes perish of grief for the loss of a husband or a child, and men have been known to starve themselves on the grave of a beloved wife. Men have also been known to give up their wives to the traders for goods and whisky; but this, though forbidden by no law, is considered disreputable, or as my informant expressed it, "only bad Indians do so."

I should doubt, from all I see and hear, that the Indian squaw is that absolute slave, drudge, and non-entity in the community, which she has been described. She is despotic in her lodge, and everything it contains is hers; even of the game her husband kills, she has the uncontrolled disposal. If her husband does not please her, she scolds and even cuffs him; and it is in the highest degree unmanly to answer or strike her. I have seen here a woman scolding and quarrelling with her husband, seize him by the hair, in a style that might have become civilised Billingsgate, or christian St. Giles's, and the next day I have beheld the same couple sit lovingly together on the sunny side of the wigwam, she kneeling behind him, and combing and arranging the hair she had been pulling from his head the day before; just such a group as I remember to have seen about Naples, or the Campagna di Roma, with very little obvious difference either in costume or complexion.

There is no law against marrying near relations, but it is always avoided; it is contrary to their customs: even first cousins do not marry. The tie of blood seems considered as stronger than that of marriage. A woman considers that she belongs more to her own relatives than to her husband or his relatives; yet, notwithstanding this and the facility of divorce, separations between husband and wife are very rare. A couple will go on "squabbling and making it up" all their lives, without having recourse to this expedient. If from displeasure, satiety, or any other cause, a man sends his wife away, she goes back to her relations, and invariably takes her children with her. The indefeasible right of the mother to her offspring is Indian law, or rather, the contrary notion does not seem to have entered their minds. A widow remains subject to her husband's relations for two years after his death; this is the decent period of mourning. At the end of two years, she returns some of the presents made to her by her late husband, goes back to her own relatives, and may marry again.

You will understand that these particulars, and others which may follow, apply to the Chippewas and the Ottawas around me; other tribes have other customs. I speak merely of those things which are brought under my own immediate observation and attention.

During the last American war of 1813, the young widow of a chief who had been killed in battle, assumed his arms, ornaments, wampum, medal, and went out with several war parties, in which she distinguished herself by her exploits. Mrs. Schoolcraft, when a girl of eleven or twelve years old, saw this woman, who was brought into the Fort at Mackinaw and introduced to the commanding officer; and retains a lively recollection of her appearance, and the interest and curiosity she excited. She was rather below the middle size, slight and delicate in figure, like most of the squaws; – covered with rich ornaments, silver armlets, with the scalping-knife, pouch, medals, tomahawk – all the insignia, in short, of an Indian warrior, except the war-paint and feathers. In the room hung a large mirror, in which she surveyed herself with evident admiration and delight, turning round and round before it, and laughing triumphantly. She was invited to dine at the officer's mess, perhaps as a joke, but conducted herself with so much intuitive propriety and decorum, that she was dismissed with all honour and respect, and with handsome presents. I could not learn what became of her afterwards.

Heroic women are not rare among the Indians, women who can bravely suffer – bravely die; but Amazonian women, female amateur warriors, are very extraordinary; I never heard but of this one instance. Generally, the squaws around me give me the impression of exceeding feminine delicacy and modesty, and of the most submissive gentleness. Female chiefs, however, are not unknown in Indian history. There was a famous *Squaw Sachem*, or chief, in the time of the early settlers. The present head chief of the Ottawas, a very fine old man, succeeded a female, who, it is further said, abdicated in his favour.*

Even the standing rule or custom that women are never admitted to councils has been evaded. At the treaty of Butte des Morts, in 1827,† an old Chippewa woman, the wife of a super-annuated chief, appeared in place of her husband, wearing his medal, and to all intents and purposes representing him. The American commissioners treated her with studied respect and distinction, and made her rich presents in cloth, ornaments, tobacco, &c. On her return to her own village, she was way-laid and murdered by a party of Menomonies. The next year two Menomonie women were taken and put to death by the Chippewas: such is the Indian law of retaliation.

The language spoken around me is the Chippewa tongue, which, with little variation, is spoken also by the Ottawas, Pottowottomies and Missasaguas, and diffused all over the

* Major Anderson.
† This was a treaty arranged by the American government, for settling the boundary line between the territories of the Menomonies and Chippewas, who had previously disturbed the frontiers by their mutual animosities.

country of the lakes, and through a population of about seventy thousand. It is in these countries what the French is in Europe, the language of trade and diplomacy, understood and spoken by those tribes, with whom it is not vernacular. In this language Mrs. Schoolcraft generally speaks to her children and Indian domestics. It is not only very sweet and musical to the ear, with its soft inflections and lengthened vowels, but very complex and artificial in its construction, and subject to strict grammatical rules; this, for an unwritten language – for they have no alphabet – appears to me very curious. The particulars which follow I have from Mr. Schoolcraft, who has deeply studied the Chippewa language, and what he terms, not without reason, the philosophy of its syntax.

The great division of all words, and the pervading principle of the language, is the distinction into animate and inanimate objects: not only nouns, but adjectives, verbs, pronouns, are inflected in accordance with this principle. The distinction, however, seems as arbitrary as that between masculine and feminine nouns in some European languages. Trees, for instance, are of the animate gender. The sun, moon, thunder and lightning, a canoe, a pipe, a water-fall, are all animate. The verb is not only modified to agree with the subject, it must be farther modified to agree with the object spoken of, whether animate or inanimate: an Indian cannot say simply, I love, I eat; the word must express by its inflection what he loves or eats, whether it belong to the animate or inanimate gender.

What is curious enough is, that the noun or name can be conjugated like a verb: the word *man*, for instance, can be inflected to express, I *am* a man, thou *art* a man, he *is* a man, I *was* a man, I *will be* a man, and so forth; and the word husband can be so inflected as to signify by a change of syllables, *I have a* husband, and *I have not* a husband.

They have three numbers, like the Greek, but of different signification: they have the singular, and two plurals, one indefinite and general like ours, and one including the persons or things present, and excluding those which are absent; and distinct inflections are required for these two plurals.

There are distinct words to express certain distinctions of sex as with us; for instance, man, woman, father, mother, sister, brother, are distinct words, but more commonly sex is distinguished by a masculine or feminine syllable or termination. The word *equay*, a woman, is thus used as a feminine termination where persons are concerned. Ogima, is a chief, and Ogimaquay, a female chief.

There are certain words and expressions which are in a manner masculine and feminine by some prescriptive right, and cannot be used indifferently by the two sexes. Thus, one man addressing another says nichi, or neejee, my friend. One woman addressing another woman says, "Nin,dong,quay," (as nearly as I can imitate the sound,) my friend, or rather, I believe, female relation; and it would be indelicacy in one sex, and arrogance in the other, to exchange these terms between man and woman. When a woman is surprised at anything she sees or hears, she exclaims, "N'ya!" When a man is surprised he exclaims, "T'ya!" and it would be contrary to all Indian notions of propriety and decorum, if a man condescended to say "N'ya!" or if a woman presumed to use the masculine interjection "T'ya!" – I could give you other comical instances of the same kind. They have different words for eldest brother, eldest sister, and for brother and sister in general. *Brother* is a common expression of kindness, *father*, of respect; and grandfather is a title of very great respect.

They have no form of imprecation or swearing. Closing the hand, then throwing it forth and opening it suddenly with a jerk, is the strongest gesture of contempt; and the words "bad dog," the strongest expression of abuse and vituperation: both are unpardonable insults, and used sparingly.

A mother's term of endearment to her child is "My bird – my young one," and sometimes playfully, "My old man." When I asked what words were used of reproach or menace, I was told that Indian children were *never* scolded – *never* menaced.

The form of salutation in common use between the Indians and the whites is the *bo-jou*, borrowed from the early French settlers, the first Europeans with whom the North-west Indians were brought in contact. Among themselves there is no set form of salutation; when two friends meet after a long absence, they take hands, and exclaim, "We see each other!"

I have been "working like beaver," to borrow an Indian phrase, and all for you! – this has been a rich and busy day: what with listening, learning, scribbling, transcribing, my wits as well as my pen are well nigh worn to a stump. But before I place before you my new acquisitions, there are a few things I must premise. I am not going to tell you here of well-known Indian customs, and repeat anecdotes to be found in all the popular books of travel. With the general characteristics of Indian life and manners you are already familiar, from reading the works of Cooper, Washington Irving, Charles Hoffman, and others. I can add nothing to these sources of information; only bear testimony to the vigour, and liveliness, and truth of the pictures they have drawn. I am amused at every moment by the coincidence between what I see and what I have read; but I must confess I never read anything like the Indian fictions I have just been transcribing for you from the first and highest authority. You can imagine that among a people whose objects in life are few and simple, that society cannot be very brilliant, nor conversation very amusing. The taciturnity of the Indians does not arise from any ideas of gravity, decorum, or personal dignity, but rather from the dearth of ideas and of subjects of interest. Henry mentions the dulness of the long winters, when he was residing in the wigwam of his brother Wa,wa,tam, whose family were yet benevolent and intelligent: he had nothing to do but to smoke. Among the Indians, he says, the topics of conversation are few, and are limited to the transactions of the day and the incidents of the chase. The want of all variety in their lives, of all intellectual amusement, is one cause of their passion for gambling and for ardent spirits. The chase is to them a severe toil, not a recreation – the means of existence, not the means of excitement. They have, however, an amusement which I do not remember to have seen noticed anywhere. Like the Arabians, they have among them story-tellers by profession, persons who go about from lodge to lodge amusing the inmates with traditional tales, histories of the wars and exploits of their ancestors, or inventions of their own which are sometimes in the form of allegories or parables, and are either intended to teach some moral lesson, or are extravagant inventions having no other aim or purpose but to excite wonder or amazement. The story-tellers are estimated according to their eloquence and powers of invention, and are always welcome – sure of the best place in the wigwam and the choicest mess of food wherever they go. Some individuals, not story-tellers by profession, possess and exercise these gifts of memory and invention. Mrs. Schoolcraft mentioned an Indian living at the Sault Ste. Marie, who in this manner amuses and instructs his family almost every night before they go to rest. Her own mother is also celebrated for her stock of traditional lore, and her poetical and inventive faculties, which she inherited from her father Waub-Ojeeg, who was the greatest poet and story-teller, as well as the greatest warrior, of his tribe.

The stories I give you from Mrs. Schoolcraft's translation have at least the merit of being genuine. Their very wildness and childishness, and dissimilarity to all other fictions, will recommend them to you. The first story is evidently intended to inculcate domestic union and brotherly love. It would be difficult to draw any moral from the second, unless it be that courage, and perseverance, and cunning, are sure at length to triumph over even magical art; but it is surely very picturesque, and peculiar, and fanciful.

The Forsaken Brother.

I T WAS a fine summer evening; the sun was scarcely an hour high, its departing rays shone through the leaves of the tall elms that skirted a little green knoll, whereon stood a solitary Indian lodge. The deep, deep silence that reigned around seemed to the dwellers in that lonely hut like the long sleep of death which was now about to close the eyes of the chief of this poor family; his low breathing was answered by the sighs and sobs of his wife and three children: two of the children were almost grown up, one was yet a mere child. These were the only human beings near the dying man; the door of the lodge* was thrown aside to admit the refreshing breeze of the lake on the banks of which it stood, and when the cool air visited the brow of the poor man, he felt a momentary return of strength. Raising himself a little, he thus addressed his weeping family: –

"I leave ye – I leave ye! thou who hast been my partner in life, thou wilt not stay long behind me, thou wilt soon join me in the pleasant land of spirits; therefore thou hast not long to suffer in this world. But O my children, my poor children, you have just commenced life, and unkindness, and ingratitude, and all wickedness, is in the scene before you. I have contented myself with the company of your mother and yourselves for many years, and you will

* The skin or blanket suspended before the opening.

find that my motive for separating myself from other men has been to preserve you from evil example. But I die content, if you, my children, promise me to love each other, and on no account to forsake your youngest brother. Of him I give you both particular charge – love him and cherish him."

The father then became exhausted, and taking a hand of each of his elder children, he continued – "My daughter, never forsake your little brother! my son, never forsake your little brother!" – "Never! never!" they both exclaimed: – "Never! never!" repeated the father, and expired.

The poor man died happy, because he thought that his commands would be obeyed: the sun sank down behind the trees and left behind a golden sky, which the family were wont to behold with pleasure; but now no one heeded it. The lodge, so still an hour before, was now filled with loud cries and lamentations.

Time wore heavily away. Five long moons had passed, and the sixth was nearly full, when the mother also died. In her last moments, she pressed upon her children the fulfilment of their promise to their departed father. They readily renewed this promise, because they were as yet free from any selfish motives to break it. The winter passed away and spring came. The girl being the eldest, directed her brothers, and seemed to feel a more tender and sisterly affection for the youngest, who was sickly and delicate. The other boy soon showed signs of selfishness, and thus addressed his sister: –

"My sister, are we always to live as if there were no other human beings in the world? Must I be deprived of the pleasure of associating with men? I go to seek the villages of my brothers and my tribe. I have resolved, and you cannot prevent me."

The girl replied, "My brother, I do not say no to what you desire. We were not forbidden to associate with men, but we were commanded to cherish and never forsake each other – if we separate to follow our own selfish desires, will it not oblige us to forsake him, our brother, whom we are both bound to support?"

The young man made no answer to this remonstrance, but taking up his bow and arrows, he left the wigwam and returned no more.

Many moons had come and gone after the young man's departure, and still the girl ministered kindly and constantly to the wants of her little brother. At length, however, she too began to weary of solitude and her charge. Years added to her strength and her power of providing for the household wants, but also brought the desire of society, and made her solitude more and more irksome. At last she became quite impatient; she thought only of herself, and cruelly resolved to abandon her little brother, as her elder brother had done before.

One day, after having collected all the provisions she had set apart for emergencies, and brought a quantity of wood to the door, she said to her little brother, "My brother, you must not stray far from the lodge. I am going to seek our brother, I shall soon be back." Then taking her bundle, she set off in search of the habitations of men. She soon found them, and became so much occupied with the pleasures of her new life, that all affection and remembrance of her brother were by degrees effaced from her heart. At last she was married, and after *that* she never more thought of her poor helpless little brother whom she had abandoned in the woods.

In the mean time the eldest brother had also settled on the shores of the same lake, near which reposed the bones of his parents, and the abode of his forsaken brother.

Now, as soon as the little boy had eaten all the provisions left by his sister, he was obliged to pick berries and dig up roots for food. Winter came on, and the poor child was exposed to all its rigour; the snow covered the earth; he was forced to quit the lodge in search of food, and strayed about without shelter or home: sometimes he passed the night in the clefts of old trees, and ate the fragments left by the wolves. Soon he had no other resource; and in seeking for food he became so fearless of these animals, that he would sit close to them while they devoured their prey, and the fierce hungry wolves themselves seemed to pity his condition, and would always leave something for him. Thus he lived on the bounty of the wolves till the spring. As soon as the lake was free from ice, he followed his new friends and companions to the shore. Now it happened that his brother was fishing in his canoe, out far on the lake, when he thought he heard a cry as of a child, and wondered how any one could exist on the bleak shore. He listened again more attentively, and heard the cry repeated, and he paddled towards the shore as quickly as possible, and there he beheld and recognised his little brother, whom he heard singing in a plaintive voice,

> Neesya, neesya, shyegwich gushuh!
> Ween, ne myeeguniwh!

That is, "my brother, my brother, I am now turning into a wolf, I am turning into a wolf." At the end of his song he howled like a wolf, and his brother approaching, was dismayed to find him half a wolf and half a human being. He however leaped to the shore, strove to catch him in his arms, and said, soothingly, "My brother, my brother, come to me!" But the boy eluded his grasp and fled, still singing as he fled, "I am turning into a wolf! I am turning into a wolf!" and howling frightfully at the end of his song.

His elder brother, conscience-struck, and feeling all his love return, exclaimed in anguish, "My brother, O my brother, come to me!" but the nearer he approached the child the more rapidly the transformation proceeded. Still he sung, and howling called upon his brother and sister alternately in his song, till the change was complete, and he fled towards the wood a perfect wolf. At last he cried, "I am a wolf!" and bounded out of sight.

The young man felt the bitterness of remorse all his days; and the sister, when she heard the fate of her little brother whom she had promised to protect and cherish, wept many tears, and never ceased to mourn him till she died.

Mishosha;

or, the Magician and His Daughters.

IN AN early age of the world, when there were fewer
inhabitants on the earth than there are now, there lived
an Indian man, who had a wife and two children, in a
remote situation. Buried in the solitude of the forest, it
was not often that he saw any one out of the circle of his
own family. Such a situation was favourable to his pursuits of hunting and fishing, and his life passed on in
uninterrupted happiness, until he found reason to suspect
the affection and fidelity of his wife.

This woman secretly cherished a passion for a young
hunter whom she accidentally met in the forest, and she
lost no opportunity of inviting his approaches; she even
planned the death of her husband, whom she justly concluded would certainly kill her, should he discover her
infidelity. But this design was frustrated by the alertness of
her husband, who, having cause to suspect her, resolved to
watch her narrowly, to ascertain the truth before he
should determine how to act. One day he followed her
stealthily at a distance, and hid himself behind a tree. He
soon beheld a tall, handsome man approach his wife, and
lead her away into the depth of the wood.

The husband, now convinced of her crime, thought of
killing her the moment she returned. In the mean time he
went home, and pondered on his situation. At last, after
many struggles with himself, he came to the determination of leaving her for ever, thinking that her own con-

science would in the end punish her sufficiently; and he relied on her maternal feeling, to take due care of his two boys, whom he left behind.

When the wife returned she was disappointed not to find her husband in the lodge, having formed a plan to murder him. When she saw that day after day he returned not, she guessed the true reason of his absence. She then returned to her lover, and left her two helpless boys behind, telling them she was only going a short distance, and would soon return; but she was secretly resolved never to see them more.

The children, thus abandoned, had consumed the food that was left in the lodge, and were compelled to quit it in search of more. The eldest boy possessed great intrepidity, as well as much affection for his little brother, frequently carrying him when he became weary, and gathering for him all the wild fruit he saw. Thus they plunged deeper and deeper into the forest, soon losing all traces of their former habitation, till they were completely lost in the wilderness. The elder boy fortunately had with him a knife, with which he made a bow and arrows, and was thus enabled to kill a few birds for himself and his brother. In this manner they lived some time, still pressing on, they knew not whither. At last they saw an opening through the woods and soon were delighted to find themselves on the margin of a broad lake. Here the elder boy busied himself to pluck some of the pods of the wild rose for his brother, who in the mean time amused himself with shooting arrows into the sand. One of them happened to fall into the lake; the elder brother, not willing to lose his time in making others, waded into the water to reach it. Just as he was about to grasp the arrow, a canoe passed him with the swiftness of lightning. An old man sitting in the canoe seized the affrighted youth, and placed him in the canoe. In vain the boy supplicated him, saying, "My grandfather," (a general term of respect for old people,) "pray take my little brother also: alone I cannot go with you, he will die if I leave him." The old magician, for such was his real character, only laughed at him. Then giving his canoe a slap, and commanding it to go, it glided through the water with inconceivable rapidity. In a few minutes they reached the habitation of Mishosha, standing on an island in the centre of the lake. Here he lived with his two daughters, and was the terror of the surrounding country. Leading the youth up to the lodge, "Here, my eldest daughter," said he, "I have brought you a young man who shall become your husband." The youth beheld surprise in the countenance of the girl, but she made no reply, seeming thereby to acquiesce in the command of her father. In the evening the youth overheard the two daughters conversing. "There again!" said the eldest daughter, "our father has brought another victim under the pretence of giving me a husband; when will his enmity to the human race cease? How long shall we be forced to witness such sights of horror and wickedness as we are daily condemned to behold?"

When the old magician was asleep, the youth told the eldest daughter how he had been carried off, and forced to leave his helpless brother on the shore. She advised him to get up and take her father's canoe, and using the spell he had observed the magician use, it would carry him quickly to his brother; that he could carry him food, prepare a lodge for him, and return before morning. He followed her directions in all respects; and after providing for the subsistence and shelter of his brother, told him that in a short time he should come to take him away; then returning to the enchanted island, resumed his place in the lodge before the magician was awake. Once during the night Mishosha awoke, and not seeing his son-in-law, asked his eldest daughter what had become of him. She replied, that he had merely stepped out, and would return soon; and this answer satisfied him. In the morning, finding the young man in the lodge, his suspicions were completely lulled, and he said, "I see, my daughter, that you have told me the truth."

As soon as the sun arose, Mishosha thus addressed the

young man: "Come, my son, I have a mind to gather gulls' eggs. I know an island where there are great quantities, and I wish you to help me to gather them."

The young man, who saw no reasonable excuse for refusing, got into the canoe. The magician gave it a slap as before, and bidding it to go, in an instant they were at the island. They found the shore covered with gulls' eggs, and the island surrounded with those birds. "Go, my son," said the old man, "go and gather them while I remain in the canoe." But the young man was no sooner ashore than Mishosha pushed his canoe a little from land, and exclaimed, "Listen, ye gulls! you have long expected something from me, I now give you an offering. Fly down and devour him!" Then striking the canoe, he darted off, and left the young man to his fate.

The birds immediately came in clouds around their victim, darkening all the air with their numbers. But the youth, seizing the first gull that came near him, and drawing his knife, cut off its head. In another moment he had flayed the bird, and hung the skin and feathers as a trophy on his breast. "Thus," he exclaimed, "will I treat every one of you that approaches me! Forbear, therefore, and listen to my words. It is not for you to eat human flesh; you have been given by the Great Spirit as food for men. Neither is it in the power of the old magician to do you any good. Take me on your backs and carry me to his lodge, and you shall see that I am not ungrateful."

The gulls obeyed; collecting in a cloud for him to rest upon, they quickly bore him to the lodge, where they arrived even before the magician. The daughters were surprised at his return, but Mishosha behaved as though nothing extraordinary had happened.

On the following day he again addressed the youth, "Come, my son," said he, "I will take you to an island covered with the most beautiful pebbles, looking like silver. I wish you to assist me in gathering some of them; they will make handsome ornaments, and are possessed of great virtues." Entering the canoe, the magician made use of his charm, and they were carried in a few moments to a solitary bay in an island, where there was a smooth sandy beach. The young man went ashore as usual. "A little farther, a little farther," cried the old man; "up on that rock you will get some fine ones." Then pushing his canoe from the land, he exclaimed, "Come, thou great king of fishes, thou hast long expected an offering from me! come and eat up the stranger I have put ashore on your island." So saying, he commanded his canoe to return, and was soon out of sight. Immediately a monstrous fish poked his long snout from the lake, and moving towards the beach, he opened wide his jaws to receive his victim.

"When," exclaimed the young man, drawing his knife and placing himself in a threatening attitude, "when did you ever taste human flesh? have a care of yourself! you fishes were given by the Great Spirit for food to man, and if you or any of your tribes, taste man's flesh, you will surely fall sick and die. Listen not to the words of that wicked old magician, but carry me back to his island; in return for which I will give you a piece of red cloth."

The fish complied, raising his back out of the water for the youth to get on it; then taking his way through the lake, he landed his burthen safely at the island before the return of the magician.

The daughters were still more surprised to see him thus escaped a second time from the snares of their father, but the old man maintained his usual silence; he could not, however, help saying to himself, "What manner of boy is this, who thus ever baffles my power? his good spirit shall not however always save him; I will entrap him to-morrow." And then he laughed aloud, ha! ha! ha!

The next day the magician addressed the young man thus; "Come my son, you must go with me to procure some young eagles, I wish to tame them; I have discovered an island on which they dwell in great numbers."

When they had reached the island, Mishosha led the youth inland, till they came to the foot of a tall pine upon which the nests were.

"Now, my son," said he, "climb up this tree and bring down the birds." The young man obeyed, and when he had with great effort got up near the nests, "Now," exclaimed the magician, addressing the tree, "stretch forth yourself to heaven, and become very tall!" and the tree rose up at his command. Then the old man continued, "Listen, ye eagles! you have long expected a gift from me; I present you this boy, who has the presumption to molest your young: stretch forth your claws and seize him!" So saying, he left the young man to his fate, and returned home. But the intrepid youth, drawing his knife, instantly cut off the head of the first eagle who menaced him, and raising his voice, he cried, "Thus will I deal with all who come near me! What right have ye, ye ravenous birds, to eat human flesh? Is it because that old cowardly magician has bid you do so? He is an old woman! See! I have already slain one of your number: respect my bravery, and carry me back to the lodge of the old man, that I may show you how I shall treat him!"

The eagles, pleased with the spirit of the young man, assented; and clustering round him, formed a seat with their backs, and flew towards the enchanted island. As they crossed the lake they passed over the old magician, lying half asleep in the bottom of his canoe, and treated him with peculiar indignity.

The return of the young man was hailed with joy by the daughters, but excited the anger of the magician, who taxed his wits for some new mode of ridding himself of a youth so powerfully aided by his good spirit. He therefore invited him to go a hunting. Taking his canoe, they proceeded to an island, and built a lodge to shelter themselves during the night. In the mean time, the magician caused a deep fall of snow, and a storm of wind with severe cold. According to custom, the young man pulled off his moccasins and his metasses (leggings) and hung them before the fire. After he had gone to sleep, the magician, watching his opportunity, got up, and taking one moccasin and one legging, threw them into the fire. He then went to sleep. In the morning, stretching himself out, he arose, and uttering an exclamation of surprise, he exclaimed, "My son, what has become of your moccasin and legging? I believe this is the moon in which fire attracts, and I fear they have been drawn in and consumed!"

The young man suspected the true cause of his loss, and attributed it rightly to a design of the old magician to freeze him to death during their hunt, but he maintained the strictest silence; and drawing his blanket over his head, he said within himself, "I have full faith in my good spirit who has preserved me thus far, and I do not fear that he will now forsake me. Great is the power of my Manito! and he shall prevail against this wicked old enemy of mankind." Then he uncovered his head, and drawing on the remaining moccasin and legging, he took a coal from the fire, and invoking his spirit to give it efficacy, blackened the foot and leg as far as the lost legging usually reached; then rising, said he was ready for the morning hunt. In vain the magician led the youth through deep snow, and through frozen morasses, hoping to see him sink at every step; in this he was doomed to feel a sore disappointment, and they for the first time returned home together.

Taking courage from this success, the young man now determined to try his own power. Having previously consulted with the daughters, they all agreed that the life of the old man was detestable, and that whoever would rid the world of him would be entitled to the thanks of the human race.

On the following day the young man thus addressed the magician. "My grandfather, I have often gone with you on perilous expeditions, and never murmured; I must now request that you accompany me; I wish to visit my little brother, and bring him home with me." They accordingly went on shore on the main land, where they found the boy in the spot where he had been formerly left. After taking him into the canoe, the young man again addressed the magician: "My grandfather, will you go and cut me a few of those red willows on the bank? I wish to prepare some kinnakinic, (smoking mixture.)" "Certainly, my son," replied the old man, "what you wish is not so very hard; do you think me too old to get up there?" And then the wicked old fellow laughed loud, ha, ha, ha!

No sooner was the magician ashore, than the young man, placing himself in the proper position, struck the canoe, and repeated the charm, "N'Chemaun Pal!" and immediately the canoe flew through the water on its passage to the enchanted island. It was evening when the two brothers arrived, but the elder daughter informed the young man, that unless he sat up and watched, keeping his hand upon the canoe, such was the power of their father, it would slip off from the shore and return to him. The young man watched steadily till near the dawn of day, when he could no longer resist the drowsiness which oppressed him, and suffered himself to nod for a moment; the canoe slipped off and sought the old man, who soon returned in great glee. "Ha! my son," said he, "you thought to play me a trick; it was very clever, my son, but you see I am too old for you." And then he laughed again that wicked laugh, ha, ha, ha!

A short time afterwards, the youth, not yet discouraged, again addressed the magician. "My grandfather, I wish to try my skill in hunting: it is said there is plenty of game in an island not far off. I have to request you will take me there in your canoe." They accordingly spent the day in hunting, and night coming on, they set up a lodge in the wood. When the magician had sunk into a profound sleep, the young man got up, and taking a moccasin and legging of Mishosha's from where they hung before the fire, he threw them in, thus retaliating the old man's artifice upon himself. He had discovered by some means that the foot and the leg were the only parts of the magician's body which could not be guarded by the spirits who served him. He then besought his Manito to cause a storm of snow with a cold wind and icy sleet, and then laid himself down beside the old man, and fell asleep again.

Consternation was in the face of the magician when he awoke in the morning, and found his moccasin and legging gone. "I believe, my grandfather," said the young man with a smile, "that this is the moon in which the fire attracts; and I fear your garments have been drawn in and consumed." And then rising, and bidding the old man follow, he began the morning's hunt. Frequently he turned his head to see how Mishosha kept up. He saw him faltering at every step, and almost benumbed with cold, but encouraged him to follow, saying, "We shall soon be through the wood, and reach the shore," – but still leading him roundabout ways, to let the frost take complete effect. At length the old man reached the edge of the island where the deep woods were succeeded by a border of smooth sand, but he could go no farther; his legs became stiff, and refused all motion, and he found himself fixed to the spot; but he still kept stretching out his arms, and swinging his body to and fro. Every moment he found the numbness creeping higher and higher: he felt his legs growing like roots: the feathers on his head turned to leaves, and in a few seconds he stood a tall and stiff maple tree, leaning towards the water.

The young man, getting into the canoe, and pronouncing the spell, was soon transported to the island, where he related his history to the daughters. They applauded the deed, and agreed to put on mortal shapes, become the wives of the two young men, and for ever quit the enchanted island. They immediately passed over to the main land, where they all lived long in happiness and peace together.

In this wild tale the metamorphosis of the old man into the maple tree is related with a spirit and accuracy worthy of Ovid himself.

The third story seems intended to admonish parental ambition, and inculcate filial obedience. The bird here called the robin is three times as large as the English robin redbreast, but in its form and habits very similar.

The Origin of the Robin.

A N OLD man had an only son, a fine promising lad, who had arrived at that age when the Chippewas thought it proper to make the long and final fast, which is to secure through life a guardian spirit, on whom future prosperity or adversity are to depend, and who forms the character to great and noble deeds.*

This old man was ambitious that his son should surpass all others in whatever was deemed most wise and great among his tribe; and to this effect he thought it necessary that his son should fast a much longer time than any of those persons celebrated for their uncommon power or wisdom, and whose fame he envied.

He therefore directed his son to prepare with great ceremony for the important event: after he had been in the sweating lodge and bath several times, he ordered him to lie down on a clean mat in a little lodge, expressly pre-

* This custom is universal among the Chippewas and their kindred tribes. At a certain age, about twelve or fourteen, the youth or girl is shut up in a separate lodge to fast and dream. The usual term is from three to five or six days, or even longer. The object which during this time is most frequently presented in sleep – the disturbed feverish sleep of an exhausted frame and excited imagination – is the tutelary spirit or manito of the future life: it is the sun or moon or evening star; an eagle, a moose deer, a crane, a bat, &c. Wawatam, the Indian friend of Henry, had dreamed of a white man, whom the Great Spirit brought to him in his hand and presented as his brother. This dream, as I have related, saved Henry's life.

pared for him, telling him at the same time to bear himself like a man, and that at the expiration of twelve days he should receive food and his father's blessing.

The youth carefully observed these injunctions, lying with his face covered, with perfect composure, awaiting those spiritual visitations which were to seal his good or evil fortune. His father visited him every morning regularly to encourage him to perseverance – expatiating on the renown and honour which would attend him through life, if he accomplished the full term prescribed. To these exhortations the boy never replied, but lay still without a murmur till the ninth day, when he thus addressed his father – "My father, my dreams are ominous of evil. May I break my fast now, and at a more propitious time make a new fast?"

The father answered – "My son, you know not what you ask; if you rise now, all your glory will depart. Wait patiently a little longer, you have but three days yet to accomplish what I desire; you know it is for your own good."

The son assented, and covering himself up close, he lay till the eleventh day, when he repeated his request to his father. But the same answer was given by the old man, who, however, added that the next day he would himself prepare his first meal, and bring it to him. The boy remained silent, and lay like death. No one could have known he was living, but by the gentle heaving of his breast.

The next morning, the father, elated at having gained his object, prepared a repast for his son, and hastened to set it before him. On coming to the door, he was surprised to hear his son talking to himself; he stooped to listen, and looking through a small aperture, he was more astonished when he saw his son painted with vermilion on his breast, and in the act of finishing his work by laying on the paint as far as his hand could reach on his shoulders, saying at the same time, "My father has ruined me as a man – he would not listen to my request – he will now be the loser, while I shall be for ever happy in my new state, since I have been obedient to my parent. He alone will be a sufferer, for the spirit is a just one, though not propitious to me. He has shown me pity, and now I must go!"

At that moment the father, in despair, burst into the lodge, exclaiming, "My son, my son, do not leave me." But his son, with the quickness of a bird, had flown up to the top of the lodge, and perched upon the highest pole, a beautiful Robin Redbreast. He looked down on his father with pity beaming in his eyes, and told him he should always love to be near man's dwellings – that he should always be seen happy and contented by the constant sprightliness and joy he would display – and that he would ever strive to cheer his father by his songs, which would be some consolation to him for the loss of the glory he had expected – and that although no longer a man, he would ever be the harbinger of peace and joy to the human race.*

* Even while these pages are printing, I learn that this tale of the Robin has already been published by an American traveller, to whom Mrs. Schoolcraft imparted it. It is retained here notwithstanding, because it is sufficiently pretty and fanciful to justify a repetition, and is besides illustrative of the custom so often referred to – of dreaming for a guardian spirit.

I T IS a mistake to suppose that these Indians are idolaters; heathens and pagans you may call them if you will; but the belief in one Great Spirit, who created all things, and is paramount to all things, and the belief in the distinction between body and soul, and the immortality of the latter – these two sublime principles pervade their wildest superstitions; but though none doubt of a future state, they have no distinct or universal tenets with regard to the condition of the soul after death. Each individual seems to have his own thoughts on the subject, and some doubtless never think about it at all. In general, however, their idea of a paradise (the land of spirits) is some far off country towards the south-west, abounding in sunshine, and placid lakes, and rivers full of fish, and forests full of game, whither they are transported by the Great Spirit, and where those who are separated on earth meet again in happiness, and part no more.

Not only man, but everything animate, is spirit, and destined to immortality. According to the Indians, (and Sir Humphry Davy,) nothing dies, nothing is destroyed; what we look upon as death and destruction is only transition and change. The ancients, it is said – for I cannot speak from my own knowledge – without telescopes or logarithms, divined the grandest principles of astronomy, and calculated the revolutions of the planets; and so these Indians, who never heard of philosophy or chemistry, have contrived to hit upon some of the profoundest truths in physics and metaphysics; but they seem content, like Jaques, "to praise God, and make no boast of it."

In some things, it is true, they are as far as possible from orthodox. Their idea of a hell seems altogether vague and negative. It consists in a temporary rejection from the land of good spirits, in a separation from lost relatives and friends, in being doomed to wander up and down desolately, having no fixed abode, weary, restless, and melancholy. To how many is the Indian hell already realised on this earth? Physical pain, or any pain which calls for the exercise of courage, and which it is manliness to meet and endure, does not apparently enter into their notions of *punishment*. They believe in evil spirits, but the idea of *the* EVIL *Spirit*, a permitted agency of evil and mischief, who divides with the Great Spirit the empire of the universe – who contradicts or renders nugatory His will, and takes especially in hand the province of tormenting sinners – of the devil, in short, they certainly had not an idea, till it was introduced by Europeans.* Those Indians whose politeness will not allow them to contradict this article of the white man's faith, still insist that the place of eternal torment was never intended for the Red-skins, the especial favourites of the Great Spirit, but for white men *only*.

Formerly it was customary with the Chippewas to bury many articles with the dead, such as would be useful on their journey to the land of spirits.

Henry describes in a touching manner the interment of a young girl, with the axe, snow-shoes, a small kettle, several pairs of moccasins, her own ornaments, and strings of beads; and, because it was a female – destined, it seems, to toil and carry burthens in the other world as well as this – the *carrying-belt* and the paddle. The last act before the burial, performed by the poor mother, crying over the dead body of the child, was that of taking from it

---

* History of the Moravian Missions. Mr. Schoolcraft.

a lock of hair for a memorial. "While she did this," says Henry, "I endeavoured to console her by offering the usual arguments, that the child was happy in being released from the miseries of this life, and that she should forbear to grieve, because it would be restored to her in another world, happy and everlasting. She answered, that she knew it well, and that by the lock of hair she should know her daughter in the other world, for she would *take it with her* – alluding to the time when this relic, with the carrying-belt and axe, would be placed in her own grave."

Do you remember the lamentation of Constance over her *pretty* Arthur?

> "And rising so again,
> When I shall meet him in the court of heaven,
> I shall not know him."

O nature – O Shakspeare – everywhere the same – and true to each other!

This custom of burying property with the dead was formerly carried to excess from the piety and generosity of surviving friends, until a chief, greatly respected and admired among them for his bravery and talents, took an ingenious method of giving his people a lesson. He was seized with a fit of illness, and after a few days expired, or seemed to expire. But after lying in this death-trance for some hours, he came to life again, and recovering his voice and senses, he informed his friends that he had been halfway to the land of spirits; that he found the road thither crowded with the souls of the dead, all so heavily laden with the guns, kettles, axes, blankets, and other articles buried with them, that their journey was retarded, and they complained grievously of the burthens which the love of their friends had laid on them. "I will tell you," said Gitchee Gauzinee, for that was his name, "our fathers have been wrong; they have buried too many things with the dead. It is too burthensome to them, and they have complained to me bitterly. There are many who, by reason of the heavy loads they bear, have not yet reached the land of spirits. Clothing will be very acceptable to the dead, also his moccasins to travel in, and his pipe to refresh him on the way; but let his other possessions be divided among his relatives and friends."*

This sensible hint was taken in good part. The custom of kindling a fire on the grave, to light the departed spirit on its road to the land of the dead, is very general, and will remind you of the oriental customs.

Here is a story not altogether new, for it has been published;† but if you have not met with it, I fancy it will amuse you.

A Chippewa chief, heading his war party against the Sioux, received an arrow in his breast, and fell. No warrior thus slain is ever buried. According to ancient custom, he was placed in a sitting posture, with his back against a tree, his face towards his flying enemies; his head-dress, ornaments, and all his war-equipments, were arranged, with care, and thus he was left. But the chief was not dead; though he could neither move nor speak, he was sensible to all that passed. When he found himself abandoned by his friends as one dead, he was seized with a paroxysm of rage and anguish. When they took leave of him, lamenting, he rose up and followed them, but they saw him not. He pursued their track, and wheresoever they went, he went; when they ran, he ran; when they encamped and slept, he did the like; but he could not eat with them, and when he spoke they heard him not. "Is it possible," he cried, exalting his voice, "that my brothers do not see me – do not hear me? Will you suffer me to bleed to death without stanching my wounds? will you let me starve in the midst of food? have my fellow-warriors already forgotten me? is there none who will recollect my face, or offer me a morsel of flesh?" Thus he lamented and upbraided, but the sound of his voice reached them not. If

* Mr. Schoolcraft.
† In Mr. Schoolcraft's Travels.

they heard it at all, they mistook it for that of the summer wind rustling among the leaves.

The war party returned to the village; the women and children came out to welcome them. The chief heard the inquiries for himself, and the lamentations of his friends and relatives over his death. "It is not true!" he shrieked with a loud voice, "I am not dead, – I was not left on the field; I am here! I live! I move! see me! touch me! I shall again raise my spear in the battle, and sound my drum at the feast!" but no one heeded him; they mistook his voice for the wind rising and whistling among the boughs. He walked to his wigwam, and found his wife tearing her hair, and weeping for his death. He tried to comfort her, but she seemed insensible of his presence. He besought her to bind up his wounds – she moved not. He put his mouth close to her ear, and shouted, "I am hungry, give me food!" she thought she heard a mosquito buzzing in her ear. The chief, enraged past endurance, now summoned all his strength, and struck her a violent blow on the temple; on which she raised her hand to her head, and remarked, "I feel a slight aching here!"

When the chief beheld these things, he began to reflect that possibly his body might have remained on the field of battle, while only his spirit was among his friends; so he determined to go back and seek his body. It was four days' journey thither, and on the last day, just as he was approaching the spot, he saw a flame in the path before him; he endeavoured to step aside and pass it, but was still opposed; whichever way he turned, still it was before him. "Thou spirit," he exclaimed in anger, "why dost thou oppose me? knowest thou not that I too am a spirit, and seek only to re-enter my body? thinkest thou to make me turn back? know that I was never conquered by the enemies of my nation, and will not be conquered by thee!" So saying, he made an effort, and leapt through the opposing flame. He found himself seated under a tree on the field of battle, in all his warlike array, his bow and arrows at his side, just as he had been left by his friends, and looking up beheld a great war-eagle seated on the boughs; it was the manito of whom he had dreamed in his youth, his tutelary spirit who had kept watch over his body for eight days, and prevented the ravenous beasts and carrion birds from devouring it. In the end, he bound up his wounds and sustained himself by his bow and arrows, until he reached his village; there he was received with transport by his wife and friends, and concluded his account of his adventures by telling them it is four days' journey to the land of spirits, and that the spirit stood in need of a fire every night; therefore the friends and relatives should build the funeral fire for four nights upon the grave, otherwise the spirit would be obliged to build and tend the fire itself, – a task which is always considered slavish and irksome.

Such is the tradition by which the Chippewas account for the custom of lighting the funeral fire.

The Indians have a very fanciful mythology, which would make exquisite machinery for poetry. It is quite distinct from the polytheism of the Greeks. The Greek mythology personified all nature, and materialised all abstractions: the Indians spiritualise all nature. They do not indeed place dryads and fawns in their woods, nor naiads in their streams; but every tree has a spirit; every rock, every river, every star that glistens, every wind that breathes, has a spirit; everything they cannot comprehend is a spirit; this is the ready solution of every mystery, or rather makes everything around them a mystery as great as the blending of soul and body in humanity. A watch, a compass, a gun, have each their spirit. The thunder is an angry spirit; the aurora borealis, dancing and rejoicing spirits; the milky way is the path of spirits. Birds, perhaps from their aerial movements, they consider as in some way particularly connected with the invisible world of spirits. Not only all animals have souls, but it is the settled belief of the Chippewa Indians that their souls will fare the better in another world, in the precise ratio that their lives and enjoyments are curtailed in this; hence, they have no remorse in hunting, but when they have killed a bear or rattle-snake, they solemnly beg his pardon, and excuse themselves on the plea of necessity.

Besides this general *spiritualisation* of the whole universe, which to an Indian is all spirit in diversity of forms, (how delighted Bishop Berkeley would have been with them!) they have certain mythologic existences. Manabozho is a being very analogous to the Seeva of the Hindoo mythology. The four cardinal points are spirits, the west being the oldest and the father of the others, by a beautiful girl, who, one day while bathing, suffered the west wind to blow upon her. Weeng is the spirit of sleep, with numerous little subordinate spirits, his emissaries, whose employment is to close the eyes of mortals, and by tapping on their foreheads *knock* them to sleep. Then they have Weendigos – great giants and cannibals, like the Ascaparts and Morgantes of the old romances; and little tiny spirits or fairies, which haunt the woods and cataracts. The Nibanàba, half human half fish, dwell in the waters of Lake Superior. Ghosts are plentiful, and so are transformations, as you have seen. The racoon was once a shell lying on the lake shore, and vivified by the sunbeams: the Indian name of the racoon, *aisebun*, is literally, *he was a shell*. The brains of a wicked adulteress, whose skull was beaten to pieces against the rocks, as it tumbled down a cataract, became the white fish.*

As to the belief in sorcery, spells, talismans, incantations, all which go by the general name of *medicine*, it is unbounded. Henry mentions, that among the goods which some traders took up the country to exchange for furs, they had a large collection of the little rude prints,

---

* I have heard the particulars of this wild story of the origin of the white-fish, but cannot remember them. I think the woman was put to death by her sons. Most of the above particulars I learned from oral communication, and from some of the papers published by Mr. Schoolcraft. This gentleman and others instituted a society at Detroit, (1832,) called the *Algic Society*, for "evangelising the north-western tribes, inquiring into their history and superstitions, and promoting education, agriculture, industry, peace, and temperance among them."

published for children, at a halfpenny a piece – I recollect such when I was a child. They sold these at a high price, for *medicines*, (*i.e.* talismans,) and found them a very profitable and popular article of commerce. One of these, a little print of a sailor kissing his sweetheart, was an esteemed *medicine* among the young, and eagerly purchased for a love-spell. A soldier presenting his gun, or brandishing his sabre, was a medicine to promote warlike courage – and so on.

The medicines and manitos of the Indians will remind you of the fetishes of the negroes.

With regard to the belief in omens and incantations, I should like to see it ascertained how far we civilised Christians, with all our schools, our pastors, and our masters, are in advance of these (so-called) savages?*

---

* "One of the most distinguished men of the age, who has left a reputation which will be as lasting as it is great, was, when a boy, in constant fear of a very able but unmerciful schoolmaster, and in the state of mind which that constant fear produced, he fixed upon a great spider for his fetish, (or manito,) and used every day to pray to it that he might not be flogged." – *The Doctor*, vol. v.

When a child, I was myself taken to a witch (or medicine woman) to be cured of an accidental burn, by charms and incantations. I was then about six years old, and have a very distinct recollection of the whole scene, which left a strong and frightful impression on my childish fancy.

Who would believe that with a smile, whose blessing
   Would, like the patriarch's, soothe a dying hour;
With voice as low, as gentle, as caressing,
   As e'er won maiden's lip in moonlit bower;
With look, like patient Job's, eschewing evil;
   With motions graceful as a bird's in air;
Thou art, in sober truth, the veriest devil,
   That e'er clench'd fingers in a captive's hair!

HALLECK.

M R. JOHNSON tells me, what pleases me much, that the
Indians like me, and are gratified by my presence,
and the interest I express for them, and that I am the
subject of much conversation and speculation. Being in
manners and complexion unlike the European women
they have been accustomed to see, they have given me, he
says, a name among themselves expressive of the most
obvious characteristic in my appearance, and call me the
white or *fair English chieftainess* (Ogima-quay.) I go
among them quite familiarly, and am always received
with smiling good-humour. With the assistance of a few
words, as ninni, a man; minno, good; mudjee, bad; mee
gwedge, thank you; maja, good-bye; with nods, smiles,
signs, and friendly hand-taking, – we hold most eloquent

conversations. Even the little babies smile at me out of their comical cradles, slung at their mothers' backs, and with the help of beads and lollypops from the village store, I get on amazingly well; only when asked for some "English milk," (rum or whisky,) I frown as much as I can, and cry Mudjee! mudjee! bad! bad! then they laugh, and we are friends again.

The scenes I at first described are of constant reiteration. Every morning when I leave my room and come out into the porch, I have to exchange *bo-jou!* and shake hands with some twenty or thirty of my dingy, dusky, greasy, painted, blanketed, smiling friends: but to-day we have had some new scenes.

First, however, I forgot to tell you that yesterday afternoon there came in a numerous fleet of canoes, thirty or forty at least; and the wind blowing fresh from the west, each with its square blanket sail came scudding over the waters with astonishing velocity; it was a beautiful sight. Then there was the usual bustle, and wigwam building, fire-lighting and cooking, all along the shore, which is now excessively crowded: and yelling, shouting, drinking and dancing at the whisky store – but all this I have formerly described to you.

I presume it was in consequence of these new arrivals that we had a grand *talk* or council after breakfast this morning, at which I was permitted to be present, or, as the French say, to *assist*.

There were fifty-four of their chiefs, or rather chief men, present, and not less that two hundred Indians round the house, their dark eager faces filling up the windows and doorways; but they were silent, quiet, and none but those first admitted attempted to enter. All as they came up took my hand: some I had seen before, and some were entire strangers, but there was no look of surprise, and all was ease and grave self-possession: a set of more perfect gentlemen, in *manner*, I never met with.

The council was convened to ask them if they would consent to receive goods instead of dollars in payment of the pensions due to them on the sale of their lands, and which, by the conditions of sale, were to be paid in money. So completely do the white men reckon on having everything their own way with the poor Indians, that a trader had contracted with the government to supply the goods which the Indians had not yet consented to receive, and was actually now on the island, having come with me in the steamer.

As the chiefs entered, they sat down on the floor. The principal person was a venerable old man with a bald head, who did not speak. The orator of the party wore a long gray blanket-coat, crimson sash, and black neckcloth, with leggings and moccasins. There was also a well-looking young man dressed in the European fashion, and in black; he was of mixed blood, French and Indian; he had been carried early to Europe by the Catholic priests, had been educated in the Propaganda College at Rome, and was lately come out to settle as a teacher and interpreter among his people. He was the only person besides Mr. Schoolcraft who was seated on a chair, and he watched the proceedings with great attention. On examining one by one the assembled chiefs, I remarked five or six who had good heads – well developed, intellectual, and benevolent. The old chief, and my friend the Rain, were conspicuous among them, and also an old man with a fine square head and lofty brow, like the picture of Red-jacket,* and a young man with a pleasing countenance, and two scalps hung as ornaments to his belt. Some faces were mild and vacant, some were stupid and coarse, but

* The picture by Weir, in the possession of Samuel Ward, Esq., of New York, which see – or rather see the beautiful lines of Halleck –

> If he were with me, King of Tuscarora!
>   Gazing as I upon thy portrait now,
> In all its medalled, fring'd, and beaded glory,
>   Its eyes' dark beauty and its tranquil brow –
> Its brow, half martial, and half diplomatic,
>   Its eye, upsoaring like an eagle's wings –
> Well might he boast that we, the democratic,
>   Outrival Europe, even in our kings!

in none was there a trace of insolence or ferocity, or of that vile expression I have seen in a depraved European of the lowest class. The worst physiognomy was that of a famous medicine-man – it was mean and cunning. Not only the countenances but the features differed; even the distinct characteristics of the Indian, the small deep-set eye, breadth of face and high cheek-bones, were not universal: there were among them regular features, oval faces, aquiline noses. One chief had a head and face which reminded me strongly of the Marquis Wellesley. All looked dirty, grave, and picturesque, and most of them, on taking their seats on the ground, pulled out their tobacco-pouches and lighted their wooden pipes.

The proposition made to them was evidently displeasing. The orator, after whispering with the chief, made a long and vehement speech in a loud emphatic voice, and at every pause the auditors exclaimed, "Hah!" in sign of approbation. I remarked that he sometimes made a jest which called forth a general smile, even from the interpreter and Mr. Schoolcraft. Only a few sentences were translated: from which I understood that they all considered this offer as a violation of the treaty which their great father at Washington, the president, had made with them. They did not want goods, – they wanted the stipulated dollars. Many of their young men had procured goods from the traders on credit, and depended on the money due to them to discharge their debts; and, in short, the refusal was distinct and decided. I am afraid, however, it will not avail them much.* The mean, petty-trader style in which the American officials make (and *break*) their

---

* Since my return to England I found the following passage in the Morning Chronicle, extracted from the American papers: – "The Indians of Michigan have committed several shocking murders, in consequence of the payments due to them on land-treaties being made in goods instead of money. Serious alarm on that subject prevails in the State."

The wretched individuals murdered were probably settlers, quite innocent in this business, probably women and children; but such is the *well-known* Indian law of retaliation.

treaties with the Indians is shameful. I met with none who attempted to deny it or excuse it. Mr. Schoolcraft told me that during the time he had been Indian agent (five-and-twenty years,) he had never known the Indians to violate a treaty or break a promise. He could not say the same of his government, and the present business appeared most distasteful to him; but he was obliged to obey the order from the head of his department.

The Indians themselves make witty jests on the bad faith of the "Big Knives."* "My father!" said a distinguished Pottowottomie chief at the treaty of Chicago – "my father, you have made several promises to your red children, and you have put the money down upon the table: but as fast as you put it upon the top, it has slipped away to the bottom, in a manner that is incomprehensible to us. We do not know what becomes of it. When we get together, and divide it among ourselves, it is nothing! and we remain as poor as ever. My father, I only explain to you the words of my brethren. We can only see what is before our eyes, and are unable to comprehend all things." Then pointing to a newspaper which lay on the table – "You see that paper on the table before you – it is double. You can see what is upon the upper sheet, but you cannot see what is below. We cannot tell how our money goes!"

On the present occasion, two orators spoke, and the council lasted above two hours: but I left the room long before the proceedings were over. I must needs confess it to you – I cannot overcome one disagreeable obstacle to a near communion with these people. The genuine Indian has a very peculiar odour, unlike anything of the kind that ever annoyed my fastidious senses. One ought to get over these things; and after all it is not so offensive as it is

* The Indians gave the name of Cheemokomaum (Long Knives, or *Big Knives*) to the Americans at the time they were defeated by General Wayne, near the Miami river in 1795, and suffered so severely from the *sabres* of the cavalry.

peculiar. You have probably heard that horses brought up in the white settlements can smell an Indian at a great distance, and show evident signs of perturbation and terror whenever they snuff an Indian in the air. For myself, in passing over the place on which a wigwam has stood, and whence it has been removed several hours, though it was the hard pebbly beach on the water's edge, I could scent the Indian in the atmosphere. You can imagine, therefore, that fifty of them in one room, added to the smell of their tobacco, which is detestable, and the smoking and all its unmentionable consequences, drove me from the spot. The truth is, that a woman of very delicate and fastidious habits must learn to endure some very disagreeable things, or she had best stay at home.

In the afternoon, Mr. Johnson informed me that the Indians were preparing to dance, for my particular amusement. I was, of course, most thankful and delighted. Almost in the same moment, I heard their yells and shrieks resounding along the shore, mingled with the measured monotonous drum. We had taken our place on an elevated platform behind the house – a kind of little lawn on the hill-side; – the precipitous rocks, clothed with trees and bushes, rose high like a wall above us: the glorious sunshine of a cloudless summer's day was over our heads – the dazzling blue lake and its islands at our feet. Soft and elysian in its beauty was all around. And when these wild and more than half-naked figures came up, leaping, whooping, drumming, shrieking, hideously painted, and flourishing clubs, tomahawks, javelins, it was like a masque of fiends breaking into paradise! The rabble of Comus might have boasted themselves comely in comparison, even though no self-deluding potion had bleared their eyes and intellect.* It was a grotesque and horrible phantasmagoria. Of their style of clothing, I say nothing –

* "And they, so perfect is their misery,
Not once perceive their foul disfigurement,
But boast themselves more comely than before."

COMUS.

for, as it is wisely said, nothing can come of *nothing:* – only if "all symbols be clothes," according to our great modern philosopher* – my Indian friends were as little symbolical as you can dare to imagine: – *passons par là*. If the blankets and leggings were thrown aside, all the resources of the Indian toilette, all their store of feathers, and bears' claws, hawks' bells, vermilion, soot, and verdigris, were brought into requisition as decoration: and no two were alike. One man wore three or four heads of hair, composed of the manes and tails of animals; another wore a pair of deers' horns; another was *coiffé* with the skin and feathers of a crane or some such bird – its long bill projecting from his forehead; another had the shell of a small turtle suspended from his back, and dangling behind; another used the skin of a polecat for the same purpose. One had painted his right leg with red bars, and his left leg with green lines: particoloured eyes and faces, green noses, and blue chins, or *vice versâ*, were general. I observed that in this grotesque deformity, in the care with which everything like symmetry or harmony in form or colours was avoided, there was something evidently studied and artistical. The orchestra was composed of two drums and two rattles, and a chorus of voices. The song was without melody – a perpetual repetition of three or four notes, melancholy, harsh, and monotonous. A flag was stuck in the ground, and round this they began their dance – if dance it could be called – the movements consisting of the alternate raising of one foot, then the other, and swinging the body to and fro. Every now and then they paused, and sent forth that dreadful, prolonged, tremulous yell, which re-echoed from the cliffs, and pierced my ears and thrilled along my nerves. The whole exhibition was of that finished barbarism, that it was at least complete in its way, and for a time I looked on with curiosity and interest. But that innate loathing which dwells within me for all that is discordant and deformed, rendered it anything but pleas-

---

* Sartor Resartus.

ant to witness. It grated horribly upon all my perceptions.
In the midst, one of those odd and unaccountable transi-
tions of thought caused by some mental or physical reaction – the law which brings extremes in contrast
together, came across me. I was reminded that even on
this very day last year I was seated in a box at the opera,
looking at Carlotta Grisi and Perrot dancing, or rather
flying through the galoppe in "Benyowsky." The oddity of
this sudden association made me laugh, which being inter-
preted into the expression of my highest approbation, they
became every moment more horribly ferocious and animated; redoubled the vigour of their detestably awkward
movements and the shrillness of their savage yells, till I
began involuntarily to look about for some means of
escape – but this would have been absolutely rude, and I
restrained myself.

I should not forget to mention that the figures of most
of the men were superb; more agile and elegant, however,
than muscular – more fitted for the chase than for labour,
with small and well formed hands and feet. When the
dance was ended, a young warrior, leaving the group, sat
himself down on a little knoll to rest. His spear lay across
his knees, and he reposed his head upon his hand. He was
not painted, except with a little vermilion on his chest –
and on his head he wore only the wing of the osprey: he
sat there – a model for a sculptor. The perfection of his
form, the graceful abandonment of his attitude, reminded
me of a young Mercury, or of Thorwaldsen's "Shepherd
Boy." I went up to speak to him, and thanked him for his
exertions in the dance, which indeed had been conspicuous: and then, for want of something else to say, I asked
him if he had a wife and children? The whole expression
of his face suddenly changed, and with an air as tenderly
coy as that of a young girl listening to the first whisper of a
lover, he looked down and answered softly, "Kah-ween!" –
No, indeed! Feeling that I had for the first time embar-
rassed an Indian, I withdrew, really as much out of coun-

tenance as the youth himself. I did not ask him his name, for that were a violation of the Indian form of good breeding, but I learn that he is called *the Pouncing Hawk* – and a fine creature he is – like a blood horse or the Apollo; West's comparison of the Apollo Belvedere to a young Mohawk warrior has more of likelihood and reasonableness than I ever believed or acknowledged before.

A keg of tobacco and a barrel of flour were given to them, and they dispersed as they came, drumming, and yelling, and leaping, and flourishing their clubs and war-hatchets.

In the evening we paddled in a canoe over to the opposite island, with the intention of landing and looking at the site of an intended missionary settlement for the Indians. But no sooner did the keel of our canoe touch the woody shore than we were enveloped in a cloud of mosquitoes. It was in vain to think of dislodging the enemy, and after one or two attempts we were fairly beaten back. So leaving the gentlemen to persist, we – that is, the young Irish lady and myself – pushed off the canoe, and sat in it, floating about, and singing Irish melodies and Italian serenades – the first certainly that ever roused the echoes of Woody Island.* Mackinaw, as seen from hence, has exactly the form its name implies,† that of a large turtle sleeping on the water. It was a mass of purple shadow; and just at one extremity, the sun plunged into the lake, leaving its reflection on the water, like the skirts of a robe of fire, floating. This too vanished, and we returned in the soft calm twilight, singing as we went.

---

* The island of Bois Blanc, or Woody Island, has never been inhabited in the memory of man.

† I believe Mackinaw is merely the abbreviation of Michilimackinac, *the great turtle*.

Vague mystery hangs on all these desert places,
   The fear which hath no name, hath wrought a spell,
Strength, courage, wrath, have been, and left no traces;
   They came – and fled! but whither! who can tell?

We know but that they *were;* that once (in days
   When ocean was a bar 'twixt man and man,)
Stout spirits wander'd o'er these capes and bays,
   And perished where these river waters ran.

BARRY CORNWALL.

July 29th.

Where was I? Where did I leave off four days ago? O – at Mackinaw! that fairy island, which I shall never see again! and which I should have dearly liked to filch from the Americans, and carry home to you in my dressing-box, or perdie, in my toothpick case – but, good lack! to see the ups and downs of this (new) world! I take up my tale a hundred miles from it – but before I tell you where I am now, I must take you over the ground, or rather over the water, in a proper and journal-like style.

I was sitting last Friday, at sultry noon-tide, under the shadow of a schooner which had just anchored alongside the little pier – sketching and dreaming – when up came a messenger, breathless, to say that a boat was going off for the Sault Ste. Marie, in which I could be accommodated with a passage. Now this was precisely what I had been wishing and waiting for, and yet I heard the information with an emotion of regret. I had become every day more attached to the society of Mrs. Schoolcraft – more interested about her; and the idea of parting, and parting suddenly, took me by surprise, and was anything but agreeable. On reaching the house, I found all in movement, and learned, to my inexpressible delight, that my friend would take the opportunity of paying a visit to her mother and family, and, with her children, was to accompany me on my voyage.

We had but one hour to prepare packages, provisions, everything – and in one hour all was ready.

This voyage of two days was to be made in a little Canadian bateau, rowed by five *voyageurs* from the Sault. The boat might have carried fifteen persons, hardly more, and was rather clumsy in form. The two ends were appropriated to the rowers, baggage, and provisions; in the centre there was a clear space, with a locker on each side, on which we sat or reclined, having stowed away in them our smaller and more valuable packages. This was the internal arrangement.

The distance to the Sault or, as the Americans call it, the *Sou*, is not more than thirty miles over land, as the bird flies; but the whole region being one mass of tangled forest and swamp, infested with bears and mosquitoes, it is seldom crossed but in winter, and in snow shoes. The usual route by water is ninety-four miles.

At three o'clock in the afternoon, with a favourable breeze, we launched forth on the lake, and having rowed about a mile from the shore, the little square sail was hoisted, and away we went merrily over the blue waves.

For a detailed account of the *voyageurs*, or Canadian boatmen, their peculiar condition and mode of life, I refer you to Washington Irving's "Astoria:" what he describes them to *have been*, and what Henry represents them in his time, they are even now, in these regions of the upper lakes.* But the voyageurs in our boat were not favourable

* As I shall have much to say hereafter of this peculiar class of people, to save both reader and author time and trouble, the passage is here given.

"The voyageurs form a kind of confraternity in the Canadas, like the arrieros or carriers of Spain. The dress of these people is generally half civilised, half savage. They wear a capote or surcoat, made of a blanket, a striped cotton shirt, cloth trowsers or leathern leggings, moccasins of deerskin, and a belt of variegated worsted, from which are suspended the knife, tobacco-pouch, and other articles. Their language is of the same piebald character, being a French patois embroidered with English and specimens of their very amusing and peculiar class. They were fatigued with rowing for three days previous, and had only two helpless women to deal with. As soon, therefore, as the sail was hoisted, two began to play cards on the top of a keg, the other two went to sleep. The youngest and most intelligent of the set, a lively, half-breed boy of eighteen, took the helm. He told us with great self-complacency that he was *captain*, and that it was already the third time that he had been elected by his comrades to this dignity – but I cannot say he had a very obedient crew.

About seven o'clock we landed to cook our supper on an island which is commemorated by Henry as the Isle des Outardes, and is now Goose Island. Mrs. Schoolcraft undertook the general management with all the alertness of one accustomed to these impromptu arrangements, and I did my best in my new vocation – dragged one or two blasted boughs to the fire – the least of them twice as big as myself – and laid the cloth upon the pebbly beach. The enormous fire was to keep off the mosquitoes, in which we succeeded pretty well, swallowing, however, as much smoke as would have dried us externally into hams or red herrings. We then returned to the boat, spread a bed

Italian words and phrases. They are generally of French descent, and inherit much of the gaiety and lightness of heart of their ancestors; they inherit, too, a fund of civility and complaisance, and instead of that hardness and grossness, which men in laborious life are apt to indulge towards each other, they are mutually obliging and accommodating, interchanging kind offices, yielding each other assistance and comfort in every emergency, and using the familiar appellations of *cousin* and *brother*, when there is in fact no relationship. No men are more submissive to their leaders and employers, more capable of enduring hardships, or more good-humoured under privations. Never are they so happy as when on long and rough expeditions, towing up rivers or coasting lakes. They are dexterous boat-men, vigorous and adroit with the oar or paddle, and will row from morning till night without a murmur. The steersman often sings an old French song with some regular burthen in which they all join, keeping time with their oars. If at any time they flag in spirits or relax in exertion, it is but necessary to strike up a song of this kind to put them all in fresh spirits and activity." – ASTORIA, vol. i. chap. 4.

for the children, (who were my delight,) in the bottom of it with mats and blankets, and disposed our own, on the lockers on each side, with buffalo skins, blankets, shawls, cloaks, and whatever was available, with my writing-case for a pillow.

After sunset, the breeze fell: the men were urged to row, but pleaded fatigue, and that they were hired for the day, and not for the night, (which is the custom.) One by one they sulkily abandoned their oars, and sunk to sleep under their blankets, all but our young captain: like Ulysses when steering away from Calypso –

> Placed at the helm he sat, and watched the skies,
> Nor closed in sleep his ever watchful eyes.

He kept himself awake by singing hymns, in which Mrs. Schoolcraft joined him. I lay still, looking up at the stars and listening: when there was a pause in the singing, we kept up the conversation, fearing lest sleep should overcome our only pilot and guardian. Thus we floated on beneath that divine canopy – "which love had spread to curtain the sleeping world:" it was a most lovely and blessed night, bright and calm and warm, and we made some little way, for both wind and current were in our favour.

As we were coasting a little shadowy island, our captain mentioned a strange circumstance, very illustrative of Indian life and character. A short time ago a young Chippewa hunter, whom he knew, was shooting squirrels on this spot, when by some chance a large blighted pine fell upon him, knocking him down and crushing his leg, which was fractured in two places. He could not rise, he could not remove the tree which was lying across his broken leg. He was in a little uninhabited island, without the slightest probability of passing aid, and to lie there and starve to death in agonies, seemed all that was left to him. In this dilemma, with all the fortitude and promptitude of resource of a thorough-bred Indian, he took out his knife, cut off his own leg, bound it up, dragged himself along the ground to his hunting canoe, and paddled himself home to his wigwam on a distant island, where the cure of his wound was completed. The man is still alive.

Perhaps this story appears to you incredible. I believe it firmly; at the time, and since then, I heard other instances of Indian fortitude, and of their courage and skill in performing some of the boldest and most critical operations in surgery, which I really cannot venture to set down. *You* would believe them if I could swear that I had witnessed them with "my own two good-looking eyes," not otherwise. But I will mention one or two of the least marvellous of these stories. There was a young chief and famous hunter, whose arm was shattered by the bursting of his rifle. No one would venture the amputation, and it was bound up with certain herbs and dressings, accompanied with many magical ceremonies. The young man, who seemed aware of the inefficacy of such expedients, waited till the moment when he should be left alone. He had meantime, with pain and difficulty, hatched one of his knives into a saw; with this he completed the amputation of his own arm; and when his relations appeared they found the arm lying at one end of the wigwam, and the patient sitting at the other, with his wound bound up, and smoking with great tranquillity.

Mrs. Schoolcraft told me of a young Chippewa who went on a hunting expedition with his wife only; they were camped at a considerable distance from the village, when the woman was seized with the pains of child-birth. This is in general a very easy matter among the Indian women, cases of danger or death being exceedingly rare; but on this occasion some unusual and horrible difficulty occurred. The husband, who was described to me as an affectionate, gentle spirited man, much attached to his wife, did his best to assist her; but after a few struggles she became insensible, and lay, as he supposed, dead. He took out his knife, and with astonishing presence of mind, performed on his wife the Cesarean operation, saved his infant, and ultimately the mother, and brought them both home on a sleigh to his village at the Sault, where, as Mrs. Schoolcraft told me, she had frequently seen both the man and woman.

We remained in conversation till long after midnight; then the boat was moored to a tree, but kept off shore, for fear of the mosquitoes, and we addressed ourselves to sleep. I remember lying awake for some minutes, looking up at the quiet stars, and around upon the dark weltering waters, and at the faint waning moon, just suspended on the very edge of the horizon. I saw it sink – sink into the bosom of the lake as if to rest, and then with a thought of far-off friends, and a most fervent thanksgiving, I dropped asleep. It is odd that I did not think of praying for protection, and that no sense of fear came over me; it seemed as if the eye of God himself looked down upon me; that I *was* protected. I do not say I *thought* this any more than the unweaned child in its cradle; but I had some such feeling of unconscious trust and love, now I recall those moments.

I slept, however, uneasily, not being yet accustomed to a board and a blanket; *ça viendra avec le temps*. About dawn I awoke in a sort of stupor, but after bathing my face and hands over the boat side, I felt refreshed. The voyageurs, after a good night's rest, were in better humour, and took manfully to their oars. Soon after sunrise, we passed round that very conspicuous cape, famous in the history of north-west adventure, called the "Grand Détour," half-way between Mackinaw and the Sault. Now, if you look at the map, you will see that our course was henceforth quite altered; we had been running down the coast of the mainland towards the east; we had now to turn short round the point, and steer almost due west; hence its most fitting name, the Grand Détour. The wind, hitherto favourable, was now dead against us. This part of Lake Huron is studded with little islands, which, as well as the neighbouring mainland, are all uninhabited, yet clothed with the richest, loveliest, most fantastic vegetation, and no doubt swarming with animal life.

I cannot, I dare not, attempt to describe to you the strange sensation one has, thus thrown for a time beyond the bounds of civilised humanity, or indeed any humanity; nor the wild yet solemn reveries which come over one in the midst of this wilderness of woods and waters. All was so solitary, so grand in its solitude, as if nature unviolated sufficed to herself. Two days and nights the solitude was unbroken; not a trace of social life, not a human being, not a canoe, not even a deserted wigwam, met our view. Our little boat held on its way over the placid lake and among green tufted islands; and we its inmates, two women, differing in clime, nation, complexion, strangers to each other but a few days ago, might have fancied ourselves alone in a new-born world.

We landed to boil our kettle, and breakfast on a point of the island of St. Joseph's. This most beautiful island is between thirty and forty miles in length, and nearly a hundred miles in circumference, and towards the centre the land is high and picturesque. They tell me that on the other side of the island there is a settlement of whites and Indians. Another large island, Drummond's Isle, was for a short time in view. We had also a settlement here, but it was unaccountably surrendered to the Americans. If now you look at the map, you will wonder, as I did, that in retaining St. Joseph's and the Manitoolin islands, we gave up Drummond's Island. Both these islands had forts and garrisons during the war.

By the time breakfast was over, the children had gathered some fine strawberries; the heat had now become almost intolerable, and unluckily we had no awning. The men rowed languidly, and we made but little way; we coasted along the south shore of St. Joseph's, through fields of rushes, miles in extent, across Lake George, and Muddy Lake; (the name, I thought, must be a libel, for it was as clear as crystal and as blue as heaven; but they say that, like a sulky temper, the least ruffle of wind turns it as black as ditchwater, and it does not subside again in a hurry,) and then came a succession of openings spotted with lovely islands, all solitary. The sky was without a cloud, a speck – except when the great fish-eagle was descried sailing over its blue depths – the water without a wave. We were too hot and too languid to converse. Nothing disturbed the deep noon-tide stillness, but the dip of the oars, or the spring and splash of a sturgeon as he leapt from the surface of the lake, leaving a circle of little wavelets spreading around. All the islands we passed were so woody, and so infested with mosquitoes, that we could not land and light our fire, till we reached the entrance of St. Mary's River, between Nebish island and the mainland.

Here was a well-known spot, a sort of little opening on a flat shore, called the *Encampment*, because a party of boatmen coming down from Lake Superior, and camping here for the night, were surprised by the frost, and obliged to remain the whole winter till the opening of the ice, in the spring. After rowing all this hot day till seven o'clock against the wind, (what there was of it,) and against the current coming rapidly and strongly down from Lake Superior, we did at length reach this promised harbour of rest and refreshment. Alas! there was neither for us; the moment our boat touched the shore, we were enveloped in a cloud of mosquitoes. Fires were lighted instantly, six were burning in a circle at once; we were well nigh suffocated and smoke-dried – all in vain. At last we left the voyageurs to boil the kettle, and retreated to our boat, desiring them to make us fast to a tree by a long rope; then, each of us taking an oar – I only wish you could have seen us – we pushed off from the land, while the children were sweeping away the enemy with green boughs. This being done, we commenced supper, really half famished, and were too much engrossed to look about us. Suddenly we were again surrounded by our adversaries; they came upon us in swarms, in clouds, in myriads, entering our eyes, our noses, our mouths, stinging till the blood followed. We had, unawares, and while absorbed in our culinary operations, drifted into the shore, got entangled among the roots of trees, and were with difficulty extricated, presenting all the time a fair mark and a rich banquet for our detested tormentors. The dear children cried with agony and impatience, and but for shame I could almost have cried too.

I had suffered from these plagues in Italy; you too, by this time, may probably know what they are in the southern countries of the old world; but 'tis a jest, believe me, to encountering a forest full of them in these wild regions. I had heard much, and much was I forewarned, but never could have conceived the torture they can inflict, nor the impossibility of escape, defence, or endurance. Some amiable person who took an especial interest in our future welfare, in enumerating the torments prepared for hardened sinners, assures us that they will be stung by mosquitoes all made of brass, and as large as black beetles – he was an ignoramus and a bungler; you may credit me, that the brass is quite an unnecessary improvement, and the increase of size equally superfluous. Mosquitoes, as they exist in this upper world, are as pretty and perfect a plague as the most ingenious amateur sinner-tormentor ever devised. Observe, that a mosquito does not sting like a wasp, or a gad-fly; he has a long proboscis like an awl, with which he bores your veins and pumps the life-blood out of you, leaving venom and fever behind. Enough of mosquitoes – I will never again do more than allude to them; only they are enough to make Philosophy go hang herself, and Patience swear like a Turk or a trooper.

Well, we left this most detestable and inhospitable shore as soon as possible, but the enemy followed us, and we did not soon get rid of them; night came on, and we were still twenty miles below the Sault.

I offered an extra gratuity to the men, if they would keep to their oars without interruption; and then, fairly exhausted, lay down on my locker and blanket. But whenever I woke from uneasy, restless slumbers, *there* was Mrs.

Schoolcraft, bending over her sleeping children, and waving off the mosquitoes, singing all the time a low, melancholy Indian song; while the northern lights were streaming and dancing in the sky, and the fitful moaning of the wind, the gathering clouds, and chilly atmosphere, foretold a change of weather. This would have been the *comble de malheur*. When daylight came, we passed Sugar Island, where immense quantities of maple sugar are made every spring, and just as the rain began to fall in earnest, we arrived at the Sault Ste. Marie. On one side of the river, Mrs. Schoolcraft was welcomed by her mother; and on the other, my friends, the MacMurrays, received me with delighted and delightful hospitality. I went to bed – oh! the luxury! – and slept for six hours.

Enough of solemn reveries on starlit lakes, enough – too much – of self and self-communings; I turn over a new leaf, and this shall be a chapter of geography, and topography, natural philosophy, and such wise-like things. Draw the curtain first, for if I look out any longer on those surging rapids, I shall certainly turn giddy – forget all the memoranda I have been collecting for you, lose my reckoning, and become unintelligible to you and myself too.

This river of St. Mary is, like the Detroit and the St. Clair, already described, properly a strait, the channel of communication between Lake Superior and Lake Huron. About ten miles higher up, the great Ocean-lake narrows to a point; then, forcing a channel through the high lands, comes rushing along till it meets with a downward ledge, or cliff, over which it throws itself in foam and fury, tearing a path for its billows through the rocks. The descent is about twenty-seven feet in three quarters of a mile, but the rush begins above, and tumult continues below the fall, so that, on the whole, the eye embraces an expanse of white foam measuring about a mile each way, the effect being exactly that of the ocean breaking on a rocky shore: not so terrific, nor on so large a scale, as the rapids of Niagara, but quite as beautiful – quite as animated.

What the French call a *saut*, (leap,) we term a *fall*; the Sault Ste. Marie is translated into the falls of St. Mary. By this name the rapids are often mentioned, but the village on their shore still retains its old name, and is called the Sault. I do not know why the beautiful river and its glorious cataracts should have been placed under the peculiar patronage of the blessed Virgin; perhaps from the union of exceeding loveliness with irresistible power; or, more probably, because the first adventurers reached the spot on some day hallowed in the calendar.

The French, ever active and enterprising, were the first who penetrated to this wild region. They had an important trading post here early in the last century, and also a small fort. They were ceded, with the rest of the country, to Great Britain, in 1762.* I wonder whether, at that time, the young king or any of his ministers had the least conception of the value and immensity of the magnificent country thrown into our possession, or gave a thought to the responsibilities it brought with it! – to be sure they made good haste, both king and ministers, to get rid of most of the responsibility. The American war began, and at its conclusion the south shore of St. Mary's, and the fort, were surrendered to the Americans.

The rapids of Niagara, as I once told you, reminded me of a monstrous tiger at play, and threw me into a sort of ecstatic terror; but these rapids of St. Mary suggest quite another idea: as they come fretting and fuming down, curling up their light foam, and wreathing their glancing billows round the opposing rocks, with a sort of passionate self-will, they remind me of an exquisitely beautiful woman in a fit of rage, or of Walter Scott's simile – "one of the Graces possessed by a Fury;" – there is no terror in their anger, only the sense of excitement and loveliness; when it has spent this sudden, transient fit of impatience, the beautiful river resumes all its placid dignity, and holds

---

* The first British commandant of the fort was that miserable Lieutenant Jemette, who was scalped at the massacre at Michilimackinac.

on its course, deep and wide enough to float a squadron of seventy-fours, and rapid and pellucid as a mountain trout-stream.

Here, as everywhere else, I am struck by the difference between the two shores. On the American side there is a settlement of whites, as well as a large village of Chippewas; there is also a mission (I believe of the Methodists) for the conversion of the Indians. The fort, which has been lately strengthened, is merely a strong and high enclosure, surrounded with pickets of cedar wood; within the stockade are the barracks, and the principal trading store. This fortress is called Fort Brady, after that gallant officer whom I have already mentioned to you. The garrison may be very effective for aught I know, but I never beheld such an unmilitary looking set. When I was there to-day, the sentinels were lounging up and down in their flannel jackets and shirt sleeves, with muskets thrown over their shoulders – just for all the world like ploughboys going to shoot sparrows; however, they are in keeping with the fortress of cedar-posts, and no doubt both answer their purpose very well. The village is increasing into a town, and the commercial advantages of its situation must raise it ere long to a place of importance.

On the Canada side, we have not even these demonstrations of power or prosperity. Nearly opposite to the American fort there is a small factory belonging to the North-west Fur Company; below this, a few miserable log-huts, occupied by some French Canadians and voyageurs in the service of the company, a set of lawless *mauvais sujets*, from all I can learn. Lower down stands the house of Mr. and Mrs. MacMurray, with the Chippewa village under their care and tuition, but most of the wigwams and their inhabitants are now on their way down the lake, to join the congress at the Manitoolin Islands. A lofty eminence, partly cleared and partly clothed with forest, rises behind the house, on which stand the little-missionary church and school-house for the use of the Indian converts. From the summit of this hill you look over the traverse into

Lake Superior, and the two giant capes which guard its entrance. One of these capes is called Gros-Cap, from its bold and lofty cliffs, the yet unviolated haunt of the eagle. The opposite cape is more accessible, and bears an Indian name, which I cannot pretend to spell, but which signifies "the place of the Iroquois' bones:" it was the scene of a wild and terrific tradition. At the time that the Iroquois (or Six Nations) were driven before the French and Hurons up to the western lakes, they endeavoured to possess themselves of the hunting-grounds of the Chippewas, and hence a bitter and lasting feud between the two nations. The Iroquois, after defeating the Chippewas, encamped, a thousand strong, upon this point, where, thinking themselves secure, they made a war-feast to torture and devour their prisoners. The Chippewas from the opposite shore beheld the sufferings and humiliation of their friends, and, roused to sudden fury by the sight, collected their warriors, only three hundred in all, crossed the channel, and at break of day fell upon the Iroquois, now sleeping after their horrible excesses, and massacred every one of them, men, women, and children. Of their own party they lost but one warrior, who was stabbed with an awl by an old woman who was sitting at the entrance of her wigwam, stitching moccasins: thus runs the tale. The bodies were left to bleach on the shore, and they say that bones and skulls are still found there.

Here, at the foot of the rapids, the celebrated white-fish of the lakes is caught in its highest perfection. The people down below,* who boast of the excellence of the white-fish, really know nothing of the matter. There is no more comparison between the white-fish of the lower lakes and the white-fish of St. Mary's than between plaice and turbot, or between a clam and a Sandwich oyster. I ought to be a judge, who have eaten them fresh out of the river four times a day, and I declare to you that I never tasted

---

* That is, in the neighbourhood of Lake Ontario and Lake Erie.

anything of the fish kind half so exquisite. If the Roman Apicius had lived in these latter days, he would certainly have made a voyage up Lake Huron to breakfast on the white-fish of St. Mary's river, and would *not* have returned in dudgeon, as he did, from the coast of Africa. But the epicures of our degenerate times have nothing of that gastronomical enthusiasm which inspired their ancient models, else we should have them all coming here to eat white-fish at the Sault, and scorning cockney white-bait. Henry declares that the flavour of the white-fish is "beyond any comparison whatever," and I add my testimony thereto – *probatum est!*

I have eaten tunny in the gulf of Genoa, anchovies fresh out of the bay of Naples, and trout of the Salz-kammer-gut, and divers other fishy dainties, rich and rare – but the exquisite, the refined white-fish, exceeds them all; concerning those cannibal fish (mullets were they, or lampreys?) which Lucullus fed in his fish-ponds, I cannot speak, never having tasted them; but even if *they* could be resuscitated, I would not degrade the refined, the delicate white-fish by a comparison with any such barbarian luxury.

But seriously, and badinage apart, it is really the most luxurious delicacy that swims the waters. It is said by Henry that people never tire of them. Mr. MacMurray tells me that he has eaten them every day of his life for seven years, and that his relish for them is undiminished. The enormous quantities caught here, and in the bays and creeks round Lake Superior, remind me of herrings in the lochs of Scotland; besides subsisting the inhabitants, whites and Indians, during great part of the year, vast quantities are cured and barrelled every fall, and sent down to the eastern states. Not less than eight thousand barrels were shipped last year.

These enterprising Yankees have seized upon another profitable speculation here: there is a fish found in great quantities in the upper part of Lake Superior, called the skevát,* so exceedingly rich, luscious, and oily, when fresh, as to be quite uneatable. A gentleman here told me that he had tried it, and though not very squeamish at any time, and then very hungry, he could not get beyond the first two or three mouthfuls; but it has been lately discovered that this fish makes a most luxurious pickle. It is very excellent, but so rich even in this state, that like the tunny *marinée*, it is necessary either to taste abstemiously, or die heroically of indigestion. This fish is becoming a fashionable luxury, and in one of the stores here I saw three hundred barrels ready for embarkation. The Americans have several schooners on the lakes employed in these fisheries: we have not one. They have besides planned a ship canal through the portage here, which will open a communication for large vessels between Lake Huron and Lake Superior, as our Welland Canal has united Lake Erie with Lake Ontario. The ground has already been surveyed for this purpose. When this canal is completed, a vessel may load in the Thames, and discharge her burthen at the upper end of Lake Superior. I hope you have a map before you, that you may take in at a glance this wonderful extent of inland navigation. Ought a country possessing it, and all the means of life beside, to remain poor, oppressed, uncultivated, unknown?

But to return to my beautiful river and glorious rapids, which are to be treated, you see, as a man treats a passionate beauty – he does not oppose her, for that were madness – but he gets *round her*. Well, on the American side, further down the river, is the house of Tanner, the Indian interpreter, of whose story you may have heard – for, as I remember, it excited some attention in England. He is a European of unmixed blood, with the language, manners, habits of a Red-skin. He had been kidnapped somewhere on the American frontiers when a mere boy, and brought up among the Chippewas. He afterwards returned to civilised life, and having relearned his own language, drew up

---

* I spell the word as pronounced, never having seen it written.

a very entertaining and valuable account of his adopted tribe. He is now in the American service here, having an Indian wife, and is still attached to his Indian mode of life.

Just above the fort is the ancient burial-place of the Chippewas. I need not tell you of the profound veneration with which all the Indian tribes regard the places of their dead. In all their treaties for the cession of their lands, they stipulate with the white man for the inviolability of their sepulchres. They did the same with regard to this place, but I am sorry to say that is has not been attended to, for in enlarging one side of the fort, they have considerably encroached on the cemetery. The outrage excited both the sorrow and indignation of some of my friends here, but there is no redress. Perhaps it was this circumstance that gave rise to the allusion of the Indian chief here, when in speaking of the French he said, "*They* never molested the places of our dead!"*

The view of the rapids from this spot is inexpressibly beautiful, and it has besides another attraction, which makes it to me a frequent lounge whenever I cross the river; – but of this by-and-bye. To complete my sketch of the localities, I will only add, that the whole country around is in its primitive state, covered with the interminable swamp and forest, where the bear and the moose-deer roam – and lakes and living streams where the beaver builds his hut.† The cariboo, or rein-deer, is still found on the northern shores.

The hunting-grounds of the Chippewas are in the immediate neighbourhood, and extend all round Lake Superior. Beyond these, on the north, are the Chip-

---

* Ante, p. 333.

† The beaver is, however, becoming rare in these regions. It is a curious fact connected with the physiology and psychology of instinct, that the beaver is found to change its instincts and modes of life, as it has been more and more persecuted, and, instead of being a gregarious, it is now a solitary animal. The beavers, which are found living in solitary holes instead of communities and villages, the Indians call by a name which signifies *Old Bachelor*.

pewyans; and on the south, the Sioux, Ottagamis, and Pottowottomies.

I might here multiply facts and details, but I have been obliged to throw these particulars together in haste, just to give you an idea of my present situation. Time presses, and my sojourn in this remote and interesting spot is like to be of short duration.

One of the gratifications I had anticipated in coming hither – my strongest inducement perhaps – was an introduction to the mother of my two friends, of whom her children so delighted to speak, and of whom I had heard much from other sources. A woman of pure Indian blood, of a race celebrated in these regions as warriors and chiefs from generation to generation, who had never resided within the pale of what we call civilised life, whose habits and manners were those of a genuine Indian squaw, and whose talents and domestic virtues commanded the highest respect, was, as you may suppose, an object of the deepest interest to me. I observed that not only her own children, but her two sons-in-law, Mr. MacMurray and Mr. Schoolcraft, both educated in good society, the one a clergyman and the other a man of science and literature, looked up to this remarkable woman with sentiments of affection and veneration.

As soon, then, as I was a little refreshed after my two nights on the lake, and my battles with the mosquitoes, we paddled over the river to dine with Mrs. Johnston: she resides in a large log-house close upon the shore; there is a little portico in front with seats, and the interior is most comfortable. The old lady herself is rather large in person, with the strongest marked Indian features, a countenance open, benevolent, and intelligent, and a manner perfectly easy – simple, yet with something of motherly dignity, becoming the head of her large family. She received me most affectionately, and we entered into conversation – Mrs. Schoolcraft, who looked all animation and happiness, acting as interpreter. Mrs. Johnston speaks no English, but can understand it a little, and the Canadian French still better; but in her own language she is eloquent, and her voice, like that of her people, low and musical; many kind words were exchanged, and when I said anything that pleased her, she laughed softly like a child. I was not well and much fevered, and I remember she took me in her arms, laid me down on a couch, and began to rub my feet, soothing and caressing me. She called me Nindannis, daughter, and I called her Neengai, mother, (though how different from my own fair mother, I thought, as I looked up gratefully in her dark Indian face!) She set before us the best dressed and best served dinner I had seen since I left Toronto, and presided at her table, and did the honours of her house with unembarrassed, unaffected propriety. My attempts to speak Indian caused, of course, considerable amusement; if I do not make progress, it will not be for want of teaching and teachers.

After dinner we took a walk to visit Mrs. Johnston's brother, Wayish,ky, whose wigwam is at a little distance, on the verge of the burial-ground. The lodge is of the genuine Chippewa form, like an egg cut in half lengthways. It is formed of poles stuck in the ground, and bent over at top, strengthened with a few wattles and boards; the whole is covered over with mats, birch-bark, and skins; a large blanket formed the door or curtain, which was not ungracefully looped aside. Wayish,ky, being a great man, has also a smaller lodge hard by, which serves as a storehouse and kitchen.

Rude as was the exterior of Wayish,ky's hut, the interior presented every appearance of comfort, and even *elegance*, according to the Indian notions of both. It formed a good-sized room: a raised couch ran all round like a Turkish divan, serving both for seats and beds, and covered with very soft and beautiful matting of various colours and patterns. The chests and baskets of birchbark, containing the family wardrobe and property; the rifles, the hunting and fishing tackle, were stowed away all round very tidily; I observed a coffee-mill nailed up to one of the posts or stakes; the floor was trodden down hard and perfectly clean, and there was a place for a fire in the middle: there was no window, but quite sufficient light and air were admitted through the door, and through an aperture in the roof. There was no disagreeable smell, and everything looked neat and clean. We found Wayish,ky and his wife and three of their children seated in the lodge, and as it was Sunday, and they are all Christians, no work was going forward. They received me with genuine and simple politeness, each taking my hand with a gentle inclination of the head, and some words of welcome murmured in their own soft language. We then sat down.

The conversation became very lively; and, if I might judge from looks and tones, very affectionate. I *sported* my last new words and phrases with great effect, and when I had exhausted my vocabulary – which was very soon – I amused myself with looking and listening.

Mrs. Wayish,ky (I forget her proper name) must have been a very beautiful woman. Though now no longer young, and the mother of twelve children, she is one of the handsomest Indian women I have yet seen. The number of her children is remarkable, for in general there are few large families among the Indians. Her daughter, Zah,gah,see,ga,quay, (*the sunbeams breaking through a cloud*,) is a very beautiful girl, with eyes that are a warrant for her poetical name – she is about sixteen. Wayish,ky himself is a grave, dignified man about fifty. He told me that his eldest son had gone down to the Manitoolin Island to represent his family, and receive his quota of presents. His youngest son he had sent to a college in the United States, to be educated in the learning of the white men. Mrs. Schoolcraft whispered me that his poor boy is now dying of consumption, owing to the confinement and change of living, and that the parents knew it. Wayish,ky seemed aware that we were alluding to his son, for his eye at that moment rested on me, and such an expression of keen pain came suddenly over his fine countenance, it was as if a knife had struck him, and I really felt it in my heart, and see it still before me – that look of misery.

After about an hour we left this good and interesting family. I lingered for a while on the burial-ground, looking over the rapids, and watching with a mixture of admiration and terror several little canoes which were fishing in the midst of the boiling surge, dancing and popping about like corks. The canoe used for fishing is very small and light; one man (or woman more commonly) sits in the stern, and steers with a paddle; the fisher places himself upright on the prow, balancing a long pole with both hands, at the end of which is a scoop-net. This he every minute dips into the water, bringing up at each dip a fish, and sometimes two. I used to admire the fishermen on the Arno, and those on the Lagune, and above all the Neapolitan fishermen, hauling in their nets, or diving like ducks, but I never saw anything like these Indians. The manner in which they keep their position upon a footing of a few inches, is to me as incomprehensible as the beauty of their forms and attitudes, swayed by every movement and turn of their dancing, fragile barks, is admirable.

George Johnston, on whose arm I was leaning, (and I had much ado to *reach* it,) gave me such a vivid idea of the delight of coming down the cataract in a canoe, that I am half resolved to attempt it. Terrific as it appears, yet in a good canoe, and with experienced guides, there is no absolute danger, and it must be a glorious sensation.

Mr. Johnston had spent the last fall and winter in the country, beyond Lake Superior, towards the forks of the Mississippi, where he had been employed as American agent to arrange the boundary line between the country of the Chippewas and that of their neighbours and implacable enemies, the Sioux. His mediation appeared successful for the time, and he smoked the pipe of peace with both tribes; but during the spring this ferocious war has again broken out, and he seems to think that nothing but the annihilation of either one nation or the other will entirely put an end to their conflicts; "for there is no point at which the Indian law of retaliation stops, short of the extermination of one of the parties."

I asked him how it is that in their wars the Indians make no distinction between the warriors opposed to them and helpless women and children? – how it could be with a brave and manly people, that the scalps taken from the weak, the helpless, the unresisting, were as honourable as those torn from the warrior's skull? And I described to him the horror which this custom inspired – this, which of all their customs, most justifies the name of *savage!*

He said it was inseparable from their principles of war and their mode of warfare; the first consists in inflicting the greatest possible insult and injury on their foe with the least possible risk to themselves. This truly savage law of honour we might call cowardly, but that, being associated with the bravest contempt of danger and pain, it seems nearer to the natural law. With regard to the mode of warfare, they have rarely pitched battles, but skirmishes, surprises, ambuscades, and sudden forays into each other's hunting-grounds and villages. The usual practice is to creep stealthily on the enemy's village or hunting-encampment, and wait till just after the dawn; then, at the moment the sleepers in the lodges are rising, the ambushed warriors stoop and level their pieces about two feet from the ground, which thus slaughter indiscriminately. If they find one of the enemy's lodges undefended they murder its inmates, that when the owner returns he may find his hearth desolate; for this is exquisite vengeance! But outrage against the chastity of women is absolutely unknown under any degree whatever of furious excitement.*

This respect for female honour will remind you of the

* "The whole history of Indian warfare," says Mr. Schoolcraft, "might be challenged in vain for a solitary instance of this kind. The Indians believe that to take a dishonourable advantage of their female prisoners would destroy their luck in hunting; it would be considered as effeminate and degrading in a warrior, and render him unfit for, and unworthy of, all manly achievement."

ancient Germans, as described by Julius Caesar: he contrasts in some surprise their forbearance with the very opposite conduct of the Romans; and even down to this present day, if I recollect rightly, the history of our European wars and sieges will bear out this early and characteristic distinction between the Latin and the Teutonic nations. Am I right, or am I not?

To return to the Indians. After telling me some other particulars, which gave me a clearer view of their notions and feelings on these points than I ever had before, my informant mildly added, – "It is a constant and favourite subject of reproach against the Indians – this barbarism of their desultory warfare; but I should think more women and children have perished in *one* of your civilised sieges, and that in late times, than during the whole war between the Chippewas and Sioux, and *that* has lasted a century."

I was silent, for there is a sensible proverb about taking care of our own glass windows: and I wonder if any of the recorded atrocities of Indian warfare or Indian vengeance, or all of them together, ever exceeded Massena's retreat from Portugal, – and the French call themselves civilised. A war-party of Indians, perhaps two or three hundred, (and that is a very large number,) dance their war-dance, go out and burn a village, and bring back twenty or thirty scalps. *They* are savages and heathens. We Europeans fight a battle, leave fifty thousand dead or dying by inches on the field, and a hundred thousand to mourn them, desolate; but *we* are civilised and Christians. Then only look into the motives and causes of our bloodiest European wars as revealed in the private history of courts: – the miserable, puerile, degrading intrigues which set man against man – so horridly disproportioned to the horrid result! and then see the Indian take up his war-hatchet in vengeance for some personal injury, or from motives that rouse all the natural feelings of the natural man within him! Really I do not see that an Indian warrior, flourishing his tomahawk, and smeared with his enemy's blood, is so very much a greater savage than the pipe-clayed, padded, embroidered personage, who, without cause or motive, has sold himself to slay or be slain: one scalps his enemy, the other rips him open with a sabre; one smashes his brains with a tomahawk, and the other blows him to atoms with a cannon-ball: and to me, femininely speaking, there is not a needle's point difference between the one and the other. If war be unchristian and barbarous, then war as a *science* is more absurd, unnatural, unchristian, than war as a *passion*.

This, perhaps, is putting it all too strongly, and a little exaggerated.

God forbid that I should think to disparage the blessings of civilisation! I am a woman, and to the progress of civilisation alone can we women look for release from many pains and penalties and liabilities which now lie heavily upon us. Neither am I greatly in love with savage life, with all its picturesque accompaniments and lofty virtues. I see no reason why these virtues should be necessarily connected with dirt, ignorance, and barbarism. I am thankful to live in a land of literature and steam-engines. Chatsworth is better than a wigwam, and a seventy-four is a finer thing than a bark canoe. I do not *positively* assert that Taglioni dances more gracefully than the Little-Pure tobacco-smoker, nor that soap and water are preferable as cosmetics to tallow and charcoal; for these are matters of taste, and mine may be disputed. But I do say, that if our advantages of intellect and refinement are not to lead on to farther moral superiority, I prefer the Indians on the score of consistency; they are what they profess to be, and we are *not* what we profess to be. They profess to be warriors and hunters, and are so; we profess to be Christians, and civilised – are we so?

Then as to the mere point of cruelty; – there is something to be said on this point too. Ferocity, when the hot blood is up, and all the demon in man is roused by every conceivable excitement, I can understand better than the Indian can comprehend the tender mercies of our law. Owyawatta, better known by his English name, Red-

Jacket, was once seen hurrying from the town of Buffalo with rapid strides, and every mark of disgust and consternation in his face. Three malefactors were to be hung that morning, and the Indian warrior had not nerve to face the horrid spectacle, although

> "In sober truth the veriest devil
>   That ere clenched fingers in a captive's hair."

Thus endeth my homily for to-night.

The more I looked upon those glancing, dancing rapids, the more resolute I grew to venture myself in the midst of them. George Johnston went to seek a fit canoe and a dexterous steersman, and meantime I strolled away to pay a visit to Wayish,ky's family, and made a sketch of their lodge, while pretty Zah,gah,see,gah,qua, held the umbrella to shade me from the sun.

The canoe being ready, I went to the upper end of the portage, and we launched into the river. It was a small fishing canoe about ten feet long, quite new, and light and elegant and buoyant as a bird on the waters. I reclined on a mat at the bottom, Indian fashion, (there are no seats in a genuine Indian canoe;) in a minute we were within the verge of the rapids, and down we went with a whirl and a splash! – the white surge leaping around me – over me. The Indian with astonishing dexterity kept the head of the canoe to the breakers, and somehow or other we danced through them. I could see, as I looked over the edge of the canoe, that the passage between the rocks was sometimes not more than two feet in width, and we had to turn sharp angles – a touch of which would have sent us to destruction – all this I could see through the transparent eddying waters, but I can truly say I had not even a momentary sensation of fear, but rather of giddy, breathless, delicious excitement. I could even admire the beautiful attitude of a fisher, past whom we swept as we came to the bottom. The whole affair, from the moment I entered the canoe till I reached the landing-place, occupied seven minutes, and the distance is about three quarters of a mile.*

My Indians were enchanted, and when I reached *home*, my good friends were not less delighted at my exploit: they told me I was the first European female who had ever performed it, and assuredly I shall not be the last. I recommend it as an exercise before breakfast. Two glasses of champagne could not have made me more tipsy and more self-complacent! As for my Neengai, she laughed, clapped her hands, and embraced me several times. I was declared duly initiated, and adopted into the family by the name of Wah,sàh,ge,wah,nó,quà. They had already called me among themselves, in reference to my complexion and my travelling propensities, O,daw,yaun,gee *the fair changing moon*, or rather, *the fair moon which changes her place:* but now, in compliment to my successful achievement, Mrs. Johnston bestowed this new appellation, which I much prefer. It signifies *the bright foam*, or more properly, with the feminine adjunct *qua, the woman of the bright foam;* and by this name I am henceforth to be known among the Chippewas.

Now that I have been a Chippewa born, any time these four hours,† I must introduce you to some of my new relations "of the totem of the rein-deer;" and first to my illustrious grand-papa, Waub-Ojeeg,‡ (the White-fisher.)

The Chippewas, as you perhaps know, have long been reckoned among the most warlike and numerous, but also

---

* "The total descent of the Fall of St. Mary's has been ascertained to be twenty-two and a half perpendicular feet. It has been found impracticable to ascend the rapid; but canoes have ventured down, though the experiment is extremely nervous and hazardous, and avoided by a portage, two miles long, which connects the navigable parts of the strait." – *Bouchette's Canada.*

† *Ant.* I know you now, sir, a gentleman born.
Clo. Ay, that I have been any time these four hours.

WINTER'S TALE.

‡ The name is thus pronounced, but I have seen it spelt Wabbajik.

among the wildest and most untamable nations of the
north-west. In progressing with the other Algonquin tribes
from south to north, they seem to have crossed the St.
Lawrence and dispersed themselves along the shores of
Lake Ontario, and Lake Huron and its islands. Driven
westward before the Iroquois, as *they* retired before the
French and Hurons, the Chippewas appear to have
crossed the St. Mary's River, and then spread along the
south shores of Lake Superior. Their council fire, and the
chief seat of the nation, was upon a promontory at the
farthest end of Lake Superior, called by the French La
Pointe, and by the Indians Che,goi,me,gon: by one name
or the other you will find it on most maps, as it has long
been a place of importance in the fur-trade.* Here was the
grand national council fire, (the extinction of which foretold, if it did not occasion, some dread national calam-
ity,)† and the residence of the presiding chief. The Indians
know neither sovereignty nor nobility, but when one family has produced several distinguished war-chiefs, the dignity becomes by courtesy or custom hereditary; and from
whatever reason, the family of Wayish,ki or the
Mudgi,kiwis, exercised, even from a remote period, a sort
of influence over the rest of the tribe. One traveller says
that the present descendants of these chiefs evince such a
pride of ancestry as could only be looked for in feudal or
despotic monarchies. The present representative,
Piz,hi,kee, (the Buffalo,) my illustrious cousin, still resides

* Henry says, "The Chippewas of Chegoimegon are a handsome, well-
made people, and much more cleanly, as well as much more regular in the
government of their families, than the Chippewas of Lake Huron." "The
women," he adds, "have agreeable features." At this time (1765) they
knew nothing of European manufactures, and were habited in dressed
deer-skins.

† Governor Cass. He adds, "that there were male and female guardians to
whose care the sacred fire was committed;" and that "no fact is better
established in the whole range of Indian history than the devotion of
some, if not all, the tribes to this characteristic feature of the ancient
superstition of the Magi."

at La Pointe. When presented with a silver medal of authority from the American government, he said haughtily, "What need of this? it is known to all whence I am descended!" Family pride, you see, lies somewhere very deep in human nature.

When the Chippewas first penetrated to these regions, they came in contact with the Ottagamies or Foxes, who, being descended from the same stock, received them as brothers, and at first ceded to them a part of their boundless hunting-grounds; and as these Ottagamies were friends and allies of the Sioux, these three nations continued for some time friends, and inter-marriages and family alliances took place. But the increasing power of the Chippewas soon excited the jealousy and apprehension of the other two tribes. The Ottagamies committed inroads on their hunting-grounds, (this is the primary cause of almost all the Indian wars;) the Chippewas sent an embassy to complain of the injury, and desired the Ottagamies to restrain their young men within the stipulated bounds. The latter returned an insulting answer. The war-hatchet was raised, and the Sioux and the Ottagamies united against the Chippewas: this was about 1726 or 1730. From this time there has been no peace between the Chippewas and Sioux.

It happened, just before the declaration of war, that a young Chippewa girl was married to a Sioux chief of great distinction, and bore him two sons. When hostilities commenced, the Sioux chief retired to his own tribe, and his wife remained with her relations, according to Indian custom. The two children, belonging to both tribes, were hardly safe with either; but as the father was best able to protect them, it was at last decided that they should accompany him. The Sioux chief and his boys departed to join his warriors, accompanied by his Chippewa wife and her relations, till they were in safety: then the young wife returned home weeping and inconsolable for the loss of her husband and children. Some years afterwards she consented to become the wife of the great chief of Chegoimegon. Her son by this marriage was Mamongazida, or Mongazida, (the Loon's-foot,) a chief of great celebrity, who led a strong party of his nation in the Canadian wars between the French and English, fighting on the side of the French. He was present at the battle of Quebec when Wolfe was killed, and, according to the Indian tradition, the Marquis Montcalm died in Mongazida's arms. After the war was over, he "shook hands" with the English. He was at the grand assemblage of chiefs, convened by Sir William Johnstone, at Niagara, and from him received a rich gorget and broad belt of wampum, as pledges of peace and alliance with the English. These relics were preserved in the family with great veneration, and inherited by Waub Ojeeg, and afterwards by his younger brother, Camudwa; but it happened that when Camudwa was out on a winter-hunt near the river Broulé, he and all his family were overtaken by famine and starved to death, and these insignia were then lost and never recovered. This last incident is a specimen of the common vicissitudes of Indian life; and when listening to their domestic histories, I observe that the events of paramount interest are the want or the abundance of food – hunger or plenty. "We killed a moose, or a bear, and had meat for so many days;" or, "we followed on the track of a bear, and he escaped us; we had no meat for so many days;" these are the ever-recurring topics which in their conversation stand instead of the last brilliant essay in the Edinburgh or Quarterly, or the last news from Russia or Spain. Starvation from famine is not uncommon; and I am afraid, from all I hear, that cannibalism under such circumstances is not unknown. Remembering some recent instances nearer home, when extreme hunger produced the same horrid result, I could not be much astonished.

To return. Waub Ojeeg was the second son of this famous Mongazida. Once when the latter went out on his "fall hunts," on the grounds near the Sioux territory, taking all his relatives with him, (upwards of twenty in number,) they were attacked by the Sioux at early dawn, in the usual manner. The first volley had gone through the lodges; before the second could be fired, Mongazida rushed out, and proclaiming his own name with a loud voice, demanded if Wabash, his mother's son, were among the assailants. There was a pause, and then a tall figure in his war-dress, with a profusion of feathers in his head, stepped forward and gave his hand to his half-brother. They all repaired to the lodge in peace together; but at the moment the Sioux chief stooped to enter, Waub Ojeeg, then a boy of eight years old, who had planted himself at the entrance to defend it, struck him a blow on the forehead with his little war-club. Wabash, enchanted, took him up in his arms and prophesied that he would become a great war-chief, and an implacable enemy of the Sioux. Subsequently the prophecy was accomplished, and Waub Ojeeg commanded his nation in all the war-parties against the Sioux and Ottagamies. He was generally victorious, and so entirely defeated the Ottagamies, that they never afterwards ventured to oppose him, but retired down the Wisconsin river, where they are now settled.

But Waub Ojeeg was something more and better than merely a successful warrior: he was remarkable for his eloquence, and composed a number of war-songs, which were sung through the Chippewa villages, and some of which his daughter can repeat. He was no less skilful in hunting than in war. His hunting-grounds extended to the river Broulé, at Fond du Lac; and he killed any one who dared to intrude on his district. The skins he took annually were worth three hundred and fifty dollars, a sum amply sufficient to make him rich in clothing, arms, powder, vermilion, and trinkets. Like Tecumseh, he would not marry early lest it should turn his attention from war, but at the age of thirty he married a widow, by whom he had two sons. Becoming tired of this elderly helpmate, he took a young wife, a beautiful girl of fourteen, by whom he had six children; of these my Neengai is the eldest. She described her father as affectionate and domestic. "There was always plenty of bear's meat and deer's flesh in the lodge." He had a splendid wigwam, sixty feet in length, which he was fond of ornamenting. In the centre there was a strong post, which rose several feet above the roof, on the top of which was the carved figure of an owl, which veered with the wind. This owl seems to have answered the same purpose as the flag on the tower of Windsor Castle: it was the insignia of his power and of his presence: when absent on his long winter hunts the lodge was shut up, and the owl taken down.

The skill of Waub Ojeeg as a hunter and trapper, brought him into friendly communication with a fur-trader named Johnston, who had succeeded the enterprising Henry in exploring Lake Superior. This young man, of good Irish family, came out to Canada with such strong letters of recommendation to Lord Dorchester, that he was invited to reside in the government house till a vacancy occurred in his favour in one of the official departments; meantime, being of an active and adventurous turn, he joined a party of traders going up the lakes, merely as an excursion, but became so enamoured of that wild life as to adopt it in earnest. On one of his expeditions, when encamped at Che,goi,me,gon, and trafficking with Waub Ojeeg, he saw the eldest daughter of the chief, and "no sooner looked than he sighed, no sooner sighed than he asked himself the reason," and ended by asking his friend to give him his beautiful daughter. "White man!" said the chief with dignity, "your customs are not our customs! You white men desire our women, you marry them, and when they cease to please your eye, you say they are *not* your wives, and you forsake them. Return, young friend, with your load of skins, to Montreal; and if there the women of the pale faces do not put my child out of your mind, return hither in the spring, and we will talk farther; she is young, and can wait." The young Irishman, ardently in love, and impatient and impetuous, after the manner of my countrymen, tried arguments, entreaties, presents, in vain – he was obliged to submit. He went down to Montreal, and the following spring returned and claimed his bride. The chief, after making him swear that he would take her as his *wife* according to the law of the white man, *till death,* gave him his daughter, with a long speech of advice to both.

Mrs. Johnston relates that, previous to her marriage, she *fasted*, according to the universal Indian custom, *for a guardian spirit:* to perform this ceremony, she went away to the summit of an eminence, and built herself a little lodge of cedar boughs, painted herself black, and began her fast in solitude. She dreamed continually of a white man, who approached her with a cup in his hand, saying, "Poor thing! why are you punishing yourself? why do you fast? here is food for you!" He was always accompanied by a dog, which looked up in her face as though he knew her. Also she dreamed of being on a high hill, which was surrounded by water, and from which she beheld many canoes full of Indians, coming to her and paying her homage; after this, she felt as if she were carried up into the heavens, and as she looked down upon the earth, she perceived it was on fire, and said to herself, "All my relations will be burned!" but a voice answered and said, "No, they will not be destroyed, they will be saved;" and she *knew it was a spirit*, because the voice was not human. She fasted for ten days, during which time her grandmother brought her at intervals some water. When satisfied that she had obtained a guardian spirit in the white stranger who haunted her dreams, she returned to her father's lodge, carrying green cedar boughs, which she threw on the ground, stepping on them as she went. When she entered the lodge, she threw some more down upon her usual place, (next her mother,) and took her seat. During the ten succeeding days she was not permitted to eat any meat, nor anything but a little corn boiled with a bitter herb. For ten days more she ate meat smoked in a particular manner, and she then partook of the usual food of her family.

Notwithstanding that her future husband and future greatness were so clearly prefigured in this dream, the pretty O,shah,gush,ko,da,na,qua having always regarded a white man with awe, and as a being of quite another species, (perhaps the more so in consequence of her dream,) seems to have felt nothing, throughout the whole negociation for her hand, but reluctance, terror, and aversion. On being carried with the usual ceremonies to her husband's lodge, she fled into a dark corner, rolled herself up in her blanket, and would not be comforted, nor even looked upon. It is to the honour of Johnston, that he took no cruel advantage of their mutual position, and that she remained in his lodge ten days, during which he treated her with the utmost tenderness and respect, and sought by every gentle means to overcome her fear and gain her affection; – and it was touching to see how tenderly and gratefully this was remembered by his wife after a lapse of thirty-six years. On the tenth day, however, she ran away from him in a paroxysm of terror, and, after fasting in the woods for four days, reached her grandfather's wigwam. Meantime her father, Waub Ojeeg, who was far off in his hunting-camp, *dreamed* that his daughter had not conducted herself according to his advice, with proper wife-like docility, and he returned in haste two days' journey to see after her; and finding all things *according to his dream*, he gave her a good beating with a stick, and threatened to cut off both her ears. He then took her back to her husband, with a propitiatory present of furs and Indian corn, and many apologies and exculpations of his own honour. Johnston succeeded at length in taming this shy wild fawn, and took her to his house at the Sault Ste. Marie. When she had been there some time, she was seized with a longing once more to behold her mother's face, and revisit her people. Her husband had lately purchased a small schooner to trade upon the lake; this he fitted out, and sent her, with a retinue of his clerks and retainers, and in such state as became the wife of the "great Englishman," to her home at La Pointe, loaded with magnificent presents for all her family. He did not go with her himself, apparently from motives of delicacy, and that he might be no constraint upon her feelings or movements. A few months' residence amid comparative splendour and luxury, with a man who treated her with respect and tenderness, enabled the fair Oshah,gush,ko,da,na,qua to contrast her former with her present home. She soon returned to her husband, and we do not hear of any more languishing after her father's wigwam. She lived most happily with Johnston for thirty-six years till his death, which occurred in 1828, and is the mother of eight children, four boys and four girls.

She showed me her husband's picture, which he brought to her from Montreal; the features are very gentleman-like. He has been described to me by some of my Canadian friends, who knew him well, as a very clever, lively, and eccentric man, and a little of the *bon vivant*. Owing to his independent fortune, his talents, his long acquaintance with the country, and his connexion by marriage with the native blood, he had much influence in the country.

During the last American war, he of course adhered to the English, on an understanding that he should be protected; in return for which the Americans *of course* burnt his house, and destroyed his property. He never could obtain either redress or compensation from our government. The very spot on which his house stood was, at the peace, made over to the United States; – himself and all his family became, per force, Americans. His sons are in the service of the States. In a late treaty, when the Chippewas ceded an immense tract in this neighbourhood to the American government, a reserve was made in favour of Oshah, gush,ko,da,na,qua, of a considerable section of land, which will render her posterity rich territorial proprietors – although at present it is all unreclaimed forest. A large tract of Sugar Island is her property; and this year she manufactured herself three thousand five hundred weight of sugar of excellent quality. In the fall, she goes up with her people in canoes to the entrance of Lake Superior, to fish in the bays and creeks for a fortnight, and comes back with a load of fish cured for the winter's consumption. In her youth she hunted, and was accounted the surest eye and fleetest foot among the women of her tribe. Her talents, energy, activity, and strength of mind, and her skill in all the domestic avocations of the Indian women, have maintained comfort and plenty within her dwelling in spite of the losses sustained by her husband, while her descent from the blood of their ancient chiefs renders her an object of great veneration among the Indians around, who, in all their miseries, maladies, and difficulties, apply to her for aid or for counsel.

She has inherited the poetical talent of her father Waub-Ojeeg; and here is a little fable or allegory which was written down from her recitation, and translated by her daughter.

THE ALLEGORY OF WINTER AND SUMMER.

A MAN from the north, gray-haired, leaning on his staff, went roving over all countries. Looking around him one day, after having travelled without any intermission for four moons, he sought out a spot on which to recline and rest himself. He had not been long seated, before he saw before him a young man, very beautiful in his appearance, with red cheeks, sparkling eyes, and his hair covered with flowers: and from between his lips he blew a breath that was as sweet as the wild rose.

Said the old man to him, as he leaned upon his staff, his white beard reaching down upon his breast, "Let us repose here awhile, and converse a little. But first we will build up a fire, and we will bring together much wood, for it will be needed to keep us warm."

The fire was made, and they took their seats by it, and began to converse, each telling the other where he came from, and what had befallen him by the way. Presently the young man felt cold. He looked round him to see what had produced this change, and pressed his hands against his cheeks to keep them warm.

The old man spoke and said, "When I wish to cross a

river, I breathe upon it and make it hard, and walk over upon its surface. I have only to speak, and bid the waters be still, and touch them with my finger, and they become hard as stone. The tread of my foot makes soft things hard – and my power is boundless."

The young man, feeling every moment still colder, and growing tired of the old man's boasting, and morning being nigh, as he perceived by the reddening east, thus began –

"Now, my father, I wish to speak."

"Speak," said the old man; "my ear, though it be old, is open – it can hear."

"Then," said the young man, "I also go over all the earth. I have seen it covered with snow, and the waters I have seen hard as stone; but I have only passed over them, and snow has melted; the mountain streams have begun to flow, the rivers to move, the ice to melt: the earth has become green under my tread, the flowers blossomed, the birds were joyful, and all the power of which you boast vanished away!"

The old man drew a deep sigh, and shaking his head, he said, "I know thee, thou art Spring!"

"True," said the young man, "and here behold my head – see it crowned with flowers! and my cheeks how they bloom – come near and touch me. Thou art Winter! I know thy power is great; but, father, thou darest not come to my country; thy beard would fall off, and all thy strength would fail, and thou wouldst die!"

The old man felt this truth; for before the morning was come, he was seen vanishing away: but each, before they parted, expressed a hope that they might meet again before many moons.

The language of the Chippewas, however figurative and significant, is not copious. In their speeches and songs they are emphatic and impressive by the continual repetition of the same phrase or idea; and it seems to affect them like the perpetual recurrence of a few simple notes in music, by which I have been myself wound up to painful excitement, or melted to tears.

A cousin of mine (I have now a large Chippewa cousinship) went on a hunting excursion, leaving his wife and child in his lodge. During his absence, a party of Sioux carried them off, and on his return he found his fire extinguished, and his lodge empty. He immediately blackened his face, (Indian mourning,) and repaired to the lodge of his wife's brother, to whom he sang, in a kind of mournful recitative, the following song; – the purport of which seems to be partly a request for aid against his enemies, and partly an excuse for the seeming fault of leaving his family unprotected in his wigwam.

> My brother-in law, do not wrongfully accuse me for this seeming neglect in exposing my family, for I have come to request aid from my brother-in-law!
>
> The cry of my little son was heard as they carried him across the prairie, and therefore I have come to supplicate aid from my brother-in-law.
>
> And the voice also of my wife was heard as they carried her across the prairie; do not then accuse your brother-in-law, for he has come to seek aid from his brother-in-law!

This song is in measure, ten and eight syllables alternately; and the perpetual recurrence of the word brother-in-law seems intended to impress the idea of their relationship on the mind of the hearer.

The next is the address of a war-party to their women on leaving the village.*

> Do not weep, do not weep for me,
> Loved women, should I die;
> For yourselves alone should you weep!

* From Mr. Schoolcraft, translated literally by Mrs. Schoolcraft.

> Poor are ye all, and to be pitied:
> Ye women, ye are to be pitied!

> I seek, I seek our fallen relations;
> I go to revenge, revenge the slain,
> Our relations fallen and slain,
> And our foes, our foes shall lie
> Like them, like them shall they lie;
> I go to lay them low, to lay them low!

And then *da capo*, over and over again.

The next is a love-song, in the same style of iteration.

> 'Tis now two days, two long days,
> Since last I tasted food;
> 'Tis for you, for you, my love,
> That I grieve, that I grieve,
> 'Tis for you, for you that I grieve!

> The waters flow deep and wide,
> On which, love, you have sail'd;
> Dividing you far from me.
> 'Tis for you, for you, my love,
> 'Tis for you, for you that I grieve!

If you look at some half thousand of our most fashionable and admired Italian songs – the Notturni of Blangini,
for instance – you will find them very like this Chippewa
canzonetta, in the no-meaning and perpetual repetition of
certain words and phrases; at the same time, I doubt if it
be *always* necessary for a song to have a meaning – it is
enough if it have a sentiment.

Here are some verses of a war-song, in the same style as
to composition, but breathing very different sentiments.

> I sing, I sing, under the centre of the sky,
> Under the centre of the sky,
> Under the centre of the sky I sing, I sing,
> Under the centre of the sky!

Every day I look at you, you morning star,
    You morning star;
Every day I look at you, you morning star,
    You morning star.

The birds of the brave take a flight round the sky,
    A flight round the sky;
The birds of the brave take a flight, take a flight,
    A flight round the sky.

They cross the enemies' line, the birds!
    They cross the enemies' line;
The birds, the birds, the ravenous birds,
    They cross the enemies' line.

The spirits on high repeat my name,
    Repeat my name;
The spirits on high, the spirits on high,
    Repeat my name.

Full happy am I to be slain and to lie,
    On the enemy's side of the line to lie;
Full happy am I, full happy am I,
    On the enemies' side of the line to lie!

I give you these as curiosities, and as being at least genuine; they have this merit, if they have no other.

Of the next song, I subjoin the music. It seems to have been composed on a young American, (*a Long-knife*,) who made love to a Chippewa girl, (*Ojibway quaince.*)

The literal meaning of the song, without the perpetual repetitions and transpositions, is just this:

Hah! what is the matter with the young Long-knife? he crosses the river with tears in his eyes. He sees the young Chippewa girl preparing to leave the place; he sobs for his sweetheart because she is going away, but he will not sigh for her long: as soon as she is out of sight he will forget her!

OJIBWAY QUAINCE.

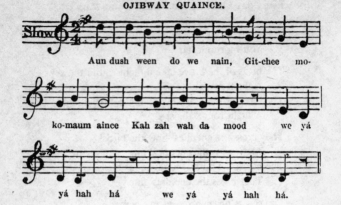

Aun dush ween   do we   nain,   Git-chee   mo-
ko-maum aince   Kah zah wah da   mood   we yá
yá hah   há   we yá   yá hah   há.

We ah, bem, ah dè,
We mah jah need dè,
We ne moo, sha yun
   We yà, yà hah hà! we yà yà hah hà!

O mow we mah ne
We mah jah need dè,
O jib way quaince un nè,
   We yà, yà hah hà! we yà yà hah hà!

Kah ween, goo shah, ween nè,
Keesh wan zhe e we ye
O gah, mah we mah zeen.
   We yà, yà hah yà! we yà yà hah hà!

Mee goo shah ween e goo
Ke bish quah bem ah de
Che wah nain ne mah de.
   We yà, yà hah hà! we yà yà hah hà!

I have been too long on the other side of the river; I must return to our Canadian shore, where indeed I now reside, under the hospitable roof of our missionary. Mrs. Mac-Murray's overflowing good-nature, cleverness, and liveliness, are as delightful in their way as the more pensive intelligence of her sister.

I have had some interesting talk with Mr. MacMurray on the subject of his mission, and the character of the people consigned to his care and spiritual guidance. He arrived here in 1832, and married Charlotte Johnston (O,ge,bu,no,qua) the following year. During the five years which have elapsed since the establishment of the mission, there have been one hundred and forty-five baptisms, seven burials, and thirteen marriages; and the present number of communicants is sixty-six.

He is satisfied with his success, and seems to have gained the good-will and attachment of the Indians around; he owes much, he says, to his sweet wife, whose perfect knowledge of the language and habits of her people has aided him in his task. She is a warm enthusiast in the cause of conversion, and the labour and fatigue of interpreting the prayers and sermons, and teaching the Indians to sing, at one time seriously affected her health. She has a good voice and correct ear, and has succeeded in teaching several of the women and children to sing some of our church hymns very pleasingly. She says all the Indians are passionately fond of music, and that it is a very effective means of interesting and fixing their attention. Mr. MacMurray says they take the most eager delight in the parables, and his explanations of them – frequently melting into tears. When he collected them together and addressed them, on his first arrival, several of those present were intoxicated; he therefore took the opportunity of declaiming against their besetting vice in strong terms. After waiting till he had finished, one of their chief men arose and replied gravely: "My father, before the white men came, we could hunt and fish, and raise corn enough for our families; we knew nothing of your fire-water. If it is so very bad, why did the white men bring it here? *we* did not desire it!"

They were in a degraded state of poverty, recklessness, and misery: there is now at least *some* improvement; about thirty children attend Mrs. MacMurray's school; many of them are decently clothed, and they have gardens in which they have raised crops of potatoes and Indian corn. The difficulty is to keep them together for any time sufficient to make a permanent impression: their wild, restless habits prevail: and even their necessities interfere against the efforts of their teachers; they go off to their winter hunting-grounds for weeks together, and when they return, the task of instruction has to begin again.

One of their chiefs from the north came to Mr. Mac-Murray, and expressed a wish to become a Christian; unfortunately, he had three wives, and, as a necessary preliminary, he was informed that he must confine himself to one. He had no objection to keep the youngest, to whom he was lately married, and put away the two others; but this was not admissible. The one he had first taken to wife was to be the permitted wife, and no other. He expostulated, Mr. MacMurray insisted; in the end, the old man went off in high dudgeon. Next morning there was no sign of his wigwam, and he never applied again to be "made a Christian," the terms apparently being too hard to digest. "The Roman catholic priests," said Mr. MacMurray, "are not so strict on this point as we are; they insist on the convert retaining only one wife, but they leave him the choice among those who bear that title."

They have a story among themselves of a converted Indian, who, after death, applied for admittance to the paradise of the white men, and was refused; he then went to the paradise of the Red-skins, but *there* too he was rejected: and after wandering about for some time disconsolate, here returned to life, (like Gitchee Gausinee,) to warn his companions by his experience in the other world.

Mr. MacMurray reckons among his most zealous converts several great medicine-men and conjurors. I was surprised at first at the comparative number of these, and the readiness with which they become Christians; but it may be accounted for in two ways: they are in general the most intelligent men in the tribe, and they are more sensible than any others of the false and delusive nature of their own tricks and superstitious observances. When a sorcerer is converted, he, in the first place, surrenders his *meta,wa,aun*, or medicine-sack, containing his manitos. Mr. MacMurray showed me several; an owl-skin, a wildcat-skin, an otter-skin; and he gave me two, with the implements of sorcery; one of birch-bark, containing the skin of a black adder; the other, an embroidered minkskin, contains the skin of an enormous rattle-snake, (four feet long,) a feather dyed crimson, a cowrie shell, and some magical pebbles, wrapped up in bark – the spells and charms of this Indian Archimago, whose name was, I think, Matabash. He also gave me a drum, formed of a skin stretched over a hoop, and filled with pebbles, and a most portentous looking rattle formed of about a hundred bears' claws, strung together by a thong, and suspended to a carved stick, both being used in their medicine dances.

The chief of this Chippewa village is a very extraordinary character. His name is Shinguaconse, *the Little Pine*, but he chooses to drop the adjunct, and calls himself the Pine. He is not an hereditary chief, but an elective or warchief, and owes his dignity to his bravery and to his eloquence. Among these people, a man who unites both is sure to obtain power. Without letters, without laws, without any arbitrary distinctions of rank or wealth, and with a code of morality so simple, that upon *that* point they are pretty much on a par, it is superior natural gifts, strength, and intelligence, that raise an Indian to distinction and influence. He has not the less to fish for his own dinner, and build his own canoe.

Shinguaconse led a band of warriors in the war of 1812, was of Fort Malden, and in the battle of the Moravian towns. Besides being eloquent and brave, he was a famous conjuror. He is now a Christian, with all his family; and

Mr. MacMurray finds him a most efficient auxiliary in ameliorating the condition of his people. When the traders on the opposite side endeavoured to seduce him back to his old habit of drinking, he told them, "When I wanted it, you would not give it to me; now I do not want it, you try to force it upon me; drink it yourselves!" and turned his back.

The ease with which liquor is procured from the opposite shore, and the bad example of many of the soldiers and traders, are, however, a serious obstacle to the missionary's success. Nor is the love of whisky confined to the men. Mrs. MacMurray imitated with great humour the deportment of a tipsy squaw, dragging her blanket after her, with one corner over her shoulder, and singing, in most blissful independence and defiance of her lordly husband, a song, of which the burthen is –

> The Englishman will give me some of his milk!
> I will drink the Englishman's milk!

Her own personal efforts have reclaimed many of these wretched creatures.

Next to the passion for ardent spirits is the passion for gambling. Their common game of chance is played with beans, or with small bones, painted of different colours; and these beans have been as fatal as ever were the dice in Christendom. They will gamble away even their blankets and moccasins; and while the game lasts, not only the players, but the lookers-on, are in a perfect ecstasy of suspense and agitation.

Mr. MacMurray says, that when the Indians are here during the fishing season from the upper waters of the lake, his rooms are crowded with them; wherever there is an open door they come in. "It is *impossible* to escape from an Indian who chooses to inflict his society on you, or wishes for yours: he comes at all hours, not having the remotest idea of convenience or inconvenience, or of the possibility of intrusion. There is absolutely no remedy but to sit still and endure. I have them in my room sometimes without intermission, from sunrise to sunset." He added, that they never took anything, nor did the least injury, except that which necessarily resulted from their vile, dirty habits, and the smell of their *kinnikinic*, which together, I should think, are quite *enough*. Those few which are now here, and the women especially, are always lounging in and out, coming to Mrs. MacMurray about every little trifle, and very frequently about nothing at all.

Sir John Colborne took a strong interest in the conversion and civilisation of the Indians, and though often discouraged did not despair. He promised to found a village, and build log-houses for the converts here, as at Coldwater, (on Lake Simcoe;) but this promise has not been fulfilled, nor is it likely to be so. I asked, very naturally, "Why, if the Indians wish for log-huts, do they not build them? They are on the verge of the forest, and the task is not difficult." I was told it was impossible; that they neither *could* nor *would!* – that this sort of labour is absolutely inimical to their habits. It requires more strength than the women possess; and for the men to fell wood and carry logs were an unheard-of degradation. Mrs. Mac-Murray is very anxious that their houses should be built, because she thinks it will keep her converts stationary. Whether their morality, cleanliness, health and happiness, will be thereby improved, I doubt; and the present governor seems to have very decidedly made up his mind on the matter. I should like to see an Indian brought to prefer a house to a wigwam, and live in a house of his own building; but what is gained by building houses for them? The promise was made however, and the Indians have no comprehension of a change of governors being a change of principles. They consider themselves deceived and ill-treated. Shinguaconse has lately (last January) addressed a letter or speech to Sir Francis Head on the subject, which is a curious specimen of expostulation. "My father," he says, "you have made promises to me and to my children. You promised me houses, but as yet nothing has been performed, although five years are past. I am now growing very old, and, to judge by the way you have used me, I am afraid I shall be laid in my grave before I see any of your promises fulfilled. Many of your children address you, and tell you they are poor, and they are much better off than I am in everything. I can say, in sincerity, that I am poor. I am like the beast of the forest that has no shelter. I lie down on the snow, and cover myself with the boughs of the trees. If the promises had been made by a person of no standing, I should not be astonished to see his promises fail. But *you*, who are so great in riches and in power, I am astonished that I do not see your promises fulfilled! I would have been better pleased if you had never made such promises to me, than that you should have made them and not performed them."

Then follows a stroke of Indian irony.

"But, my father, perhaps I do not see clearly; I am old, and perhaps I have lost my eye-sight; and if you should come to visit us, you might discover these promises already performed! I have heard that you have visited all parts of the country around. This is the only place you have not yet seen; if you will promise to come, I will have my little fish (*i.e.* the white-fish) ready drawn from the water, that you may taste of the food which sustains me."

Shinguaconse then complains, that certain of the French Canadians had cut down their timber to sell it to the Americans, by permission of a British magistrate residing at St. Joseph's. He says, "Is this right? I have never heard that the British had purchased our land and timber from us. But whenever I say a word, they say, 'Pay no attention to him, he knows nothing.' This will not do!"

He concludes with infinite politeness;

"And now, my father, I shall take my seat, and look towards your place, that I may hear the answer you will send me between this time and spring.

"And now, my father, I have done! I have told you some things that were on my mind. I take you by the hand, and wish you a happy new year, trusting that we may be allowed to see one another again."

Mrs. Johnston told me that when her children are absent from her, and she looks for their return, she has a sensation, a merely physical sensation, like that she experienced when she first laid them to her bosom: this yearning amounts at times to absolute pain, almost as intolerable as the pang of child-birth, and is so common that the Indians have a word to express it. The maternal instinct, like all the other natural instincts, is strong in these people to a degree we can no more conceive than we can their quick senses. As a cat deprived of its kittens will suckle an animal of a different species, so an Indian woman who has lost her child *must* have another. "Bring me my son, or see me die!" exclaimed a bereaved mother to her husband, and she lay down on her mat, covered her head with her blanket, and refused to eat. The man went and kidnapped one of the enemy's children, and brought it to her. She laid it in her bosom, and was consoled. Here is the animal woman.

The mortality among the children is very great among the unreclaimed Indians, from want of knowing how to treat infantine maladies, and from want of cleanliness. When dysentery is brought on from this cause, the children almost invariably perish. When kept clean, the bark cradles are excellent things for their mode of life, and effectually preserve the head and limbs of the infant from external injury.

When a young Chippewa of St. Mary's sees a young girl who pleases him, and whom he wishes to marry, he goes and catches a loach, boils it, and cuts off the tail, of which he takes the flat bone, and sticks it is his hair. He paints himself bewitchingly, takes a sort of rude flute or pipe, with two or three stops, which seems to be only used on these amatory occasions, and walks up and down his village, blowing on his flute, and looking, I presume, as sentimental as an Indian *can* look. This is regarded as an indication of his intentions, and throws all the lodges in which there are young marriageable girls into a flutter, though probably the fair one who is his secret choice is pretty well aware of it. The next step is to make presents to the parents and relatives of the young woman; if these are accepted, and his suit prospers, he makes presents to his intended; and all that now remains is to bring her home to his lodge. He neither swears before God to love her till death – an oath which it depends not on his own will to keep, even if it be not perjury in the moment it is pronounced – nor to endow her with *all* his wordly goods and chattels, when even by the act of union she loses all right of property; but apparently the arrangements answer all purposes, to their mutual satisfaction.

The names of the women are almost always derived from some objects or appearances in nature, generally of a pleasing kind; the usual termination *qua* or *quay*, immediately blending with the original signification the idea of womanhood. Thus, my Indian mother is "the green prairie," (woman). Mrs. Schoolcraft's name, Obah,bahm,wa,wa,ge,zhe,go,quà, signifies literally the "sound which the stars make rushing through the sky," and which I translate into *the music of the spheres.* Mrs. MacMurray is "the wild rose:" one of her youngest sisters is Wah,bu,nung,o,quà the morning star (woman); another is Omis,ka,bu,gu,quà, (the woman of) "the red leaf."

I went to-day to take leave of my uncle Wayish,ky, and found him ill – poor fellow! he is fretting about his younger son. I learn with pleasure that his daughter Zah,gàh,see,ga,quà is likely to accompany me to the Manitoolin Islands.

July 31.

This last evening of my sojourn at the Sault Ste. Marie is very melancholy – we have been all very sad. Mr. and Mrs. MacMurray are to accompany me in my voyage down the lake to the Manitoolin Islands, having some business to transact with the governor: – so you see Providence *does* take care of me! how I could have got there alone, I cannot tell, but I must have tried. At first we had arranged to go in a bark canoe; the very canoe which belonged to Captain Back, and which is now lying in Mr. MacMurray's court-yard: but our party will be large, and we shall be encumbered with much baggage and provisions – not having yet learned to live on the portable maize and fat: our voyage is likely to take three days and a half, even if the weather continues favourable, and if it do not, why we shall be obliged to put into some creek or harbour, and pitch our tent, gipsy fashion, for a day or two. There is not a settlement nor a habitation on our route, nothing but lake and forest. The distance is about one hundred and seventy miles, rather more than less; Mr. MacMurray therefore advises a bateau, in which, if we do not get on so quickly, we shall have more space and comfort: – and thus it is to be.

I am sorry to leave these kind, excellent people, but most I regret Mrs. Schoolcraft.

August 1.

The morning of our departure rose bright and beautiful, and the loading and arranging our little boat was a scene of great animation. I thought I had said all my adieus the night before, but at early dawn my good Neengai came paddling across the river with various kind offerings for her daughter Wa,sàh,ge,wo,nò,quá, which she thought might be pleasant or useful, and more *last* affectionate words from Mrs. Schoolcraft. We then exchanged a long farewell embrace, and she turned away with tears, got into her little canoe, which could scarcely contain two persons, and handling her paddle with singular grace and dexterity, shot over the blue water, without venturing once to look back! I leaned over the side of our boat, and strained my eyes to catch a last glimpse of the white spray of the rapids, and her little canoe skimming over the expanse between, like a black dot: and this was the last I saw of my dear good Chippewa mamma!

Meantime we were proceeding rapidly down the beautiful river, and through its winding channels. Our party consisted of Mr. and Mrs. MacMurray and their lovely boy; myself and the two Indian girls – my cousin Zah,gah,see,ga,quà, and Angelique, the child's attendant.

These two girls were, for Indians, singularly beautiful; they would have been beautiful anywhere. Angelique, though of unmixed Indian blood, has a face of the most perfect oval, a clear brown complexion, the long, half-shaded eye, which the French call *coupé en amande;* the nose slightly aquiline, with the proud nostril open and well defined; dazzling teeth; – in short, her features had been faultless, but that her mouth is a little too large – but then, to amend that, her lips are like coral: and a more perfect figure I never beheld. Zah,gàh,see,ga,quà is on a less scale, and her features more decidedly Indian.

We had a small but compact and well-built boat, the seats of which we covered with mats, blankets, buffalo skins, cloaks, shawls, &c.: we had four voyageurs, Masta, Content, Le Blanc, and Pierrot; a very different set from those who brought me from Mackinaw: they were all Canadian voyageurs of the true breed, that is, half-breed, showing the Indian blood as strongly as the French. Pierrot, worthy his name, was a most comical fellow; Masta, a great talker, amused me exceedingly; Content was our steersman and captain; and Le Blanc, who was the best singer, generally led the song, to which the others responded in chorus.

They had a fixed daily allowance of fat pork, Indian meal, and tobacco: finding that the latter was not agreeable to me, though I took care not to complain, they always contrived with genuine politeness to smoke out of my way, and to leeward.

After passing Sugar Island, we took the channel to the left, and entered the narrow part of the lake between St. Joseph's Island and the mainland. We dined upon a small picturesque islet, consisting of ledges of rock, covered with shrubs, and abounding with wortle-berries; on the upper platform we arranged an awning or shade, by throwing a sail over some bushes, and made a luxurious dinner, succeeded by a basin of good tea; meantime, on the rocky ledge below, Pierrot was making a *galette*, and Masta frying pork.

Dinner being over, we proceeded, coasting along the north shore of St. Joseph's Island. There is, in the interior, an English settlement, and a village of Indians. The principal proprietor. Major R——, who is a magistrate and justice of the peace, has two Indian women living with him – two sisters, and a family by each! – such are the examples sometimes set to the Indians on our frontiers.

In the evening we came to an island consisting of a flat ledge of rock, on which were the remains of a former camp-fire, surrounded by tall trees and bushes: here we pitched our little marquée, and boiled our kettle. The sunset was most glorious, with some floating ominous clouds. The stars and the fire-flies came out together: the latter swarmed around us, darting in and out among the trees, and gliding and sparkling over the surface of the water. Unfortunately the mosquitoes swarmed too, notwithstanding the antipathy which is said to exist between the mosquito and the fire-fly. We made our beds by spreading mats and blankets under us; and then, closing the curtain of the tent, Mr. MacMurray began a very effective slaughter and expulsion of the mosquitoes. We laid ourselves down, Mrs. MacMurray in the middle, with her child in her bosom; Mr. MacMurray on one side, myself at the other, and the two Indian girls at our feet: the voyageurs, rolled in their blankets, lay upon the naked rock round the fire we had built – and thus we all slept. I must needs confess that I found my rocky bed rather uneasy, and my bones ached as I turned from side to side; but this was only a beginning. The night was close and sultry, and just before dawn I was wakened by a tremendous clap of thunder; down came the storm in its fury, the lake swelling and roaring, the lightning gambolling over the rocks and waves, the rain falling in a torrent; but we were well sheltered, for the men had had the precaution, before they slept, to throw a large oil-cloth over the top of our little marquée. The storm ceased suddenly: daylight came, and soon afterwards we again embarked. We had made forty-five miles.

The next morning was beautiful: the sun shone brightly, though the lake was yet heaving and swelling from the recent storm, – altogether it was like the laughing eyes and pouting lips of a half-appeased beauty. About nine o'clock we ran down into a lovely bay, and landed to breakfast on a little lawn surrounded by high trees and a thick wood, abounding in rattlesnakes and squirrels. Luckily for us, the storm had dispersed the mosquitoes.

Keeping clear of the covert to avoid these fearful snakes, I strayed down by the edge of the lake, and found a tiny creek, which answered all purposes, both of bath and mirror, and there I arranged my toilette in peace and security. Returning to our breakfast-fire, I stood some moments to admire the group around it – it was a perfect picture: there lay the little boat rocking on the shining waves, and near it Content was washing plates and dishes; Pierrot and Masta were cooking; the two Indian girls were spreading the tablecloth on the turf. Mrs. MacMurray and her baby – looking like the Madonna and child in the "Repose in Egypt," – were seated under a tree; while Mr. MacMurray, having suspended his shaving-glass against the trunk of a pine, was shaving himself with infinite gravity and sang-froid. Never, I think, were the graceful, the wild, the comic, so strangely combined! – add the rich background of mingled foliage, the murmur of leaves and waters, and all the glory of a summer morning! – it was very beautiful!

We breakfasted in much mirth, and then we set off again. The channel widened, the sky became overcast, the wind freshened, and at length blew hard. Though this part of the lake is protected by St. Joseph's and the chain of islands from the swell of the main lake, still the waves rose high, the wind increased, we were obliged to take in a reef or two of our sail, and scudded with an almost fearful rapidity before the wind. In crossing a wide, open expanse of about twenty miles, we became all at once very silent, then very grave, then very pathetic, and at last extremely sick.

On arriving among the channels of the Rattlesnake Islands, the swell of course subsided; we landed on a most beautiful mass of rock, and lighted our fire under a group of pines and sycamores; but we were too sick to eat. Mr. MacMurray heated some port wine and water, into which we broke biscuit, and drank it most picturesquely out of a slop basin – too thankful to get it! Thus recruited, we proceeded. The wind continued fresh and fair, the day kept up fine, and our sail was most delightful and rapid. We passed successive groups of islands, countless in number, various in form, little fairy Edens – populous with life and love, and glowing with light and colour under a meridian sun. I remember we came into a circular basin, of about three miles in diameter, so surrounded with islands, that when once within the circle, I could perceive neither ingress nor egress; it was as if a spell of enchantment had been wrought to keep us there for ever; and I really thought we were going with our bows upon the rocks, when suddenly we darted through a narrow portal, not above two or three yards in width, and found ourselves in another wide expanse, studded with larger islands. At evening we entered the Missasagua river, having come sixty miles, right before the wind, since morning.

The Missasagua (*i.e.* the river with two mouths) gives its name to a tribe of the Chippewa nation, once numerous and powerful, now scattered and degraded. This is the river called by Henry the *Missasaki*, where he found a horde of Indians who had never seen a white man before, and who, in the excess of their hospitality, crammed him with "a porridge of sturgeons' roe," which I apprehend, from his description, would be likely to prove "caviare to the general." There is a remnant of these Indians here still. We found a log-hut with a half-breed family, in the service of the fur company; and two or three bark wigwams. The rest of the village (dwellings and inhabitants together) had gone down to the Manitoolin. A number of little Redskins were running about, half, or rather indeed wholly, naked – happy, healthy, active, dirty little urchins, resembling, except in colour, those you may see swarming in an Irish cabin. Poor Ireland! The worst Indian wigwam is not worse than some of her dwellings; and the most miserable of these Indians would spurn the destiny of an Irish *poor-slave* – for he is at least Lord o'er himself. As the river is still famous for sturgeon, we endeavoured to procure some for supper, and had just prepared a large piece to roast, (suspended by a cord to three sticks,) when one of those horrid curs so rife about the Indian dwellings ran off with it. We were asked to take up our night's lodging in the log-hut, but it was so abominably dirty and close, we all preferred the shore. While they pitched the marquée, I stood for some time looking at a little Indian boy, who, in a canoe about eight feet in length, was playing the most extraordinary gambols in the water; the buoyant thing seemed alive beneath him, and to obey every movement of his paddle. He shot backwards and forwards, described circles, whirled himself round and round, made pirouettes – exhibited, in short, as many tricks as I have seen played by a spirited English boy on a thorough-bred pony.

The mosquitoes were in great force, but we began by sweeping them out of the tent with boughs, and then closing the curtain, we executed judgment on the remainder by wholesale. We then lay down in the same order as last night; and Mrs. MacMurray sang her little boy to sleep with a beautiful hymn. I felt all the luxury of having the turf under me instead of the rock, and slept well till wakened before dawn by some animal sniffing and snuffing close to my ear. I commanded my alarm, and did not disturb those who were enjoying a sound sleep near me, and the intruder turned out to be a cow belonging to the hut, who had got her nose under the edge of the tent. We set off early, and by sunrise had passed down the eastern channel of the river, and swept into the lake. It was a lovely morning, soft and calm; there was no breath of wind; no cloud in the sky, no vapour in the air; and the little islands lay around "under the opening eyelids of the morn," dewy, and green, and silent. We made eighteen miles before breakfast; and then pursued our way through Aird's bay, and among countless islands of all shapes and sizes; I cannot describe their beauty, nor their harmonious variety: at last we perceived in the east the high ridge called the mountains of La Cloche. They are really respectable hills in this level country, but hardly mountains: they are all of limestone, and partially clothed in wood. All this coast is very rocky and barren; but it is said to be rich in mineral productions. About five in the evening we landed at La Cloche.

Here we found the first and only signs of civilised society during our voyage. The north-west company have an important station here; and two of their principal clerks, Mr. MacBean and Mr. Bethune, were on the spot. We were received with much kindness, and pressed to spend the night, but there was yet so much daylight, and time was so valuable, that we declined. The factory consists of a large log-house, an extensive store to contain the goods bartered with the Indians, and huts inhabited by work people, hunters, voyageurs, and others; a small village, in short; and a number of boats and canoes of all sizes were lying in the bay. It is not merely the love of gain that induces well-educated men – gentlemen – to pass twenty years of their lives in such a place as this; you must add to the prospective acquirement of a large fortune, two possessions which men are most wont to covet – power and freedom. The table was laid in their hall for supper, and we carried off, with their good-will, a large mess of broiled fish, dish and all, and a can of milk, which delicious viands we discussed in our boat with great satisfaction.

The place derives its name from a large rock which they say, being struck, vibrates like a bell. But I had no opportunity of trying the experiment, therefore cannot tell how this may be. Henry, however, mentions this phenomenon; and the Indians regard the spot as sacred and enchanted. Just after sunset, we reached one of the most enchanting of these enchanting or enchanted isles. It rose sloping from the shore, in successive ledges of picturesque rocks, all fringed with trees and bushes, and clothed in many places with a species of gray lichen, nearly a foot deep. With a sort of anticipative wisdom (like that of a pig in a storm) I gathered a quantity of this lichen for our bed, and spread it under the mats; for, in fear of the rattlesnakes and other creeping things, we had pitched our resting-place on the naked rock. The men had built up the fire in a sheltered place below, and did not perceive that a stem of a blasted pine, about twenty feet in length, had fallen across the recess; it caught the flame. This at first delighted us and the men too; but soon it communicated to another tree against which it was leaning, and they blazed away together in a column of flame. We began to fear that it might communicate to the dried moss and the bushes, and cause a general conflagration; the men prevented this, however, by clearing a space around them. The waves, the trees and bushes and fantastic rocks, and the figures and faces of the men, caught the brilliant light as it flashed upon them with a fitful glare – the rest being lost in deepest shadow. Wildly magnificent it was! beyond all expression beautiful, and awful too! – the night, the solitude, the dark weltering waters, the blaze which put out the mild stars which just before had looked down upon us in their tender radiance! – I never beheld such a scene. By the light of this gigantic torch we supped and prepared our beds. As I lay down to rest, and closed my eyes on the flame which shone through our tent curtain, I thought that perhaps the wind might change in the night, and the flakes and sparks be carried over to us, and to the beds of lichen, dry and inflammable as tinder; but fatigue had subdued me so utterly, that even this apprehension could not keep me awake. I pressed my hands on my eyes, breathed my prayer, and slept in peace.

The burning trees were still smouldering; daylight was just creeping up the sky, and some few stars yet out, when we bestirred ourselves, and in a very few minutes we were again afloat: we were now steering towards the south-east, where the Great Manitoolin Island was dimly discerned. There was a deep slumbrous calm all around, as if nature had not yet awoke from her night's rest: then the atmosphere began to kindle with gradual light; it grew brighter and brighter: towards the east, the lake and sky were intermingling in radiance; and *then*, just there, where they seemed flowing and glowing together like a bath of fire, we saw what seemed to us the huge black hull of a vessel, with masts and spars rising against the sky – but we knew not what to think or to believe! As we kept on rowing in that direction, it grew more distinct, but lessened in size: it proved to be a great heavy-built schooner, painted black, which was going up the lake against wind and current. One man was standing in her bows with an immense oar, which he slowly pulled, walking backwards and forwards; but vain seemed all his toil, for still the vessel lay like a black log, and moved not: we rowed up to the side, and hailed him – "What news?"

And the answer was that William the Fourth was dead, and that Queen Victoria reigned in his place! We sat silent, looking at each other, and even in that very moment the orb of the sun rose out of the lake, and poured its beams full in our dazzled eyes.

We asked if the governor were at the Manitoolin Island? No; he was not there; but the chief officer of the Indian department had come to represent him, and the presents were to be given out to the assembled Indians this morning. We urged the men to take their oars with spirit, and held our course due east down by the woody shores of this immense island; among fields of reeds and rushes, and almost under the shadow of the towering forests.

Meantime many thoughts came into my mind – some tears too into my eyes – not certainly for that dead king who in ripe age and in all honour was gathered to the tomb – but for that living queen, so young and fair –

> "As many hopes hang on that noble head
> As there hang blossoms on the boughs in May!"

And what will become of *them* – of *her!* The idea that even here, in this new world of woods and waters, amid these remote wilds, to her so utterly unknown, her power reaches and her sovereignty is acknowledged, filled me with compassionate awe. I say *compassionate*, for if she feel in their whole extent the liabilities of her position, alas for her! And if she feel them not! – O worse and worse!

I tried to recal her childish figure and features. I thought over all I had heard concerning her. I thought she was not such a thing as they could make a mere pageant of; for *that* there is too much within – too little without. And what *will* they make of her? For at eighteen she will hardly make anything of them – I mean of the men and women round her. It is of the woman I think, more than of the queen; for as a part of the state machinery she will do quite as well as another – better, perhaps: so far her youth and sex are absolutely in her favour, or rather in *our* favour. If she be but simple-minded, and true-hearted, and straightforward, with the common portion of intellect – if a royal education have not blunted in her the quick perceptions and pure kind instincts of the woman – if she has only had fair play, and carries into business plain distinct notions of right and wrong – and the fine moral sense that is not to be confounded by diplomatic verbiage and expediency – she will do better for us than a whole cabinet full of cut and dried officials, with Talleyrand at the head of them. And what a fair heritage is this which has fallen to her! A land young like herself – a land of hopes – and fair, most fair! Does she know – does she care anything about it? – while hearts are beating warm for her, and voices bless her – and hands are stretched out towards her, even from these wild lake shores!

These thoughts were in my mind, or something like to these, as with aid of sail and oar we were gliding across the bay of Manitoolin. This bay is about three miles wide at the entrance, and runs about twelve miles in depth, in a southerly direction. As we approached the further end, we discerned the whole line of shore, rising in bold and beautiful relief from the water, to be covered with wigwams, and crowded with Indians. Suddenly we came to a little opening or channel, which was not visible till we were just upon it, and on rounding a promontory, to my infinite delight and surprise we came upon an unexpected scene, – a little bay within the bay. It was a beautiful basin, nearly an exact circle, of about three miles in circumference; in the centre lay a little wooded island, and all around, the shores rose sloping from the margin of the lake, like an amphitheatre, covered with wigwams and lodges, thick as they could stand amid intermingled trees; and beyond these arose the tall pine forest crowning and enclosing the whole. Some hundred canoes were darting hither and thither on the waters, or gliding along the shore, and a beautiful schooner lay against the green bank – its tall masts almost mingling with the forest trees, and its white sails half furled, and half gracefully drooping.

We landed, and were received with much politeness by Mr. Jarvis, the chief superintendent of Indian affairs, and by Major Anderson, the Indian agent; and a space was cleared to pitch our tent, until room could be made for our accommodation in one of the government log-houses.

THE GREAT MANITOOLIN.

"Had I plantation of this isle, my lord,
And were the king of it, what would I do?

```
    .    .    .    .    No kind of traffic
Would I admit; – no name of magistrate;
Letters should not be known: no use of service,
Of riches or of poverty    .    .    .
             .    All men idle – all.
I would with such perfection govern, sir,
T' excel the golden age."
```

THE TEMPEST.

The word Manitoolin is a corruption or frenchification of the Indian *Manito,a,wahn,ing*, which signifies the "dwelling of spirits." They have given this name to a range of islands in Lake Huron, which extend from the channel of St. Mary's river nearly to Cape Hurd, a distance of about two hundred miles. Between this range of islands and the shore of the mainland there is an archipelago, consisting of many thousand islands or islets.*

The Great Manitoolin, on which I now am, is, according to the last survey, ninety-three miles in length, but very narrow, and so deeply and fantastically indented with gulfs and bays, that it was supposed to consist of many distinct islands. This is the second year that the presents to the Indians have been issued on this spot. The idea of forming on the Great Manitoolin a settlement of the Indians, and inviting those tribes scattered round the lakes to adopt it as a residence, has been for the last few years entertained by the Indian department; I say for the last few years, because it did not originate with the present governor; though I believe it has his entire approbation, as a means of removing them more effectually from all contact with the white settlers. It is objected to this measure that by cutting off the Indians from agricultural pursuits, and throwing them back upon their habits of hunting and

---

* The islands which fringe the north shores of Lake Huron from Lake George to Penetanguishine have been estimated by Lieut. Bayfield (in his official survey) at upwards of thirty-three thousand.

fishing, it will retard their civilisation; that, by removing them from the reserved land among the whites, their religious instruction will be rendered a matter of difficulty; that the islands, being masses of barren rock, are almost incapable of cultivation; and that they are so far northwest, that it would be difficult to raise even a little Indian corn:* and hence the plan of settling the Indians here has been termed *unjustifiable*.

It is true that the smaller islands are rocky and barren; but the Great Manitoolin, Drummond's, and St. Joseph's, are fertile. The soil on which I now tread is rich and good; and all the experiments in cultivation already tried here have proved successful. As far as I can judge, the intentions of the government are benevolent and *justifiable*. There are a great number of Indians, Ottawas, and Pottowottomies, who receive annual presents from the British government, and are residing on the frontiers of the American settlements, near Lake Michigan. These people, having disposed of their lands, know not where to go, and it is the wish of our government to assemble all those Indians who are our allies, and receive our annual presents, within the limits of the British territory – and this for reasons which certainly do appear very *reasonable* and politic.

There are three thousand seven hundred Indians, Ottawas, Chippewas, Pottowottomies, Winnebagos, and Menomonies, encamped around us. The issue of the presents has just concluded, and appears to have given universal satisfaction; yet, were you to see their trifling nature, you would wonder that they think it worth while to travel from one to five hundred miles or more to receive them; and by an ordinance of the Indian depart-

---

* It appears, however, from the notes of the missionary Elliott, that a great number of Ottawas and Potoganatees had been residing on the Great Manitoolin two or three years previous to 1834, and had cultivated a portion of land.

ment, every individual must present himself *in person* to
receive the allotted portion. The common equipment of
each chief or warrior (that is, each man) consisted of three
quarters of a yard of blue cloth, three yards of linen, one
blanket, half an ounce of thread, four strong needles, one
comb, one awl, one butcher's knife, three pounds of
tobacco, three pounds of ball, nine pounds of shot, four
pounds of powder, and six flints. The equipment of a
woman consisted of one yard and three quarters of coarse
woollen, two yards and a half of printed calico, one blanket, one ounce of thread, four needles, one comb, one awl,
one knife. For each child there was a portion of woollen
cloth and calico. Those chiefs who had been wounded in
battle, or had extraordinary claims, had some little articles
in extra quantity, and a gay shawl or handkerchief. To
each principal chief of a tribe, the allotted portion of
goods for his tribe was given, and he made the distribution
to his people individually; and such a thing as injustice or
partiality on one hand, or a murmur of dissatisfaction on
the other, seemed equally unknown. There were, besides,
extra presents of flags, medals, chiefs' guns, rifles, trinkets,
brass kettles, the choice and distribution of which were left
to the superintendent, with this proviso, that the expense
on the whole was never to exceed nine pounds sterling for
every one hundred chiefs or warriors.

While the Indians remain on the island, which is generally about five days, they receive rations of Indian corn
and tallow, (fat melted down;) with this they make a sort
of soup, boiling the Indian corn till it is of the consistence
of porridge – then adding a handful of tallow and some
salt, and stirring it well. Many a kettleful of this delectable
mess did I see made, without feeling any temptation to
taste it; but Major Anderson says it is not so *very* bad,
when a man is *very* hungry, which I am content to believe
on his testimony. On this and on the fish of the bay they
live while here.

As soon as the distribution of the presents was over, a grand council of all the principal chiefs was convened, that they might be informed of the will of their great father.

You must understand, that on the promontory I have mentioned as shutting in the little bay on the north side, there are some government edifices; one large house, consisting of one room, as accommodation for the superintendent and officers; also a carpenter's house and a magazine for the stores and presents, all of logs. A deal plank raised on tressels served as a table; there were a few stools and benches of deal-board, and two raised wooden platforms for beds: such were the furniture and decorations of the grand council-hall in which the *representative* of the representative of their Great Mother had now assembled her red children; a flag was displayed in front upon a lofty pole – a new flag, with a new device, on which I saw troops of Indians gazing with much curiosity and interest, and the meaning of which was now to be explained to them.

The council met about noon. At the upper end of the log-house I have mentioned, stood the chief superintendent, with his secretary or grand vizier, Major Anderson; the two interpreters, and some other officials. At some little distance I sat with Mr. and Mrs. MacMurray, and a young son of the lieutenant governor; near me I perceived three Methodist missionaries and two Catholic priests. The chiefs came in, one after another, without any order of precedence. All those whom I had seen at Mackinaw recognised me immediately, and their dusky faces brightened as they held out their hands with the customary *bojou!* There was my old acquaintance the Rain, looking magnificent, and the venerable old Ottawa chief, Kish,ke,nick, (the Cut-hand.) The other remarkable chiefs of the Ottawas were Gitchee,Mokomaun, (the Great of Long-knife;) So,wan,quet, (the Forked-tree;) Kim,e,ne,chau,zun, (the Bustard;) Mocomaun,ish, (the Bad-knife;) Pai,mau,se,gai, (the Sun's course in cloudless sky,) and As,si,ke,nack, (the Black-bird;) the latter a very remarkable man, of whom I shall have to say more presently. Of the Chippewas, the most distinguished chiefs were, Aisence, (the Little Clam;) Wai,sow,win,de,bay, (the Yellow-head,) and Shin,gua,cose, (the Pine;) these three are Christians. There were besides Ken,ne,bec,áno, (the Snake's-tail;) Muc,konce,e,wa,yun (the Cub's skin:) and two others whose style was quite grandiloquent,– Tai,bau,se,gai, (Bursts of Thunder at a distance,) and Me,twai,crush,kau, (the sound of waves breaking on the rocks.)

Nearly opposite to me was a famous Pottowottomi chief and conjuror, called the Two Ears. He was most fantastically dressed and hideously painted, and had two large clusters of swansdown depending from each ear – I suppose in illustration of his name. There were three men with their faces blacked with grease and soot, their hair dishevelled, and their whole appearance studiously squalid and miserable: I was told they were in mourning for near relations. With these exceptions the dresses were much what I have already described; but the chief whom I immediately distinguished from the rest, even before I knew his name, was my cousin, young Waub-Ojeeg, the son of Wayish,ky; in height he towered above them all, being about six feet three or four. His dress was equally splendid and tasteful; he wore a surtout of fine blue cloth, under which was seen a shirt of gay colours, and his father's medal hung on his breast. He had a magnificent embroidered belt of wampum, from which hung his scalping-knife and pouch. His leggings (metasses) were of scarlet cloth beautifully embroidered, with rich bands or garters depending to his ankle. Round his head was an embroidered band or handkerchief, in which were stuck four wing-feathers of the war-eagle, two on each side – the testimonies of his prowess as a warrior. He held a toma-hawk in his hand. His features were fine, and his counte-nance not only mild, but almost femininely soft. Alto-gether he was in dress and personal appearance the finest specimen of his race I had yet seen; I was quite proud of my adopted kinsman.

He was seated at some distance; but in far too near propinquity, for in truth they almost touched me, sat a group of creatures – human beings I must suppose them – such as had never been seen before within the lines of civilisation. I had remarked them in the morning surrounded by a group of Ottawas, among whom they seemed to excite as much wonder and curiosity as among ourselves: and when I inquired who and what they were, I was told they were *cannibals* from the Red River, the title being, I suspect, quite gratuitous, and merely expressive of the disgust they excited. One man had his hair cut short on the top of his head, and it looked like a circular blacking-brush, while it grew long in a fringe all round, hanging on his shoulders. The skins thrown round them seemed on the point of rotting off; and their attitude when squatted on the ground was precisely that of the larger apes I have seen in a menagerie. More hideous, more pitiable specimens of humanity in its lowest, most degraded state, can hardly be conceived; melancholy, squalid, stupid – and yet not fierce. They had each received a kettle and a gun by way of encouragement.

The whole number of chiefs assembled was seventy-five; and take notice that the half of them were smoking, that it was blazing noontide, and that every door and window was filled up with the eager faces of the crowd without, and then you may imagine that even a scene like this was not to be enjoyed without some drawbacks; in fact, it was a sort of purgatory to more senses than one, but I made up my mind to endure, and did so. I observed that although there were many hundreds round the house, not one woman, outside or inside, was visible during the whole time the council lasted.

When all were assembled, and had seated themselves on the floor without hurry, noise, or confusion, there was a pause of solemn preparation, and then Mr. Jarvis rose and addressed them. At the end of every sentence,

As,si,ke,nack, (the Black-bird), our chief interpreter here, translated the meaning to the assembly, raising his voice to a high pitch, and speaking with much oratorical emphasis, the others responding at intervals "Ha!" but listening generally in solemn silence. This man, the Black-bird, who understands English well, is the most celebrated orator of his nation. They relate with pride that on one occasion he began a speech at sunrise, and that it lasted without intermission till sunset: the longest breathed of our parliament orators must yield, I think, to the Black-bird.

The address of the superintendent was in these words: –

"CHILDREN! – When your Great Father, the lieutenant-governor, parted with his Red children last year at this place, he promised again to meet them here at the council-fire, and witness in person the grand delivery of presents now just finished.

"To fulfil this engagement, your Great Father left his residence at Toronto, and proceeded on his way to the Great Manitoolin Island, as far as Lake Simcoe. At this place, a messenger who had been despatched from Toronto overtook him, and informed him of the death of our Great Father, on the other side of the Great Salt Lake, and the accession of the Queen Victoria. It consequently became necessary for your Great Father, the lieutenant-governor, to return to the seat of his government, and hold a council with his chief men.

"CHILDREN! – Your Great Father, the lieutenant-governor, has deputed me to express to you his regret and disappointment at being thus unexpectedly deprived of the pleasure which he had promised to himself in again seeing all his Red children, and in taking by the hand the chiefs and warriors of the numerous tribes now here assembled.

"CHILDREN! – I am now to communicate to you a matter in which many of you are deeply interested. Listen with attention, and bear well in mind what I say to you.

"CHILDREN! – Your Great Father the King had determined that presents should be continued to be given to all

Indians resident in the Canadas. But presents will be given to Indians residing in the United States only for three years, including the present delivery.

"CHILDREN! – The reasons why presents will not be continued to the Indians residing in the United States, I will explain to you.

"First: All our countrymen who resided in the United States forfeited their claim to protection from the British government, from the moment their Great Father the King lost possession of that country. Consequently the Indians have no right to expect that their Great Father will continue to them what he does not continue to his own white children.

"Secondly: The Indians of the United States who served in the late war have already received from the British government more than has been received by the soldiers of their Great Father, who have fought for him for twenty years.

"Thirdly: Among the rules which civilised nations are bound to attend to, there is one which forbids your Great Father to give arms and ammunition to those Indians of the United States who are fighting against the government under which they live.

"Fourthly: The people of England have, through their representatives in the great council of the nation, uttered great complaints at the expense attendant upon a continuation of the expenditure of so large a sum of money upon Indian presents.

"But, CHILDREN! let it be distinctly understood, that the British government has not come to a determination to cease to give presents to the Indians of the United States. On the contrary, the government of your Great Father will be most happy to do so, provided they live in the British empire. Therefore, although your Great Father is willing that his Red children should all become permanent settlers in the island, it matters not in what part of the British empire they reside. They may go across the Great Salt Lake to the country of their Great Father the King, and there reside, and there receive their presents; or they may remove to any part of the provinces of Upper or Lower Canada, New Brunswick, Nova Scotia, or any other British colony, and yet receive them. But they cannot and must not expect to receive them after the end of three years, if they continue to reside within the limits of the United States.

"CHILDREN! – The Long Knives have complained (and with justice too) that your Great Father, whilst he is at peace with them, has supplied his Red children residing in their country, with whom the Long Knives are at war, with guns and powder and ball.

"CHILDREN! – This , I repeat to you, is against the rules of civilised nations, and, if continued, will bring on war between your Great Father and the Long Knives.

"CHILDREN! – You must therefore come and live under the protection of your Great Father, or lose the advantage which you have so long enjoyed, of annually receiving valuable presents from him.

"CHILDREN! – I have one thing more to observe to you. There are many clergymen constantly visiting you for the avowed purpose of instructing you in religious principles. Listen to them with attention when they talk to you on that subject; but at the same time keep always in view, and bear it well in your minds, that they have nothing whatever to do with your temporal affairs. Your Great Father who lives across the Great Salt Lake is your guardian and protector, and he only. He has relinquished his claim to this large and beautiful island, on which we are assembled, in order that you may have a home of your own, quite separate from his white children. The soil is good, and the waters which surround the shores of this island are abundantly supplied with the finest fish. If you cultivate the soil with only moderate industry, and exert yourselves to obtain fish, you can never want; and your Great Father will continue to bestow annually on all those who permanently reside here, or in any part of his dominions, valuable presents, and will from time to time visit you at this island, to behold your improvements.

"CHILDREN! – Your Great Father, the lieutenant-governor, as a token of the above declaration, transmits to the Indians a silk flag, which represents the British empire. Within this flag, and immediately under the symbol of the British crown, are delineated a lion and a beaver; by which is designated that the British people and the Indians, the former being represented by the lion and the latter by the beaver, are and will be alike regarded by their sovereign, so long as their figures are imprinted on the British flag, or, in other words, so long as they continue to inhabit the British empire.

"CHILDREN! – This flag is now yours. But it is necessary that some one tribe should take charge of it, in order that it may be exhibited in this island on all occasions, when your Great Father either visits or bestows presents on his Red children. Choose, therefore, from among you, the tribe to which you are willing to entrust it for safe keeping, and remember to have it with you when we next meet again at this place.

"CHILDREN! – I bid you farewell. But before we part, let me express to you the high satisfaction I feel at witnessing the quiet, sober, and orderly conduct which has prevailed in the camp since my arrival. There are assembled here upwards of three thousand persons, composed of different tribes. I have not seen nor heard of any wrangling or quarrelling among you; I have not seen even one man, woman, or child, in a state of intoxication.

"CHILDREN! – Let me entreat you to abstain from indulging in the use of fire-water. Let me entreat you to return immediately to your respective homes, with the presents now in your possession. Let me warn you against attempts that may be made by traders or other persons to induce you to part with your presents, in exchange for articles of little value. – Farewell."

When Mr. Jarvis ceased speaking there was a pause, and

then a fine Ottawa chief (I think Mokomaun,ish) arose, and spoke at some length. He said, that with regard to the condition on which the presents would be issued in future, they would deliberate on the affair, and bring their answer next year.

Shinguacose then came forward and made a long and emphatic speech, from which I gathered that he and his tribe requested that the principal council-fire might be transferred to St. Mary's River, and objected to a residence on the Manitoolin Island. After him spoke two other chiefs, who signified their entire acquiescence in what their Great Father had advised, and declared themselves, satisfied to reside on the Manitoolin Island.

After some deliberation among themselves, the custody of the flag was consigned to the Ottawa tribe then residing on the island, and to their principal chief, who came forward and received it with great ceremony.

There was then a distribution of extra presents, medals, silver gorgets, and amulets, to some of the chiefs and relatives of chiefs whose conduct was particularly approved, or whom it was thought expedient to gratify.

The council then broke up, and I made my way into the open air as quickly as I could.

In walking about among the wigwams to-day, I found some women on the shore, making a canoe. The frame had been put together by the men. The women were then joining the pieces of birch-bark with the split ligaments of the pine-root, which they call *wattup*. Other women were employed in melting and applying the resinous gum, with which they smear the seams, and render them impervious to the water. There was much chattering and laughing meanwhile, and I never saw a merrier set of gossips.

This canoe, which was about eighteen feet in length, was finished before night; and the next morning I saw it afloat.

A man was pointed out to me, (a Chippewa from Lake

Superior,) who, about three years ago, when threatened by starvation during his winter hunt, had devoured his wife and one or two of his children. You shudder – so did I; but since famine can prevail over every human feeling or instinct, till the "pitiful mother hath sodden her own children," and a woman devoured part of her lover,* I do not think this wretched creature must necessarily be a born monster of ferocity. His features were very mild and sad: he is avoided by the other Chippewas here, and not considered *respectable;* and this from an opinion they entertain, that when a man has once tasted human flesh, he can relish no other: but I must quit this abominable subject.

At sunset this evening, just as the air was beginning to grow cool, Major Anderson proclaimed a canoe race, the canoes to be paddled by the women only. The prize consisted of twenty-five pair of silver earrings and other trinkets. I can give you no idea of the state of commotion into which the whole camp, men, women, and children, were thrown by this announcement. Thirty canoes started, each containing twelve women, and a man to steer. They were to go round the little island in the centre of the bay, and return to the starting point, – the first canoe which touched the shore to be the winner. They darted off together with a sudden velocity, like that of an arrow from the bow. The Indians on the shore ran backwards and forwards on the beach, exciting them to exertion by loud cries, leaping into the air, whooping and clapping their hands; and when at length the first canoe dashed up to the landing-place, it was as if all had gone at once distracted and stark mad. The men, throwing themselves into the water, carried the winners out in their arms, who were laughing and panting for breath; and then the women cried "Ny'a! Ny'a!" and the men shouted "Ty'a!" till the pine woods rang again.

But all was good humour, and even good order, in the

* See the Voyage of the Blonde.

midst of this confusion. There was no ill blood, not a dispute, not an outrage, not even a *sound* of unkindness or anger; these are certainly the most good-natured, orderly savages imaginable! We are twenty white people, with 3,700 of these wild creatures around us, and I never in my life felt more security. I find it necessary, indeed, to suspend a blanket before each of the windows when I am dressing in the morning, for they have no idea of the possibility of being intrusive; they think "men's eyes were made to look," and windows to be looked through; but, with this exception, I never met with people more genuinely polite.

The scenes and groups around me here are merely a repetition of such as I described to you at Mackinaw, only with greater variety, and on a larger scale: – I will therefore only particularise one or two things.

There is a man here, an Englishman, settled up the lakes somewhere, who has a couple of Indian mistresses, and has brought them down to receive *their* presents. He is a man of noble family, and writes *honourable* before his name. He swaggers about in a pair of canvass trowsers and moccasins, a check shirt with the collar open, no cravat, a straw hat struck on the side of his head, and a dirty pipe in his mouth. He had a good fortune, and an honourable station in society; the one was wasted in excesses, and the other he has disgraced and abandoned. His countenance and his whole deportment conveyed an impression of reckless profligacy, of folly, weakness, and depravity, inexpressibly disgusting. There is no ruffian like the ruffian of civilised life. I turned from this man to my painted, half-naked Pottowottomies with a sense of relief.

To-day, when Mr. Jarvis was expressing his determination to keep liquor from the Indians, and enforce the laws on that subject, I heard this man mutter just behind me, "I'll be d – d, though, if I don't give 'em whisky whenever I choose!" I would write down the name of this wretched fellow, but that perhaps he has some mother or sister to whom he has already caused pain and shame enough.

After a very tiring day, I was standing tonight at the door of our log-house, looking out upon the tranquil stars, and admiring the peace and tranquillity which reigned all around. Within the house Mrs. MacMurray was hearing a young Chippewa read the Gospel, and the light of a lamp above fell upon her beautiful face – very beautiful it was at that moment – and on the dusky features of the Indian boy, akin to her own, and yet how different! and on his silver armlets and feathered head-dress. It was about nine o'clock, and though a few of the camp fires were yet burning, it seemed that almost all had gone to rest. At this moment old Solomon, the interpreter, came up, and told me that the warriors had arranged to give me an exhibition of their war-dance, and were then painting and preparing. In a few minutes more, the drum, and the shriek, and the long tremulous whoop, were heard. A large crowd had gathered silently in front of the house, leaving an open space in the midst; many of them carried great blazing torches, made of the bark of the pine rolled up into a cylinder. The innermost circle of the spectators sat down, and the rest stood around; some on the stumps of the felled trees, which were still at hand. I remember that a large piece of a flaming torch fell on the naked shoulder of a savage, and he jumped up with a yell which made me start; but they all laughed, and so did he, and sat himself down again quietly.

Meantime the drumming and yelling drew nearer, and all at once a man leaped like a panther into the very middle of the circle, and, flinging off his blanket, began to caper and to flourish his war-club; then another, and another, till there were about forty; then they stamped round and round, and gesticulated a sort of fiercely grotesque pantomime, and sent forth their hideous yells, while the glare of the torches fell on their painted and

naked figures, producing an effect altogether quite indescribable. Then a man suddenly stopped before me, and
began a speech at the very top of his voice, so that it
sounded like a reiteration of loud cries; it was, in fact, a
string of exclamations, which a gentleman standing
behind me translated as he went on. They were to this
purport: – "I am a Red-skin! I am a warrior! look on me! I
am a warrior! I am brave! I have fought! I have killed! I
have killed my enemies! I have eaten the tops of the hearts
of my enemies! I have drunk their blood! I have struck
down seven Long-knives! I have taken their scalps!"

This last vaunt he repeated several times with exultation, thinking, perhaps, it must be particularly agreeable
to a daughter of the Red-coats; – nothing was ever less so!
and the human being who was thus boasting stood within
half a yard of me, his grim painted face and gleaming eyes
looking into mine!

A-propos to scalps, I have seen many of the warriors
here, who had one or more of these suspended as decorations to their dress; and they seemed to me so much a part
and parcel of the *sauvagerie* around me, that I looked on
them generally without emotion or pain. But there was
one thing I never *could* see without a start, and a thrill of
horror, – the scalp of *long fair hair*.

Walking about early next morning, I saw that preparations for departure had already commenced; all was
movement, and bustle, and hurry; taking down wigwams,
launching canoes, tying up bundles and babies, cooking,
and "sacrificing" wretched dogs to propitiate the spirits,
and procure a favourable voyage. I came upon such a
sacrifice just at the opposite side of the point, and took to
flight forthwith. No interest, no curiosity, can overcome
the sickness and abhorrence with which I shrink from
certain things; so I can tell you nothing of this grand
ceremony, which you will find described circumstantially
by many less fastidious or less sensitive travellers.

All the Christian Indians now on the island (about nine hundred in number) are, with the exception of Mr. Mac-Murray's congregation from the Sault, either Roman Catholics or Methodists.

I had some conversation with Father Crue, the Roman Catholic missionary, a very clever and very zealous man, still in the prime of life. He has been here two years, is indefatigable in his calling, or, as Major Anderson said, "always on the go – up the lake and down – in every spot where he had the hope of being useful." I heard the Methodists and Churchmen complain greatly of his interference; but if he be a true believer in his religion, his active zeal does him honour, I think.

One thing is most visible, certain, and undeniable, that the Roman Catholic converts are in appearance, dress, intelligence, industry, and general civilisation, superior to all the others.

A band of Ottawas, under the particular care of Father Crue, have settled on the Manitoolin, about six miles to the south. They have large plantations of corn and potatoes, and they have built log-huts, a chapel for their religious services, and a house for their priest. I asked him distinctly whether they had erected these buildings themselves: he said they had.

Here, in the encampment, the Roman Catholic Ottawas have erected a large temporary chapel of posts covered in with bark, the floor strewed over with green boughs and mats, and an altar and crucifix at the end. In front a bell is suspended between the forked branches of a pine. I have heard them sing mass here, with every demonstration of decency and piety.

The Methodists have two congregations; the Indians of the Credit, under the direction of Peter Jones, and the Indians from Coldwater and the Narrows, under a preacher whose name I forget, – both zealous men; but the howling and weeping of these Methodist Indians, as they lie grovelling on the ground in their religious services, struck me painfully.

Mr. MacMurray is the only missionary of the Church of

England, and, with all his zeal and his peculiar means of influence and success, it cannot be said that he is adequately aided and supported. "The English Church," said one of our most intelligent Indian agents, "either cannot or will not, certainly *does not*, sow; therefore cannot expect to reap." The zeal, activity, and benevolence of the travelling missionary Elliott are beyond all praise; but his ministry is devoted to the back settlers more than to the Indians. The Roman Catholic missions have been, of all, the most active and persevering; next to these the Methodists. The Presbyterian and the English Churches have been hitherto comparatively indifferent and negligent.

Information was brought to the superintendent, that a trader from Detroit, with a boat laden with whisky and rum, was lying concealed in a little cove near the entrance of the great bay, for the purpose of waylaying the Indians, and bartering the whisky for their new blankets, guns, and trinkets. I exclaimed with indignation! – but Mr. Jarvis did better than exclaim; he sent off the Blackbird, with a canoe full of stout men, to board the trader and throw all the whisky into the lake, and then desire the owner to bring any complaint or claim for restitution down to Toronto; and this was done accordingly. The Blackbird is a Christian, and extremely noted for his general good conduct, and his declared enmity to the "dealers in firewater."

Yet a word more before I leave my Indians.

There is one subject on which all travellers in these regions – all who have treated of the manners and modes of life of the north-west tribes, are accustomed to expatiate with great eloquence and indignation, which they think it incumbent on the gallantry and chivalry of Christendom to denounce as constituting the true badge and distinction of barbarism and heathenism, opposed to civilisation and Christianity: – I mean the treatment and condition of their women. The women, they say, are "drudges," "slaves," "beasts of burthen," victims, martyrs, degraded, abject, oppressed; that not only the cares of the household and maternity, but the cares and labours proper to the men, fall upon them; and they seem to consider no expression of disapprobation, and even abhorrence, too strong for the occasion; and if there be any who should feel inclined to modify such objurgations, or speak in excuse or mitigation of the fact, he might well fear that the publication of such opinions would expose him to have his eyes scratched out, (metaphorically,) or die, in every female coterie, in every review, the death of Orpheus or Pentheus.

Luckily I have no such risk to run. Let but my woman's wit bestead me here as much as my womanhood, and I will, as the Indians say, "tell you a piece of my mind," and place the matter before you in another point of view.

Under one aspect of the question, all these gentlemen travellers are right: they are right in their estimate of the condition of the Indian squaws – they *are* drudges, slaves: and they are right in the opinion that the condition of the women in any community is a test of the advance of moral and intellectual cultivation in that community; but it is not a test of the virtue or civilisation of the man; in these Indian tribes, where the men are the noblest and bravest of their kind, the women are held of no account, are despised and oppressed. But it does appear to me that the woman among these Indians holds her true natural position relatively to the state of the man and the state of society; and this cannot be said of all societies.

Take into consideration, in the first place, that in these Indian communities the task of providing subsistence falls solely and entirely on the men. When it is said, in general terms, that the men do nothing but *hunt* all day, while the women are engaged in perpetual *toil*, I suppose this suggests to civilised readers the idea of a party of gentlemen at Melton, or a turn-out of Mr. Meynell's hounds; – or at most a deer-stalking excursion to the Highlands – a holiday affair; – while the women, poor souls! must sit at home and sew, and spin, and cook victuals. But what is the life of an Indian hunter? – one of incessant, almost killing toil, and often danger.* A hunter goes out at dawn, knowing that, if he returns empty, his wife and his little ones must *starve* – no uncommon predicament! He comes home at sunset, spent with fatigue, and unable even to speak. His wife takes off his moccasins, places before him what food she has, or, if latterly the chase has failed, probably no food at all, or only a little parched wild rice. She then examines his hunting-pouch, and in it finds the claws, or beak, or tongue of the game, or other indications by which she knows what it is, and where to find it. She then goes for it, and drags it home. When he is refreshed, the hunter caresses his wife and children, relates the events of his chase, smokes his pipe, and goes to sleep – to begin the same life on the following day.

Where, then, the whole duty and labour of providing the means of subsistence, ennobled by danger and courage, fall upon the man, the woman naturally sinks in importance, and is a dependent drudge. But she is not therefore, I suppose, so *very* miserable, nor, relatively, so very abject; she is sure of protection; sure of maintenance, at least while the man has it; sure of kind treatment; sure that she will never have her children taken from her but by death; sees none better off than herself, and has no conception of a superior destiny; and it is evident that in such a state the appointed and necessary share of the

* I had once a description of an encounter between my illustrious grandpapa Waub-Ojeeg and an enormous elk, in which he had to contend with the infuriated animal for his very life for a space of three hours, and the snows were stained with his blood and that of his adversary for a hundred yards round. At last, while dodging the elk round and round a tree, he contrived to tear off the thong from his moccasin, and with it to fasten his knife to the end of a stick, and with this he literally hacked at the creature till it fell from loss of blood.

woman is the household work, and all other domestic labour. As to the necessity of carrying burthens, when moving the camp from place to place, and felling and carrying wood, this is the most dreadful part of her lot; and however accustomed from youth to the axe, the paddle, and the carrying-belt, it brings on internal injuries and severe suffering – and yet it *must* be done. For a man to carry burthens would absolutely incapacitate him for a hunter, and consequently from procuring sufficient meat for his family. Hence, perhaps, the contempt with which they regard it. And an Indian woman is unhappy, and her pride is hurt, if her husband should be seen with a load on his back; this was strongly expressed by one among them who said it was "unmanly;" and that "she could not bear to see it!"

Hence, however hard the lot of woman, she is in no *false* position. The two sexes are in their natural and true position relatively to the state of society, and the means of subsistence.

The first step from the hunting to the agricultural state is the first step in the emancipation of the female. I know there are some writers who lament that the introduction of agriculture has not benefited the Indian women, rather added to their toils, as a great proportion of the hoeing and planting has devolved on them; but among the Ottawas, where this is the case, the women are decidedly in a better state than among the hunting Chippewas; they can sell or dispose of the produce raised by themselves, if there be more than is necessary for the family, and they take some share in the bargains and business of the tribe: and add, that among all these tribes, in the division of the money payments for the ceded land, every woman receives her individual share.

Lewis and Clarke, in exploring the Missouri, came upon a tribe of Indians who, from local circumstances, kill little game, and live principally on fish and roots; and as the women are equally expert with the men in procuring subsistence, they have a rank and influence very rarely found among Indians. The females are permitted to speak freely before the men, to whom indeed they sometimes address themselves in a tone of authority. On many subjects their judgment and opinion are respected, and in matters of trade their advice is generally asked and pursued; the labours of the family too are shared equally.* This seems to be a case in point.

Then, when we speak of the *drudgery* of the women, we must note the equal division of labour; there is no class of women privileged to sit still while others work. Every squaw makes the clothing, mats, moccasins, and boils the kettle for her own family. Compare her life with the refined leisure of an elegant woman in the higher classes of our society, and it is wretched and abject; but compare her life with that of a servant-maid of all work, or a factory girl, – I do say that the condition of the squaw is gracious in comparison, dignified by domestic feelings, and by equality with all around her. If women are to be exempted from toil in reverence to the sex, and as *women*, I can understand this, though I think it unreasonable; but if it be merely a privilege of station, and confined to a certain set, while the great primeval penalty is doubled on the rest, then I do not see where is the great gallantry and consistency of this our Christendom, nor what right we have to look down upon the barbarism of the Indian savages who make *drudges* of their women.

I will just mention here the extreme delicacy and personal modesty of the women of these tribes, which may seem strange when we see them brought up and living in crowded wigwams, where a whole family is herded within a space of a few yards: but the lower classes of the Irish, brought up in their cabins, are remarkable for the same feminine characteristic: it is as if true modesty were from within, and could hardly be outwardly defiled.

But to return. Another boast over the Indian savages in

* Travels up the Missouri.

this respect is, that we set a much higher value on the chastity of women. We are told (with horror) that among some of the north-west tribes the man offers his wife or sister, nothing loth, to his guest, as a part of the duty of hospitality; and this is, in truth, *barbarism!* – the heartless brutality on one side, and the shameless indifference on the other, may well make a woman's heart shrink within her. But what right have civilised *men* to exclaim, and look sublime and self-complacent about the matter? If they do not exactly imitate this fashion of the Indians, their exceeding and jealous reverence for the virtue of women is really indulged at a very cheap rate to themselves. If the chastity of women be a virtue, and respectable in the eyes of the community for its own sake, well and good; if it be a mere matter of expediency, and valuable only as it affects property, guarded by men just as far as it concerns their honour – as far as regards ours, a jest, – if this be the masculine creed of right and wrong – the fiat promulgated by our lords and masters, then I should be inclined to answer, as the French girl answered the Prince de Conti, "Pour Dieu! monseigneur, votre altesse royale est par trop insolente!" There is no woman, worthy the name, whose cheek does not burn in shame and indignation at the thought.

Such women as those poor perverted sacrificed creatures who haunt our streets, or lead as guilty lives in lavish splendour, are utterly unknown among the Indians.

With regard to female right of property, there is no such thing as real property among them, except the hunting-grounds or territory which are the possession of the tribe. The personal property, as the clothing, mats, cooking and hunting apparatus, all the interior of the wigwam, in short, seems to be under the control of the woman; and on the death of her husband the woman remains in possession of the lodge, and all it contains, except the medal, flag, or other insignia of dignity, which go to his son or male relatives. The corn she raises, and the maple sugar

she makes, she can always dispose of as she thinks fit –
they are *hers*.

It seems to me a question whether the Europeans, who,
Heaven knows, have much to answer for in their intercourse with these people, have not, in some degree,
injured the cause of the Indian women: – first, by corrupt-
ing them; secondly, by checking the improvement of all
their own peculiar manufactures. They prepared deer-
skins with extraordinary skill; I have seen dresses of the
mountain sheep and young buffalo skins, richly embroidered, and almost equal in beauty and softness to a Cash-
mere shawl; and I could mention other things. It is reasonable to presume that as these manufactures must have
been progressively improved, there might have been farther progression, had we not substituted for articles they
could themselves procure or fabricate, those which we
fabricate; we have taken the work out of their hands, and
all motive to work, while we have created wants which
they cannot supply. We have clothed them in blankets –
we have not taught them to weave blankets. We have
substituted guns for the bows and arrows – but they cannot make guns: for the natural progress of arts and civilisation springing from within, and from their own intelligence and resources, we have substituted a sort of
civilisation from without, foreign to their habits, manners,
organisation: we are making paupers of them; and this by
a kind of terrible necessity. Some very economical
members of our British parliament have remonstrated
against the system of Indian presents as too *expensive;* one
would almost suppose, to hear their arguments, that
pounds, shillings, and pence were the stuff of which life is
made – the three primal elements of all human existence –
all human morals. Surely they can know nothing of the
real state of things here. If the issue of the presents from
our government were now to cease, I cannot think without horror of what must ensue: trifling as they are, they
are an Indian's existence; without the rifle he must die of

hunger; without his blanket, perish of cold. Before he is reduced to this, we should have nightly plunder and massacre all along our frontiers and back settlements; a horrid brutalising contest like that carried on in Florida, in which the white man would be demoralised, and the Red man exterminated.

The sole article of traffic with the Indians, their furs, is bartered for the necessaries of life; and these furs can *only* be procured by the men. Thus their only trade, so far from tending to the general civilisation of the people, keeps up the wild hunting habits, and tells fearfully against the power and utility of the women, if it be not altogether fatal to any amelioration of their condition. Yet it should seem that we are ourselves just emerging from a similar state, only in another form. Until of late years there was no occupation for women by which a subsistence could be gained, except servitude in some shape or other. The change which has taken place in this respect is one of the most striking and interesting signs of the times in which we live.

I must stop here: but do you not think, from the hints I have rather illogically and incoherently thrown together, that we may assume as a general principle, that the true importance and real dignity of woman is everywhere, in savage and civilised communities, regulated by her capacity of being useful; or, in other words, that her condition is decided by the share she takes in providing for her own subsistence and the well-being of society as a productive labourer? Where she is idle and useless by privilege of sex, a divinity and an idol, a victim or a toy, is not her position quite as lamentable, as false, as injurious to herself and all social progress, as where she is the drudge, slave, and possession of the man?

The two extremes in this way are the Indian squaw and the Turkish sultana; and I would rather be born the first than the last: – and to carry out the idea, I would rather, on the same principle, be an Englishwoman or a Frenchwoman than an American or a German woman, – supposing that the state of feeling as regards women were to remain stationary in the two last countries – which I trust it will NOT.

The ways through which my weary steps I guide,
In this delightful land of faëry,
Are so exceeding spacious and wide,
And sprinkled with such sweet variety
Of all that pleasant is to ear or eye,
That I nigh ravish'd with rare thought's delight,
My tedious travel doe forget thereby,
And when I gin to feel decay of might,
It strength to me supplies, and clears my dulled spright.

SPENSER.

ON THE 6th of August I bade adieu to my good friends
Mr. and Mrs. MacMurray. I had owed too much to
their kindness to part from them without regret. They
returned up the lake, with their beautiful child and Indian
retinue, to St. Mary's, while I prepared to embark in a
canoe with the superintendent, to go down the lake to
Penetanguishene, a voyage of four days at least, supposing
wind and weather to continue favourable. Thence to
Toronto, across Lake Simcoe, was a journey of three days
more. Did I not say Providence took care of me? Always I
have found efficient protection when I most needed and
least expected it; and nothing could exceed the politeness
of Mr. Jarvis and his people; – it *began* with politeness, –

but it ended with something more and better – real and zealous kindness.

Now to take things in order, and that you may accompany us in our canoe voyage, I must describe in the first place our arrangements. You shall confess ere long that the Roman emperor who proclaimed a reward for the discovery of a new pleasure, ought to have made a voyage down Lake Huron in a birchbark canoe.

There were two canoes, each five-and-twenty feet in length, and four feet in width, tapering to the two extremities, and light, elegant, and buoyant as the sea-mew when it skims the summer waves: in the first canoe were Mr. Jarvis and myself; the governor's son, a lively boy of fourteen or fifteen, old Solomon the interpreter, and seven voyageurs. My blankets and night-gear being rolled up in a bundle, served for a seat, and I had a pillow at my back; and thus I reclined in the bottom of the canoe, as in a litter, very much at my ease: my companions were almost equally comfortable. I had near me my cloak, umbrella, and parasol; my note-books and sketch-books, and a little compact basket always by my side, containing eau de Cologne, and all those necessary luxuries which might be wanted in a moment, for I was well resolved that I would occasion no trouble but what was inevitable. The voyageurs were disposed on low wooden seats, suspended to the ribs of the canoe, except our Indian steersman, Martin, who, in a cotton shirt, arms bared to the shoulder, loose trowsers, a scarlet sash round his waist, richly embroidered with beads, and his long black hair waving, took his place in the stern, with a paddle twice as long as the others.*

The manner in which he stood, turning and twisting himself with the lithe agility of a snake, and striking first on one side, then on the other, was very graceful and picturesque. So much depends on the skill, and dexterity,

* The common paddle (called by the Canadians *aviron*, and by the Indians *abwee*) is about two feet and a half long.

and intelligence of these steersmen, that they have always double pay. The other men were all picked men, Canadian half-breeds, young, well-looking, full of glee and good-nature, with untiring arms and more untiring lungs and spirits; a handkerchief twisted round the head, a shirt and pair of trowsers, with a gay sash, formed the prevalent costume. We had on board a canteen, and other light baggage, two or three guns, and fishing tackle.

The other canoe carried part of Mr. Jarvis's retinue, the heavy baggage, provisions, marquees, guns, &c., and was equipped with eight paddles. The party consisted altogether of twenty-two persons, viz. twenty-one men, and myself, the only woman.

We started off in swift and gallant style, looking grand and official, with the British flag floating at our stern. Major Anderson and his people, and the schooner's crew, gave us three cheers. The Indians uttered their wild cries, and discharged their rifles all along the shore. As we left the bay, I counted seventy-two canoes before us, already on their homeward voyage – some to the upper waters of the lake – some to the northern shores; as we passed them, they saluted us by discharging their rifles: the day was without a cloud, and it was altogether a most animated and beautiful scene.

I forgot to tell you that the Indians are very fond of having pet animals in their wigwams, – not only dogs, but tame foxes and hawks. Mr. Jarvis purchased a pair of young hawks, male and female, from an Indian, intending them for his children. Just as we left the island, one of these birds escaped from the basket, and flew directly to the shore of the bay, where it was lost in the thick forest. We proceeded, and after leaving the bay about twelve miles onwards, we landed on a little rocky island: some one heard the cry of a hawk over our heads; it was the poor bird we had lost; he had kept his companion in sight all the way, following us unseen along the shore, and now suffered himself to be taken and caged with the other.

We bought some black-bass from an Indian who was

spearing fish: and, a-propos! I never yet have mentioned what is one of the greatest pleasures in the navigation of these magnificent upper lakes – the purity, the coldness, the transparency of the water. I have been told that if in the deeper parts of the lake a white handkerchief be sunk with the lead, it is distinctly visible at a depth of thirty fathoms – we did not try the experiment, not being in deep water; but here, among shoals and islands, I could almost always see the rocky bottom, with glittering pebbles, and the fish gliding beneath us with their waving fins and staring eyes – and if I took a glass of water, it came up sparkling as from the well at Harrowgate, and the flavour was delicious. You can hardly imagine how much this added to the charm and animation of the voyage.

About sunset we came to the hut of a fur trader, whose name, I think, was Lemorondière: it was on the shore of a beautiful channel running between the mainland and a large island. On a neighbouring point, Wai,sow,win,de,bay (the Yellow-head) and his people were building their wigwams for the night. The appearance was most picturesque, particularly when the camp fires were lighted and the night came on. I cannot forget the figure of a squaw, as she stood, dark and tall, against the red flames, bending over a great black kettle, her blanket trailing behind her, her hair streaming on the night breeze; – most like to one of the witches in Macbeth.

We supped here on excellent trout and white-fish, but the sand-flies and mosquitoes were horridly tormenting; the former, which are so diminutive as to be scarcely visible, were by far the worst. We were off next morning by daylight, the Yellow-head's people discharging their rifles by way of salute.

The voyageurs measure the distance by *pipes*. At the end of a certain time there is a pause, and they light their pipes and smoke for about five minutes, then the paddles go off merrily again, at the rate of about fifty strokes in a minute, and we absolutely seem to fly over the water. "Trois pipes" are about twelve miles. We breakfasted this morning on a little island of exceeding beauty, rising pre-

cipitately from the water. In front we had the open lake,
lying blue, and bright, and serene, under the morning sky,
and the eastern extremity of the Manitoolin Island; and
islands all around as far as we could see. The feeling of
remoteness, of the profound solitude, added to the sentiment of beauty: it was nature in her first freshness and
innocence, as she came from the hand of her Maker, and
before she had been sighed upon by humanity – defiled at
once, and sanctified by the contact. Our little island
abounded with beautiful shrubs, flowers, green mosses,
and scarlet lichens. I found a tiny recess, where I made my
bath and toilette very comfortably. On returning, I found
breakfast laid on a piece of rock; my seat, with my pillow
and cloak all nicely arranged, and a bouquet of flowers
lying on it. This was a never-failing *gallanterie*, sometimes
from one, sometimes from another of my numerous
cavaliers.

This day we had a most delightful run among hundreds
of islands; sometimes darting through narrow rocky channels, so narrow that I could not see the water on either
side of the canoe; and then emerging, we glided through
vast fields of white water-lilies; it was perpetual variety,
perpetual beauty, perpetual delight and enchantment,
from hour to hour. The men sang their gay French songs,
the other canoe joining in the chorus.

This peculiar singing has often been described; it is very
animated on the water and in the open air, but not very
harmonious. They all sing in unison, raising their voices
and marking the time with their paddles. One always led,
but in these there was a diversity of taste and skill. If I
wished to hear "En roulant ma boule, roulette," I applied
to Le Duc. Jacques excelled in "La belle rose blanche,"
and Louis was great in "Trois canards s'en vont baignant."

They often amused me by a specimen of dexterity,
something like that of an accomplished whip in London.
They would paddle up towards the shore with such
extreme velocity, that I expected to be dashed on the rock,
and then in a moment, by a simultaneous back-stroke of
the paddle, stop with a jerk, which made me breathless.

My only discomposure arose from the destructive propensities of the gentlemen, all keen and eager sportsmen;
the utmost I could gain from their mercy was, that the fish
should gasp to death out of my sight, and the pigeons and
the wild ducks be put out of pain instantly. I will, however,
acknowledge, that when the bass-fish and pigeons were
produced, broiled and fried, they looked so *appétissants*,
smelt so savoury, and I was *so* hungry, that I soon forgot
all my sentimental pity for the victims.

We found to-day, on a rock, the remains of an Indian
lodge, over which we threw a sail-cloth, and dined luxuriously on our fish and pigeons, and a glass of good
madeira. After dinner, the men dashed off with great animation, singing my favourite ditty,

> Si mon moine voulait danser,
> Un beau cheval lui donnerai!

– through groups of lovely islands, sometimes scattered
wide, and sometimes clustered so close, that I often mistook twenty or thirty together for one large island; but on
approaching nearer, they opened before us, and appeared
intersected by winding labyrinthine channels, where,
amid flags and water-lilies, beneath the shade of rich
embowering foliage, we glided on our way; and then we
came upon a wide open space, where we could feel the
heave of the waters under us, and across which the men,
still singing with untiring vivacity, paddled with all their
might to reach the opposite islands before sunset. The
moment it becomes too dark for our steersman to see
through the surface of the water, it becomes in the highest
degree dangerous to proceed; such is the frail texture of
these canoes, that a pin's point might scratch a hole in the
bottom; a sunk rock, or a *snag* or projecting bough – and
often we glided within an inch of them – had certainly
swamped us.

We passed this day two Indian sepulchres, on a point of
rock overshadowed by birch and pine, with the sparkling
waters murmuring round them; I landed to examine

them. The Indians cannot here *bury* their dead, for there is not a sufficiency of earth to cover them from sight, but they lay the body, wrapped up carefully in bark, on the flat rock, and then cover it over with rocks and stones. This was the tomb of a woman and her child, and fragments of the ornaments and other things buried with them were still perceptible.

We landed at sunset on a flat ledge of rock, free from bushes, which we avoided as much as possible, from fear of mosquitoes and rattlesnakes; and while the men pitched the marquees and cooked supper, I walked and mused.

I wish I could give you the least idea of the beauty of this evening; but while I try to put in words what was before me, the sense of its ineffable loveliness overpowers me *now*, even as it did then. The sun had set in that cloudless splendour, and that peculiar blending of rose and amber light that belongs only to these climes and Italy; the lake lay weltering under the western sky like a bath of molten gold; the rocky islands which studded its surface were of a dense purple, except where their edges seemed fringed with fire. They assumed, to the visionary eye, strange forms; some were like great horned beetles, and some like turtles, and some like crocodiles, and some like sleeping whales, and winged fishes: the foliage upon them resembled dorsal fins, and sometimes tufts of feathers. Then, as the purple shadows came darkening from the east, the young crescent moon showed herself, flinging a paly splendour over the water. I remember standing on the shore, "my spirits as in a dream were all bound up," – overcome by such an intense feeling of *the beautiful* – such a deep adoration for the power that had created it, – I must have suffocated if –

But why tell *you* this?

They pitched my tent at a *respectful* distance from the rest, and Mr. Jarvis made me a delicious elastic bed of some boughs, over which was spread a bear-skin, and over that blankets: but the night was hot and feverish. The

voyageurs, after rowing since daylight, were dancing and
singing on the shore till near midnight.

Next morning we were off again at early dawn, paddled
"trois pipes" before breakfast, over an open space which
they call a "traverse," caught eleven bass fish, and shot
two pigeons. The island on which we breakfasted was in
great part white marble; and in the clefts and hollows grew
quantities of gooseberries and raspberries, wild-roses, the
crimson columbine, a large species of harebell, a sort of
willow, juniper, birch, and stunted pine; and such was the
usual vegetation.

It is beautiful to see in these islands the whole process of
preparatory vegetation unfolded and exemplified before
one's eyes – each successive growth preparing a soil for
that which is to follow.

There was first the naked rock washed by the spray,
where the white gulls were sitting: then you saw the rock
covered with some moss or lichens; then in the clefts and
seams, some long grass, a few wild flowers and strawberries; then a few juniper and rose bushes; then the dwarf
pine hardly rising two or three feet, and lastly trees and
shrubs of large growth: and the nearer to the mainland,
the richer of course the vegetation, for the seeds are wafted
thence by the winds, or carried by the birds, and so dispersed from island to island.

We landed to-day on the "Island of Skulls," an ancient
sepulchre of the Hurons: some skulls and bones were
scattered about, with the rough stones which had once
been heaped over them. The spot was most wild and
desolate, rising from the water edge in successive ledges of
rock to a considerable height, with a few blasted gray pines
here and there, round which several pair of hawks were
wheeling and uttering their shrill cry. We all declared we
would not dine on this ominous Island, and proceeded.
We doubled a remarkable cape mentioned by Henry as
the *Pointe aux Grondines*. There is always a heavy swell
here, and perpetual sound of breakers on the rocks,
whence its name. Only a few years ago, a trader in his

canoe, with sixteen people, were wrecked and lost on this spot.

We also passed within some miles of the mouth of the Rivière des Français, the most important of all the rivers which flow into Lake Huron. It forms the line of communication for the north-west traders from Montreal; the common route is up the Ottawa River, across Lake Nippissing, and down the River Français into Lake Huron, and by the Sault Ste. Marie into Lake Superior. Pray have a map before you during this voyage.*

Leaving behind this cape and river, we came again upon lovely groups of Elysian islands, channels winding among rocks and foliage, and more fields of water-lilies. In passing through a beautiful channel, I had an opportunity of seeing the manner in which an Indian communicates with his friends when *en route*. A branch was so arranged as to project far across the water and catch the eye: in a cleft at the extremity a piece of birch-bark was stuck with some hieroglyphic marks scratched with red ochre, of which we could make nothing – one figure, I thought, represented a fish.

To-day we caught seven bass, shot four pigeons, also a large water-snake – which last I thought a gratuitous piece of cruelty. We dined upon a large and picturesque island – large in comparison with those we usually selected, being perhaps two or three miles round; it was very woody and wild, intersected by deep ravines, and rising in bold, abrupt precipices. We dined luxuriously under a group of trees: the heat was overpowering, and the mosquitoes very troublesome.

After dinner we pursued our course through an archipelago of islets, rising out of the blue waves, and fringed with white water-lilies; – Little fairy Edens, of such endless

* This part of Lake Huron, and indeed all its upper shores, are very incorrectly laid down in Wyld's map of Upper Canada. Bouchette's large map, and also a beautiful small one published by Blackwood in 1833, are much more accurate.

variety in form and colour, and of such wondrous and fantastic beauty, that I know not how to describe them.

We landed on one, where there was a rock so exactly resembling the head and part of a turtle, that I could have taken it for sculpture. The Indians look upon it as sacred, and it is customary for all who pass to leave an offering in money, tobacco, corn, &c., to the spirit. I duly left mine, but I could see by the laughing eyes of Jacques and Louis, that "the spirit" was not likely to be the better for my devotion.

Mr. Jarvis asked me to sing a French song for the voyageurs, and Louis looked back with his bright arch face, as much as to say, "Pray do," when a shout was heard from the other canoe, "A mink! a mink!"* and all the paddles were now in animated motion. We dashed up among the reeds, we chased the creature up and down, and at last to a hole under a rock; the voyageurs beat the reeds with their paddles, the gentlemen seized their guns; there were twenty-one men half frantic in pursuit of a wretched little creature, whose death could serve no purpose. It dived but rose a few yards farther, and was seen making for the land; a shot was fired, it sprang from the water: another, and it floated dead; – thus we repaid the beauty, and enjoyment, and lavish loveliness spread around us, with pain and with destruction.

I recollect that as we passed a lovely bit of an island, all bordered with flags and white lilies, we saw a beautiful wild-duck emerge from a green covert, and lead into the lake a numerous brood of ducklings. It was a sight to touch the heart with a tender pleasure, and I pleaded hard, very hard, for mercy; but what thorough sportsman ever listened to such a word? The deadly guns were already levelled, and even while I spoke, the poor mother-bird was shot, and the little ones, which could not fly, went fluttering and scudding away into the open lake, to perish miserably.

* A species of otter.

But what was really very touching was to see the poor gulls; sometimes we would startle a whole bevy of them as they were floating gracefully on the waves, and they would rise soaring away beyond our reach; but the voyageurs, suspending their paddles, imitated exactly their own soft low whistle; and then the wretched, foolish birds, just as if they had been so many women, actually wheeled round in the air, and came flying back to meet the "fiery death."

The voyageurs eat these gulls, in spite of their fishy taste, with great satisfaction.

I wonder how it is that some of those gentry whom I used to see in London, looking as though they would give an empire for a new pleasure or a new sensation, do not come here. If epicures, they should come to eat white-fish and beavers' tails; if sportsmen, here is a very paradise for bear-hunting, deer-hunting, otter-hunting; – and wild-fowl in thousands, and fish in shoals; and if they be contemplative lovers of the picturesque, *blasés* with Italy and elbowed out of Switzerland, let them come here and find the true philosopher's stone – or rather the true elixir of life – *novelty!*

At sunset we encamped on a rocky island of most fantastic form, like a Z. They pitched my tent on a height, and close to the door was a precipitous descent into a hollow, where they lighted vast fires, and thus kept off the mosquitoes, which were in great force. I slept well, but towards morning some creature crept into my tent and over my bed – a snake, as I supposed; after this I slept no more.

We started at half-past four. Hitherto the weather had been glorious; but this morning the sun rose among red and black clouds, fearfully ominous. As we were turning a point under some lofty rocks, we heard the crack of a rifle, and saw an Indian leaping along the rocks, and down towards the shore. We rowed in, not knowing what it meant, and came upon a night-camp of Indians, part of the tribe of Aisence, (the Clam.) They had only hailed us to make some trifling inquiries; and I heard Louis, sotto voce, send them *au diable!* – for now the weather lowered darker and darker, and every moment was precious.

We breakfasted on an island almost covered with flowers, some gorgeous, and strange, and unknown, and others sweet and familiar; plenty of the wild-pea, for instance, and wild-roses, of which I had many offerings. I made my toilette in a recess among some rocks; but just as I was emerging from my primitive dressing-room, I felt a few drops of rain, and saw too clearly that our good fortune was at an end. We swallowed a hasty breakfast, and had just time to arrange ourselves in the canoe with all the available defences of cloaks and umbrellas, when the rain came down heavily and hopelessly. But notwithstanding the rain and the dark gray sky, the scenery was even more beautiful than ever. The islands were larger, and assumed a richer appearance; the trees were of more luxuriant growth, no longer the dwarfed pine, but lofty oak and maple. These are called the Bear Islands, from the number of those animals found upon them; old Solomon told me that an Indian whom he knew had shot nine bears in the course of a single day. We found three bears' heads stuck upon the boughs of a dead pine – probably as offerings to the souls of the slaughtered animals, or to the "Great Spirit," both being usual.

We dined on a wet rock, almost covered with that species of lichen which the Indians call wa,ac, and the Canadians *tripe de roche*, because, when boiled till soft, and then fried in grease, it makes a dish not unpalatable – when one has nothing else.* The Clam and some of his people landed and dined at the same time. After dinner the rain came on worse and worse. Old Solomon asked me once or twice how I felt; and I thought his anxiety for my health was caused by the rain; but no; he told me that on the island where we had dined he had observed a great quantity of a certain plant, which, if only touched, causes a dreadful eruption and ulcer all over the body. I asked

---

* It is often mentioned in the Travels of Back and Franklin.

why he and not shown it to me, and warned me against it? and he assured me that such warning would only have increased the danger, for when there is any knowledge or apprehension of it existing in the mind, the very air blowing from it sometimes infects the frame. Here I appealed to Mr. Jarvis, who replied, "All I know is, that I once unconsciously touched a leaf of it, and became one ulcer from head to foot; I could not stir for a fortnight."*

This was a dreadful night, for the rain came on more violently, accompanied by a storm of wind. It was necessary to land and make our fires for the night. The good-natured men were full of anxiety and compassion for me, poor, lonely, shivering woman that I was in the midst of them! The first thought with every one was to place me under shelter, and my tent was pitched instantly with such zeal, and such activity, that the sense of inconvenience and suffering was forgotten in the thankful sense of kindness, and all things became endurable.

The tent was pitched on a height, so that the water ran off on all sides: I contrived for myself a dry bed, and Mr. Jarvis brought me some hot madeira. I rolled myself up in my German blanket, and fell into a deep, sound sleep. The voyageurs, who apparently need nothing but their own good spirits to feed and clothe them, lighted a great fire, turned the canoes upside down, and, sheltered under them, were heard singing and laughing during great part of this tempestuous night.

Next morning we were off by five o'clock. My beautiful lake looked horribly sulky, and all the little islands were lost in a cold gray vapour: we were now in the Georgian Bay. Through the misty atmosphere loomed a distant shore of considerable height. Dupré told me that what I

---

* I do not know the botanical name of this plant, which resembles a dwarf sumach: it was subsequently pointed out to me in the woods by a Methodist preacher, who told me that his daughter, merely by standing to windward of the plant while looking at it, suffered dreadfully. It is said that formerly the Indians used it to poison their arrows.

saw was the Isle des Chrétiens, and that formerly there was
a large settlement of the Jesuits there, and that still there
were to be seen the remains of "une grande cathédrale."
About nine o'clock we entered the bay of Penetanguishene, so called from a high sand-bank at the
entrance, which is continually crumbling away. The
expressive Indian name signifies "Look! it is falling sand!"

We spent the greater part of two days at Penetanguishene,
which is truly a most lovely spot. The bay runs up into the
land like some of the Scottish lochs, and the shores are
bolder and higher than usual, and as yet all clothed with
the primeval forest. During the war there were dockyards
and a military and naval depôt here, maintained at an
immense expense to government; and it is likely, from its
position, to rise into a station of great importance; at
present, the only remains of all the warlike demonstrations of former times are a sloop sunk and rotting in the
bay, and a large stone-building at the entrance, called the
"Fort," but merely serving as barracks for a few soldiers
from the garrison at Toronto. There are several pretty
houses on the beautiful declivity, rising on the north side
of the bay, and the families settled here have contrived to
assemble round them many of the comforts and elegan-
cies of life. I have reason to remember with pleasure a
Russian lady, the wife of an English officer, who made my
short sojourn here very agreeable.

There was an inn here, not the worst of Canadian inns;
and the *wee* closet called a bedroom, and the little bed
with its white cotton curtains, appeared to me the *ne plus
ultra* of luxury. I recollect walking in and out of the room
ten times a day for the mere pleasure of contemplating it,
and anticipated with impatience the moment when I
should throw myself down into it, and sleep once more on
a christian bed. But nine nights passed in the open air, or
on rocks, and on boards, had spoiled me for the comforts
of civilisation, and to sleep *on a bed* was impossible; I was

smothered, I was suffocated, and altogether wretched and fevered; – I sighed for my rock on Lake Huron.

At Penetanguishene there is a hamlet, consisting of twenty or thirty log-houses, where a small remnant of the poor commuted pensioners (in all a hundred and twenty-six persons) now reside, receiving daily rations of food, and some little clothing, just sufficient to sustain life.

From some particular circumstances the case of these commuted pensioners was frequently brought under my observation while I was in Canada, and excited my strongest interest and compassion. I shall give you a brief sketch of this tragedy, for such it truly is; not by way of exciting sympathy, which can now avail nothing, but because it is in many points of view fraught with instruction.

The commuted pensioners were veteran soldiers, entitled to a small yearly pension for wounds or length of service, and who accepted the offer made to them by our government in 1832, to commute their pensions for four years' purchase, and a grant of one hundred acres of land in Canada.

The *intention* of the government seems to have been to send out able-bodied men, who would thus cease, after a few years, to be a burthen on the country. A part of the money due to them was to be deducted for their voyage and expenses out; of the remaining sum a part was to be paid in London, part at Quebec, and the rest when settled on the land awarded to them. These *intentions* sound well; unluckily they were not properly acted upon. Some received the whole of the money due to them in England, and drank themselves to death, or squandered it, and then refused to leave the country. Some drank themselves to death, or died of the cholera, at Quebec; and of those who came out, one half were described to me* as presenting a list of all the miseries and diseases incident to humanity – some with one arm, some with one leg, bent with old age

---

* I have these particulars from the chief of the commissariat in Upper Canada, and the emigrant agent.

or rheumatism, lame, halt, and even, will it be believed, blind!* And such were the men to be set down in the midst of the swamp and forest, there to live as they could. When some few, who had been more provident, presented themselves to the commissary at Toronto for payment of the rest of the money due to them, it was found that the proper papers had not been forwarded; they were written for to the Chelsea Board, which had to apply to the War-office, which had to apply to the Treasury: the papers, after being bandied about from office to office, from clerk to secretary, from secretary to clerk, were sent, at length, after a lapse of eight or ten months, during which time the poor men, worn out with suspense, had taken to begging, or to drinking, in utter despondency; and when the order for their money *did* at last arrive, they had become useless, abandoned creatures.

Those who were located were sent far up into the bush, (there being no disposable government lands nearer,) where there were no roads, no markets for their produce if they *did* raise it; and in this new position, if their hearts did not sink, and their limbs fail at once, their ignorance of farming, their improvidence and helplessness, arising from the want of self-dependence, and the mechanical docility of military service, were moral obstacles stronger than any physical ones. The forest-trees they had to contend with were not more deeply rooted than the adverse habits and prejudices and infirmities they had brought with them.

According to the commissary, the number of those who commuted their pensions was about twelve hundred. Of these it is calculated that eight hundred reached Upper Canada; of these eight hundred, not more than four hundred and fifty are now living; and of these, some are begging through the townships, living on public charity: some are at Penetanguishene: and the greater part of those

* One of these men, stone-blind, was begging in the streets of Toronto.

located on their land have received from time to time rations of food, in order to avert "impending starvation." To bring them up from Quebec during the dreadful cholera season in 1832, was a heavy expense to the colony, and now they are likely to become a permanent burthen upon the colonial funds, there being no military funds to which they can be charged.

I make no reflection on the commuting the pensions of these poor men at four instead of seven years' purchase: many of the men I saw did not know what was meant by *commuting their pension:* they thought they merely gave up their pension for four years, and were then to receive it again; they knew nothing of Canada – had never heard of it – had a vague idea that a very fine offer was made, which it would be foolish to refuse. They were like children – which, indeed, disbanded soldiers and sailors usually are.

All that benevolence and prudence *could* suggest, was done for them by Sir John Colborne: he aided them largely from his own purse – himself a soldier and a brave one, as well as a good man – the wrongs and miseries of these poor soldiers wrung his very heart. The strongest remonstrances and solicitations to the heads of the government at home were sent over in their behalf; but there came a change of ministry; the thing once done, could not be undone – redress was nobody's business – the mother country had got rid of a burthen, and it had fallen on Canada; and so the matter ended; – that is, as far as it concerned the Treasury and the War-office; but the tragedy has not yet ended *here*. Sir Francis Head, who never can allude to the subject without emotion and indignation, told me, that when he was at Penetanguishene last year, the poor veterans attempted to get up a feeble cheer in his honour, but, in doing so, the half of them fell down. "It was too much for me – too much," added he, with the tears actually in his eyes. As for Sir John Colborne, the least allusion to the subject seemed to give him a twinge of pain.

From this sum of mischief and misery you may subtract a few instances where the men have done better; one of these I had occasion to mention.* I have heard of two others, and there may be more, but the general case is as I have stated it.

These were the men who fought our battles in Egypt, Spain, and France! and here is a new page for Alfred de Vigny's "Servitude et Grandeur Militaire!" But do you not think it includes another lesson? That this amount of suffering, and injury, and injustice can be inflicted, from the errors, ignorance, and remoteness of the home government, and that the responsibility apparently rests nowhere – and that nowhere lies redress – seems to me a very strange, a very lamentable state of things, and what *ought* not to be.†

Our voyageurs had spent the day in various excesses, and next morning were still half tipsy, lazy, and out of spirits,

---

* p. 263.

† I give the following individual case, noted at the time in my diary.

"Sept. 7, 1837. – Called on me Anthony M'Donell, invalided from the 47th, first battalion, to the 12th veteran battalion – located in the twelfth concession of the township of Emily; aged 69; twenty-one years in active service; commuted his pension of 14*l.* a year for four years; never knew what commuting meant; received 26*l.* in Ireland, and 13*l.* odd shillings at Quebec; deducting the expense of his voyage, 13*l.* remains due to him from government; does not know where to apply for it – has applied to the commissariat here in vain: *has no friend;* has a daughter aged nineteen, an idiot, and subject to epileptic fits. He brought his daughter with him; the unhappy girl is tall and handsome; the father dare not leave her for a moment, there is no lunatic asylum in Canada to receive her, only the jail, *"and I'll die,* said the father vehemently, *before she shall go there."* He cannot *sell* his land, for present subsistence, because he cannot take out his deed – cannot take out his deed, because he cannot do the duty-work on his land required by law – cannot work, because he cannot leave his poor daughter: he had come to Toronto to beg a few articles of clothing for her. The poor man cried very much, while the childish insensibility and good looks of the daughter were yet more deplorable.

Here is another case of a different kind: –

except Le Duc; he was the only one I could persuade to
sing, as we crossed Gloucester Bay from Penetanguishene
to Coldwater. This bay abounds in sturgeon, which are
caught and cured in large quantities by the neighbouring
settlers; some weigh ninety and one hundred pounds.

At Matchadash (which signifies "bad and swampy
place") we had nearly lost our way among the reeds.

There is a portage here in sixteen miles across the forest
to the Narrows, at the head of Lake Simcoe. The canoe
and baggage were laid on a cart, and drawn by oxen; the
gentlemen walked, as I must also have done, if a Methodist preacher of the neighbourhood had not kindly brought
his little wagon and driven me over the portage. We
stopped about half-way at his log-hut in the wilderness,

Dr. Winder, a gentleman who has distinguished himself by writing
cleverly in the newspapers here on what is considered the right side of
politics, (*i.e.* the support of the British supremacy in the colony,) came out
with an order from Lord Bathurst for 500 acres of land, having served in
the army twenty years. He was told, on arriving, that his papers were
irregular, and that he must have an order from the Commander-in-chief.
What is to done? "Petition the Colonial-office." – Will you forward my
petition? "You must petition *direct*" – The petition was sent – returned in
some months as irregular, because not sent through the governor: the
ministry changed – there was delay on delay, and at this time (1837) Dr.
Winder has not received his grant of land.

Colonel Fitz Gibbon, a very *preux chevalier* of bravery and loyalty, who
saved Toronto, on the fourth of December, by placing the pickets before
M'Nab came up, is likely to be involved in a similar predicament. The
House of Assembly, on meeting, voted him unanimously five thousand
acres of the waste government lands, as an acknowledgment of his services. The grant waits for royal confirmation: it is to be hoped it will not
wait long.

There is no sense of injustice that would shake the loyalty and principles of such a man as Colonel Fitz Gibbon: like the old Roman, "it were
easier to turn the sun from its course than him from the path of honour;"
but all are not like *him*: and the ranks of the disaffected are perpetually
recruited in Canada from the ranks of the injured. The commissary told
me expressly, that some of these commuted pensioners, who were respectable men, had joined what he called the "Radical set," from a sense of ill
treatment.

where I found his wife, a pretty, refined looking woman, and five or six lovely children, of all ages and sizes. *They* entertained me with their best, and particularly with delicious preserves, made of the wood-strawberries and raspberries, boiled with the maple sugar.

The country here (after leaving the low swamps) is very rich, and the settlers fast increasing. During the last winter the bears had the audacity to carry off some heifers to the great consternation of the new settlers, and the wolves did much mischief. I inquired about the Indian settlements at Coldwater and the Narrows; but the accounts were not encouraging. I had been told, as a proof of the advancement of the Indians, that they had there saw-mills and grist-mills. I now learned that they had a saw-mill and a grist-mill built for them, which they never used themselves, but *let out* to the white settlers at a certain rate.

The road through the forest was bordered in many places by raspberry bushes, bearing fruit as fine, and large, and abundant as any I have seen in our gardens.

In spite of the mosquitoes, my drive was very pleasant; for my companion was good-natured, intelligent, and communicative, and gave me a most interesting, but rather sad, account of his missionary adventures. The road was, *as usual*, most detestable. We passed a lovely little lake called Bass Lake, from the numbers of these fish found in it; and arrived late at the inn at the Narrows. Though much fatigued, I was kept awake nearly the whole night by the sounds of drunken revelry in the room below. Many of the settlers in the neighbourhood are discharged soldiers and half-pay officers, who have received grants of land; and, removed from all social intercourse and all influence of opinion, many have become reckless and habitual drunkards. The only salvation of a man here is to have a wife and children; the poor wife must make up her mind to lead a hard life; but the children are almost *sure* to do well – that is, if they have intelligent parents: it is the very land for the young and the enterprising. I used to hear parents regret that they could not give what is called a *good* education to their children: but where there are affection and common sense, and a boundless nature round them, and the means of health and subsistence, which (with common industry) all can command here, it seems that education – *i.e.* the developement of all the faculties in a direction suited to the country in which they are to exist – comes of course. I saw an example of this in the excellent family of the Magraths of Erindale; but those persons are unfortunate and miserable, and truly pitiable, who come here with habits previously formed, and unable to adapt themselves to an entirely new existence – of such I saw too many. My landlady gave me no agreeable picture of the prevalent habits of the settlers round this place; the riot of which I complained was of nightly occurrence.

Next day we went on a fishing and shooting excursion to Lake Cuchuching, and to see the beautiful rapids of the river Severn, the outlet from these lakes into Lake Huron. If I had not exhausted all my superlatives of delight, I could be eloquent on the charms of this exquisite little lake, and the wild beauty of the rapids. Of our *sport*, I only recollect the massacre of a dozen snakes which were holding a kind of conversazione in the hollow of a rocky islet where we landed to dine. The islands in Lake Cuchuching belong to the Indian chief, the Yellow-head; and I understand that he and others of his tribe have lately petitioned for *legal titles* to their reserved lands. They represent to their Father the governor that their prosperity is retarded from the circumstance of their not having titles to their lands, like their white brethren. They say, "Many of our young men, and some of our chiefs, fear that the time will arrive when our white brethren will possess themselves of our farms: whereas, if our Father the governor would be pleased to grant us titles, we should work with more confidence;" – and they *humbly* entreat (these original lords of the soil!) as a particular boon, that their "little bits of land" may be secured to their children and posterity for ever.

Next morning we embarked on board the Peter Robinson steamer, and proceeded down Lake Simcoe. This most beautiful piece of water is above forty miles in length, and about twenty in breadth, and is in winter so firmly frozen over, that it is crossed in sledges in every direction. The shores are flat and fertile; and we passed a number of clearings, some very extensive. On a point projecting into the lake, and surrounded by cleared land, a village has been laid out, and some houses built. I went into one of them to rest while they were taking in wood, and found there the works of Shakspeare and Walter Scott, and a good guitar; but the family were absent.

We reached the Holland Landing, at the southern extremity of the lake, about three o'clock, and the rest of our way lay through the Home District, and through some of the finest land and most prosperous estates in Upper Canada. It was a perpetual succession, not of clearings such as I had seen of late, but of well-cultivated farms. The vicinity of the capital, and an excellent road leading to it, (called Yonge Street,) have raised the value of landed property here, and some of the farmers are reputed rich men. Everything told of prosperity and security: yet all this part of the country was, within a few weeks after, the scene of ill-advised rebellion, of tumult, and *murder!*

Mr. Jarvis gave me an account of an Irish emigrant, a labouring man, who had entered his service some years ago as teamster (or carter:) he was then houseless and penniless. Seven years afterwards the same man was the proprietor of a farm of two hundred acres of cleared and cropped land, on which he could proudly set his foot, and say, "It is mine, and my children's after me!"

At three o'clock in the morning, just as the moon was setting in Lake Ontario, I arrived at the door of my own house in Toronto, having been absent on this wild expedition just two months.

THE END.

Afterword

BY CLARA THOMAS

And over that same door was likewise writ,
Be bold, *Be bold*, and everywhere *Be bold*;
That much she mus'd, yet could not construe it
By any riddling skill or common wit:
At last she spied at that room's upper end
Another iron door, on which was writ,
Be not too bold.

FAERIE QUEEN, book iii

This epigraph, chosen by Anna Jameson for *Winter Studies and Summer Rambles in Canada* (1838), is a doubly apt and ironic accompaniment to the text. The book is an account of Anna's experience in Canada from December of 1836 to August of 1837, months when Mackenzie's rebellion was gathering momentum towards its December climax. Anna was the wife of Robert Jameson, vice-chancellor of Upper Canada, the province's highest legal position and its holder very much a part of the governing establishment. Though her marriage was not a happy one and she had made the trip to Canada primarily to arrange for a legal separation and a living allowance, Anna enjoyed the title of Chancellor's Lady and the special treatment it assured her wherever she might roam. She walked a fine line, therefore, between writing a frank,

543

truthful and saleable account and one which might hurt
her husband's reputation – or her own. A writer much
practised in tact, she managed to tread this line, producing
a work that is personal, remarkably fresh in tone, and
exact in detail, at the same time insisting on her complete
responsibility for the opinions expressed. Though Mr.
Jameson was reported to be "much displeased" after its
publication, no dire repercussions damaged Anna's reputation or jeopardized her literary or financial future.

Secondly, the epigraph is a fitting reference to Anna's
forays into "the Woman Question," as feminist activism
was commonly known in her day. In all her work, Anna
was a tireless advocate of improved education for women,
in order to prepare them for productive, useful, and contented lives. She had become a professional writer partly
through her own predilections, partly through the necessity of being the chief support for her mother, father, and
sisters. At the age of sixteen she had begun work as a
governess, and she knew first-hand the iniquities of the
system as it existed; she wanted reform as sincerely as the
most militant feminist who ever mounted a platform. But
she had to be careful because her own living and the
comfort of her family depended on her readership and on
the goodwill of publishers and reviewers.

In 1825 she had married Robert Jameson, a rising
young barrister and at first an enthusiastic promoter of
her literary career. Her fears about their incompatibility,
however, recorded in her letters during their courtship,
proved true: in 1829 he accepted a post in Dominica, and
the couple separated with few regrets. In 1833 he became
attorney general of Upper Canada and, with the vice-
chancellorship of the province coming up in 1838, urged
his wife to join him, if only temporarily, to give his
Toronto home the appearance of married solidarity. Since
by law Anna was completely dependent on her husband,
who, in fact, could legally have demanded all the income
from her writing, she had little choice but to make the

journey, though letters to her friends before she set out are full of her lamentations.

By 1837 Anna had developed an enviable reputation as a writer, not only in England but also in America and Germany, where her books, especially *Characteristics of Women*, a study of Shakespeare's heroines, were widely read and admired. She had no real intention of staying in Canada – to her a cultural wilderness – but she had every intention of making good use of her time and a plan for a book was firmly in her mind before she ever set sail. In *Winter Studies and Summer Rambles in Canada* she was indeed "bold," going farther than she ever had before in decrying the present position of women, but as ever she was aware of the need for caution. Some critics did take her to task for her feminist zeal, but on the whole the reviews were highly favourable. She was, at least after this work's publication, an established author who could always count on an audience and who was an important influence on a group of young women who were in the forefront of the "Rights of Women" movement and instrumental in the founding of Girton College, Cambridge.

From 1848 on, in the last twelve years of her life, Anna Jameson became England's first professional art historian, producing the six-volume *Sacred and Legendary Art*, a massive compendium of useful information about art over a very wide range, from galleries to churches, from painting to sculpture, from the Ravenna mosaics to the works of the High Renaissance. Art as the handmaiden of Christianity was the basis of the volumes' plan. The series went through many editions in England and America, providing a popular, impeccably correct and lavishly illustrated guide to the development of artistic appreciation.

In common with many other aspiring women writers of her time, Anna's literary and social role model was the gifted, liberated, eccentric, and notorious Madame de Staël. Anne Louise Germaine Necker, Baroness de Staël

(1766–1817), had been a leading intellectual and writer of her day, the famous mistress of a literary salon, an enemy of Napoleon and a refugee to England during the Napoleonic wars. Her novel, *Corinne*, was a travel guide, in fictional guise, to the beauties of Italy as seen through the eyes of a beautiful, brilliant, and mysteriously brokenhearted heroine. In 1834, after the manner of her model, Anna had combined travel memoirs with social and literary criticism in *Visits and Sketches at Home and Abroad*, her account of an expedition to Germany. She related her Canadian experiences with a similar admixture of social commentary. In her very first book, *Diary of an Ennuyée* (1825), she had fictionalized an account of her first continental trip taken as a governess to a travelling family. Here she set up a broken-hearted heroine as her narrator, a female counterpart to Byron's immensely popular, suffering hero Childe Harold as well as to Corinne.

In *Winter Studies and Summer Rambles in Canada* Anna speaks in her own voice, but this time she presents herself as a woebegone exile from all those she loves. Toronto is a wasteland: "A little, ill-built town on low land, at the bottom of a frozen bay. . . . I did not expect much, but for this I was not prepared." The voice we hear is sincerely hers at that time and in that place: she had made the voyage unwillingly, not in expectation of mending a disastrous marriage, but in an endeavour to carve out an amicable and financially acceptable separation agreement. Now lonely, cold, isolated, and bereft of friends, she must get through the bleak winter months: "To use my Lord Byron's phrase, I must get 'a file for the serpent.' "

Because Anna was a close friend of Goethe's daughter-in-law, Ottilie, and much involved in the study of German literature, drama, and society, she set about translating Johann Eckermann's *Conversations with Goethe*. This became her therapy and in part the subject matter of her "Winter Studies." In it she combined penetrating descriptions of the social and political structure of Upper Canada, commentaries on German life and literature, and a new set of variations on her old theme: the character, position, and necessary reforms in education for women.

In early June of 1837, Anna began her "Summer Rambles." From Toronto to Niagara, Hamilton, Brantford, Woodstock, London, St. Thomas, Port Talbot, Chatham and Detroit engaged the first month of the tour. From Detroit she embarked on her "wild expedition" as she proudly called it. Leaving Detroit on July 19, she went by the steamer *Jefferson* to Mackinaw, still well within reach of any eager traveller. From there, however, she travelled ninety-four miles by *bateau* (a small boat which held at most fifteen persons and which was rowed by five French-Canadian voyageurs) to the Sault, arriving on July 29. On August 1, again in a *bateau*, she embarked for the annual Indian enclave on Manitoulin Island, a journey down Lake Huron of four days and three nights. On August 6, she continued by canoe to Penetang, by canoe and portage to Lake Simcoe, thence to Toronto. Few women travellers – and none who travelled alone – had undertaken the "wild expedition," and Anna was justifiably proud of it.

Once on the road she was a different person from the Anna, frost-bound in body and spirit, who was the centre-stage heroine of "Winter Studies," gallantly upholding her ideas on culture even with the temperature at twelve degrees below zero and the ink freezing in the ink-well. Anna, the practised traveller of "Summer Rambles," enjoyed all manner of people and related well to them, from the reclusive Colonel Talbot, the "Lake Erie Baron," to the picturesque voyageurs who rowed her *bateau*. Most particularly she found all the Indians fascinating cultural studies: some of them, the Chippewa Mrs. Johnston of the Sault and her daughters, Mrs. Schoolcraft and Mrs. Mac-Murray, became lasting friends. Her observations on the native peoples are both extensive and original – her judgment that Indian women were no worse and, in some cases, better off in status and self-esteem than many of

their white counterparts drew some serious critical queries, though its validity has since been attested by Native
People's historians:

> Where she [the white woman] is idle and useless by
> privilege of sex, a divinity and an idol, a victim or a toy, is
> not her position quite as lamentable, as false, as injurious to
> herself and all social progress, as where she is the drudge,
> slave and possession of the man?...

> She [the Indian woman] is not therefore, I suppose, so
> *very* miserable, nor, relatively, so very abject; she is sure of
> protection; sure of maintenance, at least while the man has
> it; sure of kind treatment; sure that she will never have her
> children taken from her but by death. . . . Hence, however
> hard the lot of woman, she is in no *false* position. The two
> sexes are in their natural and true position relatively to the
> state of society, and the means of subsistence.

Winter Studies and Summer Rambles in Canada
reveals a three-part writing scheme. Anna read before
travelling, in this case giving particular credit to Alexander Henry for the help of his work in directing the course
of her "Summer Rambles." She took notes and kept journals while travelling, these forming the personalized core
of her work. Finally, she edited and judiciously added
supplementary material, as exact as possible, ranging from
information about the Moravian missionaries to a lengthy
history of Pontiac, to minute details of Indian life and
lore. It was both perceptive and astute of her to include
the Indian folk-tales given to her by Henry Schoolcraft,
American agent at Michilimackinac and pioneer Indian
anthropologist. Interest in folk-cultures was just coming
into prominence in England, on the continent, and in
America. Anna also made sketches, sometimes water-
colours, as she travelled. Schoolcraft remembers her as an
accomplished water-colourist, "who had her portfolio ever
in hand," though he had his reservations about the extent
of the powers of observation of all his many visitors:

"Even Mrs. Jameson, who had the most accurate and artistic eye of all, but who, with the exception of some bits of womanly heart, appeared to regard our vast woods, and wilds, and lakes, as a magnificent panorama, a painting in oil." As she prepared her book for publication, Anna wrote to George MacMurray, Anglican missionary to the Sault, speaking with a justifiable confidence in her research and writing methods that may well have been intimidating to him: "You must be content to be immortalized in my fashion."

I have found no instances of reviewers quibbling as to the veracity of Anna's observations and the pertinence of her references, though complimentary comments on these facets of her work are commonplace. She combined the astuteness of the successful bookmaker with a very evident propensity for research and scholarship, qualities rare among women writers in her day, unexpected and therefore undervalued.

Of the reviews of *Winter Studies and Summer Rambles in Canada*, Anna wrote to a friend: "At this moment I have fame and praise, for my name is in every newspaper." To another she reports the words of a friend, Mrs. Procter: "The men, she says, are much alarmed by certain speculations about women; and, she adds, well they may be, for when the horse and ass begin to think and argue, adieu to riding and driving."

Anna Jameson's injunction to herself – and her readers – "Be bold, Be bold. . . . Be not too bold," was well-chosen. The deeply concerned feminism of *Winter Studies and Summer Rambles in Canada*, voiced in the course of an ostensible travel narrative, protected its author from those male critics who were involved in zealously upholding the *status quo*, while at the same time informing and exhorting her women readers – in our day as in hers.